What people are saying about

THE NEX

"*The Next Target* by Nikki Arana kept me on the edge of my seat. I loved how the suspense grabbed me from page one, but even more compelling (and convicting) was the novel's depiction of the plight of women in the Muslim world. Highly recommended!"

Colleen Coble, author of
Tidewater Inn and the Lonestar series

"US Christians in danger for sharing their faith? Terrorist cell groups on American soil? Nikki Arana's bold new novel hits on all cylinders—at times the tension was chillingly palpable."

Creston Mapes, best-selling author of *Nobody*

"*The Next Target* is *24* meets Karen Kingsbury. Nikki Arana has successfully combined the tense world of Muslim extremism with a touch of romance. Readers should prepare for interrupted sleep."

Harry Kraus, best-selling author
of *Could I Have this Dance?*

"With cultural insight and grace, Nikki Arana steps into the arena of controversy between followers of Jesus, moderate Muslims, and radical Muslims. Through her characters she clearly shows the joy of finding Jesus and forgiveness as well as the cost of choosing this new faith. A fascinating novel—a recommended read."

Gayle Roper, author of *Shadows on the Sand*

THE NEXT TARGET

THE NEXT TARGET

A NOVEL

NIKKI ARANA

David C Cook®

transforming lives together

THE NEXT TARGET
Published by David C Cook
4050 Lee Vance View
Colorado Springs, CO 80918 U.S.A.

David C Cook Distribution Canada
55 Woodslee Avenue, Paris, Ontario, Canada N3L 3E5

David C Cook U.K., Kingsway Communications
Eastbourne, East Sussex BN23 6NT, England

The graphic circle C logo is a registered trademark of David C Cook.

The website addresses recommended throughout this book are offered as a
resource to you. These websites are not intended in any way to be or imply an
endorsement on the part of David C Cook, nor do we vouch for their content.

This story is a work of fiction. All characters and events are the product of the author's
imagination. Any resemblance to any person, living or dead, is coincidental.

Matthew 24:14 and Joshua 2:1 Scripture quotations are taken from the
King James Version of the Bible. (Public Domain.) Mark 1:40–41 Scripture
quotation is taken from the New King James Version®. Copyright © 1982
by Thomas Nelson, Inc. Used by permission. All rights reserved.

LCCN 2012931542
ISBN 978-0-7814-0431-0
eISBN 978-0-7814-0827-1

© 2012 Nikki Arana
Published in association with Natasha Kern Literary Agency,
PO Box 1069, White Salmon, WA 98672.

The Team: Don Pape, John Blase, Amy Konyndyk, Renada Arens, Karen Athen
Cover Design: Nick Lee
Cover Photo: Shutterstock

Printed in the United States of America
First Edition 2012

1 2 3 4 5 6 7 8 9 10

032912

To Hasna

Who lives in the basement of an abandoned building in downtown Los Angeles. Rats often wake her from her sleep. She is a fugitive. Hunted day and night because she has committed a capital offense. She is a follower of Jesus Christ.

PROLOGUE

In the great expanse between the dimensions of space and time, a luminous form arched itself above a spiritual universe. The transparent, multifaceted figure consisted of three faces, parallel planes ablaze with the power and glory of the eternal love that begat the genesis of humanity. Above the figure shone a brilliant white light. Its name, Truth. Below the figure, a spectrum of refracted light. Rays of incandescent color: ruby, sapphire, lapis, amethyst, amber, emerald, and gold, each forming an angelic being. They were called Love, Joy, Peace, Patience, Gentleness, Goodness, and Faith. Each purposed to serve humankind.

Love heard his name called. Love, ruby red, the color of the blood shed at Calvary. Strengthened by the spittle, steeled by the nails, girded by the thrust spear.

He rose.

The air was thick with prayer. Words imbued with deep emotion and sustained by the fervent pleading of a small spirit-filled army. Followers of Christ. Devotees of the Word of God, they had discerned that the end times spoken of in the book of Revelation had begun to unfold. Persecution of Christians had begun, and the polarizing of nations was under way for a great final battle. A battle between good and evil. A battle between love and hate. Ushering in the day of judgment for all people. Their voices raised, petitioning the Lord, asking that He tarry just a little longer. Just a little longer so more might be saved.

Suddenly, Love, the only force able to defeat the principalities and powers and the demons of darkness coming against the kingdom of God, the only answer to the prayers of the saints, was lifted up by the wings of Mercy and released.

Now, unfettered by time or dimensions, transported by the Spirit already indwelling every believer, Love stands ready. Waiting only for the surrender of the human heart, the act of volition that empowers the Lord to work through the lives of His people and touch the hearts of His enemies. Changing the heart of humanity. Desiring that *none* die lost.

CHAPTER 1

Sabirah's heart pounded as she felt in the bottom of her purse for her car keys. Finally, locating the blade of the ignition key, she took them in hand. Her grip tightened. "Oh, Jesus, protect me." Then she slipped out the employee exit of the restaurant, pulling the door shut behind her.

A crescent moon provided the only light as she scanned the parking lot. She'd been careful that her family didn't know where she lived or where she'd found work. Still …

Seeing no one, she felt her heartbeat slow. She took a deep breath and raised her eyes heavenward. There was nothing to be afraid of.

A gentle breeze kicked up, teasing her with the scent of ocean air and turning her thoughts to the church picnic planned for Saturday. Paul was meeting her there. She felt heat rise in her cheeks at the thought of the handsome young man who led the singles' group. She lowered her eyes. The idea of dating was still new to her. And … well … She just didn't know what to expect. Her arm dropped to her side and a smile touched her lips as she made her way to her car. She'd decided to bring baklava, the sweet Middle Eastern pastry that Americans seemed to love. She was making it from scratch so it would be fresh. Pastor John had said she could use the church kitchen since—The hairs on the back of her neck rose as an almost-tangible malevolent energy manifested in the air around her.

A shadow fell across her shoulder.

"Sabirah."

At the sound of her uncle's voice she whirled to face him. Her eyes darted to his hands. Empty.

"Don't be afraid. Your mother has sent me with a special message."

As his words hung in the air she tried to process them.

"Your baby brother is sick."

"Uncle?" She studied his face. The man who had favored her with bangles for her wrists, the one who had tenderly taught her the daily prayers to Allah. She had been his favorite of all the nieces … until she told her family of her conversion to Christianity.

"You should be at home caring for your brothers and sisters, Sabirah."

"How is that possible, Uncle? My father has rejected me."

His face contorted with anger and his eyes hardened with hate. "Why have you shamed us? You know these Christians are infidels." He stepped closer to her, his voice rising. "Look at yourself. Look how you're dressed. Out here exposing yourself to the eyes of men."

She touched the top of her modest scoop-neck sweater. These were the lies of the Enemy and they no longer had power over her. She stood her ground and held his gaze. "I found Jesus and true peace."

His eyes widened with rage as he slapped her. "You shame your father. Disgrace your family. You disgrace Islam."

He grabbed her wrist in one hand and with the other pulled a gun from his pocket. He jabbed the muzzle of the gun into her temple. "Who is it that corrupted you?"

The certainty of death sucked her breath from her lungs and terror ran riot through her. But she would not speak. She would not betray another.

Silence was her answer.

"Tell, and save yourself. You know I have ways of finding out."
He spit on her. "And you know I will."

She lifted her chin. "I love you, Uncle. I love my parents and my
whole family. But I also love Jesus."

"Then death to you." He jerked her to her knees. "I will restore
your family's honor. It is my duty before Allah. *Allahu akbar.*"

The cold metal tip of the gun pressed into her scalp and asphalt
cut into her legs. "Jesus, help me. Jesus—"

The rush of a mighty wind encircled her, drawing her from her
body, gathering her with dominion and power to eternity and the
presence of the Father. Leaving but an empty shell in the hands of
her accuser.

The sound of a gunshot echoed far below as a legion of angels
fanned out before her and the heavens unfurled like a scroll.

CHAPTER 2

Austia Donatelli couldn't shake the intense sense of foreboding that had kept her awake most of the night. She closed her eyes a moment, trying to get in touch with the vague, disquieting feeling ... an aching ... a whisper ... it eluded her. Releasing a deep sigh, she settled back under the covers.

She'd gone to bed early because it was going to be a long day at the Career Center. Besides dealing with the usual demands of running her employment agency, she would be interviewing a number of Arabic-speaking men to act as interpreters for the job applicants. She caught her lower lip between her teeth and bit down. It would be challenging, as it always was. She was a single Christian woman living in a Muslim neighborhood on the south side of Los Angeles, running a business that required her to deal almost exclusively with men whose culture frowned upon men and women mixing in public. A job that flew in the face of the Islamic traditions that taught men a woman's place was in the home tending to the family's needs.

Rolling on her side, she brushed her long dark hair from her face and let her gaze rest on the framed photo next to the clock. *David.*

It didn't matter that the moonlight from her bedroom window caused a shadow over the picture. She knew every detail. She closed her eyes, bringing the image into focus. Alone with him, she barely breathed, searching her memory for his voice, his smile, his scent.

The truth was, she was lonely. The days were long ... and the nights longer. How she yearned for strong arms around her, security, and whispered words of comfort to soften the rough spots of this uncertain world. But the Lord's answer to her prayers had seemed elusive, the men she met unremarkable, and the memories of her husband still too precious.

Her eyes drifted open, slowly letting in the real world. *Austia, it's God's timing. The fields are ripe for harvest.* After her husband's death, she had dedicated herself to carrying on his lay ministry to Muslims. It was an agreement she'd made with God.

Throwing back the covers, she rose. Then, after stopping at the front door for the newspaper, she headed to the kitchen and made a cup of hot cinnamon-spice tea.

Taking the paper and steaming beverage to the living room, she then set the cup on the coffee table so the tea could cool, and opened the morning paper.

WOMAN MURDERED LEAVING LOCAL DINER

The headline covered the entire width of the front page. Her grip tightened as she leaned into the paper. The account was sketchy. The young woman was an immigrant from Saudi Arabia with no friends or family that her employer was aware of. She had worked at the restaurant only a short time and appeared to be living in her car. Two men in a blue Toyota had been seen driving from the parking lot at the time the shot was heard. Austia glanced at the picture accompanying the article.

Her breath caught in her throat.

She recognized the car behind the police tape. She knew the young woman who owned it.

Austia covered her mouth as a wave of nausea washed through her.

Saudi Arabia. A young woman. A blue Toyota.

Swallowing hard, Austia rose. "No." Letting the paper slide to the floor, she stormed across the living room and back to the couch. "No, God. Please, God. No." *Sabirah.*

With sickening certainty, truth settled over her like a shroud. This was an honor killing. The murderous Islamic tradition of family members killing one of their own for bringing dishonor to the family name.

Tears burned her eyes and her heart ached. Sabirah. The beautiful young girl who had attended the English-as-a-second-language (ESL) classes that Austia and her business partner Annie Lundgren taught in the evenings at the Career Center to the Muslim community.

Sabirah had sought out Austia in secret over the last few months, wanting to know more about the Jesus who Austia said loved all people. And over time Sabirah had fallen in love with the Savior who died for her sins and set her free from the judgment of Allah.

Tears streaming down her cheeks, Austia remembered the day she'd given Sabirah a special Bible. There was no bond on earth like the one formed when the Holy Spirit ministered His love and life through the heart of a believer. One body, one blood.

Austia was the one who had led Sabirah to the Lord.

Would she be the next target?

CHAPTER 3

With cold resolve and renewed commitment, Zaki opened his bed-room door and stepped into the hall. He'd had the dream again. The hot sun of the Arabian Peninsula beating down, drying his sweat before it could bead. Bloody, lifeless bodies of American soldiers scattered across the broken mountain terrain … The images feeding him, stoking the fire in his belly for his mission. He pulled the front door shut behind him and headed across the street to meet with his boss, Hussein al-Ansari.

The area was a mix of commercial and residential build-ings. Hussein had chosen the neighborhood because Hancock Community College, nearby, and the ordinary traffic of neighbor-ing businesses allowed the comings and goings of the cell's Islamic members, most of whom were in their twenties, to go unnoticed. Hussein had purchased a modest two-story duplex on a corner lot where he, his wife, Fatima, and her sister, Najah, lived, and all other female members of the extended household could gather and take care of the family. The other side of the duplex housed his frequent visitors. The arrangement allowed him to monitor the activities of everyone, family … and friends. He'd then purchased other homes within a two-block radius to house the men who worked for him, and finally he'd built an office over the garages of the duplex. It wasn't a coincidence that any route in or out of the neighborhood went past that corner or that the home's security cameras recorded every car that passed by.

Zaki knocked on Hussein's door. After a moment, Hussein's sister, Rasha, opened it. Lowering her eyes, she moved to the side as he entered.

Zaki removed his shoes, stepped into the entry, then bounded up the stairs to Hussein's office. Hussein was not a man to be kept waiting. He was on the front end of jihad. Everything and everyone was expendable.

At the top of the stairs, Zaki heard two men speaking Arabic. He recognized the voice of Shaykh al-Ansari, Hussein's father, who was the imam of the local mosque. "Does the courier have it?"

The distinctly nasal voice that answered belonged to Hussein. *"Insha'allah,* he will contact us when he reaches Yemen. We'll coordinate with him from there to get passports for the men coming out of training."

Zaki knocked twice. "It's Zaki."

The door was opened by Faisal, one of Hussein's brothers. The scars on the right side of his face gave him a dark, sinister aura. It had served him well on a number of occasions when persuasion was needed. He closed the door as soon as Zaki stepped in the room.

Zaki nodded to the three men. *"Al salamu alaikum."*

As the men responded to his greeting of peace, he took a seat in one of the chairs that surrounded Hussein's desk. The room was full of state-of-the-art computer equipment, tables, and filing cabinets. Maps of the Middle East, Yemen, and a detailed map of Los Angeles hung on the walls, while a huge computer screen, in view of Hussein's desk, silently streamed Al Jazeera, the Arabic news satellite TV channel.

Hussein turned his dark, penetrating eyes to Zaki. "My sister, Rasha, has been bothering me to let her go to the English classes that the American woman gives at the Career Center. Fatima and her sister want to go with her. I will tell them yes." He coolly narrowed his eyes. "My sister's request got me to thinking about that place." The line of his mouth tightened a fraction.

Zaki held his gaze, waiting for him to continue.

"Many of the men who move here go there looking for work."

It was true. In fact, many of the men who worked for the cell had found jobs through the Center. Busboys, janitors, construction workers. Menial jobs that originally gave them income but now gave them cover as they carried on activities for Hussein's terrorist organization.

Leaning forward, Hussein slid a folded newspaper in front of Zaki.

Zaki recognized it as a page out of the Help Wanted section of the local Arabic language weekly. Several lines were boxed in yellow highlighter. A glance told him it was an ad for an interpreter. Something his American education and Arabic-speaking parents made him uniquely qualified for.

"I think you should apply. You're looking for men who want to work." Hussein's tongue darted across his lips, removing the perpetual white crust that formed in the corners of his mouth.

The inference in Hussein's words was clear. Zaki's mission for the cell was to recruit young disenfranchised men from the community for training in Yemen and jihad in America. By working at the Career Center, Zaki would be in a position to meet Muslim men and offer them the opportunity to be part of the worldwide effort to bring down the West.

Hussein continued, "The Career Center will want references. Give them Omar's name and the phone number at the Cultural Exhibition."

Zaki smiled broadly. "As you say." He picked up the paper and rose. "Now, with your permission, I shall attend to this."

"Alhamdulillah," Hussein voiced his approval as he settled back in his chair.

As Zaki headed down the stairs, he glanced at the ad again, then took out his cell phone and dialed the number given in the paper. A woman answered.

"The Career Center."

"This is Zaki ben Hassan. I'm responding to the ad for an interpreter in today's paper."

"You can come in anytime. There is a short written test to take and then an interview."

"Thank you." He hung up and let himself out the front door.

Crossing the grass to his apartment, he heard Hussein's garage door open. He watched as Faisal got into Hussein's car.

Zaki's thoughts turned to Hussein's sudden interest in the Career Center and the English classes. Hussein had no interest in having his women become Americanized, and recruiting men for the cell had never been a problem. There was clearly some other reason for Zaki's sudden assignment.

As Zaki watched Hussein's blue Toyota disappear down the street, he felt a stirring in his gut. A nudging.

Suddenly, a number of pieces of information linked together in his mind.

Prominent among them was the blue Toyota he'd read about in the morning paper.

CHAPTER 4

"Austia?"

Austia looked up from the open newspaper lying on her desk.

"The applicant that's waiting to see you did very well on his test." Annie laid the folder in front of her.

"Oh, sorry." Austia hadn't heard her business partner come into her office. "Guess my mind was somewhere else." Seeing Annie somehow comforted her. The older woman had been with her ever since Austia had opened the Center. It was Annie's wisdom, godly council, and unfailing support that had helped Austia through the difficult days after David's death. A true blessing from God.

Annie rested her hand on Austia's shoulder. "I loved her too."

Austia nodded, afraid to speak, not wanting to lose her composure again. She and Annie had not discussed the fact that Sabirah's death had almost certainly been an honor killing. Stating the obvious wouldn't change it. And it would only play into the hands of the Enemy. Instead they'd set aside some time when they'd first arrived at the office and prayed that God would station His warring angels around them so they could continue their work, and that the Career Center would not become involved in the police investigation. There was no doubt that if the radicalized Muslims in the community learned Austia was sharing her faith with the women who attended the classes, the building would be burned to the ground. And there was little doubt that a fatwa would be put out on her life.

Annie straightened and gestured to the folder. "Zaki ben Hassan is waiting in the conference room. He's a great prospect. He used to work at the Arabic Cultural Exhibition. They gave him a wonderful reference. And that job gave him a lot of experience working with Americans and Muslims. So he's someone who can bridge not only the language barrier but also the cultural differences during job placement. He worked there for over a year and his background check was clear."

Background check was code for the extensive vetting they had to do on anyone who worked for them. It included email address searches, social media "friend" network searches, and certain Arabic website searches.

"The Exhibition! That's wonderful training for this job. I've been there many times. I've visited all the displays. I've probably spoken to him there." Austia opened the file and looked at the test. "These dialogues he interpreted show a very good grasp of American language and culture. I'm not surprised."

"That's exactly what I thought." Annie dropped into the chair next to the desk. "We've been interviewing for two days. When he finished the written test and I read what he wrote, I was pretty excited and spent some time talking to him." She paused. "I think we should offer him the job."

Austia rose and began to rifle through the papers on her desk. Finding her legal pad, she laid Zaki's folder on top of it, then she tucked both under her arm. She started toward the door. "Oh, I forgot to tell you. My brother's coming to dinner tonight so I've got to head home a little before we close. If you need me for any reason, just call me on my cell."

"Don't worry about a thing. I'm planning to stay late anyway and catch up on a few things."

Austia stepped toward her and gave her a quick hug. "Thank you. You're such a blessing to me." Catching up on a few things meant trying to work through the dispute they currently had with the IRS over the first quarter's payroll report. According to the government, they'd underdeposited. Thankfully Annie did the books and they wouldn't have to pay an accountant to straighten it out. Annie was a godsend.

"Oh, Austia. I went ahead and put a hire sheet in the folder."

"Well, that's a subtle hint." Austia gave her a wicked smile and headed for the conference room.

All interviews with men were conducted in the conference room with its floor-to-ceiling windows, keeping the meeting in view of everyone in the office. And gender issues, such as avoiding eye contact, were always strictly observed when dealing with Muslim men. If she or Annie were not meeting Zaki in a professional capacity, it would have been completely unacceptable for them to meet with him alone. In fact, for most Muslim men, working for a woman was frowned upon and was one of the reasons they'd had such a hard time finding and keeping an interpreter.

As Austia rounded the corner of the conference room she felt the top of her blouse, making sure the small gold cross with the tiny mustard seed encased at its center wasn't visible. She let her fingers rest a moment on the hidden necklace. It was the first … and last … anniversary gift she'd received from her husband.

After giving it to her, he'd tapped the little seed and said, "With just that much faith, you can say, 'Mountain, move.' And it *will* be moved." He'd kissed her forehead. "Jesus said so."

But that was before his death, before Sabirah's murder, before the mountains God had given her to climb threatened to crush her.

Zaki stood as she entered.

The familiar scent of his aftershave distracted her for a moment. *David.*

She recaptured her focus. "Good morning. Thank you for coming. I'm Austia Donatelli." She nodded toward him, careful to avoid eye contact. Though his uncommon good looks didn't escape her. "You scored very well on your test." She laid the legal pad on the table and slid the test sheets in front of him as they both sat down.

Her cell phone chirped. "Oh, sorry. I meant to leave my phone in my office." She pulled it from her skirt pocket and glanced at the screen. Her pulse quickened. Abdur Rahman. A dear elderly man whom she'd known ever since she'd moved to Agua Viva. His wife had recently become quite ill. A call from him could mean he had new concerns about his wife.

"Excuse me a second. I have to take this call."

"Yes, of course." Zaki nodded.

After walking outside the room, she closed the door and answered her phone. "This is Austia."

"Al salamu alaikum."

Austia smiled at the formal greeting of Abdur Rahman.

"Wa alikum alsalam. Is your wife feeling all right, Mr. Rahman?"

"As God wills it." Emotion textured his voice. There was a moment of silence. Then he cleared his throat. "I call you to ask if you're going to the meeting Tuesday night."

"About the call-to-prayer issue the Planning Commission is taking up?"

"Yes. I'm sorry to have to trouble you. I cannot leave my wife, but I want to speak. Would you take a letter for me and read it to them?"

She hadn't been planning to go to the council meeting; the matter was too divisive. There had been another article in the paper just this morning, and it was clear that the issue was continuing to split the community. The story had referred to the two sides as the citizens and the Muslims. As though they were two different things. Personally, she preferred that the call to prayer be confined to inside the mosque, but she was willing to accept whatever the Planning Commission decided.

Citizen or Muslim, Mr. Rahman deserved to be heard. If Austia didn't respond, it would have the effect of silencing him.

"Of course, it will be no trouble whatsoever to do that for you. I'll come by sometime before the meeting, pick the letter up, and present it to the Planning Commission."

"Thank you so very much."

Austia said a quick good-bye to Mr. Rahman, shut the phone, and returned to the table. "Sorry for that interruption. It was a friend whose wife has been ill. I was concerned."

"Of course." His eyes met hers. "I understand completely."

For a split second she couldn't look away.

"Anyway, as I was saying." She pointed to the test sheets. "You did very well on these translations."

He looked at the few notes Annie had made on the papers. His closely shaved beard hugged his jawline, his dark eyes momentarily on the test sheet. He had an air of self-assurance about him, as did many of the Muslim men she came into contact with, yet … Somehow he was different. Ordinarily she had an extremely good sense about people. It's what had made her agency successful. But this time, she couldn't put

her finger on it; there was something different about Zaki ben Hassan.
"We checked your references at the Arabic Cultural Exhibition and
they were quite good." She glanced at him, waiting for a response.

She cleared her throat. "I'd like to offer you the position."

He looked up, his gaze briefly meeting hers. "When do I start?" A
smile spread across his straight white teeth.

"Tomorrow if possible." Austia pulled the hire sheet from the file
and extended it to him. "This confirms the specifics of the job."

Zaki read it, then signed it and handed it to her.

"Thank you." Austia rose. "You'll have your own office." She
turned and pointed across the hall. "It's right over there. When applicants come in, we'll ask if they need an interpreter. If they do, we'll give
them their paperwork and send them to you." She unclipped the key
from the folder and handed it to him. "Here is a key to the back door.
You'll be working under a deadline and I think you'll find that requires
you to come in early and stay late from time to time."

Zaki stood and took the key. "Very well."

She nodded and smiled. "See you tomorrow."

Watching him walk out the door, she tapped her pen on her lower
lip. The Arabic Cultural Exhibition's loss would be her gain.

She tilted her head and pursed her lips.

The Arabic Cultural Exhibition.

Thinking about it for a moment, Austia realized she'd never seen
him there.

Her breath caught in her throat. What if Zaki's appearance at the
Career Center and application for the job had really been prompted
by Sabirah's family?

CHAPTER 5

Austia's pounding heart set off multiple internal alarms. What did she really know about Zaki ben Hassan? Sabirah had just been murdered—if not by her family then by someone doing their bidding. What if the family had decided to trace back Sabirah's activities and find out how she had become a Christian? What if they had found the Bible Austia had given her and somehow traced it back to Austia?

A dagger of fear sliced through her chest. She took hurried steps after him.

"Excuse me."

He turned toward her.

She averted her gaze, still careful to observe the cultural edict that forbade eye contact with any man who was not a member of her household. Willing herself to remain calm, she smiled.

"When my partner gave me your file and a recommendation to hire, she neglected to tell me what your position was at the Cultural Exhibition."

"I handled all the correspondence." His quick answer and easy smile reassured her. "We often received inquires to speak at schools and make presentations at libraries."

She'd been to the Cultural Exhibition many times and knew those offices were on the third floor. They were not part of the public displays. She felt her heartbeat begin to slow. Of course, it made perfect sense.

"Why do you ask?" His voice interrupted her thoughts.

"Oh …" Her mind raced to find some plausible answer. "I was just thinking maybe they would be looking for someone to replace you. We do have some bilingual clients."

He quirked his mouth. "They hired the director's brother to fill the position."

"I see. Well, I'm sure that will work out well for them." With a nod of acknowledgement, she turned to leave.

"Ms. Donatelli—"

She turned back toward him.

"I worked with a lot of Westerners at the Exhibition, and my brother is married to an American woman who converted to Islam." He tilted his head and caught her eye. His smile widened. "I'm quite comfortable in both cultures."

Dark, mysterious eyes, deep tan, charming smile—what was the matter with her? She couldn't allow even a hint of impropriety here at the Career Center. She'd worked for years to build credibility and respect from the community. Straightening, she summoned her most professional tone. "Thank you. I appreciate that."

"I'll see you tomorrow, then." He tipped his head.

She watched as he walked across the lobby and out the door. Zaki ben Hassan certainly wasn't typical of the Muslim men she worked with every day. A sliver of uneasiness returned.

Striding across the room to the window by the door, she watched him make his way to a white Mazda. As the car disappeared down the street, she glanced at his application and noted his home address. Perhaps she would drive by it. With all that had happened, one couldn't be too careful.

She huffed a sigh and chided herself. There had been several men who had responded to the ad. And there would be more men coming into the Center today, tomorrow, and the next day looking for jobs. She couldn't live in fear of every new person who happened to cross her path. Her ministry must continue. Now it seemed more important than ever.

Tears stung her eyes. Sabirah's faith had cost her her life … just as David's had cost his.

Adrenaline and anxiety rushed through Austia at the memory of her husband's death two years before.

She'd been married to David a little more than a year when he'd decided to go to the Middle East. It was something he felt he had to do. She'd understood. This was so like her husband—humble, tolerant, caring, looking at the world through the eyes of Christ. Desiring that none should die lost.

Her heart ached. It was impossible to believe how much she'd hated Muslims when they'd first met. And she'd told him so, recounting the death of cherished friends on 9/11. Her attack on him and his ministry had hurt him deeply.

She squeezed her eyes shut; she wouldn't go there. She was a different person now. He had taught her to forgive. He'd taught her that from deep wounding can come deep love. Love steeled through suffering. This was what had drawn her to him: his beautiful spirit, his extraordinary capacity not only to love but to forgive. The example of his life kept her on her knees seeking the heart of God. She wanted what he had.

Just before going through security at the airport on his way to Kuwait he'd taken her into his arms. "We're in a battle, you know. We're on the front lines. We're watching the end times unfold."

Austia had searched his eyes. "Promise me you'll take care of things while I'm gone." She'd nodded.

"Things" meant his ministry. It meant checking on the Nassers down the street, helping the neighbors' daughter, Hasna, with her homework, and making sure that Zara, a Muslim widow, had a ride to get her children to their doctor's appointments.

"I promise," she'd answered. The last words she had spoken to him before he walked through the security checkpoint.

Word of his death had come ten days later.

The phone next to her bed had rung in the middle of the night, and a heavily accented voice told her that her husband had earned his fate, coming into the man's home and speaking blasphemy. A capital offense. And there had been a veiled reference to the vigilant network of radical Muslims that stretched worldwide. She'd changed her phone number, her address, and the locks on her house. She'd even returned to her maiden name.

The year that followed had been a nightmare. Despite the efforts of her senator, Ricardo Amende, David's body was never returned to the United States. The senator and his wife had become dear friends and she would forever be grateful to them.

Her husband's death had first rekindled, then fanned to a rage, a burning hatred toward Muslims and Islam. But as the months passed, she realized that not only had the radical Muslims killed her husband, she was allowing them to destroy her relationship with the Lord as well. The relationship that the example of David's life of love, tolerance, and peace had forged.

Steadying herself, she rested her hand on the windowsill and closed her eyes ... remembering. Remembering the months of soul-searching and days on her knees before God before she finally found peace one night in the long hours between dusk and dawn. Immersed in the healing words of Jesus Christ and the benevolent power of prayer, as clear and sure as the rising sun of that unforgettable morning, she heard the Lord speak to her heart, reminding her of her husband's legacy. The only answer to such spiritual blindness, the only way to stop the killing, whether it be for honor or for jihad, was to seek the hearts of the Muslim people. And God willing, touch them and change them with the love of Christ. A spiritual truth rooted in her heart. She could make of the rest of her life what she wished. The choice was hers.

She had chosen to keep her promise.

That very day she contacted her business partner and began her plans to open their office nights and weekends for ESL classes. It was a way to gain access to the people she knew she was being called to serve now that David was gone. Yes, it was dangerous positioning herself in the middle of a Muslim conclave and choosing to spend day and night working behind enemy lines. Nearly everyone close to her had begged her not to do it. Islam was becoming radicalized around the world, and moderate Muslims living in the United States were under pressure to join their fundamentalist brothers. Any Christians who dared to reach out to the unsaved, the lost followers of Islam, could lose their lives. There was such a thing as true evil in the world, one who still stalked the earth, seeking to destroy all that was godly.

She knew that was true. But for her there was a greater truth. To be cowed by fear would be to let the terrorists win. It was in that moment she'd realized this was no longer her husband's ministry. It was hers. And she would trust God to sustain her.

Straightening her shoulders, she lifted her eyes heavenward for a moment. Then turning, she headed back to her office.

"Austia!"

Face ashen, Annie ran toward her. "I've got a call holding on line two. You'd better take it."

Austia quickened her steps. "Who is it?"

"The police. They're asking about Sabirah."

CHAPTER 6

Zaki found an open spot around the corner from the duplex, parked, and headed to Hussein's office above the garage.

The phone call Austia had taken was a bonus. And her decision to step outside of the room they were meeting in and close the door had been especially helpful. She'd felt free to speak freely out of his earshot. He grinned, remembering how easy it had been to read her lips through the glass wall of the conference room.

When the call-to-prayer issue had started to heat up, he'd made it his business to connect to all the Islamic activists who were working to advance the mosque's call to prayer because those who were dedicated to the furthering of the Islamic presence in Agua Viva were possible candidates for the network of jihadists he was building for Hussein al-Ansari.

But no one named Rahman had attended any of the mosque meetings where they'd planned a strategy to ensure that the Planning Commission voted in their favor. He made a mental note to find out more about the man. Mr. Rahman had asked Austia to read a letter to the council. He pursed his lips. He looked forward to hearing it.

As he approached his front door, he could smell the odor of garlic and onions. Preparations were under way for lunch, which was always served after one o'clock prayers.

As he raised his hand to knock on the door, Hussein's sister, Rasha, opened it. He removed his shoes and headed for Hussein's office above the garages. Reaching the office, he knocked twice.

"It's Zaki."

"Enter."

Opening the door, he saw Hussein was alone.

Without looking up from his computer screen, Hussein waved toward the chairs around his desk. "Sit."

The moment Zaki settled in a chair, Hussein swiveled toward him, his eyes as dead and hard as black stones. "What news do you have for me?"

"I start the job tomorrow morning."

The corner of Hussein's mouth twitched with pleasure. "Good. Then it is as Allah wills it." Hussein leaned back in his chair, eyes narrowing, sweeping Zaki with an appraising look. He paused a moment, then spoke. "I believe they may be involved in some other business there. I trust you will find out."

Zaki gave a quick half nod. "As you wish."

From Zaki's years in the cell he knew there would be no more information forthcoming. By giving him only the barest details, Hussein could maintain control of all the information being gathered. It was very likely that he'd assigned other members of the cell to spy on Austia. This allowed Hussein to compare all his men's reports. Any discrepancies would be ferreted out. Any deception anywhere would be treated as a capital offense. It kept the cell secure. And it would keep Austia Donatelli from having any secrets.

Including that cross she wore beneath her blouse.

Hussein's tongue darted across his lips. "The sooner the better. The clock is ticking." He raised his hand, long slender fingers waving Zaki away. A surgeon's hands. One of the things Zaki had noticed when they'd first met. The almost-feminine, refined hands were freakish extensions of the leader's muscular arms.

Zaki glanced at the machete hanging on the wall as he stepped out of the office.

CHAPTER 7

Austia put the phone in its cradle.

Dealing with the police had been dicey. She'd managed to answer all of their questions truthfully without revealing anything that would cast suspicion on the Center. But the conversation had caused the shocking reality of Sabirah's death to coalesce into an irrefutable truth. Honor killings were no longer something that was "over there" in Kuwait or Saudi Arabia. They were clearly being carried out over here. Sharing the love of Christ with Muslims now carried an additional responsibility. Safety would have to be provided for those whose lives were in danger. Homes where they could be hidden.

A blade of grief cut through Austia as the sobering thought brought to the forefront what she had so desperately tried not to think about. Sabirah had been killed because Austia hadn't provided a safe place for her to go.

Austia would never forget that night at the Career Center when, during a break, Sabirah had asked if they could speak privately in Austia's office. She'd trembled as she confessed how she'd been secretly reading the Bible and the many accounts of Jesus healing people, laying hands on the sick and unclean, and even raising the dead. The stories had touched her deeply, especially the story about the woman with the issue of blood. "The woman was unclean, Austia. Untouchable. And He healed her and He … He … He called her … daughter." She broke down as she spoke the words that told her Jesus had not only chosen to heal the woman, but the prophet had done it selflessly, out of heartfelt compassion.

Sabirah's brow was creased, her eyes questioning. "Why? Why did He do these things?"

Austia had asked Sabirah to sit, then taking the frightened girl's hands into hers, she had answered. "Because He loved them." She brushed Sabirah's hair from her face. "Sabirah, love's touch heals. Not only the body but the heart." Sabirah had wept as the reality that Jesus had paid the penalty for her sins became truth to her. The sacrificial love of Christ breaking through the punitive message of Islam. The tenets that taught her every transgression against Islamic law she had committed since birth was being recorded in a book whose pages would be read at the judgment. Balancing her good deeds against her sins and leaving her still not knowing if she had earned her salvation. The Islamic traditions confirming her inferiority and condemning her to Hell.

When Austia had answered all of Sabirah's questions, the young woman had dropped from her chair to the floor and pressed her forehead into her knees. "Thank You, Jesus. Thank You, Jesus."

Finally, raising her eyes to Austia, the grace and power of God shining in them, with a halting voice she'd professed, "Jesus died to set me free."

Her freedom had cost her her life.

I'm sorry. I'm so sorry.

Wiping the back of her hand over her eyes, Austia clenched her jaw. It would never happen again. She would contact Christians in the community who would want to help. Who would partner with her. Who would be willing to hide and help a Muslim Background Believer whose life was in danger.

She glanced at her watch. She had a lot of work yet to get done if she hoped to leave early to meet her brother for dinner. She hoped this meal would not end as so many others had—with harsh words spoken in anger and fear.

She paused, then pushed a stack of waiting files to the side of her desk and pulled her wireless keyboard in front of her. Positioning her hands on the keys, she faced the computer screen and began to type out the names of all the churches, charities, and organizations she could think of that would be in a position to respond to a request for safe houses. Then she looked up their phone numbers and recorded them on her growing list. She searched her memory for people she knew who loved the Lord and would probably welcome the chance to help new believers. By the time she finished, she had two pages of ideas. She hit the print key, then retrieved the papers from the printer.

Laying the two sheets side by side, she reviewed her list. It would be best to start with some of her Christian friends. Women she'd attended Bible studies and retreats with in the Los Angeles area. Women she knew loved the Lord. Women she could trust with her secrets.

She reached for the phone, then hesitated; now wasn't the time. She needed uninterrupted privacy to engage in a discussion like this. Tonight after Steve left would be a much better time. She titled the Word document *The Saints* and emailed it to herself so she could pick it up from her computer at home. Then, after pulling the stack of files within easy reach, she took the first one and set to work. The next time she looked at the clock it was after one.

Austia laid down her pen and leaned back in her chair. She was starving. Rubbing the back of her neck, she rose. A quick trip to Little Piggy's Deli would be the perfect break. She retrieved her purse from next to the desk.

As she started out the office door, a piece of paper lying on the floor caught her eye. Picking it up, she realized it was Zaki's job application. Apparently she'd missed her mark when she'd thrown it toward the corner of the desk on her way to answer the call from the police.

She pursed her lips and glanced at her watch. If she hurried, she could drive by his address before grabbing a bite to eat and get a little more information about him. Tucking the application under her arm, she headed to her car.

The usual noon-hour traffic had thinned, and knowing the general area where the address was located, she made her way to the nearby neighborhood quickly. Zaki's address was on one of the avenues. She checked to make sure her doors were locked.

Keeping to the right of the main artery, she watched the street signs as their numbers entered the twenties. She turned right onto Twenty-Seventh.

Trying not to slow down and draw attention to herself, she looked for an address to get an idea of where she was. But the build-ings were crowded together in the mixed-use area, and the addresses weren't prominently displayed. Spotting an abandoned house next to a thrift store, she searched the side of its mailbox as she drove past. Bingo. The number, crudely scrawled on the broken box, gave her her bearings. She was getting close.

Beyond the house was a restaurant-equipment company, its parking lot surrounded by a chain-link fence with two strands of barbed wire capping it. Beyond that a filling station next to a brown duplex.

Without turning her head she cut her eyes to the residence. Above the door of the unit on the right were the numbers she was looking for. Her grip tightened on the steering wheel and she continued on. At the end of the block she turned left. As she rounded the corner, she caught her breath. Zaki's white Mazda was parked at the curb and the local imam was leaning against the side of the car reading something. Her eyes widened. She fought the urge to step on the gas and get out of the area. Instead, she looked straight ahead and maintained her speed. At the end the block she found herself dead-ending into a one-way street.

Unsure where she was, and unfamiliar with the neighborhood, she decided to turn and make her way to the road she'd come in on. That would take her back to the main arterial.

As she neared the corner of Zaki's block, she found herself facing a stop sign. A car pulled up behind her. She glanced in her rearview mirror. It was a man in a blue compact.

She scanned the duplex as she stepped on the gas. At just that moment the front door opened. There was Zaki. Her heart began to pound. Her eyes flew to the rearview mirror. The blue car was right behind her.

As her car approached the front of the duplex, Zaki turned toward the row of shoes lined up next to the front door.

He braced himself with one hand on the doorjamb and slipped his feet into a pair of the shoes just as Austia passed directly in front of the building. He bent over to tie them. The back vent of his coat split open, revealing a holstered gun.

Panic zigzagged through her.

The car behind her honked, waking her to the realization that, momentarily stunned, she'd let up on the gas. She slammed her foot down on the accelerator.

Who was Zaki? Why had he come to work at the Center? Had he been carrying a concealed weapon when he'd been in her office? Her eyes darted again to her rearview mirror.

She watched the car following her as it turned into the driveway of the duplex.

It was a blue Toyota.

"Oh, God, help me."

CHAPTER 8

Zaki seated himself at the small desk he had in his bedroom and turned his attention to his computer screen. It had been a productive day. Annie had demonstrated how the Career Center computer system worked during his interview.

He grinned. He'd picked up her password from the reflection of the keyboard in her glasses. After she assigned him a password, she logged out and left him to write two ads from two sample job descriptions. The fifteen minutes she'd left him alone had been the most profitable time he'd spent there.

He placed his hands on his keyboard and began to type. He quickly signed on to the Career Center network and identified himself as the administrator. A few keystrokes later he was viewing a list of deleted files, memos, and business letters written by Austia. The creation dates identified them as two years old. There were several exchanges about the death of her husband.

Hussein's cryptic directive to find out what other business Austia might be doing had deepened the scope of his mission for the cell. But it was a double-edged sword. Being entrusted with the task might make it possible for him to be present in the leaders' inner circle, a position coveted by every man in the cell. But failure to execute the mission to Hussein's satisfaction could put him in the presence of God. He googled Austia's husband's name.

He located and read newspaper articles that detailed the circumstances of her husband's death. He pieced together announcements of the ESL classes and other community events that she'd organized, and determined her outreach to Muslims had started a few months after her husband's memorial service. A picture of the service accompanied one of the articles and, to his surprise, a senator, Ricardo Amende, who chaired the senate's Homeland Security Committee, was sitting next to her brother. Living by the code that there was no such thing as a coincidence, he considered the possibility that her community involvement was a front and that her association with the senator went beyond that of a constituent to a politician. Perhaps Homeland Security was involved. She had personal information through her employment records on hundreds of Muslims in the community. He shifted in his chair, red flags going up everywhere. Was this what Hussein suspected? He clenched his fist. If the woman had any connection to any feds, he would have to take her out. Immediately. He lifted an eyebrow. That would be messy.

He began an exhaustive probe of every Internet resource available to him. But he found nothing definitive. The portrait that emerged was that of a woman who was deeply involved with the Islamic community in Agua Viva, both through the Career Center and volunteering in various capacities at the Friendship Center, the Recreation Department, and other service organizations. Nothing he found connected her or her late husband to any person or organization outside the immediate area. Everything he found made it clear she was dedicated to serving the very people who had killed her husband. Yet another red flag. No one would devote herself to helping the very same group of people who had killed her loved one unless she had an ulterior motive. He had to find out what that was.

He returned to the Career Center network and extended his search into Austia's email account. Still, that brought him no closer to knowing what Hussein was after. He sat back in his chair and steepled his fingers under his chin.

Finally, he rose and felt his pants pocket for the key Austia had given him to the back door of the office. He looked at his watch. He knew what he needed to do. What he had learned had revealed the possibility of wider implications of Hussein's interest in the Career Center. Though the specifics were a mystery to Zaki, it was clear that Austia was in danger.

Tonight he would go to the Career Center and take the steps necessary to make sure nothing Austia did escaped his notice. He wasn't going to squander the opportunity Hussein had given him.

CHAPTER 9

Steve Donatelli looked in his rearview mirror. "We're almost there, Harvey."

Harvey panted gleefully at the news.

Steve eyed the two Take 'n' Bake pizzas on the seat next to him. One was an extra-large cheese pizza and one was a small Hawaiian Delight. Ham and pineapple and cheese rolled into the crust. His sister's favorite. He smiled. The pizzas would be baking in the oven when she arrived home.

He'd been wrong to let things escalate into an argument the last time they'd had dinner together. Since she started the Career Center, they'd had an unspoken arrangement to agree to disagree about Muslims and Islam. She was determined to save them. He … well … He didn't trust them. Not after watching the Twin Towers come down from his office window in New York. He'd lost a lot of good friends that day, some he and Austia had known in college.

Ever since he'd moved to California, her involvement with the Muslims had been a sore spot between them. Most of the time when the two of them got together she came to his house. He didn't care for the part of Los Angeles she lived in.

But lately he'd been giving it a lot of thought. Maybe Austia was right, maybe it was time to forgive. He'd been a Christian all his life, and lately it seemed like every radio program he listened to, every devotional he read, and every church service he attended, the subject was always forgiveness. He released a deep sigh. If she could care about them after the loss of friends on 9/11 and what they'd done to her husband, maybe he could too.

Since their last argument, he'd spent time with the Lord every morning to think and pray about what had happened. Serious soul-searching had brought him to a decision. He would try and make friends with some of the Muslims his sister was always trying to help. Not only would it please her, it would also give him an opportunity to witness about Christ. There was nothing offensive about openly sharing the gospel. Jesus said to preach it to all nations. That meant the Muslims, too.

Austia spoke often about the family who lived next door to her. They were from Saudi Arabia, and he knew she'd had them to dinner in the past. He'd told Austia he'd be over after work, but he'd actually taken the afternoon off so he could arrive early enough to introduce himself to her Arab neighbors and invite them to dinner as a surprise. He looked at the temperature display in the corner of his rearview mirror. It was going to be warm enough to eat outside.

He'd picked out his shirt specifically for the occasion. It was a subtle way to make a statement about his faith. The white T-shirt had a small cross on the pocket with the words *Jesus is Lord* in block letters under it. He'd purposely stayed away from his other shirts that had large graphics with Christian themes in deference to Austia's fear of offending the Muslims. He shifted in his seat. He couldn't shake the nagging feeling that somehow he'd compromised. It just didn't seem right to downplay one's faith.

Approaching Austia's house, Steve began looking for a parking place. If she'd been home he could have parked in her driveway. But with a single-car garage, that would have left her in the street. He

released a deep sigh. Parking was always a problem when he visited her, though before he'd bought his vintage Mustang it hadn't
mattered.

What luck. He eyed a long empty spot next to the curb across the
street from her house. He pulled into it.

As he unbuckled his seatbelt, he noticed some men sitting on the
porch of the house next to hers watching three young boys kicking
a soccer ball. He parked the car and observed them for a moment.
All the men had beards and dressed like they still lived in the Middle
East. A wave of conviction flashed over him. He should have gone
ahead and worn the large graphic of Jesus on the cross that he'd felt
drawn to. After all, these men weren't afraid to dress exactly as they
wanted. He climbed out of the car and waved.

The men waved back.

For some reason he flashed to the Twin Towers coming down. *I
wonder what they thought about that?*

He turned back to the car and rolled the window halfway down,
then leaned across the front seat and grabbed the pizzas. "You wait
here, Harvey. I'll be right back. We'll go introduce ourselves and you
can play with the kids."

He set the pizzas on the roof of the car for a moment as he felt
in the pockets of his shorts for Austia's key. Finding it, he stuck it
between his front teeth, then hurried to the house.

After taking the time to preheat the oven and get the pizzas
unwrapped and onto cookie sheets, Steve returned to the car and put
Harvey on a leash. Ignoring the anxiety that stirred in his stomach,
he started toward the neighbors' house. He saw that the men and the
boys had gone inside.

Austia wouldn't be home for another hour, plenty of time to visit with them—Zahid was the man's name, as he recalled, extend the dinner invitation, and return to the house in time to get the pizzas in the oven and set the patio table. He took a deep breath, paused a moment, then crossed the porch and rang the doorbell.

As he waited for someone to answer, he observed the shoes lined up next to the door. He'd never understood why Muslims always took their shoes off before entering their house, no matter what the weather. He frowned. Surely they wouldn't expect him to do the same. He paused … nah … they were in America now. If they didn't accept the American way, frankly, they should. He rang the bell again.

After the third ring, a young boy answered the door.

"Hi. Is your mom or dad home?" He glanced over the top of the boy's head into the front room of the house.

A look of concern came over the child's face.

Steve loosened Harvey's leash, and Harvey, tail wagging, stepped up to the little boy and licked his cheek. The child jerked away.

"It's okay. He likes you. He—"

The boy turned on his heel and ran toward the back of the house, leaving the door open.

Steve waited for what seemed like several minutes, then tightened his hold on Harvey's leash. For a moment he thought about leaving. He knew nothing about these people, but what he knew about Muslims in general gave him the distinct impression they didn't like Americans. Still, he was here to build a bridge and serve the Lord. Ignoring the apprehension that held him on the porch, he stepped just inside the threshold, calling out, "Is anybody here?"

He would apologize for Harvey's unmannerly greeting. That should smooth things over.

As he waited, he glanced around the room. There were pillows on the floor surrounding a low table. Immediately to his right was a small table with a few pieces of mail on it. He took a small step to get a better look and make sure of the name. The envelope on top had a single line: Hussein al Ansari.

Hussein?

Steve was sure Austia called her neighbor Zahid. He rolled his eyes. Most Muslims he'd heard about called themselves Muhammad. Maybe Zahid was what his friends called him.

Voices came from the back of the house.

Craning his neck, he called out, "Hello?"

The muffled shuffle of feet sounded in the hall, and then a woman appeared. The little boy who had answered the door clung to her skirt.

"Hi." He extended his hand. "I'm Steve." He nodded toward the black lab. "And this is Harvey."

The woman moved her hand behind her back, reaching protectively for the child.

Seeing her odd behavior, it occurred to him that maybe she didn't speak English. He smiled to put her at ease, then pronounced each syllable clearly. "My name is Steve. What is your name?"

A loud voice sounded behind him. "What is the meaning of this?"

Steve turned. "Oh. Hi." He extended his hand. "You must be Zahid. I'm Austia's brother. I—"

"What are you doing in my house?"

The tone of the man's voice and the anger on his face changed the question to an accusation. Steve let his hand drop to his side.

"I was going to ask your wife to dinner. I mean, ask your fam—"

"Get out."

Steve flinched as Zahid's arm swung from his side, thick forefinger pointing to the front door.

"Get out, now." Zahid stepped toward him.

Fear winged across Steve's shoulders. He tightened Harvey's leash, and pulling the dog to his side, he hurried from the house, his mind racing as he tried to understand what had just happened.

Austia might be well-intentioned, but she was naive and misguided. The Muslims had no desire to assimilate into American society. Somehow he had to convince her that if she didn't distance herself from these fanatics, she might well meet the same fate her late husband had. He loved his sister. And he feared for her. He had to protect her no matter what it took.

As he quickened his steps, he looked over his shoulder. Zahid was standing on the porch with a cell phone to his ear. Even from a distance Steve could see the anger on the big man's face. What if he was calling friends, telling them about what Steve had done—whatever that was—and rallying them to retaliate against him? Or worse, Austia.

How he wished he hadn't identified himself as Austia's brother.

They knew she lived alone.

CHAPTER 10

Fatima closed the door of her bedroom, and letting her *hijab* fall from her head, she held her baby boy in front of her and kissed his forehead. "I can't believe it, Sami. I'm going to learn to speak English properly." She had studied some English while at school in Qatar, but had had little chance to use the language since then.

She dropped to the edge of the bed, cradling her son in her arms and covering his chubby cheeks with kisses. "And your grandmother is going to watch you while I'm in class." Fatima had thought long and hard about what relinquishing her son's care to his grandmother, even for a few hours, would mean. The woman had never liked her and held the opinion that Fatima's usefulness in regards to her grandson ended in the delivery room.

Fatima had no idea what had changed Hussein's mind about letting her, her sister Najah, and her sister-in-law, Rasha, go to the English classes at the Career Center. But when her husband had announced it at lunch, she'd been thrilled. It had been Fatima's idea, though she had convinced Hussein's sister, Rasha, to ask him. Fatima had learned very quickly after she'd married Hussein that it was unwise to ask her husband's permission to do anything that took her away from their home. Hussein expected a certain level of service from her and had many rules for her to follow. She'd been the oldest daughter, yet the last to get married. Being born with a slight curve in her spine that caused her to limp had set her apart from her pretty sisters. Something Hussein reminded her about often. And her body had further betrayed her when it had refused to make milk for her baby. But having been blessed with his birth, she accepted this condemnation with humility.

She had not seen her family since she stopped to visit them in Qatar on her way to America. She'd been six months pregnant with Sami. Accompanied by Hussein's brother, they had gone to her parents' house to pick up her recently widowed sister. Najah's husband had been killed in a bus accident the year before, just weeks after they'd married. Fatima didn't know if it was the stress of seeing how her sister had wasted away since her husband's death or if it was simply another episode in what had become a difficult pregnancy, but she became extremely ill the day after arriving. Her family had taken her to the hospital and the doctor had immediately admitted her. Though they didn't tell her anything specific, there seemed to be an undercurrent of urgency as the doctor and nurses settled her in her room, took blood samples, and hooked her up to machines. After everyone had left, she'd been unable to sleep. And as the hours passed a feeling had settled over her, a knowing. Something was wrong with her baby.

Her thoughts took her back to that night in the hospital. It had been both terrifying ... and beautiful ...

"How are you doing, sweet lady?"

Fatima, lying on her side, turned toward the voice, surprised to see a pretty Filipina nurse standing next to her bed. Fatima hadn't heard anyone enter the room.

"My name is Rosalie."

Fatima took the tissue knotted in her hand and wiped her eyes again. "I'm so frightened. There's something wrong with my baby. I haven't felt him move since yesterday." The fear that had plagued her since she'd come to the hospital surged through her.

The nurse seated herself in the chair next to the bed. "Don't be afraid."

The three simple words were spoken with a quiet confidence that drew Fatima's attention. She searched the nurse's face as the young woman took her hand. Rosalie's gentle brown eyes were filled with compassion. "Would you like me to pray with you?"

Fatima had grown up in Qatar and knew that most of the nurses were Christians. Unexpectedly, words that she'd once heard read from the Qur'an drifted through her mind, reminding her that Jesus was the son of Mary, an honored prophet, and one whom God had empowered to perform miracles.

In a way she could not explain, she felt drawn to Rosalie. "Yes." Her voice came out a whisper.

Rosalie released Fatima's hand and raised her own hands to her chin, palms turned upward in supplication. "Almighty God, Lord of Heaven and earth. You alone are worthy of all our praise and worship. Thank You for all of Your blessings. Thank You for this child You are knitting together in Fatima's womb. In faith I humbly ask that You stretch out Your hand and touch this child and bless him. I invoke the name of Your Holy Servant, Jesus the Messiah, and believe for a complete healing. Amen."

As Rosalie finished, she slowly lowered her hands. But instead of letting them rest in her lap, she passed her right hand across Fatima's forehead. Beneath that motion, Fatima felt her eyes grow heavy. Try as she might, she could not keep them from closing. As they drifted shut, she heard the sound of singing. Glorious high voices singing praises.

And then she saw the light.

It touched her.

An overwhelming sense of love and peace enveloped her, filling her with unspeakable joy. And there, through the cadence of the music and the current of pure love she saw her unborn child, a baby boy, resting in the hand of Jesus.

Then Jesus breathed on him.

As she watched, the baby suddenly began to stretch, as though awakening. His tiny feet pushing outward …

An excited squeal brought her back to the present. Sami's eyes were fixed on her face. He flailed his chubby arms and legs, opening his mouth wide in a smile. As though he too remembered.

She tickled his chest, then rose and laid him in his crib. Many times since that night she'd wished she could learn more about the Prophet Jesus. She had heard things about Him. Forbidden things. But she didn't dare ask anyone about it, and there was no way she could ever have a Bible.

Fatima knew about the English classes because she and Najah and other ladies who lived nearby went to the park with their children on Tuesdays, following afternoon prayers. Some of the women attended the classes and had told her about them and the teacher, Maryam. Fatima walked to the window. She could see the line of trees at the park from her upstairs bedroom.

One day as they had been walking home, an American woman was standing at a crosswalk, waiting for the light to change. The ladies had recognized her as Maryam, and she had spoken to them. Just as they had been about to cross the street, Maryam had dropped the mail she was holding. Fatima had stooped next to her to help her pick it up.

That's when Fatima had glimpsed the cross beneath the woman's blouse.

Fatima glanced toward the crib where Sami giggled as he played with his hands.

She wanted to know more about the Jesus who had saved her baby's life. The ESL classes were her only hope.

As she drew in a deep breath, her gaze returned to the distant park. She knew Hussein well. If he ever realized the true reason she wanted to attend the classes, he not only wouldn't let her leave the house. He would kill her.

CHAPTER 11

As Austia turned onto the boulevard that would take her home, an icy shiver crept up her spine. There were just too many coincidences. The ad had been in the paper several days. Yet the morning after Sabirah's death, a man carrying a concealed weapon had come to her office to apply for a job. And now that she'd seen someone driving a blue Toyota pull into his driveway, there was little room for doubt. Zaki was connected to Sabirah's killer in some way. Austia's heartbeat faltered—what if *he* was Sabirah's killer?

She should call the police.

She'd almost done it when she'd first returned to the office, but had decided against it because it would only draw attention to the Career Center. The last thing she wanted was the police asking questions about her business. It would cause all kinds of complications. Not the least of which involved the fact that there were Muslims on the police force. Even moderate Muslims would be deeply disturbed if they learned she was sharing the gospel with their women. No, involving the police was just too dangerous.

And what about the imam? What had he been doing at Zaki's car? What was their connection? She'd even tried to look up the ownership of the duplex through the county assessor's website to see if she could glean some information. But it had shown the owner's name was an attorney's office.

Her stomach churned. What a day it had been. She hadn't even had a moment alone with Annie to tell her in detail what had happened. But one thing she'd decided for sure was that tomorrow, Zaki's first day at work, would also be his last. Though she had no idea what reason she would give him. She tightened her grip on the steering wheel. After Zaki was gone, maybe she could anonymously point the police toward him and the blue Toyota.

She forced herself to turn her thoughts toward home. She wanted to be sure she arrived before Steve did because he was bringing his new black lab, Harvey, for her to meet. Muslims didn't like dogs. Especially black dogs. They believed angels of blessing didn't enter homes where dogs were kept. The thought of Harvey running loose in the neighborhood made her knees weak.

Despite her best efforts, Steve's last visit had ended in an argument with him trying to convince her to give up the ESL classes at the Career Center. When he'd called last week to ask to visit, they both knew it was just an excuse to mend their relationship, and she'd immediately wished she'd been the one who put forth the first effort. She'd gladly accepted the overture and she hoped that tonight she could welcome Harvey to the family and take her brother out to dinner. They'd always had a special connection. It was Steve who had led her to the Lord. And when their parents had died unexpectedly in a car accident, he'd moved from New York to be near her. Still, she kept hidden from him how deeply involved she was in sharing Christ with Muslim women.

Austia skirted the downtown, and as she made her way home, her thoughts once again returned to the need for safe houses. This was the dichotomy of Islam: For every radicalized Muslim there were hundreds of good, decent people of the Islamic faith. And for those who converted to Christianity, most Americans knew little or nothing about the terrible price Muslim Background Believers paid for becoming followers of Jesus. But everyone she asked to shelter a former Muslim would have to be told what the risks were and enter into the agreement realizing they had stepped onto a battlefield. As she knew only too well, countering the spread of radical Islam was spiritual warfare. And those God called would need His full armor.

Her cell phone chirped, interrupting her thoughts. "Hello."

It was the police. She listened to the voice on the phone, a wave of uneasiness rippling through her stomach.

"I'm so sorry, Chief Peterson. I'm sure he meant no harm."

Pulling into her driveway, she turned off the ignition. Deep, unsettling concern had turned into alarm as the chief of police told her about the complaint he'd received from her neighbor. Zahid had made clear his concerns about her brother but he hadn't wanted the police to do any follow-up. Apparently Zahid had been visiting with friends, and after driving them home, he'd returned to his house and found Steve in the house alone with his wife. Their son had been frightened to death by the man who had broken into their home with a huge black dog.

When Austia was sure the chief had finished, she closed her eyes a moment. "I'll speak to Steve immediately. It won't happen again. And thank you so much for letting me know about this." She was sure it was her long history of community involvement that had prompted Chief Peterson to give her a call. They'd crossed paths from time to time over the years.

After the chief hung up, Austia snapped her phone shut and got out of the car, her mind spinning. Why on earth would Steve have gone to her neighbors' house? And beyond that, why would he go into their house uninvited, especially when Zahid wasn't home? Whatever had happened, she knew Steve would never intentionally start a fight with anyone. One thing she was sure of, whatever had happened had sprung from the vast differences in their cultures. Each man would see himself unequivocally in the right.

As she headed toward the house, she tried to gather her thoughts. Maybe it wasn't as bad as it had sounded. She could only hope. "Lord, please give me wisdom. Help me build bridges between these people."

As Austia opened the front door, she feigned an ease she didn't feel.

"Hey, you beat me here," she called out as she stepped into the living room. The smell of baking pizza drifted to her from the kitchen.

Ordinarily the scent would have caused her mouth to water, but the call from Chief Peterson had set her stomach churning. "Yum. Something smells good. Hawaiian?" She hoped her cheerful tone didn't sound as forced to Steve as it felt to her.

A big black dog bounded toward her.

"You must be Harvey." She knelt and wrapped her arms around the dog's neck.

Steve appeared behind him.

Austia rose. The sight of his familiar face brought the sharp realization that they hadn't seen each other in months … and she'd missed him terribly. "Oh, it's so good to see you."

"Hi." His stiff, clipped response infused tension in the air.

Seeing him standing in front of her in his *Jesus is Lord* T-shirt gave Chief Peterson's phone call a lot more context. The shirt would have been very offensive to Zahid. To him the cross represented horrific

things that had happened throughout history, beginning with the
Crusades. And for a Muslim, stating "Jesus is Lord" was the same as
saying "Jesus is God," which amounted to blasphemy. It was tanta-
mount to Zahid going to Steve's home wearing a shirt emblazoned
with a crescent moon and star, underlined with the words: *There is
one God and his name is Allah.*

"It's good to see you, too." Steve's voice was brisk and he quickly
added, "I wish I could say the same about your neighbor."

Austia walked to the living room couch and sat down. "Oh?"
Why did this have to happen just as Steve and she were mending
their relationship?

As Steve recapped the events, Austia was able to see how things
had gone so horribly wrong. Her heart went out to both men.

As he finished his story, he threw up his hands. "All I did was go
over to ask them to dinner."

A picture of Steve standing in Zahid's house with a large black
dog, alone with Zahid's wife, flashed through her mind. She stifled
a shudder. "Steve, that was a lovely gesture. But there are certain
traditions and customs that Muslims observe that probably led to
the misunderstanding."

Steve folded his arms across his chest. "Like what? And don't
tell me there was a language barrier, because your neighbor speaks
perfect English."

She waited a moment, hoping Steve would calm down. "Being
alone in his house with his wife is a very serious offense in Muslim
culture."

"That's ridiculous." Steve's mouth dropped open. "Are you saying that that man thought …?" His face turned beet red.

"I know you only had the best intentions when you went over there, but gender etiquette is extremely sensitive in Islam." She paused, choosing her words carefully, remembering how mad it had made her the first time a similar situation had been explained to her. "As impossible as it is to believe, and as horrific as it sounds, a woman could be killed by her own family members if they thought she dishonored them by promiscuous behavior."

He threw up his hands. "Only in Islam could something as innocent as inviting people to dinner become something as offensive as what you're talking about. Thank God we live in America." Anger singed every word. "Why do you even want to be associated with those people?"

Tears sprang to her eyes. Her relationship with her brother was disintegrating in front of her. "Steve, I completely understand how you feel. I even agree with you that an insinuation like that is way out of line, but that's how they've been taught. And we'll never be able to show them that tolerance and love is the better way if we sit in judgment. Believe me, the rigidness of their beliefs is something I've struggled with many times over the years. But we have to come to them where they are."

And the truth was, she still struggled … especially when things like this happened. "I'm sorry, but you shouldn't have gone over there when Zahid wasn't home."

"Well, he was home when I pulled up, and it couldn't have been more than ten minutes before I walked over there."

"That's when he drove the men visiting him home."

Steve studied her a moment. His face darkened. "How do you know what he was doing?"

"A friend of mine at the police station called and told me what happened."

"The police called you?" His voice rose in disbelief.

"You have to realize, from his point of view you were trespassing … or worse."

"So you're basically saying this guy Zahid is completely justified acting like he did." Steve grabbed Harvey's leash and snapped it on the dog's collar. "I've suddenly lost my appetite."

He stormed to the front door and yanked it open. Not bothering to shut it, he yelled over his shoulder. "Now that I know where your loyalties lie, I can move on."

CHAPTER 12

"Please, please, don't do this." Sobbing, Austia ran after Steve and grabbed his arm. "You're my brother. You're the only family I have in this world."

His steps slowed.

She let go of his arm.

He stopped, then turned around and faced her. Pain etched his face.

It was her pain.

Inflicted on him through that invisible cord that bound their hearts. Anchored in love that ran deep as their blood.

Oh, how she wished she could tell him what he wanted to hear. That she would give up the Career Center, that she would move out of the area, that she would leave the Muslims to their fate.

But she couldn't.

Moments passed.

Steve's stance softened almost imperceptibly. "You're wasting your time trying to save the Muslims. You can't change who they are." His voice was textured with emotion.

"You're right, Steve. Only the Holy Spirit can do that. And He will. Can't you see that?" *Please, hear me.* "We have to look for opportunities to model Christ's love to them."

"Austia, Jesus hasn't given me a love for them like He's given to you." Steve loosened his hold on Harvey's leash.

Austia sought her brother's eyes. "It isn't a love for the Muslims that drives me to serve them. It's my love for Him."

Tears glistened in Steve's eyes. As he lowered his gaze, a spark of hope that their relationship could be repaired kindled within her.

Several moments passed, then he lifted his chin. "What can I do to make this right?"

"Well." She hesitated. "We could be peacemakers."

Steve's face clouded.

Before he could speak, she continued. "Shouldn't we?"

"But Austia, I didn't do anything wrong. They took offense over nothing."

"Of course you didn't do anything wrong. But it doesn't matter whether or not they should be offended. The Muslims who know me, know I'm Christian. I never want to do anything that reflects poorly on Jesus. I find I can speak volumes without opening my mouth if I just try to live out the love of Christ."

Steve glanced at Zahid's house.

"Could you apologize for offending his family?"

Steve slowly reached down and rubbed Harvey's ears. "I guess you'll have to wait here." He unhooked Harvey's leash, then straightened. "We could take them the pizza."

Austia tilted her head and gave him a sheepish grin. "Er. They don't eat pork."

"That's okay. I knew that." He looked rather proud of himself. "One of them is cheese."

She paused. "From their point of view, anything that touches ham is unclean. The chances are pretty good that the pizza cutter that cut my Hawaiian pizza also cut their cheese pizza."

"Come on." Steve clucked his tongue. "They wouldn't know that."

"But *I* do." She gently poked his chest. "Let's just leave the pizza here, and you can take it home. Come on, let's go."

Steve put Harvey in the car, then they quickly made their way to Zahid's house.

When they arrived on the porch, Steve stepped to the side and waited for Austia to ring the doorbell.

"Oh, no you don't." She playfully pointed her finger at him. "You're the one who needs to take the lead here."

Steve gave her a glare of mock contempt.

Stepping around behind him, she nudged him in front of the door. "Go ahead. Ring the bell."

Just as he lifted his finger, the door opened.

Zahid's face darkened. "You."

Steve glanced at Austia, then back to Zahid. He squared his shoulders. "I've come to say I'm sorry, Mr. al Ansari. I didn't—"

Zahid's voice rose. "Why do you call me Mr. al Ansari?"

"Isn't that your name? Earlier I saw a piece of mail. I—"

Zahid stepped through the doorway, towering over Steve. "You came in my house when my wife was alone." He knotted his fists. "And now I find out you looked through my mail." He grabbed Steve by the arm and pushed him. "Pig. Get off my property, you pig." His head swiveled to Austia. "You, too. Go."

The hostility that raged in Zahid's eyes transformed him into a stranger. A myriad of conflicting emotions broke over Austia, rooting her to the spot.

"Go," he bellowed.

Her feet moved of their own accord and she found herself stumbling down the porch stairs and across the grass as the door slammed behind them. By the time she reached her yard, Steve was storming to his car.

Steve stopped and turned to her. "What is it going to take for you to learn that those people are best left alone? They don't understand us, and we don't understand them." He jerked his head toward her. "Go ahead. Explain how something as civilized as an apology deserves that kind of reaction."

Before she could answer, Steve strode to his car, pulled open the driver's door, and climbed behind the wheel. Rolling down the window, he shouted out to her, "Wake up. This isn't a war against flesh and blood. Let the Lord handle it."

Heartsick, she watched as he burned rubber down the street.

Suddenly, she realized she was holding her breath. Slowly releasing it, she let her gaze drift to the ground. How had this happened?

Dropping to her knees, she covered her face with her hands. Sobs shook her as the reality of her situation overwhelmed her. She had been the catalyst for an innocent woman's death. Her desire to reach Muslim women for Christ had made her a target and could cost her everything. The goodwill she'd worked so hard to build with her neighbor was in ruins, with hatred emerging from the ashes. And now the fragile relationship she had with her brother, the only remaining member of her once-close family, was shattered.

Her heart lurched as these deadly facts crystallized into a dark and ominous truth.

This was a spiritual battle.

She was not at war with her brother or the Muslims or Islam, but against principalities and powers, and the rulers of the darkness of this age.

The single avid eye of Hell was focused on her every move. She was at war with the Enemy himself.

"Uncle?"

He waited for the code words.

"It's Taj. He just left her house. I'll be heading back to LA now."

He threw his phone on the empty seat next to him and watched the Mustang disappear down the street.

CHAPTER 13

Zaki slipped through the back door of the Career Center and closed it behind him. Feeling the knob, he calmly engaged the lock, then moved stealthily to Austia's office.

In the thin flickering light of the screensaver, he crossed the room to her computer and signed in with her password. A click on the Outlook Express icon and three keystrokes later, he exported all her email to his online storage service.

He returned her screen to its original status and then took a moment to observe the room. He scanned the bookcase behind her desk. Seeing a photograph, he stepped closer. The picture was of Austia in a wedding dress, playfully feeding a piece of cake to a grinning groom. The frame was inscribed with a date and their first names.

Zaki pursed his lips. Little did they know then what their future held. She, soon to be a widow. He, soon to be dead.

Zaki stared at the man in the picture. The image spurring memories ... *Neryda* ... and fresh resolve for this mission.

Neryda. Beautiful. An innocent woman. Murdered.

Zaki clenched his jaw and turned toward Austia's desk. A large file caught his eye. He flashed his light on it. The tab was lettered: *The City of Los Angeles.* He lifted the cover, revealing a thick stack of job applications.

He fingered through them, reading the names. About a third of the way through one caught his eye. Ma'amoon Abdullah. Zaki took snapshots of the application and the accompanying head shot. The man worked for Hussein, but didn't live in the area. Zaki had only been able to glean that they were related in some way by family. Zaki quickly looked through the rest of the applications but nothing else caught his eye.

Using the flashlight, he methodically scanned the contents of the drawers. One held client files, another had ESL handouts. In the bottom left drawer he found a Bible. There was a leaflet tucked beneath the cover. Pulling the cover back, he saw it was a handout from Unity and Grace Community Church. He lifted it out and checked the address, then placed it back exactly where it had been.

Zaki straightened. After a final scan of the room, he turned off his flashlight and exited the office.

Zaki was familiar with the church. Hussein's latest target in the master plan to spread Islam in Agua Viva was to monitor the church closely. He was delighted to see how quickly Christians were moving out of the area. The church had recently been moved to the list of area churches in the final phase of takeover. It was anticipated that the church would soon be put up for sale. Within six months Hussein's father, the imam, would oversee the purchase of the land and building and direct the placement of a dome over the cross. This would be the third successful takeover of a Christian church since Zaki had joined the cell. Every church in Agua Viva was on Hussein's list.

Austia sat curled up in the corner of her couch in the darkening living room, her Bible on the coffee table, her cell phone in her hand. Steve still wasn't answering.

Spidery shadows crawled on the wall opposite her as a car engine slowed outside her house.

A car door slammed shut.

She jumped up and ran to the window. Staying out of sight, she peered into the dimly lit street.

It was empty.

Her eyes drifted to the front doorknob. Jamming her phone in her pocket, she ducked under the window and crawled across the room to check and be sure it was locked.

It was.

She straightened. This was ridiculous. There was no reason to feel frightened in her own living room. She was just upset over the argument with Steve and the terrible scene at Zahid's house. That kind of thing robbed her of her joy. She was committed to live in peace with all people. Besides, Steve was the only family she had; she loved him dearly. She shouldn't have been so anxious to set him straight.

Oh, well. There was no sense in beating herself up over it. She'd call him in the morning and apologize. And somehow she needed to mend her relationship with Zahid. Though, with the rage on his face still burning in her memory, she knew right now her time would be better spent working out a plan to set up safe houses. She snapped on the light.

Before doing another thing, she needed to call her business partner. Austia picked up the phone and dialed her friend's number. Annie listened silently while Austia recounted all that had happened when she'd gone to drive by Zaki's house.

Austia began to pace. "Do you see the problem? What possible reason could I give him for letting him go tomorrow?"

"Austia, you don't have to give him any reason. Did he sign the hire sheet?"

"Yes. It's in the file."

"Then when he arrives tomorrow just tell him that you won't be needing him after all. It says right on that hire sheet that there is a ninety-day probationary period. You don't have to give him a reason."

Austia paused. "Hmm. I don't think that will work. He's going to want to know why. And I certainly can't say, 'I'm afraid you murdered a friend of mine and I might be next.'"

"Maybe he won't ask."

Austia seated herself on the couch. She knew her friend was grasping at straws, trying to put the best face on a terrible situation. But that wasn't going to help either of them. They were caught up in a very dangerous situation and facing it head-on was their best chance of surviving it. "Think about it. He's obviously connected to Sabirah's death in some way. And frankly it makes me sick to my stomach to think of how he would have connected me to her." Tears stung her eyes at the thought of Sabirah being forced to reveal who had told her about Jesus. "He's come to work at the Center to find out if something is going on there. I'm positive of it."

She heard Annie release a shaky breath.

"Oh, Austia. I hope you're wrong."

"I hope I'm wrong too. But right now we have to find a way to fire him."

They spent the next thirty minutes playing out different scenarios, but the more they talked, the more they realized that any excuse to fire him was weak and would only raise his suspicions if he indeed had taken the job to spy on them. And any excuse that could not be challenged would require Austia to lie. She couldn't do that. It would be stepping out from under God's protection. It was something her husband had talked to her about many times in regards to his ministry to Muslims. "If you're trusting God, He'll never ask you to lie."

But those conversations hadn't been about matters that threatened her life. Surely, this was different. And it wasn't only her life, it was Annie, family members, and the Muslim women who attended the classes.

Like the point of a tine, doubt pricked her conscience. Maybe just this once it would be okay.

CHAPTER 14

Austia said good-bye to Annie and released a deep sigh. *Oh, Lord, help us. Only You can provide a way out.* Zaki's presence made the need for safe houses for the precious women the Lord sent to her ESL classes even more urgent.

She rose from the couch and walked to the bedroom she'd converted to an office. After seating herself at her desk, she opened her email account and clicked on the Word document *The Saints.*

Drawing a deep breath, she set her mind to the task before her.

The first name on the list, Jill Dixon.

She dialed the number.

After saying hello she gave the reason for her call. "You know how you've asked in the past how you could be of help with my ministry to Muslims?"

There was a moment of silence.

"Of course. I think it's just awesome how you're trying to reach Muslims for Christ. What can I do?" Her words were stilted.

Austia hitched her chair forward. "I'm setting up a network of safe houses. Private homes that would be willing to shelter Muslims who become believers, take them in and help them get a new start."

"Do you mean people arriving here from overseas? Like exchange students?" Her voice lightened.

"No, I mean people who live here."

"Why do they need a new start?"

It never ceased to amaze Austia how many Christians failed to understand what it cost a Muslim to accept Christ as Savior.

"When Muslims leave Islam it usually means that their families disown them and sometimes it can put their life in danger. They need to be relocated to another area and helped to get a new start."

There was a pause.

"Exactly what kind of danger?"

Austia wasn't sure how to answer. She didn't want to give the worst-case scenario and unnecessarily frighten Jill, but she didn't want to give the best case and mislead her. "That's the reason we need houses outside of Agua Viva. Places that would make it difficult for their families to find them."

"Are you saying that these people are actually going to be hunted?" Jill's voice sounded incredulous.

"No, not necessarily. It's possible, but the idea of the safe house isn't just to shelter them, but to help them get reestablished in a new community. Help them find a job or job training or education. Disciple them and connect them to a church. They're basically starting over."

"The job market in our area isn't very good right now. I don't think I could be of much help." Jill's voice was firm. "And besides, I only live about two hours from you. That seems a little too close for something like you're talking about. I have a responsibility to my own family. I mean what if their family did decide to hunt them down? They could end up taking out their revenge on us."

Before Austia could speak, Jill added, "I'll be praying for you, Austia. And good luck." Then she hung up.

Austia refused to accept the weight of disappointment that pressed on her chest. Instead, she drew a deep breath and deleted Jill's name, then moved the cursor down the list.

She stopped at Martha Hillman. A devout Christian. She'd been Austia's Sunday school teacher when Austia's family had lived in Santa Barbara. They'd stayed in touch over the years. Austia dialed the number.

After catching up on the time since they'd last talked, Austia got to the point of her call. "As God blesses my ministry, I'm feeling like I need to put some safeguards in place for Muslims who become believers."

"I would think so. It can be dangerous for them. I've heard about what can happen when a Muslim leaves Islam."

Austia felt a weight lifting from her shoulders. This was so like Martha, compassionate and understanding. "I'm trying to set up a network of safe houses. Christians who are willing to open their homes to Muslims. Hide them if necessary and help them get on their feet." She swallowed. "In fact, that's one of the reasons I called. Would you be open to helping out?"

"In what way?"

"Would you be willing to offer a Muslim Background Believer a home for a few months?"

Martha didn't answer immediately.

Finally she spoke. "Our grandson served in Iraq. He dealt with the Muslims on a daily basis. We learned quite a bit about Islam and that culture from him. You know he went there hoping for opportunities to witness to them, but he soon learned that their hearts are hardened against the Lord." She hesitated. "Did you know that their religion teaches that it's all right to lie if it furthers Islam? That you don't have to keep any agreements made with infidels?"

Austia knew what Martha was saying was partly true. How many times had she heard Christians making the case against Islam by referring to a verse in chapter 8 of the Qur'an that urges Muslims to do whatever possible to inflict terror and destroy the enemy for the cause of Allah and Islam? Extremists used it to justify any immoral act, from lying to the killing of innocents. But most Muslims viewed such verses as no longer relevant since Islam was now recognized as a world religion and it was unnecessary to spread it by conquest and colonialism as was done in the first centuries. Unfortunately, they feared the radicals as much as any westerner, and their reluctance to speak out against their militant brothers gave people like Martha the impression that they agreed with the radicals, or even worse, quietly supported them. "Yes, but Muslim Background Believers aren't following the Qur'an anymore. God has lifted the veil from their eyes."

"How would you know, Austia? How could you be sure? Particularly when you're talking about someone who says they're a 'new' believer. Maybe they're just saying that and it's just one more way to try and spread Islam. You can't trust them."

Austia slowly closed her eyes, searching for words to put things in perspective, but nothing came to mind. Finally, she just spoke from her heart.

"Martha, Muslims who convert pay a huge price. Most have no jobs because they live in a Muslim community and are shunned. Sometimes they have to flee and their families hunt them down and kill them."

Austia paused, hoping Martha would comment or give some sign that she understood.

But she didn't.

As the moments passed, something Austia hadn't thought about since her husband's death occurred to her. "I'll share with you something the Lord showed me when David died." She blinked back tears. "My Christianity cost me nothing."

"What on earth are you saying?"

"That I can never know Jesus like a Muslim believer does. They pay a great price to know Him. And they love Jesus as you would love someone who has saved you from certain death."

"Austia, He saved us all from certain death."

"Oh, I know He saved me from sin and death. But I don't know it experientially like they do. I know because I have read about it in the Bible. But I have never lived under the threat of eternal damnation like they have. Islam is an unforgiving religion, and God is perceived as cold and unpredictable, judging you every moment, noting your sins, waiting for your death to exact His judgment. And there is no way to escape Him. That is as real to them as God's redeeming love is to us. When they meet Jesus, and often He comes to them personally to overcome their fear of Allah, and they find out that He died in their place, that God exacted His judgment on Jesus, that Jesus suffered so they will never have to, they fall on their knees and worship Him. They worship and love Him in a way I never can. I have never experienced what life and death would really be without Jesus and Calvary. I've known about Jesus' love and forgiveness since I was just a kid."

Oh, Lord God, let her hear me.

"Well, if Jesus actually appeared to them He might break through. But how would you know? I mean really know."

Though it was frustrating, Austia understood where Martha was coming from. It was exactly the way Austia had felt when she first met David. She'd harbored a deep distrust, even hatred, of the Muslims after 9/11. And it had returned with a vengeance after his death. Her thoughts lingered a moment, then she straightened, pulling back from the precipice. Hatred was what had killed David.

The image of the imam leaning on Zaki's car suddenly loomed in her mind's eye. Only this time he raised his head and his dark eyes focused on her.

Fear zigzagged through her chest. "Martha, would you pray for me? Will you pray that I will have wisdom and if this is God's will I won't be deceived by the Enemy?"

"Of course I'll pray. And will you call me from time to time and let me know how this is going?"

Austia promised she would, and then said good-bye.

Austia hung up, then returned to the list. She set her lips in a firm line and deleted Martha's name. She dialed the next number. "God doesn't call everyone to serve in that way. I'm called to help the poor. Christ said when you minister to the least of us, you minister to Him. But it's awesome that He's called you to minister to Muslims. Frankly, the whole idea scares me." ... And the next one ... "My boss is very anti-Muslim because one of them is suing the company for the right to wear native dress in the office. The office has received threatening emails. I want nothing to do with those people. I will definitely pray for you though." ... And the next one ... "What if their people found out where they were? Our organization could be targeted by them, our offices blown up, and our employees killed." … And the next one … "I would love to get involved. But I know my husband won't let me. We have a wonderful life with our church friends and are involved with the worship music and Friday night potluck. What you're talking about could ruin that kind of open fellowship." … And the final one … "Would they be wearing that rag on their head?"

She put the receiver in the cradle and stared at it. This wasn't working. Flopping back in her chair, she let her arms drop to her sides. Closing her eyes, she leaned her head against the back of the chair and searched her memory. There had to be somebody willing to help.

Just one believer. Somewhere.

CHAPTER 15

Austia bolted upright. Pastor Bill. Unity and Grace Community Church. The church she attended. She picked up the phone and pressed the numbers to reach Pastor Bill Nelson.

He answered on the second ring.

"Hi, Pastor Bill, it's Austia."

"Oh, thanks for returning my call."

Austia hesitated.

"I left a message at your office late this afternoon."

Austia paused. "Oh, I left a little early so I didn't get it. How can I help you?"

"I wanted to remind you that the Planning Commission meeting is next Tuesday night, and they're hearing public comment about the proposed noise ordinance change that will allow the mosque on Second Street to broadcast their call to prayer over a loudspeaker."

Austia had followed the controversy closely, but she had mixed feelings. She loved hearing the church bells chime on Sunday mornings, and the call to prayer was just as pleasing to the Muslim ear. Still, the church bells only rang one day a week, not five times a day. Though it would be lovely if the church bells did.

"Are you going?" the pastor prompted her.

"Yes, I am."

"Great. You're respected here in the community and you've done a lot for the Muslims. Teaching them English is a good first step in helping them assimilate, after all, they *are* living in America. They have the freedom to worship as they wish, but we're a Christian nation. There is nothing American about forcing a community to listen to a call for prayer in a foreign language, five times a day."

There was an edge to the pastor's voice that surprised Austia. "I understand how you'd feel that way."

He drew a breath and continued. "Beyond that, it will set a precedent. Today it's Agua Viva, but tomorrow it will be another town, then another town after that. Then it will no longer be a matter of the Planning Commission taking up the issue, because it will have become the right of Muslims to broadcast their call to prayer anywhere they live."

Austia frowned. She could see his point. "Maybe the call to prayer could be allowed once in the morning or once in the afternoon."

"Unfortunately, I'm afraid a compromise would only be taken by them to be a sign of weakness and the first step in achieving what they really want. Which is to recreate their homeland right here on the West Coast. I hope you'll pray about this."

Sensing this was not the right time to bring up the issue of safe houses, she closed the conversation. "I promise I will give it some prayerful thought."

"Will I see you in church Sunday?"

"I'm not sure. I was thinking I might go visit my brother, Steve."

"Well, in case you don't attend, I'll tell you now. I'll be announcing that we're going to be cutting back to one Sunday service in the sanctuary. Eleven o'clock, starting the first Sunday of next month."

"Thanks for letting me know. Have a good night."

After hanging up, she leaned back in her chair. She didn't have to ask why the services were being cut. It was painfully clear to anyone who went there regularly. The attendance had diminished dramatically over the past year.

And during the same period of time, her ESL classes had grown. The simple truth was, as more Muslims moved into the area, many middle-class, churchgoing Christians had moved out. Mosques were multiplying and churches were closing.

She shut down her computer, then rose and went into the living room. Dropping onto the couch, she picked up the remote control and turned on the television to FOX News. A Middle Eastern man in native garb was speaking on the right half of a split screen. On the other side was the talk show's host.

"Islam is a religion of peace. We don't believe in killing innocents."

The host slowly shook his head. "If that's true, you people aren't getting that word out. And where are your leaders, why aren't we hearing from them?"

That was a question she used to ask. One of the questions she'd asked David when she first met him, before she'd fallen in love with him.

Austia spoke to the television screen. "You aren't hearing from them because they are afraid too." She studied the face of the Muslim guest. Dark eyes intent, shoulders hunched forward in earnestness, trying to salvage his religion. Moderate Muslims everywhere were suffering the consequences of the actions of their radical brothers.

Her thoughts went to Walid at the gas station, Faruq the baker, and Nasir with his vegetable stand. All good, kind, honest men who loved America and considered it their home. Giving a resigned sigh, she switched off the television and got ready for bed.

She turned off her bedroom light, then stepped to the open window. The moon backlit the clouds that dotted the sky and a strong breeze moved through the leaves of the maple tree just a few feet away. Somehow tonight the safe, familiar world beyond her window seemed menacing.

Suddenly, a cloak of fear enveloped her.

She climbed into bed and pulled the sheet up under her chin. Too keyed up to sleep, she watched as the moon mirrored the leaves and limbs of the tree outside her window on her bedroom wall.

Her imagination observed the shadow figure. The trunk looked like a huge body, and the branches like great pinions sprouting from its shoulders. Outlined by the big, rustling leaves, they became massive wings.

In the silence of the dark room it was a frightening presence, spread across the wall like some huge, dark, supernatural being hovering over her. She tucked the covers around her, chiding herself. God was with her. Wasn't He? She turned toward the empty space next to her.

David was gone. Sabirah had been murdered. Her brother wouldn't answer her phone calls. And now, a mysterious and dangerous Islamic man who was likely connected to Sabirah's murder would be arriving at the Career Center tomorrow morning to start work.

As exhaustion overcame her and she slipped away to that transient passage between waking and sleeping, her eyes fluttered closed. Glimpsing the wall as sleep overtook her, the huge transcendental image seemed to come into stark relief.

Fusing into a dream, it became a sulfurous, pulsating mass arcing over her.

Then it vanished.

CHAPTER 16

Finding an empty space near the back door to her office, Austia parked and turned off the engine. On edge and tired after a restless night, she found herself scanning the parking lot.

Annie's car was in its usual spot; the cleaning people from the business next door were loading their van and preparing to leave. She waved at them through the windshield.

Feeling the tightness in her shoulders ease a little, she took in the deep blue skies woven with pristine white clouds—a beautiful tapestry of nature that she often thought of as the outer garments of God. Everything seemed just as it did on any other morning.

But this wasn't just any other morning. Zaki ben Hassan was coming to start his job.

Not only could the ministry be uncovered, but she and every one of the women who attended the ESL classes would fall under suspicion from their families. In some cases it would mean interrogations and beatings. She drew a deep breath. That wasn't going to happen. She would take the steps necessary to protect them. God was with her.

Austia closed her eyes a moment. She believed in God and the truth of His Word. And several times during the night she'd thought about the Scripture in Matthew when Jesus told His disciples not to worry about what they would say when they were in difficult situations because the Holy Spirit would give them the words. But right now blindly clinging to a few sentences in Scripture didn't seem like enough.

In fact, she'd awoken during the night dreaming that she was calling a former employee. Someone she was still in touch with. Omar Malik, a former Muslim who was now a Christian. He'd done translations for her in the past. The dream led to an idea, a reason she could give Zaki to let him go that would hold up even if Zaki checked it. She could tell Zaki that Omar was returning to the area and would be taking his job back.

She'd agonized over the idea because she didn't want to foster a lie. Finally, she'd called Omar before she'd left for work and explained the situation. He'd completely understood her fear and why she was asking for his help. He reminded her that Rahab had lied to save the spies and he saw nothing wrong, should he ever be asked, to say he had planned the move, but it hadn't worked out.

After gathering her purse, her lunch, and the stack of files she'd hoped to finish working on at home, she climbed out of the car. Arms full, she bumped the car door closed with her hip and made her way across the parking lot. As she neared the back door, she heard chirping. A glance to the little ledge under the overhang revealed a mama sparrow feeding her little brood. There was something about the sweet scene that calmed her. Everything was going to be all right.

After hesitating a moment to pull herself together, she jostled the load in her arms and grabbed the door handle to the office's back entrance.

"Can I help you with that?"

She jumped at the sound of the accented voice just behind her.

"Zaki!" She took a step back.

"Oh, sorry. I didn't mean to startle you. Here, let me help you." He took three-quarters of the files from her before she could answer and tucked them under his arm. Then, with his free hand, he gripped the door handle and pulled the door open.

A very familiar scent of aftershave rode silently on the rush of air from the opening door. *David.* Her stomach clenched. Such intimate and precious memories being sparked by the dangerous man before her was deeply unsettling. Almost as if he were signaling her he knew of her husband and his death. She wanted to run.

Instead, careful to keep her eyes from his, she lowered her head and walked past him into the back hall of the office. "Thank you."

"You're welcome." He let the door close behind them, then silently followed her down the hall to her office. As she set her files on the desk, he stepped around her and started to put his stack on top of her file cabinet.

"Zaki. Would you mind putting those here?" She pulled out a deep drawer on the left side of her desk. "I still have work to do on them."

"Of course."

As he dropped the folders into the drawer, Austia stepped toward the office door, ever mindful of the strict Islamic requirement of separation of genders. And on this day, extremely grateful for it. She put distance between them and made herself visible from the hallway. "I'd like to take a moment and meet in the conference room."

Zaki nodded. "Of course. I can't wait to start."

"I'll be there in a minute." Austia moved to the side and Zaki walked passed her and down the hall. She stared at the back of his jacket, trying to determine if there were any irregularities in how it lay.

Austia stepped into her office and closed the door. Leaning against it, she tried to gather her thoughts about the plan she'd made with Omar.

She jumped at the sound of a knock on the door behind her.

"It's Annie."

Austia opened the door and Annie stepped in.

"Oh, honey. I have some bad news. I'm just getting to yesterday's mail and we got a notice from the IRS."

"Are you talking about that payroll deposit dispute you've been working on for a month?"

"Yes." Annie rested her hand on Austia's arm. "And they still say we owe them about eighteen hundred dollars. I'm positive about my filings and know when this finally gets straightened out we'll get that money back. But in the meantime I have to pay it … again."

Austia felt tears sting her eyes. How much more could she take? They ran the Center on a shoestring. They didn't have an extra eighteen hundred dollars. This meant other obligations would have to wait. Why was the Lord allowing this to happen, especially now?

Annie patted Austia's arm. "I know, honey, and I hate having to tell you. But I've got to get this check out this morning and it means using the overdraft." She handed Austia a check and a pen. Then, tilting her head and shrugging her shoulders, she smiled. "James says to consider it pure joy when you face trials."

Austia rolled her eyes. There was nothing joyous about finding out you weren't going to have enough money to pay your bills. "You know I support whatever you need to do." Resting the check on the back of the door, she signed it. "Now I've got to go meet Zaki ben Hassan."

Turning on her heel, she headed to the conference room. As she entered the meeting room she absently touched the cross beneath her blouse.

Zaki rose and smiled.

Austia seated herself across from him.

After he took his seat, she folded her hands and rested them on the conference table. "I'm sorry, I have some bad news."

She glanced toward him and found his eyes keenly focused on her. His smile gone.

Her resolve ebbed away. "Uh." She dropped her gaze to her hands.

He was taking control of the situation. He was a man, and she only a woman. The culture she chose to live and work in asserted itself. An aggressive and unseen participant injecting itself into the crisis Sabirah's death had brought to her. She stumbled over her thoughts.

"I need to talk to you about something." The words didn't sound like hers. They were loud and hasty.

He made no response.

The silent hand of intimidation rested on her mouth. A hard pit formed in her throat. She shifted in her chair. She was going to have to lie. A vice tightened around her heart.

Please help me, God. The desperate, silent prayer felt empty. And they both knew why. He would not help her lie. Rahab had not given her life to Christ with a promise to obey Him. Christ would never lie.

Suddenly, a memory surged. Zaki ben Hassan had made a point of telling her that his brother was married to an American and that he was very comfortable in both cultures. The thought strengthened her. Well then … A firm face-to-face meeting with his boss should not seem disrespectful. She lifted her gaze to meet his.

He blinked.

As mysterious and certain as the Spirit of God, words formed on her lips.

"I received an unfortunate piece of news this morning from my business partner."

He sat silently.

She opened her mouth again. "We've had an unexpected expense levied against us by the government and we won't be able to afford to fund your position. I'm sorry."

His eyes coolly narrowed.

"I see."

"I will certainly keep your file, and if things change we'll be looking again."

He lifted one hand, palm up, suddenly relaxed. "These things happen. I understand completely. In fact, this happened to my brother's wife where she worked. But since it was only a temporary problem, she agreed to stay on a volunteer basis until funds became available." He leaned forward, taking control. "I will be glad to do that for you. It's important to me to help my people find employment."

His brother's wife! She didn't believe him. Her mind raced.

"That is so kind of you." She held her voice steady against the gnawing sense of danger that spurted through her. "But our insurance doesn't allow us to have volunteers work here."

He raised his eyebrows, and in the silent seconds he gathered his thoughts, the look in his eyes told her he knew she didn't want him working for her.

"As it happens, that was the case with my sister-in-law." He paused as his words formed a steel trap. "She signed a hold-harmless agreement with her employer. If you think that is necessary, I'll be glad to do it." He watched her as the trap closed.

Somehow the conversation was no longer about the job or his sister-in-law. The set of his jaw, the predatory tone of his voice, and the quick pat answer stripped away pretense. She felt like she was breathing through mud. She was afraid of him, afraid to confront him, afraid of what he was going to find out … and he knew it. A bolt of fear ricocheted through her. She had to get out of the room.

She rose. "Well, since you are willing to be so accommodating, let me talk to my partner. Perhaps we can have you come in a couple of hours a day until we get our finances straightened out."

He rose. "That sounds like a good plan." He picked up a newspaper from the chair beside him. "I'll be in my office. I was reading your ads in this morning's paper. Those in Arabic had some errors. I thought you'd want them corrected. I called the paper and had that done."

He strode across the room, then turned. "Oh, my sister-in-law's job worked out very well. She worked for her boss until the day he died."

CHAPTER 17

Austia set her cup in its saucer and pushed it away, her stomach in a knot. "Annie, if that isn't a veiled threat, I don't know what is. Besides, I'm positive someone was in my office. You know how I always read the suggested daily Scripture from church when I first get to work?"

Annie nodded.

"This morning I didn't because of that meeting with Zaki. But later I took my Bible out of the drawer and the ribbon that's set into the spine was moved."

Annie leaned forward in the booth. "How can you be sure?"

"I keep the little leaflet that the church prints with the month's Scripture readings in the front of the Bible and I run the ribbon down the page I'm on. The ribbon wasn't in the leaflet. It was behind it, partially off the page. I'm positive someone was in that drawer looking at my Bible. And Zaki ben Hassan is the only person I have any reason to suspect."

"But why would he want to look at your Bible?"

Austia shifted in the booth. "I don't know. Maybe it's not even about the Bible or that drawer. Maybe he was snooping around my office for something else." The disturbing thought sent a wave of apprehension through her. "Something to connect me to Sabirah."

Annie's eyes widened with fear.

"For all I know, he was in there planting a microphone." Her eyes locked onto Annie's. "We will be very careful what we talk about in there from now on."

"Austia, you have to go to the police."

"You know I can't do that. There are too many Muslim officers and detectives."

The waitress laid the tray with their change in it on the table.

"Then just tell Chief Peterson you want to talk to him confidentially."

Austia scooted out of the booth. "I don't know."

Annie grabbed her purse and followed her. "Look, Zaki left shortly after you met with him. When I get back to the office I'll call him and tell him we want to use him for our interviews. In fact we have someone scheduled for tomorrow. I'll tell him to come in for that."

"I just don't know, Annie."

Annie stepped in front of her and opened the door. They walked to the parking lot.

"Austia, go on. At least feel the chief out. Do it for me."

Reluctantly, Austia nodded. "Maybe I should."

Annie gave her a hug, then climbed into her car. Waving through the windshield, she pulled onto the street.

Austia started her car.

She shouldn't do it. She felt it in every fiber of her being. Going to the police about Zaki and the threat he presented meant revealing her connection with Sabirah. If word got out that she was witnessing to the Muslim women who came to her classes, there would be huge repercussions from the radical members of the community. It would taint every Muslim woman who'd ever come to class. It would cast suspicion on them. It could even lead to another murder. She shuddered at the thought of bringing the innocent women who trusted her such trouble and grief. Perhaps even death.

Would God have brought her this far to have it end like this? Had she somehow wandered so far out of God's will that He was slamming doors shut, or was she so deeply in God's will that she was under attack?

Bowing her head, she prayed. "Lord, I'm so confused and frightened."

Voicing the words seemed to give them life, and fear flooded through her, pricking her like fiery darts, resurrecting the reality of Sabirah's murder.

She confessed the secret fear that had dogged her since she first read of Sabirah's death. Things were too dangerous now. Her work for the Lord might be found out, and she too might be killed. And now, with the appearance of Zaki at the Center ... She wanted to leave her ministry.

Letting her heart utter all that she could not find words to express, she asked the Lord to make His will known to her, while through her tears she implored Him to remember all it had already cost her.

The old, familiar ache rose in her heart. The weeping wound that held her memories of David. He had loved people with the love of Christ. And with life-changing clarity she suddenly realized ... she didn't.

She loved Sabirah and the other women she'd shared Christ with in the natural, with human love. She lowered her eyes. Now it was not enough to sustain her.

The love of Christ was the answer.

The only thing that could change people's hearts and stop the killing.

With the power of conviction, the words cut deep, circumcising her heart.

Then, in a way that she had never understood before, she knew she must choose to surrender all to God if she wanted to be used by Him. Going to the police would be selling out.

Austia slowly dropped her chin to her chest, desperately wishing the fear would subside. The stakes were so high and eternity hung in the balance.

Dropping her head into her hands, she prayed. "Jesus. Jesus, I'm so afraid."

She heard a whisper as gentle as the brush of an angel's wing.

"Trust Me."

She felt for the cross David had given her. As she touched it, a flame of light, glowing red, ruby red, cut through her line of vision. And though she could not say how, she knew that it contained the truth of Calvary. Love that was stronger than death.

The choice was hers.

In a deliberate act, she surrendered her heart to the only thing that would allow her to endure. "Give me Your love for them. There is no way I can do this on my own."

Time seemed to stop and peace enveloped her as Love cast out Fear.

A flash of heat rushed through her, filling her with a profound sense of passion so sweet and pure she wept. Lifting her face to her Savior, she cried out her demand. "Yes. Give me *Your* love."

In the beauty of the moment she knew that from deep wounding *can* come deep love.

And it was worth the cost.

She would go to battle with the enemies of His kingdom. Desiring that none would die lost.

She would not depend on the police to protect her. She would trust God.

Moments passed as the certainty of her decision found root in the sterile ground of reality. The people she was up against were killers, and her actions could endanger not only her life but those of the women the Lord had entrusted to her. It was as David had told her when he'd taken her into his arms at the security gate on his way to Kuwait. They were living in the "final days" Jesus had prophesied when He said, "And this gospel of the kingdom shall be preached in all the world for a witness unto all nations; and then shall the end come." A cold chill gripped her. It was not until she'd met David that she'd realized "all nations" included the nation of Islam.

Suddenly anxious to return to the office, she started the car. As she drove, she tried to think of ways to convince Zaki that there was no reason for him to focus on the Center. Once he was satisfied that there was nothing going on out of the ordinary, he would leave.

She pulled into the parking lot and took an open space next to Annie's car. She noticed Zaki's car just in front of her. As she reached across the seat to get her purse, a movement caught her eye. Looking through her passenger window and over Annie's hood, she realized one of the baby birds had fallen from the nest over the back door.

"Oh, dear."

The little bird floundered.

Just as she straightened, the back door of the office opened.

It was Zaki.

When he spotted the baby bird, he stopped.

After watching it a moment, he scooped it into his hand and began walking toward her, his expression intense. As he neared her car, he saw her.

His expression didn't change as his eyes rested on her.

Then, inexplicably, he slightly raised the hand with the baby bird and closed his fingers around it.

Austia gasped.

He'd killed it.

CHAPTER 18

Zaki kicked off his shoes, then, with his hand in his pocket, took the stairs two at a time to his bedroom.

After shutting the door behind him, he lifted the tiny bird from his pocket and gently set it on his bed. "Don't be afraid."

He'd hated frightening Austia like he had, but this was a high-stakes game, and by making her fearful it was much more likely that she would curtail whatever it was she was doing. She had become an unexpected complication. His mission was to infiltrate Hussein's cell and feed their plans to his FBI handler. Which wasn't easy. Hussein kept all his activities compartmentalized. He revealed information on a need-to-know basis only, and information was shared between men only if there was a specific directive from Hussein. He ruled from the top down with an iron fist.

So far, all Zaki had been able to determine was that jihadists were being trained in Yemen for a strike in the US, and that Hussein's obsessive interest in the call-to-prayer issue was somehow tied to that.

The baby bird made a weak noise. Zaki knelt beside the bed. "Hang on. Don't you die on me."

He'd bandaged mangled bodies on the battlefield; he'd kept wounded men alive until the medics arrived; he'd even improvised a splint from a piece of shrapnel. But this had him stumped.

He shook his head, clearing it of the images of bloody, lifeless bodies—foot soldiers for jihad—lying on a runway hidden in the mountain terrain of Yemen. They'd underestimated the courage of the Americans who'd surprised them, but their dream of radicalizing the world had not died with them.

That had been a turning point in his life, even now hardening his resolve to accomplish his mission.

He stood back and raked his fingers through his hair. "What am I going to do with you?"

Little black eyes peered back at him.

Quickly rising, he dashed to his computer and typed "nurse baby bird" into the search bar. Whatever he was going to do, he had to hurry. In the cell he was known as ruthless and calculating. And that reputation had served him well. He should have disposed of the bird while driving home.

But he hadn't.

Clicking on the top link, the screen filled with instructions. The first one read: *Keep bird warm.*

He scanned the room. A shaft of light shone through the open window across from his bed. He carefully carried the baby bird across the room and gently laid it on the carpet below the window in the sunlight. "You're going to be okay." He straightened.

His mind flashed back to the mountains of Yemen and the brave Rangers who'd died in that godforsaken place. His American brothers who'd laid down their lives for the love of their country and the cause of freedom. Jimmy Lee, an Asian from San Francisco; Isaiah Jones, an African American from Harlem; and Zak Genzberger, his buddy from New York, and others. All dead. Christian, Muslim, or Jew, it hadn't mattered. They were Americans. In the heat of those battles he'd fought not for his country or to kill the enemy but to keep his buddies alive. In combat one's bond to a brother soldier didn't lessen with death; it was forever fused in memory and reawakened with palpable clarity by certain sounds, smells, emotions.

In Yemen, his last mission had been to destroy a network of tunnels that the jihadist movement used to move weapons and fighters around the capital as they increased their efforts to create a safe haven for their group. Miraculously, he'd survived the tunnel blast that had taken place beneath the streets of the capital during the final bloody battle with the Islamist militants.

He was awarded the Medal of Honor for his bravery. He'd given it to Zak's wife. Accolades and tributes meant nothing. He had a score to settle with the radicalized Muslims who were proliferating their hate around the world. And whatever the price, he would pay it.

Though he'd survived, his injuries had permanently sidelined him from seeing any further action. And he hadn't re-upped when the time came. Instead he'd connected to other patriots, former Navy Seals and Rangers who, like himself, were of Middle Eastern descent. Their language skills and cultural background were sought-after commodities in the war on terror. They shared job information, and those connections led him to the FBI and a case agent, Madani, who worked for the Weapons of Mass Destruction Directorate. Madani managed a case investigating the development and production of an undetectable poison. US intelligence believed the source of this plot was al-Qaeda in the Arabian Peninsula, based in Yemen, and they had uncovered a cell operating in the US that tied back to them.

Now the FBI's mission was to infiltrate the cell. They tried to recruit Zaki, but he rejected their offer and the rules that went with it. Instead, using his Arab roots, he posed as a jihadist, and over time penetrated the cell and became a confidential informant for them.

This protected his identity while keeping him from being under the thumb of the FBI. He wanted to do things his way. And he had.

Still, that the beautiful young woman had garnered the attention of Hussein al-Ansari was something he needed to let them know.

Fortunately, her showing up at the duplex yesterday and then trying to fire him had tipped him off that she was suspicious of him. But she wouldn't go to the police. She was clearly extremely bright and unusually perceptive. If she felt free to go to the cops, she would have already done it. And if she were connected to any state or federal agencies, she would have sought them out. Whatever she was hiding, she didn't want the police or anyone else to know about it.

Zaki set his lips in a firm line. She was in Hussein's crosshairs. And he was the only one who could save her. But jeopardizing his mission was not an option.

Thousands of innocent people would lose their lives if he lost his focus.

CHAPTER 19

"Come on, Sami, we're going to the park with Aunt Najah." Fatima lifted Sami from the playpen by her bed and settled him on her hip.

"And you know what?" His large dark eyes searched her face. "When we get back your grandmother will be coming to take care of you. That way I can go to school and learn to speak English so people can understand me."

Her heartbeat quickened as thoughts of the evening class at the Career Center sparked memories of her husband's niece, Sabirah. Hussein had told Fatima that Sabirah had been murdered by some American teenagers who hated Muslims. His voice had been caustic as he delivered his tirade that this kind of attack was to be expected for Muslim women who chose to leave the protection of their families. And he was quick to add that he'd predicted Sabirah would come to this end long ago.

Despite Hussein's constant admonitions about the girl since Fatima first arrived in America, she had secretly become close to the free-spirited young woman whom the family considered a black sheep for embracing the American culture. Sabirah's interest in the ways of the West was a constant source of shame to her parents, and they had banished her from their home before she finished high school. But Fatima had found her bright and curious mind endearing and encouraged her to go to the English class that was offered locally. She and Sabirah had prepared many family meals together when they'd first met, talking about Sabirah's dreams of becoming a teacher and how she admired the woman who taught the ESL classes. Fatima could not say why, but those conversations always ended with her feeling that things were being left unsaid. That there was more Sabirah wanted to share.

Especially the last few times they had visited. Fatima's usual good-bye of "I love you. See you later" had brought tears to Sabirah's eyes. And Sabirah's cryptic answer still came to Fatima's mind from time to time: "Remember, love's touch heals."

As Fatima started out the door, the sound of voices came through the open bedroom window. She turned and shuffled back across the room. Peering down at the driveway, she caught her breath.

Sabirah's car.

Hussein and Faisal, Sabirah's father, and an American man she didn't recognize were standing next to it. She leaned toward the window, watching and listening, now recalling that she had overheard her husband say he was going with his brother to pick up the car from the police.

Hussein put his arm around his brother Faisal's shoulder. "The police don't seem to have any leads."

Faisal stepped away from him. "As Allah wills it."

The three men started toward the house. As they walked out of her sight, Hussein's voice drifted through the window. "I'll have Najah come and clean out all that junk in the car. The garbage man can haul it off."

Tears sprang to Fatima's eyes and she stepped back, dropping to the edge of the bed. Why such cold words, and why were they sending Sabirah's things to the dump? Fatima tightened her grip on Sami. Why wouldn't Sabirah's parents and sisters and brothers want to go through everything and keep any items that held special memories? Yes, Sabirah's teen years had been trying, but she was still their daughter. If something had happened to Najah, Fatima would have carefully selected from her sister's belongings items that would be precious keepsakes for herself and their family in Qatar.

She rose. "It looks like we won't be going to the park after all." She kissed her son's cheek. "Let's go help Aunt Najah."

Fatima hurried down the steps as quickly as she could and got Sami's stroller from the front hall. After slipping him into the seat, she walked him outside to the driveway. Najah was opening the trunk.

"Fatima, I've been told to clean out this car. I won't be able to go to the park."

Fatima parked Sami's stroller on the nearby lawn. "Don't worry about that. Let me help you." As she walked away, Sami began to fuss. She returned to him, and seeing his eyes were heavy, dropped the back of the stroller down. By the time she positioned the stroller in a shady spot near the flowerbeds, he was asleep. She smiled, thinking that the first thing he would see when he opened his eyes was the beautiful rose bush blooming nearby. She kissed his cheek, then returned to the car.

Najah tore some plastic bags off the roll she'd set on the ground by the back tires. "Here, you can start in the backseat."

The garage door opener began to hum, and a moment later Hussein appeared. He brushed past Najah and pushed in front of Fatima. "Move. I need to get the registration."

As Fatima stepped aside, he opened the passenger door. Reaching into the car, he opened the glove compartment, removing all its contents and throwing them on the front seat.

Suddenly Hussein stiffened. His jowly face reddened.

Fatima followed his gaze to a book lying amid the papers strewn on the seat.

Her eyes widened at the Arabic lettering. *New Testament and Psalms.*

"May Allah damn her soul in Hell." Though his curse came out a whisper, the venom that delivered it was palpable. Fatima shrank back as her husband knocked it off the seat to the floor, then quickly picked through the papers.

Having found what he wanted, he walked away, shouting a directive as he disappeared into the garage. "Get that trash out of here."

Fatima and her sister exchanged glances.

Najah snapped her bag open. "I wonder what set him off?"

Fatima's eyes cut to the book. "You know him. He doesn't need anything to set him off." … He'd told them to throw it out … "He considers every problem in the family his problem." … No one would know.

She pulled the back of the passenger seat forward and reached behind it, pulling some clothes out, making a little pile between her feet and the car. Then she pulled the seatback upright. She glanced at Najah. Her sister was folding a small blanket.

Najah matched the corners. "Do you think they'll catch those dogs who killed her?"

Fatima glanced around. Hussein was gone. Leaning back, she quickly looked down the street. No sign of her in-laws or the blue

Toyota that Faisal had taken to pick them up. She opened her bag and began filling it from the pile of clothes at her feet. "I hope so."

As she bent down to get more clothes she reached into the car and moved the book from the floor back to the seat. Then she squatted down and eyed the book more closely. If only her *abaya* had pockets. Her mind raced. Maybe it would fit up her sleeve.

With a quick look toward Najah, she leaned forward, grasped the book with her right hand, and began working it up the back of her forearm. It fit tightly. If anyone looked at her closely they would see the rectangular silhouette below her elbow.

She rose, moving her right arm behind her back. She only had to get past Najah, then she'd have a clear shot to the stroller where she could hide the book. There was no need to involve her sister in what she was doing. If Hussein ever found out it would be impossible to explain. Najah could honestly say she knew nothing about it. "I'm going to go check on Sami."

As Fatima took her first steps, she heard a car pull in behind her. "Oh, look, it's your in-laws."

Heart pounding, Fatima whirled around and came face-to-face with a black Toyota. Her mother-in-law peered from the backseat as Imam al-Ansari coolly observed Fatima through the windshield.

A rush of heat washed through her and her heart beat wildly as they exited the car. "*Al salamu alaikum.*"

"*Wa alikum alsalam.*" Her mother-in-law moved toward her, arms outstretched.

"*Alhamdulillah.* It looks like a new car." Hussein called out as he strode across the front lawn smiling broadly, stopping next to Fatima, his shoulder touching hers.

A high-pitched scream suddenly pierced the air.

Fatima gasped.

Sami!

Fear strapped her feet to the ground as every thought fled from her mind.

Finally, she willed her herself forward. As her awkward, stumbling limp took her to her baby, Sabirah's book slipped from her cupped fingers.

CHAPTER 20

What a day it had been. Austia threw her purse in the passenger's seat and climbed behind the wheel. Annie's insistence that she go to the police was a point of contention between them. And the incredibly unsettling incident with Zaki when she had come back from coffee with Annie still haunted her. She'd spared her friend the retelling of that event. The one bright spot of the day had been when Steve had returned her call.

She hadn't fully realized how concerned her brother was about her until that conversation. But then, she'd kept him at a distance since David's death, knowing he didn't support what she was doing.

She'd kept a lot of people at a distance. And the truth was, right now she felt isolated and lonely. She had walked closely with the Lord for years. And the one thing she had learned was that whenever she had cried out for confirmation that she was indeed on the path He had chosen for her, He would answer by giving her peace.

But where once she had felt direction, certainty, and passion, she now felt fear.

"Lord, I need a clear sign from You. Something that removes every doubt I have about going forward with this ministry."

Signs. It seemed the Lord wasn't in the mood for giving signs these days. How many times had she prayed for Him to send her a man to love her? A man who would be there for her when the bite of life stung. A man with a heart of compassion who would hold her and comfort her. A man who was noble and good, who would put his life on the line for what mattered in this world. Someone who could share in the pain and joy that came with living on this earth. Then today a little ray of light had come beaming through the phone call from Steve. She felt a little tug at the corner of her mouth. He had hinted that he had someone he wanted her to meet. She broke into a smile. He knew she hated blind dates.

She turned on the car radio. The local Christian "talk" station, KJCL 95.5 FM, was in the midst of a discussion about the call-to-prayer issue that the Planning Commission was taking up Tuesday night. As she listened, she remembered her promise to pick up Mr. Rahman's letter. A glance at the clock on the dash told her it was not too late to stop by his house.

At the bottom of the freeway exit to Agua Viva, she pulled to the shoulder of the road, picked up her cell phone, and called him. He answered on the second ring.

"*Al salamu alaikum*, Mr. Rahman."

"*Wa alikum alsalam.*"

"Mr. Rahman, this is Austia. I was wondering if I could come by and pick up your letter."

"Oh, yes. Please come." There was a note of urgency in the old man's voice.

"Is everything okay?"

He hesitated. "Yes—yes, everything is fine, *alhamdulillah.*"

"I'll be there in about half an hour."

"*Insha'allah.*"

After saying good-bye, she closed her cell phone, her thoughts filtering back through the many visits she'd had with the sweet couple over the years. Him proudly showing her his retirement letter from the Ford Company in Detroit, thanking him for forty years of service in the janitorial department. "We come with nothing. I work hard."

His wife's eyes shone as though she were hearing the story for the first time.

"America. She is good," he'd said, his hand slowly smoothing the face of the letter. It was his appreciation for the country and her freedoms that had caused him to become involved over the years in issues that sometimes caused conflict in the community. Like special accommodations in the public schools for daily prayer and now the call to prayer being broadcast. He was always a voice of reason looking for common ground. And he had often expressed feelings of shame about the terrorist acts that received so much media coverage. He'd wept with her when the Twin Towers fell.

Austia huffed a sigh. She couldn't put her finger on it, but it was clear from the phone call that Mr. Rahman wanted to say more than he had. Her heart went out to him. He was a man. She was a woman. There was a certain line that could not be crossed. Still, she could be supportive in other ways. With Mrs. Rahman so ill, Austia decided she'd stop at the grocery store near their house and pick up something for them to eat.

During their friendship she'd shared many beautiful times with the childless couple and had made it a point to learn the traditions and practices that were important to them. There were required social formalities to be observed, and she was careful to avoid the casual familiarity that was acceptable in Western culture. She had become especially close to Mr. Rahman's wife, Safia, helping her with her crocheting projects, joining her in the preparation of special foods for the Muslim holidays, and even going to the park with her for afternoon strolls.

It was during these walks that Austia had learned how well-read Safia was. Without children and with her husband gone all day, she had educated herself through weekly trips to the library near her home in Detroit. Though, knowing her place and respecting the authority of her husband, she kept what she learned to herself. She fully accepted the strictures of her beloved Islam, the religion of peace that brought her inner tranquility. She openly expressed her shame at the killing of innocents being done in the name of her faith. Her eyes misting, she had told Austia, "I pray for peace among all people."

Austia would never forget the day Mrs. Rahman asked her to call her *khalama*. The term of endearment meant "auntie," but the gesture carried a far deeper meaning. They had been sitting on the couch visiting. Mr. Rahman was sitting nearby repairing an old lamp cord. And though his eyes never left the task at hand, Austia saw him smile and nod. Even in this matter, Safia respected the authority of her husband.

As their relationship deepened, Austia continued to pray for their salvation. But as close as she had grown to the Rahmans, the Rahmans were closer still to Islam.

After a quick stop at the store, Austia continued on to their home. As she turned onto their street, a deep sense of foreboding suddenly sucked the oxygen out of the air.

Headlights flashed in her rearview mirror from a car turning off the main street behind her. She caught her breath, eyes glued to the mirror, trying to discern what kind of car it was.

She stepped on the accelerator and drove past the Rahmans' house, then turned right to circle the block.

The car behind her continued down the street, seemingly headed to its own destination.

Austia pulled over, keeping her eyes on the rearview mirror.

As the minutes passed, she became convinced she was just on edge and being silly. She continued on around the block, then parked at the curb in front of the Rahmans' house.

Mr. Rahman answered the door before she could knock. Slipping her shoes off, she stepped into the living room. The sweet smell of incense greeted her. *"Al salamu alaikum."*

"Wa alikum alsalam. It is so kind of you to take the trouble to stop by."

"It was no trouble at all. We haven't had a chance to visit in a while, and I wanted to pick up the letter."

He stepped to the side of the door and gestured to the couch. "Please, Austia, have a seat."

Austia crossed the room and set the small bag of fruit and yogurt she'd purchased on the coffee table. "Here's just a little something for you and Mrs. Rahman to snack on."

"Masha'allah! You should not have taken the bother."

"You and *Khalama* have been so good to me. It was no bother at all."

Mr. Rahman took the bag from the table. "One little moment, please. Let me put this away."

She watched him shuffle to the kitchen. His chin down, his limp a bit more pronounced, his shoulders rounded from the weight of his wife's illness. *Bless him, Lord.*

Austia seated herself on the couch at the end closest to Mr. Rahman's recliner. He was hard of hearing, and she had discovered long ago that sitting close by him made conversation easier for both of them. Had it been acceptable, she would have pulled one of the straight-backed chairs from the kitchen up next to him so they could chat. But without his wife in the room it would have made Mr. Rahman extremely uncomfortable. Austia's respect for the boundaries of Islam was the foundation of their friendship. She loved them and considered it a small price to pay to be part of their lives.

Glancing around the room, she could see that he was trying to keep the house up as Safia would have, but the afghan that covered the couch was askew and the ordered clutter of their small home had become chaotic without the loving touch of his sweet wife. Gently lifting the afghan, she folded it just the way Safia did and laid it on the arm of the couch.

Turning to the coffee table, she straightened some magazines. She noticed some mail and a flyer from the local mosque written in Arabic, outlining all the reasons that it was so important for every Muslim to support the public call-to-prayer ordinance and attend the meetings so they could volunteer to help where needed. Her heart went out to him. It wasn't easy taking a position against the mosque leadership.

"Here you are." Mr. Rahman set the tray he was carrying on the coffee table.

Austia knew the routine and reached for the cup of steaming mint tea he offered her.

She recognized the serving piece. It had lost its luster long ago and there was a crack that ran along one side, but Henry Ford's profile was still clearly visible in the center. It had been one of Mr. Rahman's retirement gifts and a prized possession. She knew he kept it for special occasions. No matter how many times she visited, she was always touched that they chose to serve her from it.

He seated himself in his recliner. "My wife was awake when you called and insisted that I move her to the chair by the window in our bedroom, but she fell asleep as she waited." His eyes misted. "She sleeps a lot now."

Apprehension flickered across his face and he shifted in his chair. For the second time that evening Austia had the feeling there was something he wanted to say.

"Did you want to give me the letter for the council?"

Mr. Rahman's face went blank for a moment, then he turned to the table next to his chair. "Oh, I have it right here."

After rummaging through the papers and magazines, he reached across the coffee table and handed her a sealed envelope. She slipped it into her purse and set her purse on the floor. "I saw that your imam, Shaykh al-Ansari, was interviewed by the paper."

Mr. Rahman nodded, but didn't offer any comment. His gaze drifted to the wall opposite him, unfocused and unseeing, lost in his own thoughts.

Now, certain there was something on his mind, Austia sipped her tea and waited.

When her teacup was empty, she held it in her lap instead of putting it back on the tray, not wanting to disturb Mr. Rahman as he considered his words. Whatever he wanted to say, it was clearly of great importance to him.

Finally, he spoke.

"I've been listening to the radio more since Safia has been ill."

She waited for him to continue.

"And I happened to come across a radio station last week."

He hesitated and a few more moments passed.

"The callers were talking about a place called Real Life Community Church and about some kind of prayer meeting they have there."

Austia knew exactly which program he was talking about. It was on the station she always listened to, KJCL 95.5, on noon weekdays when she took her lunch break. She was also familiar with the church's gifted pastor, who loved the unlovely and drew his congregation from the homeless population of South Central Los Angeles.

"Yes, I have heard of that church." Austia leaned forward and set her teacup on the table, hoping to get an unobserved glimpse of the radio on the stand next to Mr. Rahman's chair. The light from its clock illuminated the current channel selection—95.5. *Praise You, Jesus.*

He cleared his throat. "They talked about Prophet Jesus, peace be upon Him, and how He is healing people of addictions and all kinds of sicknesses.

"I am terribly concerned about my wife." He drew a deep, shaky breath as he struggled to give voice to his thoughts. "Her doctors say the cancer has spread to her lymph nodes and … and … I fear there is no hope."

Austia caught her breath. She had known that Mrs. Rahman was being treated for colon cancer, but she had not known the details. Nothing had been volunteered, and it would have been inappropriate to ask.

Suddenly Mr. Rahman rose, grabbed her teacup, and hurried to the kitchen. As muffled sounds of grief made their way to the living room, it was all Austia could do not to run to him, take his hand, and comfort him. But to violate the rigid separation of men and women outside of family would not be a comfort to him. She would honor him more by keeping her emotions in check.

After a few minutes, Mr. Rahman returned, carrying a fresh cup of tea. He put it on the coffee table in front of her, then seated himself in his recliner. "As a Muslim, I am told to accept and submit to everything in my life as the will of Allah. But I cannot lose my wife, Austia. She is all I have."

He paused, then leaned forward in his chair. "Do you think Prophet Jesus, peace be upon Him, could heal Mrs. Rahman, even though we are Muslims?"

Austia took a sip from her cup, then set it down, her spirit soaring. The Holy Spirit was drawing him. She had spent years building a relationship with the Rahmans that had originally come from an act of obedience to God. But it had prospered into an abiding love for the elderly couple. And her most fervent prayers were that they would come to know Christ.

Sensing the presence of the Holy Spirit, she felt goose bumps rise on her arms and love filling her heart. She gathered her thoughts. This moment was the culmination of years of prayer. She reached down and took her New Testament from her purse. Then, pushing her purse aside, she set the book on her lap.

"Mr. Rahman." She hesitated, suddenly aware of how culturally inappropriate it would be to read to Mr. Rahman from the Bible. Her ministry was with Muslim women. Somehow she'd always imagined that Mrs. Rahman would be the one to raise a question with her about Jesus. She closed her eyes a moment.

Again she felt the strong presence of the Holy Spirit.

"Mr. Rahman, before I answer that question, would you permit me to show you something in the Holy *Injil?*" She opened her New Testament to Matthew 4, then turned to verse 23, which spoke of Jesus' Galilean ministry of help and healing for all people, even outsiders. "Here, you can read for yourself of God's love for all people." She laid the book on the coffee table within his reach, pointing to the passage.

A knock sounded at the front door.

"Who could that be?" Mr. Rahman rose and crossed the room.

As he opened the door, he stiffened. *"Al salamu alaikum,* Shaykh al-Ansari."

It was the imam from the local mosque. Another man was with him.

CHAPTER 21

Austia's heart lurched.

The imam stepped into the living room.

With her eyes on the unexpected visitor, she slipped her free hand under the New Testament and folded it closed as she slid it into her lap. The imam glanced at her.

Leaning forward to hide the pocket-sized book, she pretended to take a sip of her tea. She didn't dare reach for her purse for fear the activity would draw one of the men's attention to her. Instead, in a furtive movement she prayed would not be noticed, she pushed the New Testament off her lap and between the afghan and the arm of the couch.

Heart pounding, she stood and picked up her purse, acutely aware that just being alone with Mr. Rahman in his living room would be viewed as highly suspicious by Shaykh al-Ansari.

The three men turned toward her—Mr. Rahman's eyes locked on the coffee table.

She stepped around the table and approached the doorway. "Thank you so much for allowing me to visit Mrs. Rahman, but I must be going." As she lowered her eyes, she noticed that the imam was holding a flyer. She saw the words "Planning Commission" and Tuesday's date.

Mr. Rahman nodded toward her, then addressed the imam. "This is Austia Donatelli, a friend of Mrs. Rahman." Turning back to Austia, he continued, "I am sorry you cannot stay longer to visit with her."

Keeping her gaze on the floor, she stepped past the men and out the door into the moonlit night.

As the door closed behind her, dread rose in her chest. Her teacup was still on the table.

"You should be very careful about letting Christians into your home, Mr. Rahman."

Austia froze at the ominous tone of the voice behind her. Turning, she realized it was coming from the open living room window.

"They are infidels and they will corrupt our people."

The elderly man's response was muffled.

"I was wondering, Mr. Rahman, if there is some reason you have not been at the mosque for Jumma prayers these last two Fridays."

Shaykh al-Ansari's tone was accusatory and intimidating. Dread in Austia's chest coalesced into fear. *Oh, Lord, protect Mr. Rahman.* She didn't know whether to stay or run.

The old man's voice was conciliatory. "It is only because my wife has been very ill. I will be sure to attend next Friday."

"Since when does a woman come before Allah and our religious duty? You almost sound like a *kafir.*"

Glancing to her right and left, Austia realized she was completely exposed standing on the front steps in view of the living room window with its open curtains. *Lord God, what should I do?*

The imam moved directly in front of the window facing her. If he took his eyes off Mr. Rahman he would be looking directly at her. She slowly rolled her eyes toward the street. Moonlight bathed her car.

Suddenly a shadow fell across the steps, hiding her. Austia looked up and saw a large cloud had drifted across the face of the moon. A wind sprang up and the trees in the yard began to sway, their leafy limbs casting shadows that deepened the darkness that hid her.

The imam's voice resonated in the night air. "Already, some of our sisters have apostatized. Do they think they can escape the retribution of Allah? They will die for their infidelity. This is just another reason sounding the prayer call five times a day is so important. Our people must stay focused on Islam. We are called to change America, not to be changed by America."

The imam's specific mention that "sisters have apostatized" and "they will die for their infidelity" filled her with foreboding. In light of what she and Mr. Rahman had been talking about it almost seemed as if the imam were obliquely referencing their conversation. The hair on her arms rose. Why had he come right at the time she was visiting and precisely at the moment Mr. Rahman asked about Jesus? It was almost as if he'd known she was there.

The car that had been behind her! How on earth could they have known she would come here? She had only decided herself at the last moment while on her way home. Had she been followed?

Her thoughts flashed to the day before when she'd driven by Zaki's address. The imam had been leaning on Zaki's white Mazda reading something. And at Zaki's interview, he'd heard her talk to Mr. Rahman. Had he reported what he'd heard to this imam? How was Zaki tied into these people?

She tensed in the shadows, her brother's words returning to her. *"This isn't a war against flesh and blood. Let the Lord handle it."*

The words fostered uncertainty, then grew stronger. Waves of fear engulfed her, drowning her in doubt. What if God was not protecting her? What if the imam had stood at the door listening through the open window, and she had witnessed to Mr. Rahman about Christ and he had embraced the truth? She went weak in the knees at the thought.

Austia lifted her eyes heavenward as the night sky, thickening with clouds, blotted out the moon and stars. Her eyes cut to her car, now concealed in the inky darkness. Realization bolted in her chest as the gentle whispered words she'd heard as she prayed in her car returned to her. *"Trust Me."*

She returned her gaze to the open window.

And found the imam looking directly at her.

CHAPTER 22

"I was scared to death." Austia pulled out one of the chairs that surrounded the small table in the little kitchen at the Career Center. She seated herself, then nudged the chair across from her with the toe of her shoe. "Here, sit for a second, Annie. It's a few minutes before we open."

Annie pulled the chair out opposite Austia's and dropped into it.

Setting her coffee cup on the table, she suppressed a shiver. "The timing couldn't have been worse. I was in the living room alone with Mr. Rahman. And it occurred to me later that it's even possible Imam al-Ansari could have been at the window for some time listening to us." Remembering the possibility set her stomach churning again. "I didn't dare try calling Mr. Rahman last night to see if he was okay for fear the imam was still there." She glanced at her watch. "I thought I'd try him later this morning. I just pray that nothing more happened after I left."

Annie's brow creased. "You don't actually think they'd hurt Mr. Rahman, do you?"

"Before I saw the imam leaning on Zaki's car I would have said no. But now I'm not so sure. Besides, you know what a strong hold community identity and belonging have on Muslims in America since so many of their cultural practices are different from ours. I'm sure by the time that imam left, Mr. Rahman was quite aware that he'd better change his ways about mixing with Christians if he wants to be a part of the brotherhood." Austia's gaze connected with Annie's. "Mr. Rahman was asking me about Jesus when the doorbell rang."

Annie leaned forward and put her hand on Austia's arm. "Go, God."

Her friend's eyes first sparked, then blazed as Austia recounted all that had happened.

"Well, thank heavens you went to the police yesterday. What did Chief Peterson say?"

Austia avoided her friend's eyes.

Annie withdrew her hand. "You did go, didn't you? You said you would."

"I said, '*Maybe.*'" Austia closed her eyes a moment. She should have told Annie of her decision. "But I thought more about it and I can't. It would put all of my students at risk. It's just too dangerous."

"Well," Annie's voice rose, "I've thought more about it too. And after what you've just told me, I'm more convinced than ever that the police need to be involved. The radicals are becoming bolder and bolder here in Agua Viva. The call-to-prayer issue is a perfect example of how it's beginning to change. A few years ago that idea was brought up, but the imam didn't pursue it because of the protests it sparked. He said he wanted to be a good neighbor. Look how things have changed with the new imam, Shaykh al-Ansari. Have you noticed how you see fewer and fewer Muslim women in Western dress? And he doesn't hide his support of the Council on American-Islamic Relations, which Congress has said has ties to radicals.

"And the number of churches they've bought and turned into mosques. You can't help but think that ultimately that will mean even more towers broadcasting the call to prayer and giving them an even greater presence here." Anger flashed across Annie's face. "Domes replacing steeples. Crescents replacing crosses. And now an honor killing." Annie's eyes cut to Austia's, making a silent statement about what she was really saying: *We might be next.*

"I understand your point." Austia tried to keep her voice calm. They'd been through a lot over the years—David's death, the opening of the Career Center, the secret discipleship of Muslim women, common causes that had only drawn them closer. Until this moment it had been unthinkable that she would find herself at odds with her closest friend. "Can't you see that going to the police would be the same as giving up? We've got to continue to reach out. If every Christian in Agua Viva would reach out with the love of Christ to a Muslim neighbor, maybe we'd see churches being built instead of being closed. Not only that, if most Muslims coming to America were being converted to Christianity, Muslim countries would try to stop them from coming here." She leaned forward. "That would stop them from tasting freedom and us from reaching out to them. But they're not worried about that in the least. And countries like Saudi Arabia send thousands of 'exchange students' here every year so those 'students' can establish homes, marry American women, convince them to convert, and then have American Muslim children who must follow Islam."

Austia swallowed hard and lifted her chin. "They're focused on spreading Islam throughout the world. But we have the Holy Spirit and God's promise that all things are possible with Him." She said the words with far more conviction than she felt, fighting the fear that the recent events had triggered in her. The same fear that now caused Annie to insist Austia go to the police. Zaki's presence keeping fresh in their minds what had happened to David and now Sabirah. Daring them to continue bringing the truth to Muslims. Reminding them that the hardened hearts of radical Islamists were formidable foes and would go on killing in the name of Allah.

Austia's phone chirped.

She pulled the phone from her pocket, then drew a deep breath. "Hello."

It was Mr. Rahman.

She was so relieved to hear his voice she forgot the required formalities and blurted out. "Are you all right?"

"I'm quite all right, Austia. But I must ask you not to take that letter to the Planning Commission meeting Tuesday night."

Austia's heart sank.

This was the outcome of the imam's visit. Her chest tightened. What more might he have convinced Mr. Rahman to change?

"Of course. Would you like me to bring the letter to you or just throw it away?"

"If you would mail it to me that would be fine."

So there had been more.

"Of course, I'd be glad to. Give my best to Mrs. Rahman."

"I will. That's all for now." He disconnected.

She put her phone away and looked at Annie. "That was Mr. Rahman. He doesn't want me to take his letter to the Planning Commission meeting; he wants me to mail it back to him."

Annie's expression mirrored her own concern. They both knew this was the result of the imam's intimidation. And without a doubt, the imam would continue to try to isolate Mr. Rahman from outside influences.

"I have an idea." Austia taped her phone on the table. "I'll mail him the letter as he asked and then attend the meeting myself. That will give me the perfect excuse to call him. I know he'll want to know what happened at the meeting."

Annie looked at her askance.

Austia met her friend's gaze. "I'm not about to let that imam steal what the Holy Spirit has begun in that precious man." Austia shoved the phone into her pocket. "What did you end up telling Zaki yesterday?"

"I told him that for now we would schedule his hours to coincide with the scheduled interviews with the applicants who speak only Arabic." Annie paused. "But that was when I thought you were going to the police. I'm not comfortable at all with his being here with no one but the two of us knowing about it."

"Are there any interviews on Monday?"

Annie swallowed hard. "First thing in the morning. He's coming in at nine and I'm going to show him where we keep the supplies and forms in the storage room. Then we have an interview and he'll interpret."

Annie's eyes searched Austia's face. "So what are you going to do?"

The fear in Annie's voice sent an icy chill up Austia's spine. "I'm sorry." Austia met Annie's gaze. "Nothing, right now."

Annie turned on her heel. "Then *maybe I* will."

Tears rose in Austia's eyes as she watched her friend storm from the room.

If only David were alive to advise them … protect them. She steeled herself. No point in indulging in such thoughts. David was gone and she was on her own. And as far as she could tell, her recent prayers for a chance to love again, to face life with a strong partner beside her, would go unanswered. She ignored the anger that sparked in her heart.

Right now the only man God had allowed into her life was Zaki ben Hassan.

CHAPTER 23

After positioning her hands on the keyboard, Annie turned to Zaki. "Would you ask him his name and address?"

Zaki introduced himself to the young man. "My name is Zaki ben Hassan," he said in Arabic.

The man's shoulders relaxed. "My name is Tawfeek Aziz."

"What is your address?"

"It's 1109 Third Avenue."

Zaki tilted his head. "Didn't I see you at the meeting about the call to prayer last Saturday at the park?"

"Yes." Tawfeek hesitated, then brightened. "Yes, I remember you."

Zaki turned to Annie. "His name is Tawfeek Aziz. His address is 1109 Third Avenue."

Annie began typing. "Which ad is he answering?"

Zaki continued the interview. Speaking quickly to ensure that Annie could not understand what he was saying, he carried on a dual conversation with Tawfeek. When the interview was finished, Tawfeek had an appointment to interview for a job at the dry cleaners, and Zaki had all the information he needed to give Hussein another name for recruiting. More important, it was another name for his handler to enter into the FBI database.

Still, Hussein was a master of deception. Zaki couldn't rule out the possibility that this was a setup. That Tawfeek Aziz had already been recruited by Hussein and it was Zaki who had just been evaluated. Even though he was an Arab, and his childhood in Iran gave him the Islamic background that was so imperative to his credibility for this mission, underestimating Hussein would be a mistake.

With enough infiltration, Hussein would find out that Zaki was not an American by blood, but he was a patriot by conviction. That conviction had been nurtured by his mother. With her Christian family's blessing and help, she and his Muslim father had escaped from the repressive Islamic government of the madrasa-trained cleric Khomeini after the fall of the Shah of Iran, amid the chants of "death to America." And even though the dangerous journey to the shining beacon of freedom in New York's harbor had taken her husband and left her struggling alone to make a new life, not a morning had passed that his mother didn't get on her knees and thank God for delivering her and her son from the fundamentalist Islamic rule of her home country and the iron fist of Sharia law. Not a day had passed that she didn't remind Zaki of the dangers of Islam in the hands of radical clerics. Though she grieved for her people, her culture, and her country until the day she died, she was the one who had instilled in him a love for their adopted homeland, helped him study for his citizenship, and birthed the idea of a career of service to his country. Her strength and her faith in God had gotten him through the dark days after Yemen.

He reined in his thoughts. The truth was, bringing down Hussein al-Ansari was personal. But he knew better than to indulge those thoughts. Keeping his emotions in check was the key to surviving this game of life and death.

As Annie rose from the table, Austia hurried into the conference room. "We just got a walk-in. I thought since Zaki's here you could go ahead and do another interview."

Zaki saw the tremor in Austia's hand as she extended the file toward Annie. She feared him.

Good … He saw Tawfeek on the other side of the conference room glass stop and observe them. It could save her life.

After taking Hussein's sister, Rasha, and Fatima's sister, Najah, to the Career Center for the ESL class, Zaki headed to the meeting at the mosque per Hussein's orders. Unfortunately the two women had immediately seen other women they knew and it had not been necessary to take them into the building. He'd hoped to run into Austia. Had she seen the women with him it would have immediately put her on guard.

He welcomed the silence of the car as he drove. On the way to the class, the two women had commiserated endlessly about the fact that Fatima had suddenly decided not to come. Najah felt certain that it had really been Hussein who had stopped her, though she didn't know why he had changed his mind.

Zaki had listened with interest. Najah was right.

He'd been outside checking out the imam's freshly painted black Toyota in the driveway when he'd heard voices coming through the open upstairs window. He'd heard Hussein cursing Fatima and slapping her as she begged for mercy. It had taken every ounce of discipline and training Zaki had not to interfere. *I promise you, Fatima. His day is coming.*

Hussein's sudden interest in the Career Center was still a mystery. Zaki had been unable to discern from the cryptic fragments of conversations he'd picked up exactly what it was that had caught Hussein's attention. But Zaki had recently pieced together, from increased courier activity and Hussein's inordinate number of trips into Los Angeles, that the planned attack on American soil was escalating. Still, Hussein's paranoia made any overt method of getting details a death sentence, and intervening too soon would mean that valuable information and leads to stop future attacks would be lost.

He bit down on his lower lip. What had drawn Hussein's attention to the Career Center? Was it related to the unknown scheme incubating in Los Angeles? Why at this particular time had the imam's blue Toyota suddenly been painted black? Linkage. There had to be linkage.

And what of Austia's involvement with Senator Amende? Did Hussein know about that? What possible reason would Austia have for being involved with the Muslims after they killed her husband unless it was to join in the fight against them? But that didn't ring true to him. During the limited amount of time he'd spent with her, he'd been struck by her genuineness and dedication to finding jobs for the Muslim immigrants in the community.

Zaki forced his thoughts to the hastily organized meeting at the mosque. Hussein had decided it was needed before the Planning Commission meeting about the call-to-prayer ordinance the following night. Hussein had been deeply, though quietly, involved in pushing for the prayer call to be sounded for each of the five daily prayers. Five times a day, every day of the week. This effort to broadcast the prayers was clearly tied to the cell's mission, though Zaki did not know how. And apparently some members of the Muslim community were willing to compromise and settle for just the midday call each day. Like a spider sensing the vibration of an intruder on his web, Hussein had discerned that the discord was a threat to passing the ordinance and called the meeting.

Arriving at the mosque, Zaki quickly parked and entered the building. From the looks of the parking lot, word had spread. A few well-placed flyers in the local Muslim shops were as good as posting it on the front page of the paper. And, undoubtedly, personal visits had encouraged the dissenters to attend.

Zaki bounded up the stairs to the prayer room. He took off his shoes and entered.

Hussein was sitting on the carpeted floor at the head of a large semicircle of men that was several rows deep. Zaki seated himself toward the front side, which allowed him a clear view of most of the men. He wanted to commit their faces to memory.

Faruq, the Palestinian who owned the bakery, was speaking.

"I've got a lot of Americans who come into my shop for my baklava and Turkish coffee. I know they don't want the prayer call sounded at all. My shop's only a block from here, so the *adhan* will be heard clearly by people in my store. I'm afraid anything more than the midday call will cost me business."

Hussein gave the baker a friendly smile. "I understand how you might think that. But this is a democracy. The Americans will accept the vote of the Planning Commission if we unite as one voice and demand our rights. They'll complain for a while, but they'll still tell each other that we're entitled to our religious freedom."

A man called out from the middle of the group. "Hussein is right. America is so proud of its democracy. Let the government grant us our rights. If Christians can ring their church bells, then we can have our prayer calls."

Heads nodded. Murmurs of agreement and *amins* filtered through the crowd.

When Faruq didn't respond, a second man began speaking. Zaki recognized him as Nasir. He had a farm on the outskirts of town and his children ran a vegetable stand.

"The Qur'an instructs us to invite all people to join Islam. If we make an issue out of this, we may alienate the very people we are trying to attract. It's hard enough with the militants overseas getting themselves in the papers every day. We don't want to be identified with the extremists who've perverted Islam's message of peac—"

"Anybody else want to speak?" Hussein scanned the room.

A young, clean-shaven man Zaki had not seen before pushed himself up onto his knees. "He's right. Come on. We all have watches. We don't need a prayer call. It just creates unnecessary fear among our Christian friends. It's old-fashioned. It's time to bring Islam into the twenty-first century."

"You sound like you've sold out to the Americans and their Christian nation." Hussein stood, color rising in his cheeks as he addressed the young man, then, eyes smoldering, he coolly studied other faces. "It seems some of you are more concerned about being Americans than being Muslims. If you are, you are inviting the wrath of Allah." Hussein's face darkened. "You need to ask yourself these questions." He jabbed his finger at them. "Who are the greatest distributors of pornography in the world? The Americans. Who are the greatest providers of abortions in the world? The Americans. Who fights for the right of two men to marry? The Americans. Their democracy exalts wickedness and the desires of men."

Someone shouted, "America is the Great Satan. The American pigs want to take their democracy and their Christianity to our homelands. If we allow it, soon our laws will be replaced by man-made laws, and God's laws will be mocked."

The men murmured among themselves. This was truth.

Another voice called out, "These people are obsessed with material things, Hollywood celebrities, and alcohol. Their women roam the streets half naked. What is meant for their husbands' eyes, they give to any man. They have no respect for God or His commandments."

The men's voices grew louder, pulsating through the air.

Hussein raised his fist. "Remember, America must not change us. We must change America. In Islam there is no compromise. There is only full surrender to Allah, his laws, and his messenger. Anything less than the right to all our prayer calls is to surrender to the infidels. We must demand what Allah commands."

Faruq, who only moments before had been concerned about his bakery, began to shout out, *"Allahu akbar. Allahu akbar."* He rose, lifting a clenched fist in the air. *"Allahu akbar."*

Within moments, every man attending was on his feet, thrusting his fist up and down. The chant grew louder and louder, building to a pitched frenzy. *"Allahu akbar. Allahu akbar."*

Zaki rose, joining them, clenching his jaw as he feigned support. He'd heard Hussein's speech before. It was given to every young man recruited for jihad.

And the irony never failed to anger him. The country that had been founded on godly principles, whose citizens had shed blood here and abroad for the cause of freedom, and whose ingenuity, courage, and faith had made it the most powerful country in the world, was now known across nations as the champion of abortion, drunkenness, pornography, and gay marriage.

Zaki knotted his fists, eyes burning, wishing Hussein's points could be disputed.

America.

For truths that were self-evident, for rights endowed by the Creator, for equal justice under the law, for the freedom of men and women who lived and breathed amid her frailties, she was still the greatest nation on earth. And he would fight, even die, to save her.

Unobserved, Zaki began to scan the room. The men now whipped into a frenzy. The air charged with hatred. Silently outraged and inwardly repulsed, he felt the bite of tears sting his eyes as images of dead Americans strewn in the mountains of Yemen oozed from the weeping wound that was his past. He clenched his jaw and lifted his chin.

As his sweep of the room ended on Hussein, Zaki's heart leaped from his chest.

The despot's fierce, probing gaze was focused directly on him.

CHAPTER 24

Hussein had left for the evening. A glance at the clock told Fatima he'd been gone for more than an hour.

Finally feeling safe, she switched on the lamp by the bed. Leaning across the mattress, she examined her sleeping son's swollen hand.

"Oh, Sami, Mommy didn't know." She hadn't seen any bees anywhere when she had left him sleeping by the garden in his stroller. She teared up again at the thought of how she'd foolishly, thoughtlessly, left her precious baby in harm's way. For this Hussein felt he had every right to beat her. He'd even said it might be better to let his mother raise his child. Hussein considered his mother superior to her in every way and treated his mother like a queen. Fatima tossed her head. His mother had raised him. That was all Fatima needed to know about her.

She lightly kissed Sami's forehead. His cry had saved her. Everyone had rushed to him, pushing her out of the way. After realizing he'd been stung by a bee, Hussein had carried him into the house, his family trooping after him. She'd found herself behind them, and it was then she'd realized the New Testament had fallen from its hiding place in her sleeve and was lying in plain sight in the grass not ten feet from where Sami's stroller had been. She'd grabbed it and stuck it in the stroller's pouch, then followed the family into the house.

Straightening, she scanned the room. The stroller lay on its side, having been kicked over by Hussein during his fit of rage. Her heartbeat quickened as she remembered seeing the edge of Sabirah's book show itself as the stroller flew across the room and hit the wall. It was a miracle that the little book hadn't fallen out.

Fatima walked to the bedroom door and locked it. Then she hurried back to the window to be sure that Hussein had not come back to the house for some reason. Just the thought of his returning unexpectedly and showing up at their locked bedroom door sent a wave of nausea through her. She wiped her palms on the skirt of her *abaya* and hurried to the stroller. Righting it, she removed the New Testament from the pouch.

After pulling the rocking chair next to the window, she positioned it so she could watch Sami and hear any activity in the driveway. Sitting on the edge of the rocker, she looked the book over. How had it gotten into Sabirah's car?

She opened it.

The first page was blank. On the second page there was an inscription written in English. "For Sabirah"—a gasp escaped her lips—"my sis-ter in the Lo-rd."

She stared at the words.

Fatima continued, sounding the words out as best she could. "... Love's tou-ch he-als." ... tou-ch he-als. The English words didn't sound familiar at all.

Her eyes returned to the opening words. *For Sabirah.*

Who would write her sweet friend's name in such a book? Fatima blinked slowly. Sabirah had always been different from the other girls in the family, her dark eyes often dreamy and distant, gazing at visions only she could see. Visions that had drawn her away from the world of her conservative family and Islam. Fatima ran her forefinger over Sabirah's name. Who had written it?

Fatima read the words again. " ... *my sis-ter in the Lo-rd.*"

Sis-ter. She furrowed her brow. *My sister.*

An alarm spiraled through her stomach.

Sabirah's sisters would never write in such a book. What did the words mean? Was this an American expression?

She fanned through the pages of the book, looking for clues. But she found nothing.

Her gaze returned to the inscription: *Love's touch heals.*

What did the words mean?

She closed the book and gazed at the front of it. This was Sabirah's Bible. She wished Hussein hadn't seen it in the car. If she had found it while cleaning the car out, she would have kept Sabirah's secret. Had Hussein seen the writing? If he had, he would undoubtedly tell Sabirah's father. What did it matter now that she was dead?

Fatima slowly shook her head. Why would anyone want to kill Sabirah?

Hussein's words suddenly played back to her. *"May Allah damn her soul in Hell."*

Spidery fingers of fear crawled down Fatima's spine as fragments, vignettes spliced together from the past few weeks, fanned out before her like light through a prism: Sabirah running away from home. The news that she had been murdered by unknown young men. The emptying of her car. Hussein's arm casually on his brother's shoulder while saying, *"The police don't seem to have any leads."* The immediate disposal of her belongings ... The unclean possessions of an infidel.

The pieces fell into place. Sabirah had converted to Christianity.

Another thought occurred to her. The person who had written in the book must be the one who had told Sabirah about Jesus.

Suddenly, a bolt of fear shot through her chest. There had been no young men. Hussein and his brother had avenged the family's name.

A loud knocking on the bedroom door broke into her thoughts. Frozen with terror, she stared at it. The doorknob rattled.

She stood, holding Sabirah's Bible, her eyes frantically searching the room.

The doorknob rattled again.

She rushed to the window. Was it possible she hadn't heard Hussein return?

Her eyes darted to the driveway below.

Hussein's car shone in the moonlight.

"Fatima."

Fist pounding the door, her husband bellowed her name.

CHAPTER 25

Zaki took the last open chair, next to Faisal. He glanced around the crowded room. It buzzed with the fervor of the men still high from the rally at the mosque. It was rare that Hussein called all his men together. But after the rally, Hussein had demanded they gather immediately in his office for final instructions regarding the Planning Commission meeting that was taking place the next night. As it happened, the man himself was late.

Suddenly, the door burst open and Hussein strode to his desk, then seated himself behind it. "I stopped to check on my wife and son." He absently rubbed his knuckles.

The gesture silenced the room. All eyes turned to him.

Hussein had divided the town and its outskirts into quadrants. He'd assigned several men to each section, and apparently they'd gone to each Muslim home and questioned the occupants. Zaki directed his eyes to the street map of Agua Viva that had been pinned to the wall at the front of the room. The map was divided into four sections with a highlighter. There were black numbers written on every block. The cell had developed a list and knew which homes were occupied by Muslims.

Hussein went around the room and questioned each of the men one by one about his specific task. From Hussein's questions it was clear he even knew certain families by name, how many children they had, where they worked, and their opinion about the call to prayer. As the men answered his queries they referred to pages of printouts. And as they talked a man named Mustapha typed into a laptop.

When Hussein finished his interrogations, he dismissed all but ten of the group of men. Next, he called out the remaining names. Zaki's was one of them.

Zaki straightened, his full attention on Hussein.

"Mustapha will give you a list of people you are to pick up and take to the Planning Commission meeting tomorrow night."

Mustapha rose from his spot behind the laptop and handed out the papers.

Zaki's sheet had only one name. Abdur Rahman.

An image of Austia answering her cell phone immediately replayed in Zaki's mind. Her voice echoed: *"Wa alikum alsalam. Is your wife feeling all right, Mr. Rahman?"*

Hussein had connected Austia, Mr. Rahman, and the Planning Commission meeting.

As though he had spoken his thoughts out loud, he was suddenly aware that Hussein's eyes were on him. It was only his years of working undercover that allowed him to keep any sign of apprehension from his expression as his mind followed the fine thread that laced together the name on the paper, Austia Donatelli, and Hussein's request that he take the women to the ESL class. He casually folded the paper and put it in his pocket.

Hussein dismissed the second group of men. As Zaki rose to leave, Hussein called to him. "Stay here."

Shutting down any outward sign of alarm by sheer force of will, he strode confidently to his chair. As the door closed behind the last man, Zaki found only he and two other men remained:

Hussein's father, the imam Shaykh al-Ansari, and Hussein's brother, Faisal.

Hussein turned to Zaki, his eyes cold and hard. "We picked up the women at the Career Center tonight after the meeting."

Zaki nodded. He'd thought nothing of it when Hussein had told him as they left that Faisal would be picking up the women. Now, it took on an ominous tone.

"Unfortunately, tonight Sami's mother couldn't go. But she will go next time. I want her to learn to speak English so she can speak it to my son." A crooked smile twisted Hussein's lips. "He has a bright future, you know?"

Zaki nodded.

"The women brought home notebooks and papers. I want you to read them and see what that woman is teaching." Hussein leaned forward and put his elbows on the desk, steepling his fingers under his chin. "I want you to find out everything about her."

Zaki nodded. "Of course."

"You know, Faisal's daughter Sabirah went to the English classes there." Hussein let his hands fall to the desktop. "I'm not sure that was good for her."

Zaki had not known Faisal had a daughter named Sabirah. He'd never heard the name spoken by Faisal or any of the family during his time with the cell.

At the mention of the name, Faisal lowered his eyes.

The atmosphere in the room changed. The air suddenly charged with some unseen energy.

The hairs on the back of Zaki's neck rose. He watched as the imam and Hussein exchanged a silent glance. As though of their own

accord, his thoughts filtered back through his memory ... the blue
Toyota, freshly painted black. A pit formed in his throat.

They'd killed her.

Why? And what did Austia have to do with it?

The imam stroked his chin, regarding Zaki carefully. "That
woman at the Career Center seems quite friendly with Abdur
Rahman."

Hussein's gaze sharpened as he turned back to Zaki. "Find out
why. You can start by taking him to the Planning Commission meeting on Tuesday. For some reason he hasn't been responsive to the
information we've made available to everyone in his neighborhood
about this most important matter of the call to prayer. I will inform
him you're coming."

Hussein's tongue darted across his lips. "And tell Faisal what you
learn."

CHAPTER 26

Zaki stepped soundlessly to the doorway that led to the Rahmans' hallway. Taking shallow breaths, he listened.

"I wished I didn't … commission tonight … you felt better …" Zaki shot a glance at the rows of prescription bottles lined up on the table next to the recliner.

A woman's voice responded, her words urgent with fear. "Imam al-Ansari demanded … you … go … frightens … He will come back …"

Zaki strained to catch more of the conversation.

At the sound of movement, he quickly returned to the couch.

Sliding over the arm of the couch into the cushion, he heard something drop to the floor. He picked up the book by his feet. A New Testament! He shoved it in his pocket.

Mr. Rahman entered the room.

Zaki rose. "Shall we go now?"

Mr. Rahman nodded. After they put on their shoes, the two men walked to Zaki's car. Zaki helped Mr. Rahman with his seat belt, then climbed behind the steering wheel and started the engine.

After backing out of the driveway, he deliberately took the turn that would take him through town and past the Career Center. "We should get a good turnout at the meeting."

His comment went unanswered.

He wished he could simply have let Mr. Rahman stay home. But showing up at the Planning Commission meeting without him would not have gone unnoticed. Zaki clenched his jaw and pushed down the compassion that rose in his heart. He was a professional. He was not allowed the luxury of his emotions. He would perform as though he were the devoted adherent he pretended to be. Dragging a frail old man from his ailing wife was the very least that was expected for the cause of the prayer call. And it was far better for Mr. Rahman that Zaki had been chosen to do it instead of one of Hussein's other henchmen.

His grip tightened on the steering wheel as he turned onto the main street of Agua Viva, thinking of what would be required of him to find out the nature of Austia's relationship with Mr. Rahman. And beyond that, what the consequences would be should that relationship not be to Hussein's liking. His gut wrenched as he glanced at his passenger. Whatever was motivating Hussein, it was rooted in his fundamentalist interpretation of Sharia law. People like Mr. Rahman were not permitted to live out their faith from the moderate perspective of most Muslims. This was the curse the radical Islamists had brought to their people. The curse they now wished to spread throughout the civilized world.

Zaki's mother had been a Christian, but his father had been a Muslim. This was permitted by the Qur'an, and before the Iranian Revolution those marriages had been accepted in his birth country. But the leaders of the revolution branded the Iranian Christians as accomplices to the Western infidels, and mandated that Muslims married to Christian women convert the women to Islam. As the pressure had intensified, and the future had become more ominous, his parents had fled the country.

Zaki had attended the madrasa in the years before they left, learning the rituals and mind-set of Islam. Their home life had been peaceful, and he treasured his memories of large family gatherings with tables of food, lively conversation, and laughter. But the iron fist of Khomeini had shattered his world.

In Iran, Zaki had lived the life of a Muslim, but after fleeing to America his mother had secretly shared with him the stories of Jesus from the Gospels. One evening, a year or so after they'd arrived in America, they had been sitting on the steps of their back porch. She put her arm around him. "You know that crescent moon?" He wondered if she meant the one in the sky above them or the symbol of Islam. But he didn't ask. There was something beautifully sweet about the moment. Something that drew him to her words. "That crescent is how much your father knew about Allah. But all the rest of the moon, what cannot be seen with the human eye, is what is revealed about God by His Spirit and by His Word." And beginning with that simple explanation, she told him of God's love and of His Son, Jesus. In divine obedience, truth knocked on the door of his young and open heart. And he believed.

But as he and his mother continued to live in poverty in New York in the tough neighborhood of 101st and Amsterdam, Zaki began to question the truth of her message about God's love, forgiveness, and the assurance that the Lord was his Shepherd. Then, when he was sixteen, she died unexpectedly from a brain aneurism.

If it had not been for the first ... the only ... girl he ever loved, Neryda, who was a committed Christian, his life could easily have defaulted to the drug dealers and gangs that frequented his neighborhood. He'd met her through a mutual friend. She was studying music at Juilliard. On their first date she'd been practicing when he approached her door. The music had drifted down the hallway of the old building, moving him in a way he didn't understand and taking him far away from the cursed existence that was his life. A place that her eyes and her smile would take him again as their love deepened.

But then, less than a year later, she was murdered while walking home from the night-shift waitressing job that supported her while she went to school. Her nude body dumped in an alley. An innocent, slaughtered and discarded.

Whatever faith he had in God died with her.

Living in tough neighborhoods, with no family, he could rely on only himself. He used his bright mind and the academic scholarships that went unnoticed by his peers to forge a way out of the hell that was his childhood. College doors opened to him, and he graduated at the top of his class. From there he went into the military, where 9/11, his Islamic heritage, and his street smarts had put him on the fast track. But the fast track had led him to the Arabian Peninsula, Yemen, and more lessons of death and loss. Yet it was there in the trenches with his buddies, fighting for freedom, fighting for a cause that was noble and good and right, that all the events of his life connected, leading him not to the God of his mother's heart, for the wounds were too deep, but to the conviction that the men who fell beside him, his only family, would not die in vain. He would fight on.

Mr. Rahman gazed silently out the window, his brows knitted, absently smoothing the top of his wedding band, fully absorbed in his thoughts. Still present with his wife. Preparing for the inevitable.

Zaki focused on the road ahead of him, trying to ignore the long-buried feelings that Mr. Rahman's silent vigil stirred within him. He needed to stay emotionally distant. He'd learned that lesson long ago. He drew a deep breath, filling up the empty places.

Zaki saw the Career Center ahead of him. He casually pointed through the window as they drove by. "I just started working there at the Career Center as a translator."

Mr. Rahman nodded silently.

"Have you taken any of the English classes?"

Mr. Rahman folded his hands in his lap. "I know nothing about the place and have no interest in what they do there. I've spoken English all my adult life."

His words were short, telling Zaki any further discussion about the Career Center, including the woman who ran it, was closed. And because Zaki had overheard Austia's phone conversation with him, it also told Zaki that something had changed dramatically since that call. Mr. Rahman's wife's frightened voice echoed in his thoughts *"Imam al-Ansari … He will come back."* Zaki shifted in his seat. He would have to wait until the Planning Commission meeting to learn more about Mr. Rahman, Austia, and the letter. They drove in thick silence the rest of the way to city hall.

The parking lot was jammed, and Zaki ended up letting Mr. Rahman off at the door and finding a parking spot two blocks away. As he jogged to the building, he scanned the parked cars, looking for Austia's gray Taurus.

Uneasiness rippled through his stomach. He didn't see it anywhere.

CHAPTER 27

By the time Zaki and Mr. Rahman entered the meeting chambers the meeting was being called to order. They sat through the consent calendar, the minutes, and some miscellaneous bills that had been processed for council approval.

Zaki wasn't surprised to see that the crowd had divided itself. Muslims on one side, everyone else on the other. Not only was the floor full, but people lined the walls. He carefully scanned the room, but he didn't see Austia. He looked at his watch and shifted in his seat. Hussein's sudden interest in her, Mr. Rahman's declaration that he knew nothing about the Career Center, and now her absence from the meeting ... He tried to glean something from the fragments of information.

A snippet of conversation in the imam's voice suddenly echoed through his thoughts—*"That woman at the Career Center seems quite friendly with Abdur Rahman."*

A piece clicked into place. Hussein's father, the imam Shaykh al-Ansari, knew about Austia's involvement with the Rahmans and had forbidden it.

Zaki took a second look around the room. Or had Hussein taken steps to ensure Austia would never again have contact with anyone?

A dispute broke out across the aisle from Zaki. A tall, dark-skinned woman with an emerald-green scarf covering her hair had attempted to take one of the last seats in the row of folding chairs that had been added behind the "townspeople." A heavyset man in the chair next to the empty seat rose and pushed into her, changing seats. "I'm saving this seat for a friend. Go sit with your own people."

The tall woman paused a moment, then without speaking a word, stepped back and found a spot to stand against the wall.

"The Planning Commission has received one hundred forty-three letters as of five o'clock this afternoon." The mayor's voice sounded across the room. "They will be entered into the public record. Now, for those wishing to speak, when you come to the microphone, please state your name and address for the record."

The mayor had hardly taken his seat before a man Zaki didn't recognize stepped in front of the podium. He had on an American Legion hat.

"My name is Peter McDonald, Colonel US Air Force retired. I live at 15427 Ramsey Road here in Agua Viva. My acreage is next door to Nasir al-Din. He's a great neighbor and a good man. But this prayer call isn't about our good Muslim neighbors. I'm not prejudiced against anyone. But I don't want to hear someone shouting that Mohammed is God's messenger five times a day in a foreign language. I had a military career and fought for this nation and the freedom of these Muslims to worship as they choose. But that doesn't include beating me over the head with it five times a day." He paused, then turned from the podium. A man wearing a white prayer cap immediately took the microphone.

"My name is Nur-ul Islam. I move here from New York." His accent was thick and Zaki guessed his native tongue was Bengali rather than Arabic. "Me and my wife, we come here because we visit and see young girls wearing hijabs and burkas. It is beautiful, just like our village back home. We don't want that our children become corrupt. They need to hear *azan* so they not forget who they are. It too much easy for them to see and hear bad things. We want that we obey Muhammad's teaching. It is our right."

A man standing in the back, whom Zaki recognized as a teacher at the local high school, shouted across the room. "Everybody wants to talk about their rights, but my rights are being stripped away. Last week there were Muslims praying in the school auditorium. If Christians gathered and did that, the ACLU would sue us." The crowd on his side of the room began to murmur and nod.

One of the commissioners' voices boomed through the speakers. "If you want to speak, please follow the rules of order." Within moments there was a line at the podium.

Zaki eyed each face. Austia's was not among them.

And so the evening wore on. Impassioned statements back and forth, each of the speakers defining the issue from their own perspective. Each believing God was on their side. There seemed to be no common ground. Finally, the line dwindled to just a few.

"Good evening. My name is Ayesha Hashim. I live at 3480 Drake Drive here in Agua Viva." It was the tall, dark-skinned woman with the green scarf. "I am an Arab American and I'm opposed to amending the noise ordinance to accommodate the request for a call to prayer being delivered five times a day through a loudspeaker." The room became silent.

"Devout Muslims already know when it is time to pray. If they need reminding, they can find other ways to do that without disrespecting the wishes of the general public who do not want to hear the praising of a God in whose name the death and destruction of 9/11 was committed. This is just another attempt to test the tolerance and goodness of America. They know that in most Muslim countries Jewish synagogues and Christian churches are not even permitted to be built, much less be promoted via a public-address system."

She scanned the faces of the seven commission members. "Capital cities all over the Middle East use these loudspeakers as tools to incite and indoctrinate by broadcasting sermons that call for the destruction of infidels and Jews. How tolerant do you want to be?" Her gaze rested on the commissioners for a moment, then she turned and sat down.

Zaki looked toward the heavyset man in the aisle across from him. The man sat, eyes staring straight-ahead, color rising in his cheeks.

Hussein's voice booming across the room drew Zaki's attention back to the podium.

"Good evening, gentlemen." He had a presence about him that spoke of authority. A charisma that both intimidated and fascinated. After just three words, all eyes had turned toward him.

"Islam is a religion of peace and I come in peace. We are neighbors and should be friends. We all want the same thing. To raise our families, enjoy our freedoms, and worship our God." A few heads began to bob in agreement.

"Not to forget, it is the duty of every Muslim to pray, as it is for every Christian. Still, it's easy to get busy and lose track of time and …" He raised his hand, palm up. "The next thing you know, the day has passed." Dropping his hand, he tilted his head. "It's the times that we are living in. No?"

A few of the commissioners chuckled and others began to move their heads in assent.

The hairs on the back of Zaki's neck stood up as Hussein took control of the room with stealthy cunning.

"The prayer call lasts just a little more than a minute. We are asking for just five minutes out of the day to remind our people of their religious obligation."

Zaki heard a woman across the aisle say to the man next to her. "You know, their prayer call could be a way of reminding *us* we need to pray."

"We want to be good neighbors." Hussein paused, the few moments of silence serving to underscore his next words. "And I would like to announce that once this very minor issue is resolved, I have Middle Eastern investors who are eager to meet with your city officials to negotiate some worthwhile projects that will benefit us all."

People straightened in their chairs; others leaned forward.

He continued. "Our community should have state-of-the-art schools for our children, and clinics and hospitals with the latest technology. We also hope to establish a university someday in order to nurture the growth of the community and foster greater understanding. And endowments for future development are readily available." Then he made a final statement. "It's up to you."

He gave a congenial nod, then stepped away from the podium.

As he returned to his seat, murmuring broke out among the crowd. Zaki caught snatches of conversations: "They have the money to make it happen." … "Think of the jobs this will create." … "It's only five minutes out of the day."

Slowly the atmosphere of the room began to change as the fruit offered from the hand of Hussein al-Ansari ripened in the minds of the people. By the time the Commission called for a vote, except for a few of the local pastors and the woman with the green scarf, no one could remember why the request for a call to prayer had been so objectionable.

When the last commissioner said aye, and the passage of the ordinance to allow five prayer calls from six a.m. to ten p.m. was made official, Zaki shot a glance at Hussein.

Hands coiled in his lap, Hussein watched as the gavel fell. His tongue darted across his lips … tasting victory.

With the meeting adjourned, Hussein rose and surveyed the room with cold, unblinking eyes.

Observing him, Zaki silently vowed, *You're the son of Satan himself, and I'm going to take you down.*

Hussein gave a start and his face darkened.

Suddenly, his sharp, penetrating eyes cut to Zaki.

Taj reached from under the covers and grabbed the phone from the nightstand. "Yes?"

"It's time to execute your mission."

"I understand." Taj put the phone back in its cradle.

"Who was that?" He heard the concern in his wife's voice.

Turning toward her, he whispered. "Nothing that concerns you. Just family business." Then, putting his arms around her, he pulled her into his chest and rested his chin on the top of her head.

He had been setting up Steve for over a month and now was well positioned to carry out the plan. It would be easy. Taj smirked.

His uncle would be proud.

CHAPTER 28

Zaki glanced at Mr. Rahman, who was leaning slightly forward, hands folded in his lap, eyes tracking the road that was taking him back to his beloved wife.

Passing the Career Center, Zaki noted it was dark. Apparently it wasn't Austia's job that had kept her away from the Planning Commission meeting. "The woman who runs the Career Center is very active in the community. I thought maybe she'd speak at the meeting tonight."

Mr. Rahman shrugged. "She has done a lot of good things here."

Zaki considered the old man's words. Maybe they were nothing more than friends. Maybe this assignment from Hussein was just another example of the extreme paranoia with which the despot viewed the world around him. Any one of Hussein's many spies, or any one of their wives or children, could have reported something that was nothing more than gossip. Zaki set his lips in a tight line. He'd worked with Hussein long enough to have witnessed that gossip was enough to get a person killed. How a slanderous word could worm its way into Hussein's thoughts, then fester there until it became truth.

Zaki settled back in his seat. Tomorrow he would do further checking at the office in Austia's files and on her computer to see if there was anything that might connect her to Abdur Rahman. The sooner he could get Austia out of Hussein's crosshairs, the better.

As they turned the corner to Mr. Rahman's street, Zaki heard him gasp.

Following the old man's gaze, Zaki saw Austia's car was parked in the Rahmans' driveway.

Zaki pulled in next to the Taurus. "It looks like you have company."

The wail of a distant siren filled the silence.

Eyes wide, Mr. Rahman straightened. "Safia."

Without waiting for the car to come to a complete stop, the elderly man opened his door. Stumbling out, he fell.

Jamming the gearshift into park, Zaki raced around the back of the car to help Mr. Rahman. But he had already managed to pull himself up, and with awkward, uneven steps was racing toward the front door.

As the two men reached the steps, an ambulance blazed to a stop behind them. Mr. Rahman ran into the house, but Zaki stepped aside as the paramedics bounded to the porch, carrying medical equipment.

Zaki followed them into the house. Stopping in the living room, he watched them disappear down the hall. He could hear their voices.

"What happened, miss?"

"I was on my way to the Planning Commission meeting and she called me. Said she wasn't feeling well. I came right away."

"BP 102 over 72, pulse 98, respirations 10, O2 85 percent."

"After I got here I sat with her. She wanted me to hold her hand. She seemed to be resting. Then … then …" Austia's voice broke. "She told me she felt like she couldn't breathe."

"Safia. Safia." Mr. Rahman's desperate plea overarched the commotion.

"We need to go."

Zaki moved next to the couch as the paramedics rounded the corner, pushing the gurney through the living room, Mr. Rahman at their heels and Austia close behind. She stopped when she saw him, her face pale and troubled, her eyes teary. His heart went out to her.

"I didn't know anyone was here." Her hands shook as she wiped the tears from her cheeks.

"I brought Mr. Rahman home from the Planning Commission meeting."

Her eyes were guarded. "Thank you."

There was something about the raw emotion on her face, and the sudden reminder of the frailty of life that touched Zaki deeply, stirring memories. He wanted to comfort her.

Instead he checked his emotions and stepped to the side, letting her pass, then fell into step behind her.

After Mrs. Rahman had been loaded into the ambulance, Mr. Rahman tried to follow the paramedic inside with her.

The young paramedic gently put his hand on the old man's shoulder. "You need to ride up front."

Mr. Rahman's brow furrowed, and his back stiffened. "No, that would not be proper. She is my wife."

The paramedic dropped his hand to his side. "She'll be fine. I'll take good care of her."

Mr. Rahman didn't move.

"Look, I've answered calls in this neighborhood before and I understand where you're coming from, but there's nothing to worry about. Nothing is going to happen." Frustration punctuated the paramedic's words.

"No." Mr. Rahman knotted his small hands beside him and lifted his chin. "What if she wakes up and finds she is alone with you and I have abandoned her?"

The young man moved toward the ambulance door. "Sir, please get in the cab. This is for your wife's safety. If you were in the back and something should happen on the way to the hospital, it would only complicate things."

Zaki understood the terrible turmoil the elderly man was in. Coming from both worlds, Zaki had witnessed this kind of cultural conflict many times. Not only did the paramedic's request transgress the rigid separation of men and women mandated by Islamic law, it was also about Mr. Rahman's sense of love and duty to his wife. To protect and care for her, especially in this situation. And his concerns were justified. The elderly Mrs. Rahman would be confused and terror-stricken to wake up and find herself alone with a strange man, in a vehicle filled with equipment, and the sound of a siren blaring. The young paramedic understood where Mr. Rahman was coming from only in the narrowest sense. Mr. Rahman was more than a Muslim, he was a human being. Vulnerable and frightened, trying to be strong for his beloved wife.

But there was nothing Zaki could do. An attempt to convince him that the paramedic was right could raise questions about Zaki in Mr. Rahman's mind later. To him, Zaki was an orthodox Muslim who would never suggest such a thing.

Finally, Mr. Rahman's shoulders slumped and his chin dropped to his chest. Austia stepped beside the old man and gently guided him to the cab.

Keeping his eye on them, Zaki spoke to the paramedic. "What would you have done if that was your father?"

The young man stared at him a moment, then silently climbed into the back of the cab.

As the doors closed, Austia returned to the sidewalk next to Zaki.

With siren blaring, the ambulance sped away.

"*Khalama. Khalama.*" The word came out in stuttered sobs. Austia covered her face with her hands and turned away from the street.

He now fully understood the nature of Austia's relationship with Mr. Rahman. Calling Mrs. Rahman *khalama* told him all he needed to know. The endearing term was only for special family members or dear friends. She cared deeply for the couple and they for her. Mr. Rahman had asked her to take the letter to the meeting because they were close. And somehow Hussein had learned of their friendship.

Austia's genuineness and sincerity arrowed through his heart. She was a woman without pretense. And there was something else. Austia's interest in the Muslims of Agua Viva had nothing to do with Senator Amende or the government. There was some other reason that she lived here, served the community, and helped the people who had killed her husband. And he needed to find out what it was before Hussein did.

Whether it was because she was lost in her grief or because she didn't realize how close she was standing to him, Zaki wasn't sure, but her first step took her into his chest. He felt her trembling. Without conscious thought he raised his arms to hold her, to comfort her.

Suddenly aware of the indifferent moon illuminating them to any in the Muslim neighborhood who might still be standing at their windows after the sounds of the commotion in the street, he dropped his arms to his sides. He must not respond. He was deeply involved in a game of life and death and no corner of Agua Viva was out of Hussein's sight.

His gut clenched as he shoved his hands in his pockets. Austia had lost her parents and her husband, and now this. He knew about the pain of loss. Losing Neryda to the streets of New York, his friends to the battle in Yemen, his mother to the cruel hand of fate—the memories scorched his heart.

"Excuse me." He stepped aside, careful not to touch her, careful to maintain the illusion demanded by the mission. Still, the compassion that squeezed his heart mixed the pain of the past with the present. And unexpected feelings stirred that had nothing to do with his duty to protect her.

Her head lowered, she quickly sidestepped onto the curb, then turned to watch the ambulance disappear down the street.

As he watched with her, he took note of the street. With a start he realized a car was parked near the corner, facing them.

A black Toyota.

CHAPTER 29

Eyes riveted on the black Toyota, Zaki's mind raced. He was positive it hadn't been there when he'd turned onto the street to bring Mr. Rahman home. How long had it been parked? Who was in it … and why? What had Austia's brush against him and his response looked like from that distance?

If the car had been positioned to observe him, he needed to leave immediately, to draw whoever was lying in wait away from Austia. "It's time for me to go." He delivered his words with a coolness he didn't feel.

Austia nodded, then started toward the house. "I'll get my purse, turn off the lights, and lock up. Good night."

Zaki hurried to his car, climbed in, quickly backed out of the drive, and headed toward the main boulevard. As he approached the Toyota, he took his foot off the accelerator. Rolling down his window, he came to a stop parallel to the driver's door.

The driver's window of the Toyota was already down and the man inside the Toyota slowly turned his head toward Zaki.

It was Faisal.

Black eyes glittering with accusations, Faisal raised his eyebrows. In a deliberate motion, he lifted his hand where Zaki could see it, paused, then set the infrared camera he was holding on to the passenger seat. With an unseen press of a button, Faisal's window went up, silently terminating their encounter. The message clear: The camera would be doing the talking to Hussein about the incident at the Rahmans'.

As Zaki stepped on the gas, a suffocating shroud of apprehension wrapped around him. His eyes darted to his rearview mirror. Headlights off, the black car crept along the curb toward Mr. Rahman's house. He shifted his focus. Austia's car was still parked, but he was too far away to make out any movement. She was probably still in the house. His gaze returned to the black car; its red brake lights, like two demonic eyes, flashed intermittently.

Zaki's heart pounded as revelation sent adrenaline spurting through his chest. Faisal had seen the embrace with Austia and had immediately become suspicious about their relationship. Suspicions had become conclusions. The cell was exposed. Austia would be dead within the hour. He would be next.

Zaki stopped at the intersection, his mind and body on a razor's edge, aware that Austia's life depended on him. Options. What were his options?

Go to the Rahmans' house, lie in wait, and kill Faisal?

Zaki clenched his jaw. He was the only US contact who'd penetrated Hussein's inner circle. A terrorist attack was imminent. If Hussein had sent Faisal, his death would only cast suspicion on Zaki, threaten the mission, and mean certain death not only for Austia but for thousands of innocents.

Like a kaleidoscope's shards of glass and mirrors, his mind rotated through fragments of information, piecing together scenario after scenario. All led him to one conclusion. He had to let it play out. There was too much at stake. He would watch and see what Faisal did.

Turning left, Zaki circled the block until he was behind the Rahmans' house. He found himself in front of a school. He pulled to the curb and shut off the car's engine. He quickly shed his white shirt and loafers. He took off his thin dress socks and put them on his hands, then he slipped out the door and sprinted behind the buildings. A large sports field sprawled in front of him. The Rahmans' distinctive single-story house was on the other side of the field's fence. Lights still on.

As the moon dimmed behind unexpected clouds, Zaki pressed close to the low bushes that lined the cyclone fence. Within moments he stood facing the Rahmans' backyard.

Forcing himself to quiet his breathing, he crouched, listening as he scanned the property before him. Suddenly, the house went dark.

He scaled the fence and dropped soundlessly into the yard.

An engine hummed on the other side of the detached garage.

Zaki fingered the revolver strapped to his ankle.

His bare back skimming along the wall of the residence, he edged toward the front of the house. The vibration of a door being pulled shut sounded on his bare shoulders. Then the *clack* of footsteps on the front porch confirmed it. Austia was leaving.

The steps stopped.

The engine sputtered into silence and a car door opened and shut. Faisal's heavily accented voice snaked through the air. "Good evening."

"I'm sorry, the Rahmans aren't here. Mrs. Rahman has been taken to the hospital." The sound of her footsteps resumed, bringing her across and just past the open space where Zaki stood in the shadows.

She stopped.

"I am not here to see the Rahmans. I am here to see you."

Zaki heard Austia gasp.

Edging deeper into the shadow that the garage cast on the open space between the house and the driveway, Zaki had a clear view of Faisal. He was holding a gun, pointed at Austia. "You seem to have a habit of sticking your nose where it doesn't belong."

Faisal was going to kill her.

As Zaki's pulse pounded, all but the present was snuffed out by a single consuming thought. He would not let her die.

He raced to the other side of the garage, then pocketed a few pebbles from the dirt in the flowerbed.

Soundlessly he braced his foot on a trellis and hoisted himself to the roof of the garage. Silently maneuvering to the edge of the roof, he positioned himself behind Faisal. Then took a pebble from his pocket. He tossed it into the shadows near the killer.

Faisal's head snapped in the direction of the noise. He slowly backed up, his gun still trained on Austia.

In one seamless, precise motion, Zaki leapt onto Faisal, stripping the gun from the man's hand. As Faisal thrashed wildly, Zaki's strength and training pulled the terrorist to his feet and brought the crushing force of a choke hold to Faisal's carotid arteries.

As Zaki exerted more pressure to Faisal's throat, he heard a car start. Glancing over his shoulder, he saw Austia's car bounce out of the driveway and tear down the street.

Faisal's body grew limp.

Zaki dropped him.

How much she had seen Zaki didn't know. But without a doubt she would call the police to protect the Rahmans.

Zaki bent down and hurriedly felt for Faisal's pulse.

Nothing.

He rose. He would get his car and put the dead man in the trunk. He would dispose of the body and the camera, and then he'd have to deal with the Toyota.

Within moments he was over the back fence and once again moving down the fence line of the sports field, his head spinning.

Had Faisal acted alone?

Doubtful.

Did Faisal know more about Austia's relationship with Sabirah than he'd let on and decided to exact vengeance instead of waiting for Hussein's probe into the Career Center?

Never.

Had Hussein sent Faisal to spy on him? To record whatever he could and then compare it to whatever Zaki reported?

Yes. That had to be it. A wheel within a wheel. One more device to be sure no one escaped the web. Thank God Faisal was dead. If he wasn't, Zaki surely would be.

Back at his car Zaki stripped the socks from his hands, and started the engine. He waited for an approaching car to move past him, then he pulled out and continued to the corner. He made another left.

As he turned onto the Rahmans' street, adrenaline spiked through every vein in his body. More irrational and surreal than the most horrific nightmare he'd ever had, the black Toyota screamed backward out of the Rahman's driveway, onto the street, and moved erratically down the block to the main boulevard. He watched transfixed.

Faisal's fat, blocky silhouette visible through the back windshield.

CHAPTER 30

Zaki glanced at the clock on his nightstand. It was almost three a.m. He still hadn't slept. He threw his legs over the edge of the bed and rose.

Austia was on his mind … for a lot of reasons.

Frowning, he walked to the bedroom window and leaned against the window frame, careful not to stand too close to the opening. Even here, alone with his thoughts, he knew better than to assume he had any privacy.

His slip at the Rahmans' house had been disastrous. He'd allowed himself, for one moment, to be a human being instead of an undercover informant for the United States government. And it had cost him. Though he still wasn't sure how much.

When he'd left the Rahmans' house he had taken the shortest route home. He'd driven about a mile when he'd come upon an accident. He parked and mingled with the crowd. Apparently the black Toyota had run a red light and been broadsided by an SUV. Both drivers had been badly injured, and when the driver from the Toyota was wheeled to the ambulance, a shot of adrenaline raced through Zaki's body. It was Faisal.

Not knowing if Faisal had already phoned Hussein from the Rahmans' and reported what he'd seen, Zaki decided to place a call to Hussein from the accident scene. When Hussein answered, Zaki explained how he'd taken Mr. Rahman home from the meeting and had been returning home when he came upon the accident. Hussein seemed genuinely surprised by the news, and nothing in his voice betrayed any knowledge of what had happened at the Rahmans'. But that did little to ease Zaki's mind. Hussein kept everything compartmentalized, and if Zaki's actions had been reported to him, it would have gone no further until Hussein decided what to do with the information. Calculating and shrewd, he would take his time to make a plan, and then, web tightly woven, strike with deadly precision. This was Hussein's diabolical modus operandi.

Being in charge of recruiting for the cell made Zaki part of the first tier of the organization, so the revelation that Faisal was watching him had taken him off guard. What had he missed? He flashed on the dark and penetrating look Hussein had given him just as the Planning Commission meeting ended. He shifted on his feet. Was that when Hussein had decided to have Faisal follow him? He shook his head to clear it, then walked across the room. Maybe. But his gut told him it was something else. Something he was missing.

Once again he began to reexamine every meeting and discussion with Hussein since he'd begun working at the Career Center. One by one he filtered back through every action he'd taken, trying to determine what could possibly have raised suspicion about him. But there was nothing. The only slight deviation from the ordinary was the meeting in Hussein's office when the despot gave him the assignment of tracking Austia. It was the only time since joining the cell that he had been included in a meeting between Hussein and Faisal. Hussein's father, the imam, and brother made up Hussein's inner circle, and all meetings among them were closed. In fact, Hussein had instructed him, "And tell Faisal what you learn."

Zaki caught his breath.

And tell Faisal what you learn.

This was about Austia. Faisal was the point man … for Austia. He slapped his fist on his leg. Faisal hadn't been following him; he'd been following her—must have followed her there while Zaki was at the Planning Commission meeting with Mr. Rahman. Then Faisal had parked down the street, watching and waiting for her to leave. It was one more way for Hussein to double check what Zaki reported about Austia. Zaki clenched his jaw. That had paid off for Faisal. He had seen plenty.

Cursing his stupidity, he rose. But why the interest in her?

Hussein had originally mentioned Austia when he'd said that the three women wanted to go to the English classes at the Career Center. Zaki pursed his lips, suddenly remembering how that first night Hussein and Faisal had told him not to pick the women up, and the two men had gone instead.

The thought of Hussein in the Career Center sent an unexpected rush of anger through Zaki. Had they been doing some kind of reconnaissance? His eyes drifted to the nightstand that held his gun. Austia was being drawn deep into Hussein's tangled web. Why? He closed his eyes and dropped his chin to his chest, taking himself back to the meeting with Hussein and Faisal, when he'd first realized they were the ones who had killed Sabirah.

"You know Faisal's daughter Sabirah went to class there," Hussein's voice echoed. *"I'm not sure that was good for her."*

The pieces began to fall into place. Hussein told Zaki to find out about Austia and Mr. Rahman. But Hussein knew that Sabirah had some kind of relationship with Austia, even if it were only teacher to student. Yet he made no direct mention of that. Instead, he'd allowed his sister and Fatima and Fatima's sister go to the ESL classes at the Center and then asked Zaki to look at the papers they brought home. Hussein was using the three women as his eyes and ears. There was no doubt his sister would tell him anything that she thought was suspicious. Hussein's real interest wasn't in Austia and Mr. Rahman; his interest was in Austia, Sabirah, and the ESL classes. Austia had Hussein's full attention.

And now Zaki knew why.

He strode to his closet, felt for the jacket he'd been wearing at the Rahmans', and took the New Testament from the pocket. Taking it back to the window, he opened the cover and read the inscription again: "To Austia. Celebrating this day of His birth, David."

She was witnessing to the Muslims of Agua Viva. And Hussein suspected it.

Did he suspect Mr. Rahman, too? Did he see Mr. Rahman's opposition to the call-to-prayer ordinance as proof that he was against Islam? Zaki quirked his mouth. No, Hussein would see it as opposition to Hussein's plan and that would be more than enough reason to target an elderly man who had harmed no one and whose only concern was his ailing wife.

Snapshots of Austia clicked through his mind: in the office conference room helping job applicants fill out forms, gently guiding Mr. Rahman to the ambulance cab, the ESL forms in her desk drawer—suddenly the images took on a new dimension. This demure and unassuming woman was made of steel. She was on a mission behind enemy lines.

But the truth raised more questions than it answered. Why? Why would she seek to help the very people who had killed her husband?

His eyes drifted to the starry night sky, seeking an answer. And in the silence of the moment, words he had not thought of since before his mother's death replayed in his memory, taking him back to New York, to a summer evening on the porch of his boyhood home. He heard his mother's voice as sweet and clear as it had been then: "So many believers risked their lives to help us escape Ayatollah Khomeini."

"Why, Mother?"

"Because they love. They will lay down their lives for a friend."

Zaki's thoughts returned to the present. He understood that. It was why he had been willing to lay down his life for his brothers in Yemen, and even now, for his country.

But as his gaze returned to the New Testament, he was suddenly aware he was driven by anger and vengeance. Desiring the death of his enemies.

Austia was doing it for Christ. Desiring the death of no one. Instead, life for all.

The full impact of that realization stunned him for a moment. Her courage in the context of her circumstances filled him with admiration and respect for her.

At a different place, a different time … maybe …

The thought came before he could stop it. Who was he kidding? He'd known when he'd committed to the clandestine world of working undercover for his country that he was opting out of the American dream. That's why he'd done it. His work took him underground for years at a time and his life was in constant jeopardy. He had nothing to offer a woman.

He closed his eyes a moment. Not even children.

Deep down in his belly, beyond the facade of his daily life, something stirred. He cared deeply about her. He tried to push the unsettling truth behind the concrete wall that protected him from feeling, from caring, from needing. But the events of the night were too fresh, the inequity of Neryda's death too caustic.

He steeled himself against the raw emotions that gripped him. To indulge them was more dangerous than the mission that lay before him.

He clenched his fist, crushing the seed trying to root in his heart. Yes, he would do everything in his power to protect Austia. But only because it was his duty.

Moving silently across the room, he returned to the closet and secreted the book in his jacket pocket.

The air suddenly became thick with a dark and malevolent presence. His work for love of country, his commitment to a nation of people, now somehow seemed deeply personal. The danger that threatened all seemed to be coming to focus on one particular person. Austia Donatelli.

Zaki's heartbeat quickened. Had she recognized him when he'd struggled with Faisal? She hadn't wasted a moment making her escape, and he could only hope that even if she had stopped to try to see what was happening, she could have discerned little in the shadowy side yard.

Deeply troubled, he walked to his bed. He needed to get some sleep. Mistakes could happen if he didn't.

Now he would have to be more vigilant than ever. When he'd spoken to Hussein about Faisal, Hussein said he would be calling a meeting to discuss what had happened. The choice of words had

made them sound accusatory. Zaki's stomach churned. Knowing
Hussein, Zaki guessed the meeting wouldn't be held for a few
days. Hussein would want time to investigate the incident himself. Zaki could not even be sure that Faisal hadn't been subject
to some bizarre redundancy Hussein had ordered, still someone
else watching Faisal. By the time the meeting was called, Hussein
would know everything that could be gleaned about the situation.

Lying down on top of his covers, he returned his gaze to the cold,
distant stars. He wasn't a praying man. God had let him down his
whole life. But this bold young woman, who willingly walked in the
shadow of death, gave him pause.

Please, watch over her.

He turned on to his back. Who would be the new point man to
carry out Hussein's investigation of Austia?

Zaki tensed. He heard the noise again.

Throwing his legs over the edge of the bed, he grabbed his phone
from the nightstand. A text message. From Hussein.

He opened the message.

His grip tightened on the phone as the five words sent a thousand volts of fear pulsating through him.

"Come to my office now."

CHAPTER 31

Drawing on years of discipline, Zaki took control of his emotions. Any delay in responding would raise suspicion. He stepped into a pair of jeans and pulled on a polo shirt, then headed to the duplex next door.

The front door opened just before he reached it.

The imam motioned him in, then followed him up the stairs and into Hussein's office.

Hussein sat behind his desk. To his right was Ma'amoon Abdullah.

Zaki's heartbeat quickened. Ma'amoon Abdullah was involved with Hussein in some other tier of the organization. Zaki had only been able to glean that he was related to Faisal's wife's family in some way. He often accompanied Hussein on his trips into Los Angeles, and Zaki was aware that Ma'amoon's American wife frequently couriered information to the Arabian Peninsula and Pakistan. The content of his messages and his precise role in the cell remained unknown to Zaki, but in recent months it had become clear that he played a primary role in the planned terror attack. He also had a son who Zaki had seen with him on one occasion. Zaki had reported all he learned to his government contacts; still, the specifics of Ma'amoon's role in the attack remained secret.

On the desk in front of them lay an infrared camera exactly like the one Faisal had made a point of showing Zaki.

Hussein's hard eyes locked on to Zaki. "Sit."

Hussein tapped the camera. "A friend of mine at the police

171

department found this in Faisal's car and was kind enough to return it to its rightful owner."

As Zaki took a seat, Hussein opened his desk drawer, pulled out a gun, and laid it on the desk.

Zaki heard the imam close the office door. Then the unmistakable click of the lock being engaged.

Zaki shut down every open thought in his mind, leaving only the persona of Zaki ben Hassan, terrorist, to live and breathe in him. "As he should."

His words sounded in the room with calm confidence.

Almost imperceptibly, uncertainty shadowed across Hussein's eyes.

Hussein reached into his shirt pocket, then, pushing the camera to the side, casually laid a handful of bullets on the desk.

Zaki recognized them. Dum-dum bullets, banned since the late 1800s, were designed to splinter in the body with devastating effect on the victim. Their hollowed, open tips—and their message—clearly in view for Zaki's benefit.

Zaki nodded. "A favorite choice of mine."

Hussein began to pick them up, one by one, loading the gun, a smile inching across his face.

Suddenly finished, he slammed the gun down on the desk, rose, and in a movement Zaki could not completely follow, produced a picture and threw it in front of him.

Though the faces were dim, the images were clearly Zaki and Austia. Austia leaning into his chest, Zaki's hands partially raised around her.

Zaki looked at the picture a moment. If they had this picture, they had others. Yet seeing the picture out of context suddenly made what had seemed like a difficult sell very plausible. He shrugged indifferently. "Women."

Hussein didn't blink.

The moment etched in his mind, Zaki recalled how he'd immediately stepped away. He grinned. "You know American women. Needy. Lonely." He tilted his head back slightly, let his lips part, and touched his tongue to his front teeth as though reconsidering the opportunity, then shifted in his chair. Giving a nod to the camera, he narrowed his eyes coolly. "Any man could see that."

Hussein picked up the gun from the desk and openly examined it, his face inscrutable but for the fractional tightening of his jaw. Then he sat back down in his chair, gun still in his hand.

Leaning forward, he rested the heel of his hand on the desk. The muzzle of the gun pointed directly at Zaki.

Zaki rose. If he was going to die, it would be on his feet, not on his knees.

Hussein steadied his grip on the gun and his breathing became labored.

Zaki tilted his head slightly and gave Hussein an easy smile. "But the timing wasn't right. I want her to be comfortable and tell me about herself and her English classes."

Hussein tilted the gun upward. "A friend of mine at the hospital says Faisal is in critical condition."

Zaki summoned an appropriate expression of concern.

Lifting the gun, Hussein used the muzzle to scratch his lower lip. "Until he recovers, I want you to report directly to me about this woman and her involvement with the Rahmans."

Hussein's shift in focus from the Career Center to the Rahmans did not escape Zaki. It explained Faisal's presence at their house and possibly even Faisal's threatening Austia's life. Hussein's area of interest had expanded.

Casually turning the gun back toward Zaki's chest, Hussein continued, "If my suspicions are confirmed, and I think they will be ..."

His lips pulled into an easy smile as he pushed the gun toward Zaki.

"Kill her."

CHAPTER 32

Leaning forward toward the bathroom mirror, Austia patted a little more makeup under her eyes, then stepped back. The dark circles were still visible.

The events of the night before thundered into her consciousness, as horrific and frightening as the moment they'd happened. Who was the man who'd confronted her? She was sure she'd never met him before, but in some oblique way his face was familiar. That made it all the more terrifying. Was he someone she occasionally crossed paths with? She shuddered at the idea.

His comment about sticking her nose where she shouldn't made it seem like he was talking about the Rahmans. The more she thought about it, the more it seemed this must somehow be connected to the imam's finding her visiting Mr. Rahman the week before. Had the imam learned of Mr. Rahman's interest in Jesus? Her heart raced.

And who had been lying in wait for the man with the gun? She rubbed her forehead. The whole night had been terrifying.

And confusing. She was sure that she'd heard Zaki chastise the ambulance driver as she'd walked Mr. Rahman to the cab. And then later, when she'd accidentally stepped into Zaki, for just a split second it almost seemed as if he were going to comfort her. She'd sensed his stance soften. He'd almost moved toward her.

She tossed her head, dismissing the memories. Ridiculous. There was nothing gentle or good in that man.

When she'd finally been sure she was not being followed, she'd driven to the hospital and found Mr. Rahman waiting to learn of his wife's condition.

Under the circumstances she'd hated burdening him with such horrific news, but she felt she had to warn him. His reaction went beyond surprise and concern. His eyes had widened with raw fear. It was obvious that he had his own thoughts about the incident, but it was not her place to press him and he offered nothing. By the time she left, Mrs. Rahman had been stabilized. But when the doctor delivered the good news, Mr. Rahman's face had not registered relief.

Returning to her bedroom, Austia finished dressing.

Ready for work, she gathered the homework papers she'd brought home from the previous ESL class. She'd planned to correct them after the Planning Commission meeting, but the bizarre turn of events had made that impossible. She'd have to do it at lunchtime in order to have them ready for tonight's class. Slipping her purse on her arm, she hurried to her car and headed for the office.

Idling at the light a few blocks from the office, Austia glanced at the rearview mirror.

Zaki was behind her.

Her heart lurched. Dread smothered her.

She focused on the road in front of her. Sometime during the long night she'd decided she would not go to the police. That would only lead to questions about why she might be accosted in the middle of the night by a Muslim man she didn't know. And those questions would eventually focus not only on her, but on every area of her life.

In the safety of her bedroom, the risk had seemed too great. But now …

Her eyes cut back to the mirror.

Feeling in her purse, she retrieved her phone and entered a number. "Is Chief Peterson in?"

She would tell him everything.

Steve pressed the "lock" button on his key fob and headed toward his apartment. He glanced at his watch and picked up his step. He didn't have much time before he needed to leave for Bible study and he wanted to call Dave Miller before he left.

At the sound of shouting, he stopped and turned toward the grassy open space between the parking area and his building. Two boys were taunting a smaller boy. He recognized one of the two boys as Isaiah Dunne. His father was on the city council. Steve had worked with him the past two Christmases as part of Community Volunteers, doing toy drives to provide gifts for the children in battered women's shelters. He'd even been to their home.

Steve strode across the lawn. As he neared the scene he saw Isaiah lean into the face of the smaller child. "Better not see you in the park again, Burka Boy."

The young boy clenched his fists and raised his chin, trying to stand his ground. But the fear on his face gave him away. Steve recognized him as from one of the families who lived in the complex. The only Muslim family he'd seen there. They wore traditional Islamic dress and kept to themselves. As he approached the three boys, Isaiah stepped back nonchalantly.

"Hey, Isaiah, what's going on here?" Steve put his hand on Isaiah's shoulder.

"Oh, nothing really." Isaiah grinned. "Just kidding around." A horseshoe nail cross hung from a leather band around his neck. Apparently more for style than as a statement of faith.

Steve looked at the younger child, who still stood ramrod straight, facing his attackers. "What's your name?"

No response.

Isaiah folded his arms across his chest and leaned back on one heel. His smile widened.

The unspoken message to the frightened boy was as clear as words. Steve had been on the receiving end of that kind of intimidation. Instead of a park, a playground. Instead of neighborhood kids, classmates. Instead of Burka Boy, it had been Fat Boy.

Steve knelt beside the boy and put his arm around his shoulders. "It's okay. These boys were way out of line, and I know they want to apologize." He looked toward Isaiah and his companion. "Right, boys?"

They stared back at him.

"Kalid." Steve barely heard the boy whisper his name.

Steve rose and moved behind Kalid, placing his hands on the boy's shoulders. "Isaiah, when I talk to your father I know he'll be disappointed that you didn't set things right with Kalid." Steve looked directly into Isaiah's eyes. "Don't you think so?"

Isaiah held Steve's gaze but didn't answer.

Steve felt Kalid press into him.

The boy standing next to Isaiah took a step forward. "I'm sorry, Kalid."

Steve felt Kalid's shoulders relax slightly. Steve tilted his head at Isaiah in silent expectation.

Isaiah clenched his jaw. "Sorry." The word chilled the air.

Steve continued to observe Isaiah silently.

Isaiah, his expression still cool, dropped his arms to his sides. "I'm sorry."

"Thank you for that." Steve nodded toward the two bicycles lying by the sidewalk. "Why don't you two get going. I'm sure you have better things to do."

The boys turned and sauntered toward their bikes.

Steve turned Kalid toward him. "I'm sorry that happened."

Kalid averted his eyes and his shoulders slumped.

A rush of emotion washed through Steve, sweeping out of hidden places that had been closed off for years.

He brushed the boy's hair from his eyes. His thoughts went to the cross Isaiah was wearing, wishing it hadn't been visible.

He stepped away from Kalid. "People don't always act as they should, and I hope those boys leave you alone. But you know what?"

Kalid shook his head.

"Look over there. Do you see that building, number five?"

Kalid nodded.

"I live there in number 2180. If you have any more trouble from anyone and you need help, come and get me. Okay?"

Kalid gave a slight nod.

"Bye now." Steve waved as he hurried to his condo and ran up the stairs. As soon as he unlocked his door he pulled his cell phone out of his pocket and pressed in Dave Miller's number.

No answer.

Steve waited for the beep at the end of the voice-mail greeting.

"Hey, Dave, it's Steve. Remember me telling you about my sister? I'm thinking about having a little get-together at my place this weekend and I'd like you to meet her. Give me a call back."

Steve smiled as he hung up the phone. He'd known the first time he met Dave that he'd be a perfect match for his sister. Dave had told him he was a Christian and had confided to him how he was looking for a girl he could spend the rest of his life with.

The incident with Austia's neighbor had really driven home the reality of how dangerous the life she'd made in Agua Viva was. But, if she met the right guy, she'd forget about running that employment agency.

Steve began to whistle. He was going to do everything in his power to ensure his sister's safety.

And he would start by introducing her to Dave.

CHAPTER 33

Heart pounding, Fatima could hardly keep her mind on the conversation taking place between Najah and Rasha as Zaki parked the car at the Career Center. She gripped her notebook to hide her trembling hands. The feel of the hard cover reminding her of the paper she'd hidden between its pages.

Hussein's showing up at the bedroom door last Monday night while she was looking at Sabirah's New Testament had been a terrifying reminder of how dangerous it was for her to seek information about Jesus or Sabirah. She wasn't even sure Hussein believed her story that the door must have accidentally locked when she shut it. He'd forced her to shut the door over and over to show him how it had happened. Poking her in the shoulder and screaming "Do it" each time she failed, he'd given her deep purple bruises that were now a daily reminder that should he have any idea of what she was doing, the cost could be—

Blinking rapidly, she raised her chin. When she'd finally fallen asleep that night, she'd had a dream. It had taken her back to the hospital in Qatar, back to that room and her nurse, back to the vision she'd had there. The sound of music and glorious high voices singing praises had surrounded her. And once again, she'd seen Jesus.

But this time He'd looked at her. The love and compassion in His eyes unconditional, consuming, life-giving.

And then He had extended His hand to her. "Come, My daughter," He said, speaking to her in the dialect of her homeland, *"Ta'ali ya binti.*" The swathe of His breath wrapping her in love, filling her with a peace that passed her understanding, and a yearning to know exactly what He meant.

The desire to run to Him had been overwhelming. She wanted to know Jesus. And suddenly she knew He wanted to know her, too. But the moment she lifted her foot to step toward Him, she had been awakened by Hussein rising from their bed, saying he'd had a terrible dream. That he had been trapped in a lake of fire and though his flesh burned, he did not die. He spit to the side of the bed and cursed the evil that had disturbed his sleep, then, murmuring verses from the Qur'an, he'd returned to bed. But he had not slept the rest of the night.

As the long night wore on, Fatima's thoughts filtered back to the dream Hussein had awakened her from, the vision of Jesus holding her unborn son in His hand, and the inscription in Sabirah's Bible. Conviction rooted in her heart. She would learn more about Jesus.

And as the dawn broke, she knew where she would start. She must find out who had written in Sabirah's Bible. How that would ever be possible, she didn't know. She had only the hope of Jesus' outstretched hand and the words He'd breathed.

"Didn't she, Fatima?" Her sister-in-law's voice jolted her back to the present.

"Oh, sorry. Sorry, Rasha. I wasn't listening." Fatima's mind raced. "I was just thinking about how important this class is and how much I want to be here. I want to do well and start speaking English to Sami right away."

Rasha's mercurial black eyes sharpened, studying her. "I said Sabirah was always talking about the teacher when she came to these classes."

"Uhh." Just as Fatima felt heat rising in her cheeks, her car door opened.

"Let's go." Zaki's voice was impatient.

Rasha shouldered her bag as the women climbed out of the backseat. They followed him through a back door and down a hall.

Soon Fatima saw a big room with a glass wall. Women were seated at long tables, and Fatima recognized several of them from the Tuesday afternoon walks in the park. Cala bint Alwalid, whose husband was Faruq, the baker. And Jamila, who worked as a maid at the Holiday Inn Express. She had been a doctor in Yemen and she had once told Fatima she and her husband hoped to open a clinic in Agua Viva. "Only here could we live our dreams. We will work hard and we will learn the language. We will become Americans." In the back she saw Habiba. Rasha had told her that Habiba had married an American man who had studied at the University in Beirut.

There was an air of excitement and the room buzzed with chatter. She heard bits and pieces of familiar English phrases. "How are you?" "I am fine." "Thank you very much." A swell of delight surged through her as she realized she recognized some of the words from her classes as a young woman in Qatar. There weren't three empty seats together, and she ended up sitting next to Cala.

Cala turned to her. "How are you?"

Carefully pronouncing each word, Fatima responded. "I am fine." Then, in a flash of inspiration, she added, "And you?"

Cala giggled. Then, slipping back into Arabic, asked, "What'd you say?"

Suddenly the room began to quiet.

"Welcome." The woman Fatima knew as Maryam stood at the

front of the room. The two women turned to the front and folded their hands on the table. "I'm so glad you have come to learn English. My name is Austia, but please call me Maryam." She pointed to a white tag near her shoulder. "That is the name my husband gave me."

Then Maryam repeated the English in Arabic. She had an American accent, but Fatima understood her easily.

Maryam continued. "Please excuse my Arabic. Like you, I am still learning. My husband and I tried to speak it at home."

Fatima noticed that Maryam spoke of her husband in past tense and wondered if he had died. Or maybe he had gone back to his village ... and she hadn't. Maybe she had been unable to bear him any children.

"While we are in class we will always try to speak English." Cala caught Fatima's eye and smiled broadly. "But for those of you who are new, I give the evening's instructions in Arabic. Tonight we will spend the first hour on things we might find in a child's room." Maryam took a stack of papers from the end of the table next to her and began to pass them out. "The last hour is for individual help and study, including help filling out documents for citizenship, driver's licenses, or anything else that is needed. I am here to help you. And if I can't, I will try to find someone who can." Once the papers were handed out, Maryam returned to the front of the room. "If this is your first class, be sure to write your name and address in the front of your notebook. They sometimes get left behind or lost."

Sabirah had loved her teacher, and Fatima could see why. She always smiled and she seemed so humble. Not at all like most of the Americans Fatima had come across, who stared at her, then turned silently away. Her parents had warned her about coming to

America. Telling her that since 9/11 Muslims weren't welcome. That not only would she not be accepted, but she would find they hated Islam. They would talk about religious freedom, but that was only for other faiths. She fingered her notebook again, wondering about the paper she'd hidden there. She studied Maryam's face. If it were not for Sabirah's testimony about the woman, she would not dare ask Maryam her question.

Cala passed the papers coming down the row to her. She took one and passed them on.

For the next hour Fatima listened as others in the class spoke of books and crayons and balls. Smiles and giggles punctuated the lesson, and through it all the lovely Maryam gently corrected and openly praised every woman, no matter how small her effort.

Finally, she turned off the overhead projector. "Very good. What a bright group of ladies you are. For those of you leaving now, I'll see you next time. For those of you staying for study time, just raise your hand and I'll be glad to help."

Fatima scanned the room looking for her sister and sister-in-law. She finally saw them standing in the back of the room talking with some of the Tuesday afternoon ladies.

"See you next time." Cala gathered her things and left.

Fatima pulled Cala's empty chair close to hers and then raised her hand, all the while watching the movements of Najah and Rasha.

Maryam nodded toward her, but as she neared Fatima another woman intercepted her. While Maryam spoke to her, Fatima quickly double checked her notebook, smoothing the sheet of paper she'd hidden in it and glancing at the words she'd copied from Sabirah's New Testament.

She laid the handout from class over it, making sure it covered the sheet of paper she'd written on, then she glanced again at her two relatives.

They were moving toward her.

Maybe it was too risky. Maybe she should wait. Half rising, she started to gather her things.

If she didn't do it now, when would she? What if Hussein suddenly decided she shouldn't come to class? She looked toward Maryam.

Gently patting the arm of the woman she had been speaking to, Maryam made eye contact with her and mouthed, "I'm coming."

Najah and Rasha were right behind her.

It was too dangerous. What if the words meant something forbidden and Rasha heard her asking? What if Rasha wanted to know where she had seen the words and then told Hussein?

When Maryam reached her, Najah and Rasha stopped at her heels, waiting for Fatima to speak.

Fatima knotted her hands into fists to keep them from shaking. As she tried to find her voice, a breath of air encircled her. And as a cloak of peace settled on her shoulders she heard a woman's voice call out, "Rasha. Najah."

It was Cala. "I want you to meet my cousin." Cala was signaling them from the glass door.

Rasha turned to Fatima and nodded toward the door, signaling her that it was time to leave. Then the two women headed toward Cala.

Maryam slipped into the empty seat next to Fatima. "What is your name, dear one?"

"My name is Fatima."

"How can I help?"

Fatima swallowed hard, then slowly turned her gaze to Maryam. "I have a question."

Time stopped. The eyes. Maryam's eyes. She had seen them before … loving … compassionate. … But where … where?

"Did you have a question?" Maryam's gentle voice interrupted her thoughts.

She looked toward the glass wall. Rasha and Najah were watching her, waiting. What if Rasha found out and told Hussein?

"Um. No. No. I'm sorry. I must go."

"Perhaps I can help next time. Or stop here at the Career Center anytime during the week and ask for me." Maryam's smile drew her.

That would never be possible. And what if Hussein decided not to let her come back? Her chance to find out more about the inscription, and her chance to possibly find the person who had written it, would be gone forever.

Fatima lifted the handout and pointed to the words she had copied from Sabirah's Bible. "Could you translate this for me?"

As the moments passed and the teacher didn't answer, Fatima looked from the paper to the teacher.

Maryam had turned her face away.

Concern rose in Fatima's chest. She shouldn't have asked. The words were not meant for her. They were not meant to be shown to others. They were in a holy book and they had been written for Sabirah. But she had so desperately hoped they might give a clue to who had written them.

As she began to close the notebook, Maryam spoke to her.

"Love's touch heals."

The cryptic Arabic words took Fatima's breath away.

CHAPTER 34

Austia glanced at the clock in the task bar of her home computer: 6:15 a.m. The last two hours had flown by.

Love's touch heals. The words that had kept her awake most of the night returned to her. When the young woman had shown her the sentence, Austia had hardly been able to keep it together. The whole incident had been shocking and unsettling.

It had been obvious the girl was nervous, and at first Austia had thought nothing of it. Many of her Muslim students were shy until they got to know her. Though there was something vaguely familiar about this girl, try as she might, Austia had been unable to place her. She was sure she'd seen her somewhere. Watching her walk from the room she'd noticed the young woman had a slight limp, and that had stirred something in her memory. Something about the park or the post office. But she was unable to follow the fleeting feeling anywhere concrete and had finally given up.

Rising from her desk, Austia picked up her cup of coffee and walked to the kitchen. The words that were written on the paper were the very same words Austia had written in the New Testament she'd given Sabirah. It was the last time she'd seen her alive. But how had this girl gained possession of the book, and why on earth had she copied that sentence from it?

The link to Sabirah filled Austia with apprehension. Was this some kind of a setup? Had someone linked Sabirah's conversion back to the Career Center and sent this girl to get information?

Austia poured herself another cup of coffee and returned to her desk. That didn't seem to make sense. Anyone involved in Sabirah's death who suspected Austia was involved in her conversion would know that a reference to the Bible would only be a huge red flag.

So was the girl trying to reach out to her in some way? She took a sip of the coffee, then set the cup down. There was no way to be sure.

And that uncertainty had kept her in prayer most of the night, never resolving itself, but leading her to three decisions: She would pursue finding out if the girl was seeking help, and if she was wrong, accept the consequences; she would step up her efforts to find safe houses; and if Chief Peterson returned her call, she would not tell him of her fears. If the girl last night had approached her to seek help, bringing the chief of police's attention to the Career Center could put both of them in immediate danger.

Austia cut and pasted the final name, address, and phone number into her document.

Her first attempt at making phone calls to believers had been discouraging, but it had taught her something. It would be wiser to seek out people and organizations that were already set up to do outreach ministry. She'd searched the Internet for churches that ran battered women's shelters or programs for the homeless. Then she'd read their mission statements, noting those who emphasized a reliance on the Holy Spirit.

And during her prayer time she'd felt a leading about something else. She needed to meet with the pastors face-to-face. She clicked on the email address of the first church listed in her document. The box came up on the screen. Moving the cursor to the subject line, she typed: A Question.

Moving to the body of the email, she continued:

> *My name is Austia Donatelli. The Lord has given me*
> *a special ministry and I find myself in need of help. I*
> *am looking for churches that would be willing to adopt*
> *immigrants who have recently become Christians.*
> *They will need to be housed and will need assistance*
> *in finding jobs.*

She stopped and reread what she'd written, then sat back in her chair. How much should she say?

She closed her eyes a moment. Once again she had the strong impression that she was not to reveal the fact that the new Christians were Muslim Background Believers before meeting the people she would be partnering with. Straightening, she continued:

> *If you think you would be able to help, I'd like to set up*
> *an appointment to meet with you.*
> > *Blessings, Austia*

Austia reread her note, then pressed Send.

One by one she wrote to each of the handful of churches on her list. All were in a day's driving distance from Agua Viva, a requirement that came from another specific impression she'd had during her prayer time.

Keeping her eye on the clock, she quickly finished the last of the emails and rose. It was time to get ready for work. She wanted to share with Annie all that had happened. Thank God for that woman.

As she walked to her bedroom the thought of talking with Annie suddenly brought forth a deep sense of loneliness. How she missed having those special moments with David. They had talked about everything. He was her spiritual covering, and there was a security in knowing that his counsel was ordained by God.

Tears stung her eyes. It never seemed to get any easier. And this recent turn of events just drove home how dangerous it could be to try to bring the truth to the Muslims. She knotted her fists. Jesus was her covering now. She must love with His love ... Love's touch heals.

Love's touch heals. Had the young woman been brought to her by the Lord or by the Enemy? Once again apprehension rose in her chest. She must be very careful.

She pursed her lips. She hadn't noticed who had brought the young woman to class. At the next class she would make a point of watching to see who the girl came in with. When Sabirah had first started coming to class, she had been brought by various male family members, in a blue Toyota. Austia stopped midstride. In fact, she had seen the local imam with them on at least one occasion. She'd thought nothing of it then—but now it seemed important. The image of the imam standing in the Rahmans' living room flashed through her mind.

Sabirah had been killed. Her New Testament had somehow come into this young woman's possession. And now the woman was in her class asking about the words Austia had written in the book. The linkage sent a chill down her spine.

Austia drew a deep breath. She would watch and see who brought the girl to class.

Whoever it was must be regarded with extreme caution. Her husband's ministry had led him to Kuwait, his family ... and his death.

CHAPTER 35

Fatima sat down on the bed next to Sami, then carefully scooted back against the headboard, not wanting to wake him from his nap.

Thankful for the few extra minutes before she had to go downstairs to help prepare the evening meal, she picked up the ESL handouts from the nightstand and studied the line of pictures and the words typed neatly beneath them.

"B-all," she whispered. "Ba-bee."

Her gaze moved to Sami, dark lashes nestled on chubby cheeks, pink lips resting in a sweet smile. Tears welled in her eyes; she loved him so much.

She set the papers aside, gently picked him up, and cradled him in her arms. His eyes fluttered open for a moment, but upon seeing her face, they drifted closed.

As so often happened, the sight of her sleeping son stirred memories of the hospital in Qatar and the incredible vision she'd had of Jesus. The Jesus who had called to her so recently in her dream.

Quietly rising, Fatima crossed the room and put her son in his crib. Then silently moving to the window, she checked to see if Hussein's car was still gone. He hadn't come home last night. He'd probably stayed at the hospital with his brother, Faisal. She dismissed the thought. It wasn't a wife's place to question her husband, especially being a woman lucky to have found one. Absently, she placed her hand on her lower back and leaned into it. It was her duty to show him how much she'd missed him when he did return.

Reassured that Hussein was still gone, and knowing the other women were not yet back from the park, Fatima knelt beside the bed. Feeling deep between the mattress and box springs, she found Sabirah's Bible and slid it out. Sitting back on her good leg, she opened it to the page she had been reading the last time she'd had a moment alone.

> Now a leper came to Him, imploring Him, kneeling down to Him and saying to Him, "If You are willing, You can make me clean." Then Jesus, moved with compassion, stretched out His hand and touched him, and said to him, "I am willing; be cleansed."

Tears sprang to her eyes as they had the first time she'd read the passage.

Scooting off her heel, she stretched her legs out in front of her. She didn't know why she limped. It had been that way since childhood. Some of her relatives said she was cursed. And often it seemed that was true. When she was a young girl, friendship eluded her, while humiliation dogged her. Had it not been for her father's extremely generous offer to Hussein, marriage, too, would have been denied her. But the many struggles that marked her past had only strengthened her resolve to make a life with what she'd been given.

She rubbed her leg and sighed. At times marriage to Hussein was hell on earth—she glanced at the crib—but for all she had been through, she would gladly suffer it again, a thousand times over, if that was what was required to give her her son. She loved him more than life itself.

She lowered her eyes. She was not the only one who adored Sami. Hussein's mother was ever vigilant, watching Fatima like a hawk whenever she saw Fatima carrying the baby. Constantly voicing her fear that Fatima's uneven gait was a danger to her grandson, and often calling out after her to no one in particular, "Just a matter of time till she takes a fall and kills that baby."

Pulling her legs back under her, Fatima rose. Her mother-in-law's public concern was just another way to gain favor with Hussein and keep Fatima in her place. Hussein was his mother's only financial security in this life. Fatima tossed her head. She was Sami's mother, and as long as she was Hussein's wife her son would remain hers to raise. And there was nothing her mother-in-law could do to change that.

After checking to be sure Hussein had not returned home, Fatima sat on the edge of the bed and read until she heard women's voices downstairs. Knowing it was time to start preparing the evening meal, she returned the book to its hiding place, took Sami into her arms, and started down to the kitchen. Nearing the bottom of the stairs, she heard her mother-in-law talking to someone. Fatima slowed her steps.

"Another wedding?" Fatima recognized Rasha's voice.

"Yes, the arrangements should be finalized next week."

A zigzag of excitement danced through Fatima's chest. Who was getting married? Maybe it was Zainab, Hussein's cousin, or the beautiful Hafsah, daughter of Abdul Aziz, the wealthy businessman from Riyadh who had visited not long ago. She leaned forward, against the railing. Weddings were such joyous times.

Her mother-in-law continued. "What a delight to the eyes she is. She has her mother's beautiful face."

Fatima suppressed a giggle. It must be Hafsah. How wonderful.

"Why is he taking another wife so soon?" Rasha's voice sounded up the steps.

Fatima drew back. Oh dear, it must be a second marriage. A deeply unhappy time for the first wife, though whoever she was, she would suffer in silence. To speak of her pain to anyone would be to speak against her husband. Forbidden. To do such a thing would only invite more trouble. Not only the possible loss of her marriage, but her children. Fatima's grip tightened on Sami.

She heard her mother-in-law's short, loud laugh. "Hah. You can't blame Hussein for wanting another wife. I encouraged him to do it. Fatima isn't worthy of our family honor. She doesn't obey me, she's so slow to get any work done, and she rarely lets me spend time with my grandson."

Suddenly weak in the knees, Fatima grabbed the banister to steady herself.

Hussein?

Hussein was taking another wife?

"He's going to divorce Fatima. He says it's necessary because of the Americans' laws."

Heart pounding, Fatima leaned into the railing, her mind racing. It was her fault. She should have been a better wife. She should have been more attentive to Hussein and treated his mother with greater respect. And how many times had she gone out in public and forgotten to fully cover herself? Her mother-in-law was right. It was shameful.

Rasha gave a short, haughty laugh. "I thought something was up. He asked me to watch her closely at that English class." Her voice dropped. "And it's a good thing I did. I told him she was whispering to that teacher about something."

Fear seized her. She *was* cursed. Or maybe … maybe she had brought on Allah's wrath by reading the holy book of the Christians. Even hiding it under her mattress.

She shouldn't have copied the words out of it. She shouldn't have even touched it.

The reality of what she had done sent hot bolts of fear through her, filling her with certainty. She had brought all this on herself.

She must burn the book.

Yes, that's what she would do, and she would say all her prayers, every day. She would even keep the fast of Ramadan until the very end, no matter what. Somehow she would earn Allah's favor.

Sharp prods of panic jabbed her like unseen fingers. She must get the book and burn it … now.

She whirled around to race to her room. Her weak leg gave way. Using her free arm she tried to catch herself, but it was too late. Her head hit the wall and her back scraped down the steps.

When she finally slammed into the floor below, her mother-in-law's scream pierced the air. *"Ya Allah!* Look what's happened. She's killed my grandson."

CHAPTER 36

Las Vegas 40 Miles.

Austia pulled to the side of the road just past the sign. Picking up her copy of the email lying on the seat next to her, she double checked her directions.

Pastor Brown had responded within hours to the email she'd sent out Thursday morning asking if his church was open to adopting immigrants who had recently become Christians. They'd ended up talking on the phone, and the insightful pastor's questions had soon brought out in the open her real purpose for contacting him. He said his church's primary ministry was to the homeless and that sounded like a good description of Muslim Background Believers. They'd agreed to meet early the following Saturday morning. He'd given her directions to Deep Spring, where the church had a thrift store and soup kitchen. As Austia neared her destination, she noticed bars on some of the storefront windows. She checked to be sure her car doors were locked.

Craning her neck, she tried to catch a glimpse of some of the addresses as she moved down the street. "It's one block past the bus station," she murmured as she drummed her fingers on the steering wheel, glancing right and left.

Finally, convinced she'd somehow missed the building, she took a right turn so she could loop around the block and head back where she'd come from. Approaching the intersection that took her to the main road, she saw two men walking on the sidewalk. One had on a purple knitted cap pulled down over his ears. Rather odd for a summer California morning. She slowed, pulled up next to them, and cracked her window. "Do you know where the bus station is?" The man with the cap turned toward her.

The sight of his dark eyes, deep olive skin, and closely cropped beard took her by surprise. She hesitated a moment then said, *"Al salamu alaikum."*

The man nodded to her, his eyes guarded. *"Wa alikum alsalam."*

"Do you know where the bus station is?" she asked him in Arabic.

Finding she was only a few blocks away, she thanked him and started back the way she had come. She didn't know why, but the encounter made her uneasy. She shifted in her seat. It seemed odd that two Arab men happened to be walking down the street, right where she was driving, in a town she'd never been in before.

She shook her head to clear it. She was being silly. Arabs lived all over the United States, and there were certainly many in the Las Vegas area. Still, Pastor Brown hadn't said a word about there being an Arab or Muslim population in Deep Spring when she'd talked about her ministry. Spotting the bus station, she turned her attention to the building next to it.

Thrift Shop. The hand-painted sign was nailed above the door. A heavyset, dark-skinned man waved at her from the doorway.

Pulling into the small parking lot on the side of the building, she turned off the ignition and climbed out of the car. The large man bounded toward her with surprising ease. "Welcome, Austia."

"Good to meet you, Pastor." Austia extended her hand.

The big man's firm handshake, wide smile, and gentle, earnest eyes returned her greeting. "Do come in. I want you to meet my wife."

Austia followed him into the old building.

He stopped, made sure the Closed sign was in place on the front door, then moved on through a large open area filled with racks of clothes and shelves stocked with everything from dishes to plumbing parts. At the back of the shop there was another door. He opened it, leading Austia into a small office. Gesturing to a petite woman sitting at a wide oak desk surrounded by large boxes of what looked like … junk. He spoke. "This is my wife, Omaima."

The woman rose and stepped toward Austia. "We are so glad you are here." Austia recognized her appearance and accent as Middle Eastern. For the second time since arriving, she found herself taken by surprise. Omaima embraced Austia and whispered, "God bless you."

"Here." Pastor Brown pointed to a sturdy wooden chair. "Sit. Please, sit."

Austia seated herself, and Omaima took the chair next to her. Pastor Brown sat behind the desk.

"So, this is a divine appointment." Pastor Brown's gaze rested on her.

Not sure what he meant, Austia waited for him to continue.

Omaima reached out and rested her hand on Austia's arm. "We've been praying God would prosper our ministry. The need is greater now than ever."

Pastor Brown leaned forward. "My wife is Palestinian. Her family are missionaries in the Palestinian territories. As Hamas has gained power and land, there is greater and greater persecution of Christians."

Austia turned toward Omaima, thoughts of David's trip to the Middle East bringing tears to her eyes. "Are you planning to bring your family here to the US?"

Omaima furrowed her brow and shook her head. "Oh, no. It is more important than ever that they continue their work there. Those they lead to the Lord need support. And for those who have the means to get out, we must help them."

Suddenly the conversation she'd had with Pastor Brown on the phone took on a new light. No wonder he had understood her request so easily and embraced it so quickly.

The pastor's smile was gentle. "We, too, are in the business of finding homes for immigrants who have recently become Christians." Austia couldn't believe what she was hearing. "And we've had good luck finding them homes and jobs in the Las Vegas area."

Austia felt as if a weight were being lifted from her shoulders. "You have no idea how excited I am to hear this. In many ways I have to contend with the same oppression in Agua Viva that Omaima's family does in the Palestinian territories. I'm sure you've heard Agua Viva referred to as America's Muslim capital."

"I have." Pastor Brown straightened in his chair. "But we meet with resistance here, too. Ever since discussions heated up again about dividing Jerusalem and allowing a piece of it to become part of a Palestinian state, some members of our own congregation have voiced concern about what we're doing. We're a community church and have people from many different backgrounds. The fear is that the Palestinians will attack Israel once they get a state right next door. And that's a legitimate concern. Many believe that to take a stance against the Palestinians is to take a stance for Israel. But our response is to work harder to try and reach the Palestinians." He glanced at his wife. "Recently Jake, a man who attends our church, actually took his family and left the church. Though the details of our work are not public, it is commonly known that we have a heart for the Palestinian people." The big man looked down at his hands and drew a deep breath. "Jake is absolutely on fire for the Lord and a passionate supporter of Israel. He's traveled there many times. He strongly believes the increasing power of Hamas and their agenda to wipe out Israel is being advanced on all fronts. He recently quit his job to devote himself full-time to raising public awareness about the push to divide Jerusalem between the Palestinians and the Jews. He sees his calling in conflict with ours. We love him and pray he and his family will come back." Pastor Brown's eyes sought hers. "You know, Austia, Jesus said that a kingdom divided against itself cannot stand. I can't help but feel that any approach to solving our problems that is not motivated by Christ's message of love will only serve to divide God's kingdom here on earth."

The pastor's genuine expression of love and loss for the man named Jake and the desire to draw him back to the church touched Austia. "The Muslims I work with need to be relocated because they are in danger from their own families."

Pastor Brown nodded. "We understand. You aren't the first person working with Muslims here in the US that God has sent across our path."

"What do you mean?"

"We have worked with people in Michigan and New Mexico. We started a network of safe houses a few years ago."

Austia sat stunned, trying to grasp the pastor's words. Her voice came out a whisper. "Praise God. This *is* a divine appointment."

Bound by their common interest, she told them all that had happened. They wept with her as she spoke of David, and prayed with her when she recounted Sabirah's fate. They shared with her their own dreams and disappointments, but most important of all they confirmed to her that she was not alone in answering God's call to minister to the Muslim people and provide safety for those who chose to follow Him. As the hour passed, each understood that it was no coincidence that their paths had crossed.

Pastor Brown glanced at his watch. "We must open the store now. And I'm going to be taking some men to a job interview." He rose. "We'll need to meet again and put some concrete plans in place. Though I think it's unwise to use email and the telephone to discuss our plans. This is dangerous work, as you know. Recently we have had reason to take extra precautions. When can you return?"

His words didn't surprise her. Whether in Palestine, Los Angeles, or Deep Spring, Nevada, a Muslim Background Believer was never beyond the reach of the Islamic faithful. And neither were she or the Browns. "How about the same time next Saturday?"

"Why don't you come at closing time? We can take all the time we need. I'll prepare a list of our safe houses and our contacts." He grinned at her. "I keep them here." He tapped his forehead. "It's the only place I can be sure they are truly safe. Oh, and we'd love to have you stay with us for the night."

Austia welcomed the invitation and chance for fellowship. "I'll plan that." She rose and hugged her new friends, then Pastor Brown walked with her to the front door.

When he opened it, a small group of people were waiting to get in. Austia noticed that the two Arab men she had seen walking on the sidewalk were among them. One of them was wearing a back-pack. Her eyes shot to Pastor Brown. But he seemed unconcerned, smiling at the two men as he and she stepped to the sidewalk so the people could enter.

"Drive safely." The pastor waved as she walked away. "Jake?"

Austia stopped and turned back toward the store. The pastor was embracing a short man who had a bouquet of flowers in his hand. It must be the Jake they'd mentioned.

She watched for a moment as Jake stepped back and handed the flowers to the pastor. She studied the distant figure. What had changed Jake's mind? Surely, it was the Brown's unconditional love for the man.

Her thoughts returned to the man with the backpack who had disappeared into the store. A niggle of concern caused her to shift on her feet. She hesitated, waiting several more minutes.

Finally, the tension easing, she turned on her heel and started toward her car and the long drive home.

"Oh, Lord, please don't let those two men harm the Browns."

"We're going to have a baby."

Taj replayed his wife's words in his mind as he pulled into the employee parking lot and parked his truck. He'd almost called in sick so he could have the day off to celebrate. But today they were doing maintenance and it was imperative that he be at the site.

He lifted his security ID from the rearview mirror and lowered it over his head. It would be a boy, of course. Soon another American soldier in Allah's army. To take his place if Allah so willed it.

CHAPTER 37

As the traffic thinned and miles of highway stretched ahead, Austia's thoughts turned to the Rahmans. She had called Mr. Rahman the day before and learned that Safia had been released from the hospital after the doctors determined that the frightening episode had been caused by one of the medicines she was taking. Mr. Rahman's voice had been warm, but he said nothing about her stopping by. "Oh, Lord, I'm trusting you to make a way."

Just outside of Agua Viva, her cell phone rang. She flipped it open. "Hello."

It was Steve.

"Austia, how about coming by after church tomorrow? I'm having a couple of friends over and we're going to barbeque."

"Sure, I'd love to. Want me to bring anything?"

"Nope, just yourself."

"Okay, see you then." Austia closed the phone and threw it on the seat.

It would be good to see Steve ... A couple of friends. It suddenly occurred to her that that could mean a guy and a girl. A girl as in Steve's date, and a guy as in a blind date for her. She reached for the phone and called him back. She knew her brother well. They'd been down this road before. If he didn't answer, it would be a dead giveaway that he was setting her up.

There was no answer. Argh. She'd fallen for it, again. She could just see him looking at his cell phone screen at this very moment, saying, "Gotcha."

When voice mail picked up, she hung up.

Oh well, how bad could it be? She grinned. Actually, getting together with a few people sounded really good. And maybe the guy would be Mr. Right. The Lord knew, she was more than ready for that. To be in love. To be loved in return. Security and covering that only a husband could give. God would provide.

A vague sensation drifted through the back of her mind. A hard, strong chest … arms seemingly rising to hold her.

Zaki.

She straightened, gripping the steering wheel. Everything about that night at the Rahmans' had been deeply unsettling. She'd been frightened and vulnerable. And he had been—

His stance had softened—

Impossible.

He'd been different—

Dangerous.

She set her lips in a firm line and reached over and pressed the CD button on the radio. That's what he was. Lethally dangerous. That moment of contact with him resurfacing was beyond annoying.

Arriving home, she parked the car and headed for the kitchen. She was starved. Passing through the living room, she flipped on the television, saw it was still on FOX, and turned up the volume so she could listen as she fixed herself something to eat.

She opened the refrigerator and took out some turkey slices, mayonnaise, lettuce, and tomato.

"… Deep Spring, Nevada." The sound from the television caught her attention. She cocked her head, listening. "… explosion." Turning on her heel she hurried into the living room, grabbed the remote, and turned up the volume.

As she backed up to the couch and dropped on to the cushions, a picture of the building she had been in only that morning flashed onto the screen. The windows were blown out; fire trucks and ambulances filled the street.

Her mind raced, recalling the two Arab men she'd seen first on the sidewalk, and then later going into the store. Why hadn't she said something? Why hadn't she warned the Browns? The Browns had even commented on how dangerous their work was and how recently they'd had to take precautions. She would call the police in Deep Spring. She reached across the couch to the end table, for the phone. Eyes still glued to the television screen.

The camera zoomed in. The face of popular reporter Jerri Rivas filled the screen. "I have here the individual who chased the suspect, Jake Richards, and held him until the police arrived. He has asked that his face not be shown."

As the camera pulled back, Austia's mouth dropped open. Turned away from the camera so his face was not visible was a man with a purple knit cap pulled down over his ears.

Jerri tilted the microphone toward him. "You're being called a hero."

The man made no response.

"Did you know the victims?"

"They very good people. They help me and my family many times. Me and my brother come to see them today. They taking us to a job interview." His voice cracked.

Austia's hand slid off the phone and she sank back into the couch. The two men were the people the pastor had spoken of. She dropped her gaze to her hands.

"Did you know the suspect?"

Turning back to the television, she watched the man shake his head. Then, lowering his chin to his chest, he turned and walked away.

The shot cut to a residential street. A voice-over stated Jake Richards had been a member of the victims' church. A reporter spoke to an elderly couple. "Did you know Jake Richards?"

"We've been neighbors a couple of years."

"What kind of man is he?"

"He was a good neighbor, and we considered them friends. But lately he had become very vocal about the political situation in Israel. In fact, a few months ago he came back from a trip there to visit his parents. Apparently they were displaced when the government gave up the land they were living on to the Palestinians. They lost their home and everything." The man looked down. "It changed him. He seethed when he talked about it. And he talked about it often."

Austia stared at the screen, stunned.

The reporter turned to the camera. "There are still many unanswered questions. There have been reports that the church was involved in some kind of underground mission in the Palestinian territories and had received death threats in the past from a radical right-wing Christian group that opposes the creation of a Palestinian state. But that remains unconfirmed and doubtless we'll be discussing it for days to come." The channel cut to a commercial.

Austia turned the television off. She had misunderstood Pastor Brown when he'd told her they'd had reason to take extra precautions.

It was she who had assumed he meant the threat was from radicalized Muslims. Tears filled her eyes. And that thought had been fed from her encounter with the two Arab men on the street. They had made her uneasy, and she had assumed they were Muslims. She hadn't even tried to speak English to them. The reporter's interview now revealed that they were Christians. Brothers in the Lord.

Heat rose in her cheeks as the revelation laid bare her own prejudices. They had blinded her.

She glanced at the telephone. What if she hadn't seen the interview? What kind of trouble might she have brought to the two brothers had she singled them out to the police? Would the police have believed her, or them? "God, forgive me."

She slipped from the couch to her knees and lowered her head to her chest. "Oh, Lord, brood over this chaos." Austia prayed in the Spirit, petitioning God to take the scales from her own eyes, to send His warring angels to deliver both Muslims and Christians from Satan's blinding darkness that sought to divide God's kingdom on earth.

CHAPTER 38

Driving through the entrance of Steve's condo complex, Austia released a deep sigh. It felt so good to get away for a little while and just have some fellowship with other Christians. And the truth was, her suspicion that Steve had invited someone for her to meet only made it sweeter.

In the two years since David's death, time had not dulled her memory of him, his beautiful spirit, his exceptional capacity to love. But that same benevolent agent of memory moved the living on, and over the past months she had begun to ask the Lord to let her love again.

God's timing was perfect and so maybe it was finally time. In light of all that had happened, a strong partner to face the world with was something she needed now more than ever.

The events in Deep Spring had shaken her. She'd desperately wanted to talk about it and had tried to call Annie. But there had been no answer.

She'd even debated about calling the police in Deep Spring. At one level she felt she should. While at the same time, telling them she was there would likely only raise more questions than it would answer. Last night, as the news reports continued, she realized she had nothing to add. The media was reporting far more about Jake Richards and his activities than she had learned from Pastor Brown.

Pulling into an open space near Steve's unit, she blinked back tears. God bless that sweet man and his precious wife. They had laid down their lives for the Arabs living in Palestine. Not just for the saved, but even more so for the unsaved.

She closed her eyes a moment. The spiritual battle raged on.

For a moment the reality of that truth threatened to overwhelm her, taking her back to the loss of her husband. But she clenched her jaw and lifted her chin. It didn't matter what the Enemy did. It mattered what she did. She had long ago come to an understanding that it was not the Muslim extremists who hated and killed. It was the Enemy at work through them. It wasn't that she absolved them of their actions, but it allowed her to separate them from the spiritual darkness that ruled their lives. This is what Jesus meant when He said "love your enemies." She must look at them through the eyes of Christ. But for the grace of God, she herself could have been born into the bondage of radical Islam and blinded to the gospel of Jesus.

She turned off the engine and climbed out of her car. Though her chance of receiving the list of safe houses had died with Pastor Brown, she must not give up. Especially now that she knew there were other warriors out there. Other Christians whom God had called to fight against the fundamentalist Islamic war that was being waged against the world. The Lord was building a network of safe houses. As she closed the car door a thought struck her. She'd met Pastor Brown and his wife only an hour or so before their death. God had known what would happen that day. Through the forty or fifty years the Browns had lived, through the thousands of days, the Lord had brought her there at the last *hour* of their journey.

She raised her eyes toward Heaven. In a way she had never understood before, she knew she was not alone in her ministry to the Muslims. No matter how things looked, no matter what came against her, no matter what she saw happening in the physical world, God was at work in the spiritual world. She voiced the truth that spoke to her heart. "The things that are seen are temporary; the things that are unseen are eternal."

Her eyes still on the infinite blue sky above, she slowly smiled, suddenly realizing … the Browns, too, understood.

She lowered her gaze and headed toward Steve's condo.

Approaching Steve's door, she heard laughter. She stopped a moment, drew a deep breath and smoothed her hair, then knocked. Harvey gleefully announced her arrival.

The door swung open and Steve swept his arm in a big semicircle. "Come in. We've been waiting for you."

As Austia stepped into the living room, a tall, slender young woman rushed from the kitchen with a large tray holding three glasses filled with iced drinks. She quickly set them on the coffee table and stepped toward Austia. "You must be Austia. Steve speaks so highly of you." Her warm, wide smile came easy. "I'm Sue Callen." The two women hugged.

As a tall, clean-cut man with dark hair and sun-browned skin rose from the couch, Sue stepped back. "What can I get you to drink?"

"Diet anything will be fine."

"Coke it is, then."

Steve closed the door and then turned back to Austia. "This is David Miller."

David. For the briefest moment the name seemed to hang in the air, releasing a cacophony of emotion—family, love, laughter, security … loss—taking her to a place deep in her heart.

He stepped toward her.

With sheer force of will, Austia smiled and extended her hand. "Nice to meet you."

She noticed his strong, firm grip.

"Just call me Dave." Dropping his hand, he winked at her. His deep-set, dark eyes were veiled behind short, thick lashes.

The moment seemed to linger until she realized he was waiting for her to sit. She quickly chose the chair nearest Dave's end of the couch.

After setting her purse on the floor, she cupped her hands in her lap and received Harvey's big nose. Roughing up his jowls, she kissed the top of his head. "I've missed you, boy. You should come and see your Auntie Austia more often."

Sue returned from the kitchen and handed Austia a Coke, then served the others from the tray. For the next few minutes, talk turned to the community baseball league. Austia learned that all three played in the league and saw how their common interest bound them together.

Suddenly, Sue lifted her chin and sniffed the air. "Hey, those steaks are smelling good. Come on, Steve. Let's go check on them."

Austia hoped their exit didn't seem as obviously planned to Dave as it did to her.

Dave set his glass on the table. "Steve tells me you live in Agua Viva."

"Yes, I have a business there."

Dave nodded. "So he said. Says you're very involved in that community."

"I am. It's very rewarding."

"I know what you mean." He leaned forward. "I did a tour in Iraq. Worked a lot with the locals." He grinned. "Helped build schools for the Iraqi children. Those people's lives were destroyed during the war.

It felt good to make a difference." He settled back into the couch. "And I love kids anyway."

Answered prayer? Was it possible? Her heartbeat quickened at the thought. "Love *is* the answer, isn't it?"

He looked at her blankly for a moment, then laughed. "Yeah, that's right."

"I teach an English as a Second Language class three nights a week at my office. Teaching is kind of my ministry. I've thought about maybe offering some kind of tutoring for the local kids."

"What a great idea."

David. Those had been David's exact words when they had talked about her tutoring children the day he left. She felt as if she were in a dream, as if a magic wand were waving over her.

"Time to eat." Sue's voice came from the kitchen, breaking the spell.

Dave rose. "Shall we?"

Steve's condo backed to the common area and the large deck had a fabulous view of the open space. The food was perfection and the afternoon was filled with a sense of camaraderie that Austia realized she hadn't experienced for … well, since David's death. She absolutely loved Sue and knew they would be friends whether Steve dated her or not. As the afternoon passed, she found herself sorry to see it coming to a close.

After helping clean up, she gathered her things.

"It's been so much fun. Thanks, Steve, for inviting me."

Sue planted her hands on her hips. "Do you have to go? It's still early."

"I really must." She gave Sue a quick hug, then hugged Steve.

"Can I walk you to your car?" Dave stepped toward the door.

"I'd like that." Austia waited for him to open the door, then stepped through it.

"See you later." She waved as she and Dave started to the steps.

Walking side by side to the car in silence with him, she suddenly felt awkward. "Well, that sure was good food."

"It was. I haven't had a meal that good since I ate at South of Dixie."

Nearing her car, Austia slowed her steps. "South of Dixie? Where's that?"

"It's a restaurant in Westwood. The best southern-fried chicken anywhere. And it is the only place I've ever found my absolute favorite dessert."

Austia stopped next to her car door and turned to face Dave. "What might that be?"

"Black bottom pie." He rubbed his stomach. "My grandmother used to make it when I was a kid, every time she visited us."

"No." Austia stared at him in disbelief. "That is my absolute favorite dessert in the whole world."

"Hey, that's a good sign."

For some reason his words seemed to be asking for a response. But she didn't know what to say. She shifted on her feet. This seemed to be right from the hand of God, but all of a sudden things were happening too fast.

Dave stuck his hands in his pockets. "Could I take you there for dinner sometime?"

She pushed away the little wave of uneasiness that nudged her. Why not? He was a nice guy, a good friend of Steve's. And best of all, he loved kids. It was almost as if he were tailor-made for her. There was no earthly reason she should discourage him. If this wasn't answered prayer, she didn't know what was.

She opened her purse. "Here's my card. My phone number's on it." She hesitated. "That sounds like fun."

As she turned toward the car, he stepped around her and opened her car door. "Drive carefully."

Austia slipped behind the steering wheel, and he closed the door. He waved a last time as she drove away.

His concerned parting words, the image of him waving good-bye—there was something about it that filled her with a sense of deep loneliness.

How ridiculous. She shook it off. What was the matter with her? Here was a nice guy showing some interest in her. This was the very thing she'd been praying for. And now that the Lord was blessing her, she was acting like an idiot. In fact, she felt a grin pulling at her lips. His name was David for heaven's sake. How much clearer could the Lord be? And his concern for the people in Iraq. Little pieces of their conversations came flooding to her. He'd even liked the idea of the homework program.

From out of nowhere, that subtle suggestion sparked a thought she hadn't entertained in a long time. An ESL class for Muslim men. It was something she and David had talked about before his death. She slapped her hand on the steering wheel. Wouldn't it be too wonderful for words if Dave was willing to lead one? Her mind was racing. Gender issues had made it an impossibility. Until now. She would talk to him about it. She'd find out where he was in his walk with the Lord. It had been so long … so long since she'd had a man to share her life with. To listen to her, to hold her, to understand her. She merged onto the freeway.

Suddenly she couldn't wait to see him again and share about her ministry.

Taj turned out the light on the nightstand and climbed into bed, being careful not to awaken his sleeping wife. Locking his hands behind his head, he reflected on the very interesting afternoon he'd spent at Steve's house.

Up until now his assignment had seemed sterile, gathering information from Steve about Austia as they'd become friends. But today had been different. There had been something about the people at the barbeque. He'd felt it. But he couldn't put his finger on it.

He turned onto his side and slowly drew a deep breath. Whatever it was, it didn't matter. They were the enemy. He would perform his mission, make his father proud, and gain the favor of Allah.

His eyelids growing heavy, he felt himself drawn to the precipice of sleep. As he relinquished his will, he felt himself slipping into a familiar dream. His grandfather's arms drew him close.

A child once again, he heard his *jadd's* gentle voice. "Spiritual seekers do not learn from books alone, my child. But also from the companionship of others. Islam is grand enough to stand on its own."

Long-buried feelings of love stirred for the man of deep conviction who lived out his Islamic faith through a life of tolerance and peace.

In the freedom of his dream, his heart ached.

CHAPTER 39

Zaki stepped into the storage room and flipped the light on. After partially closing the door so he could get to the wall behind it, he squatted and grabbed a ream of copy paper. As he rose, he heard Austia's voice. "Dave Miller, that guy Steve introduced me to, and I are meeting at a place called South of Dixie. There's no point in having him drive all the way out here to pick me up and then drive halfway back into LA."

"Makes sense. Besides it'll give you a chance to get to know him a little better before you give him too much personal information."

Zaki recognized the other voice as Annie's. The two women were in the kitchen. Silently moving toward the partially opened storage-room door, he listened.

"Oh, Annie, I feel completely comfortable with Dave. He's a friend of Steve's and he really has a heart for people. He called me last night just to be sure I got home safe."

Zaki felt his shoulders tense.

"And he loves kids. How perfect is that? And you know what else?" Austia didn't wait for Annie to respond. "He even knows some Arabic. He picked it up while he was serving in Iraq. That got me to thinking." She paused. Her voice became husky. "Do you remember how David always dreamed about starting an ESL class for Muslim men when he was alive?"

"I do. Your brother sure set you up with the perfect guy. How does he know him?"

"They met through the baseball league."

Alarm sliced through Zaki's stomach. This was too pat. Austia's brother just happening to find a perfect guy who spoke Arabic was too much of a coincidence.

Austia cleared her throat. "Well, when I see Dave tonight I'm going to talk to him about it. About having a men's class here one night a week."

"What a blessing that would be. And I've got everything ready for the class tonight, so don't worry about that." Annie's voice dropped and Zaki leaned closer to the door, straining to catch her words. "The harvest truly is plentiful, but the laborers are few."

Austia's words came softly. "And David's constant prayer was that the Lord of the harvest would send out His laborers." Her voice caught at the end.

Anger kindled in Zaki's chest. He didn't believe for a minute that Dave Miller was sent to her by God in answer to her late husband's prayers. He would bet his life that Hussein had orchestrated it. The despot was a genius of manipulation and deception.

"It's always in God's timing, isn't it, Annie?" Austia's voice strengthened. "And right now I need to give the Secret Garden a call and have a spring bouquet sent to Mrs. Rahman now that she's home. I sent them once for her birthday and she still talks about it. Then it's time to get to work."

Zaki waited, and when the women's footsteps faded, he switched off the light, opened the door and returned to his office.

After putting paper in the printer, he closed his office door and leaned against it, a deep sense of foreboding settling over him. There was no denying it. Austia was being sucked into the dark and dangerous plan of Hussein al-Ansari.

Zaki strode to his desk and sat down.

He steepled his fingers under his chin and stared at the blank computer screen. Angle by angle, he considered every word of the conversation that had taken place in Hussein's office. Slowly, an idea crystallized. It was a long shot, but perhaps there was a local paper that reported on the league. He remembered where Steve lived from his research on Austia.

With no other options, he brought up his Google homepage and typed into the search box: *local baseball leagues west LA.*

Results 1–10 of 53,023,648 filled the screen. He scanned them, then went to the next page.

He filtered through the site blurbs page after page, looking for anything that might hold information about local baseball. When he found something, he went to the site. An hour into it he found a clue: The Community Sports Bulletin. He clicked on it.

A PDF file opened on the screen. A glance at his browser field told him he was looking at an archived bulletin. He moved his curser to the search box and typed *Steve Donatelli.*

Nothing.

An exasperated sigh escaped his lips.

He moved the cursor back to the search box. *David Miller.*

It hit *New Member Spotlight On: David Miller.*

Zaki maximized the text and began to read the interview. "… recently moved to the area … had always loved the game … learned of the league through some coworkers … was currently employed with the City of Los Angeles." Then at the end of the article was a picture of David Miller in his uniform. It sent a rush of adrenaline through Zaki.

The smiling face was that of Ma'amoon Abdullah's son, Taj.

There had to be some way to help Austia. He opened his laptop and clicked on the address book icon.

But scanning the list of Arabic names only brought to the surface the very truth he was trying to ignore. He had spent years penetrating the cell, cutting ties with the outside world, and living out a full commitment to his mission. For all practical purposes he was a Muslim and a terrorist. Any attempt to help Austia could jeopardize everything, potentially putting untold numbers of innocent people in danger of death and destruction.

His mission was to find out when and where the al-Ansari cell planned to attack the United States. The revelation that "Dave" worked for the city had been a huge break, though it raised more questions than it answered. It would take much more work to connect the dots and give his contact any actionable intelligence.

He drew a ragged breath past the dagger of truth lodged in his chest. Fulfilling his mission meant a death sentence for Austia.

Zaki knotted his hand against the potent emotions of a man and not a soldier that suddenly vied to define him, then slammed his fist into the desk.

He had not allowed himself to feel since Neryda's death.

He would not allow it now.

CHAPTER 40

Austia checked her lipstick in the rearview mirror one last time, grabbed her purse, and climbed out of the car. Thankfully, South of Dixie had been easy to find. She hurried to the restaurant.

As she reached the door, it swung open. "Hey, beautiful." Dave grinned at her.

She felt herself blushing. "It's good to see you." She gave him a quick hug.

He put his hand on her back and guided her into the dining room. "I already got us a table." Taking her hand, he led her toward a spot by a window with a view of a garden area. Then he pulled out her chair. As she sat down, she noticed a single sterling silver rose by her plate.

"Oh, this is lovely." She waited for him to take his seat. "Thank you so much."

How sweet. He must have gone to the trouble of asking Steve what flowers she liked. She hadn't felt so special in a long time.

When the waitress came to take their drink orders, Austia noticed he ordered iced tea. While they waited for her to return, Austia asked, "Do you drink?"

Dave laughed. "Sure do. Mostly tea and milk."

Austia grinned at his play on words.

"Seriously?" He tilted his head. "No. Never have."

By the time they had their drinks and had ordered the house special of fried chicken, mashed potatoes, and gravy, the initial awkwardness had vanished. It seemed like the right time to broach the subject of the ESL class for Muslim men.

"You know how you were telling me about serving in Iraq and building schools for kids, and then I told you I teach ESL classes for Muslim women?"

He nodded.

"Well, I was thinking." She hesitated, having trouble getting her thoughts together. What *did* she want to say? Her ESL classes were about a lot more than teaching English. David, Sabirah, safe houses—the words coalesced into their emotional equivalents, overwhelming her. She found herself unable to speak.

Dave leaned toward her. "Something wrong?"

"Uh. No." *Just slow down. One step at a time.* She took a sip of her Coke. "Did you actually work with the Muslim people in Iraq?"

"Yes. Made some friends. They are the most hospitable people in the world."

"Isn't that the truth?" She stirred her Coke with her straw. "When you visit their homes, they can't do enough for you. And if you get invited to dinner, you'd better be prepared to eat."

Dave raised his hand, palm out. "You're telling me? I still wake up nights thinking about baklava. My mom …"

He lowered his hand.

"Your mom?"

She noticed Dave's neck redden.

"My mom loves the stuff too."

"Do your parents live near you?"

Dave shifted in his chair. "No, they live back east. My dad's really down on Muslims."

He suddenly seemed distant, but she couldn't quite put her finger on it. "I'm sorry to hear that. If only people knew how much we have in common with them."

The look on Dave's face became incredulous.

"Didn't you find that to be true in Iraq?"

His eyes narrowed slightly. "How do you mean?"

"I mean how they are so family oriented and have such deep family values. Especially how the young men respect their mothers. Well, how the children respect their parents for that matter. And working with them at the Career Center I've really come to appreciate their work ethic." She hesitated. "But you know …"

He waited for her to continue.

"The thing that I think the most about is how they shame me as a Christian."

"What are you talking about?" There was an edge in his voice.

"Well, for one thing, how devout they are. They pray five times a day. Sometimes I don't even pray once. And their reverence for their holy book, the Qur'an. It's so important to them. Some Muslims even memorize the whole thing. I've only memorized a handful of Bible verses." She slowly shook her head. "Only the best is good enough for Allah. They truly worship him and they willingly die for him."

Dave's face held an odd mixture of emotions. "It's true."

"I totally respect them as people. Well, I can't say I feel that way about the radical fundamentalists. How can you respect people who are so intolerant that killing is their answer to everything? But the moderate Muslims are precious people who deserve a lot more than Islam allows them."

"Here you are." The waitress put a huge plate of food in front of Austia.

"Wow. That looks delicious."

Dave smiled at the waitress. "Thank you."

Austia put her hands in her lap and waited.

Dave followed suit, then looked at her.

Finally, she spoke. "Did you want to say grace?"

For the briefest moment Dave seemed at a loss for words. Then blurted out, "Prayer is kind of a private thing for me."

"Well then." Austia folded her hands together. "In honor of our Muslim friends, *Bismillah.* Lord, bless this food and our time together."

Austia picked up a piece of the fried chicken and took a bite. Chewing slowly, she savored it. "This is fantastic."

As they ate, the conversation drifted to Steve and Sue, then base-ball. But Austia couldn't help notice that Dave seemed reluctant to talk much about anything beyond that, other than his time in Iraq. He must have his reasons for being such a private person, though she found herself hoping he would open up in time. Just as they finished eating, he brought the subject back to the ESL classes.

"So tell me, how is it you decided to teach English to Muslim women?"

Once again, she felt unsure what to say. *Because I love my husband. Because God called me to it. Because of women like Sabirah.*

"Because I love them."

Dave raised an eyebrow.

"They're my neighbors and my friends. They need help and I'm in a position to give it to them."

"I see."

"In fact, I'd love to have a class for the men. But I need a man to teach them."

"Really?"

"Yes, I need a man who has at least some experience with their culture and if he knew a few words of Arabic, that would even be better."

Dave stared at her a few moments, then a broad grin broke across his face. "Really?"

"Just something to think about." Austia pushed her plate away.

"I'll do that."

"Dessert?" The waitress began clearing the table.

"Black bottom pie," they answered in unison.

The waitress left with their order.

Austia folded her arms on the table. "Do you live near Steve?"

"Not far. Why?"

"Well, Agua Viva is about an hour from there. It would be kind of a long drive. But it would only be one night a week."

"That sounds totally doable to me." He winked at her.

The waitress suddenly appeared with two huge pieces of pie.

Austia put her fingers to her lips. "Oh, my."

"Don't worry, you can get a doggy bag."

As Austia lifted her fork and cut into the flaky crust, she felt Dave's eyes on her.

"So tell me about the women in your class."

With a tight grip on the steering wheel, Taj stared at the stretch of freeway in front of him. His jaw clenched as he thought about the time he'd just spent with Austia.

Steve had talked about her as being a sharp businesswoman, but adrift since the death of her husband. When he'd met her at Steve's house she'd seemed quite unremarkable. And her comment "Love *is* the answer, isn't it?" when he'd said he loved kids, had confirmed to him exactly what he suspected. She was naive and weak. Tonight, when she'd asked him about teaching a class at her business, he knew she'd bought into everything he'd told her. Yet now, though he hated to admit it, there was something about Austia Donatelli that made him uneasy.

Her chattering about how much Christians had in common with Muslims had been disturbing. No Christian believed that and he didn't believe it either. And saying she taught the Muslim women English because she loved them was beyond belief. There wasn't a doubt in his mind that she was being paid for her time one way or the other, either directly by the students or by some government program. Money in America was *shirk*, idolatry. Her goal was to teach them English and then Americanize them. Eventually convince them that church and state should be separated, and that the will of man should displace the will of God as the law of the land. Which was surely a plan laid out by Satan himself. This is exactly what Hussein said had happened to his niece, Sabirah. She had taken up the ways of the West and then converted to Christianity. And it had all started when she began the English classes. But Hussein was a good and fair man. He would get the facts about what happened to his niece before taking any action.

Taj felt honored that Hussein had called him to *jihad*, had paid to have him trained in Afghanistan, and had given him an important assignment. It was beyond an honor to be chosen to report directly to Hussein, first in the Los Angeles project, and now this one. It was imperative that the world be set up as an Islamic state. Let old men like his grandfather sit and pray while the Jews occupied Palestine, the Americans occupied Iraq, and the Great Satan tried to spread democracy around the world. His own father had told him that grandfather didn't really know what was in the Qur'an, that he got caught up with some mystic brotherhood. That the difference between him and his grandfather was that he was a true Muslim. True Muslims shaped their ideologies, their every thought, and even their desires after the *sunnah*, the model of Prophet Muhammad, keeping God's laws with unyielding allegiance. He would excel. He would earn the respect of his father and Hussein—and more importantly the favor of Allah. Death would be honor. Paradise a certainty.

As his thoughts turned to Austia and how he would arrange to see her again soon, the vague sense of uneasiness returned to him. He cursed it. He had nothing to fear from her. She was no match for him. He was Allah's sword. God's power, and implementation of God's explicit laws, would silence people like her and put the world right.

When he'd told her that he helped build schools for the Iraqi children, she'd said, "Love is the answer, isn't it?"

The statement had been so ridiculous; he hadn't known what to say.

Taj reconsidered the weak, pathetic words for a moment.

Then he laughed out loud.

CHAPTER 41

Fatima sat on the edge of the bed, her hands clasped in her lap and her eyes riveted on Sami's empty crib. Hussein had spoken to her only once since she'd fallen down the stairs. And that had been to berate her for her carelessness and to tell her that his mother would be caring for Sami during the day. He'd said nothing about his plans to divorce her or to take a second wife.

Then this morning, when her mother-in-law came to take Sami away, she'd told Fatima that Hussein wanted to speak to her and that she should wait in the room until he came. It was now almost noon.

Fatima lifted the baby blanket she had taken from Sami's crib and once again pressed it to her cheek. Closing her eyes, she breathed deeply, seeking a trace of his scent. "Mama loves you." She rocked back and forth, imagining him in her arms.

Heartsick, she rose and walked to the window. Hussein's car was still in the driveway. That he was in the house but had not chosen to see her fueled her fears of what was to come. She knew nothing about the Americans' laws that restricted a man to one wife. Maybe an American divorce was something Hussein had to do to satisfy the government so he could take a second wife. Like the thing Cala had told her about having to take off your *hijab* for a driver's license picture. She would go along with whatever was necessary to satisfy Hussein so he could have his second wife … and she could have Sami.

"What are you looking at?"

Fatima whirled around at the voice behind her.

"Oh, I didn't hear you come in."

Hussein's mouth curved in reproach. "You should pay more attention."

Fatima's eyes drifted to the floor. "Yes, I should. I'm sorry."

"I've noticed that you seem to be tired lately. Unable to help the other women as much as you should."

Fatima kept her eyes riveted on the floor.

"I think it would be good for you to take a rest." His voice was matter-of-fact.

"A rest?" She raised her eyes.

He gave her a bland smile. "Yes, I'm going to send you and Najah home to visit your family. Not only will it be good for you, but your parents are aging and you should spend some time with them."

Her chest tightened with apprehension at his suggestion of kindness. "When?"

"There are arrangements to be made and you need to pack. It will be a week or so."

A hard pit of fear formed in her throat as Hussein turned on his heel and strode across the room.

Steeling herself, she turned toward him. "Sami will need a passport."

Hussein stopped at the door and faced her. "Sami will be staying here. My mother will care for him. And if she decides to take him to see our family, we'll get him a passport then."

He leveled his gaze at her and stared, daring her to say more. Then he grabbed the doorknob and closed the bedroom door as he left the room.

Heart pounding, Fatima pulled her son's blanket to her chest. "Sami." Her voice cracked. "Sami."

All the pieces fell into place. Hussein was divorcing her. And not as some manipulation of American laws so the new wife could live with them. If that were the case, he would not be sending her away. She didn't believe for a moment that he had any true concern for her or her parents. Her mother-in-law was finally getting what she had wanted since the day Fatima had arrived. A new daughter-in-law. And Sami.

Suddenly, Fatima felt like she was breathing through mud. She would never see Sami again. A wave of nausea rocked her stomach.

Covering her mouth, she stumbled to the bathroom. Barely able to stay on her feet, she vomited through deep, violent sobs that shook her body. Why hadn't Hussein just killed her? Death would be welcomed.

The answer razored through her gut. He'd known that.

Leaning heavily on the bathroom sink, she straightened, then turned, slowly making her way back to the bedroom.

With a shaking hand, she pushed her hair from her sweaty brow, then sank to her knees, letting her face press into the carpet. She would be sent home, disgraced and tainted. And her shame would be imputed to her family. Najah would have difficulty ever finding another husband. And Fatima would become an unwanted burden to her parents ... as long as they were alive. Hopelessness enveloped her. She was as alone now as she would be then. No one could help her.

"Sami." She raised her head, and with eyes on the empty crib, crawled across the room. She would never see him again after she was sent away. He would never know his mother or what he meant to her. "Sami. I love you so much."

At the foot of the crib, she huddled, clinging to its wooden leg. Shunned by all. Stripped of any reason for living. A cripple waiting to be cast into the street. And no one could help her.

If You are willing.

The words she'd read in Sabirah's book whispered to her, drawing her memory to the story she'd returned to time and again since she'd first read it.

The leper, calling out to Jesus, "If You are willing."

Suddenly, the room faded from her vision and snapshots, vignettes of time, flashed through her mind: Sami resting in Jesus' hand. Jesus calling to her in a dream, "*Ta'ali ya binti*." Maryam sitting next to her, gentle eyes filled with love, her sweet voice speaking, "Love's touch heals."

"Oh, Jesus." Fatima lifted her face, barely able to speak. "If You are willing. Help me." The words came out in choked fragments as she sobbed.

"If You are willing." She cried out the words again.

There on the floor, broken and alone, she sensed a presence surrounding her. As her tears subsided and her breathing slowed, the presence intensified, becoming an impression so strong she perceived it as words, not spoken, but pressed into her heart.

"I am willing."

CHAPTER 42

Zaki quietly took his seat at the meeting Hussein had called, noting the presence of Hussein's father, the imam.

As the days had passed and Faisal continued to languish in a coma at the hospital, Zaki had become cautiously optimistic that his cover had not been blown that night on the street in front of the Rahmans'. But then, almost as if Hussein sensed there was a tear in the broad net he'd cast over his cell, he had shrewdly engineered the introduction of Dave to Austia. The cunningly clever move created more cross-checks for Hussein and even greater problems for Zaki. In effect, when Austia spoke to Dave she was speaking directly to Hussein. That Hussein had set up Dave's chain of command through Zaki was a buffer of sorts. But even that was suspect. It was more than possible that Dave actually reported directly to Hussein and the myth that Dave reported go Zaki was so that Hussein would know if anything Zaki said was deceptive.

Hussein leveled his eyes at Zaki. "So, what have you learned about the woman Austia and Abdur Rahman?"

She left her Bible in his couch. "She's friendly with his wife, who has been ill. Seems to think it's her Christian duty to visit them from time to time."

Hussein raised his eyebrows. "I see. Anything else?"

"I know of nothing significant." *Khalama. Khalama.* Austia's stuttered sob rang out in his memory. The howl of the ambulance's siren wailed over it. "Taj has visited with Austia twice but reported nothing back to me."

"It seems that the woman sent some flowers to the Rahmans' house."

"I'm not surprised," Zaki answered evenly.

"But you didn't know that."

Holding Hussein's gaze, Zaki spoke. "A spring bouquet, delivered by the Secret Garden yesterday morning."

Surprise flickered in Hussein's eyes.

"It didn't seem worth mentioning, since the woman didn't go there herself."

Hussein shrugged. "Nevertheless, I believe it is only a matter of time until she does. Some of Mr. Rahman's neighbors have said that in the past she has visited quite often. Odd behavior for a stranger, don't you think?"

Zaki lifted his chin, still holding Hussein's gaze. "There's no explaining the Americans."

"A close inspection of his house might be helpful. Perhaps you'll discover what is so fascinating to the woman."

"As you wish."

Hussein settled back in his chair. "I have the feeling that Mr. Rahman is going to have an unfortunate accident. When Mr. Rahman's imam hears of it"—Hussein glanced at his father—"he will want someone to visit him in the evenings for a few days."

Zaki walled off the emotions that pressed hard within him.

"An excellent plan." Zaki tipped his head to the despot.

Hussein's eyes coolly narrowed, observing Zaki. Then he spoke. "Faisal has been asking for you."

"Really?" Zaki forced himself to breathe.

"Yes, it seems your name is the only word he has spoken from his mindless sleep."

"Strange." Zaki managed to keep his voice steady.

Hussein's tongue darted across his lips. "Yes, I thought so."

CHAPTER 43

Austia drummed her fingers on the water glass.

"Is something the matter?" Annie pushed her lunch plate to the side. "You hardly ate and you seem distracted."

"I just keep thinking that I have to find a safe house."

Annie settled back in the booth. "You've been doing all you can. And after what happened in Deep Spring, I'd think you would take it slowly. Maybe even put things on hold for a while."

"I can't tell you how many times that thought has occurred to me over the last few days. But I just can't get any peace about it. I suddenly have this feeling of urgency." She chewed on her lower lip. "Still, it isn't like a Muslim woman is going to walk up to me and say, 'Tell me about Jesus.' And then suddenly she has to be hidden away."

"That's certainly true." Annie grinned at her. "It takes months of building a friendship, not to mention trust. For now, there's plenty of time." Compassion filled Annie's eyes. "It's going to work out."

"You know, after having dinner with Dave last night and finding out that he'd like to help me with a class for Muslim men, I feel like I ought to put my energy into working on that with him." She began to tap her glass again as vague feelings of uncertainty skittered through the back of her mind.

"So how *did* it go last night?"

"Umm." Austia tilted her head. "Actually there was something about it that I can't quite put my finger on."

"What do you mean?"

"I don't know." She huffed a sigh. "I guess one thing … It kind of took me by surprise that he was uncomfortable saying grace." She hesitated. "And there was something else that seemed kind of odd. That first time I met him." She closed her eyes a moment, then shrugged. "I can't think of it right now. It was something about when he was speaking of being in Iraq and building schools for the Iraqi children. But, hey." She drew an invisible pattern on the tabletop. "It's been a long time since I've been out with anyone. I'm probably being too picky."

"Oh, Austia. Lots of Christians are shy about praying in public."

"I know that. I guess I'm being silly." Austia shifted in her seat. "But it's hard. David was such an awesome husband. At some level it always comes back to that. I don't want to settle for less." She felt tears sting her eyes. "He truly loved me like Christ loves the church. Without a doubt he would have laid down his life for me." She blinked back her tears and met Annie's gaze. "Let's face it. He was involved in things that might have put him in that position." Austia lowered her eyes. "I'll never find another man like that."

"Of course, no one will ever take David's place." Annie reached across the table and patted Austia's arm. "And you just met Dave. Give it some time. I bet his shyness will go away after you get to know him better. If nothing else, you could end up with a great friend."

"You're right." Austia straightened and gave her friend a weak grin. "And there are lots of things I like about him. Especially his willingness to serve the Muslim people. Since David died, any outreach to men has been out of the question."

"Did you say anything to Dave about how it would give him opportunities to share the gospel? If he's not comfortable saying grace, he might be the type of person who's private about his faith all the way around."

"Oh, you know that doesn't matter." Austia clasped her hands in her lap. "If it turns out he loves teaching the men, they'll feel it. And that's really the only way to begin sharing the gospel with Muslims anyway. Living it. But there is something else I've thought about that might interest him."

"What's that?"

"The safe houses. I had never even considered that there might already be a safe house network set up. But after meeting the Browns I realized there was. Dave could be a real help if I was able to connect to them because then we could help shelter Muslim men."

"If he has his own place, that would be perfect."

"Exactly my thinking. I'm going to talk to him about it."

"By the way." Annie leaned forward and crossed her arms on the table. "Did that girl you told me about, the one who asked you to translate 'Love's touch heals' show up at the class Friday night?"

"No." Austia pressed her hand to her chest. "And that whole thing really concerns me. I mean I'd like to think she's someone that Sabirah might have reached out to and shared with. Maybe she even gave her the little New Testament. But it didn't feel that way. The girl was incredibly nervous. And, the more I've thought about it, I don't believe that Sabirah would have parted with the book. Besides that, when she first saw the words, why wouldn't she have just asked Sabirah what they meant? It has to be that the girl saw the writing after Sabirah's death." Austia dropped her hand in her lap and searched Annie's face. "How could that have happened, and why would she come to me? I purposely didn't sign the inscription. There is nothing I know of that ties me to that book."

"Well, it stands to reason that Sabirah's personal belongings would have been returned to her family." Annie's brows drew together. "And, without a doubt, they would have immediately gotten rid of the book."

"Right. Think about it. How did that girl come to see the inscription, and what would possess her to write it down? She has to be connected to Sabirah's family. She didn't come to class Friday and we didn't have class last night. I'm going to watch for her and try to reach out to her. And I'm going to try and see who brings her next time. If the radicals who live in Agua Viva ever got wind of what we're doing at the Career Center, we could both be ..." Her voice trailed off.

"Austia, I counted the cost long ago, just as you have."

"I know that. And in fact, in fairness to Dave, it's something I need to be sure he understands before he commits to teaching the men or getting involved with the safe houses." She gave a resolute nod. "I'll lay it all out the next time I see him."

CHAPTER 44

He had to do it.

Zaki lay in the darkness of his bedroom, eyes fixed on the ceiling. He could feel the noose resting around his neck. And with diabolical cunning Hussein would soon be tightening it.

It was apparent that the young man was quickly working his way into Austia's confidence. It would only be a matter of time before she confided in Dave the real reason she ran the ESL classes. And that revelation would end her life.

He rose from the bed. Anything Dave discovered that Hussein believed Zaki should have discerned would immediately raise Hussein's suspicion, putting Zaki's entire mission in jeopardy and his life at risk.

He walked quietly to the window and stared into the starry night. For himself, so be it. He had come into the mission knowing the danger. He had no attachments and had long ago come to terms with the fact that he might be asked to pay the ultimate price. But Austia was an innocent.

He bit down on his lower lip. He was going to have to communicate with his FBI contact. Something that he was to do in only the direst circumstances. He would tell him that Austia had to be removed from the nexus.

Drawing a long, deep breath, he put his hands on the windowsill and lowered his head. Removing her would surely put him in extreme peril. But let the chips fall where they may. He would not let his mission take Austia's life ... even if it took his.

He raised his head and lifted his eyes to the night sky. Austia Donatelli believed in God. He shook his head slowly. Little did she know how much she needed Him now.

Inexplicably, tears sprang to his eyes.

Disconcerted by the sudden emotion, he brushed the back of his hand across his eyelids.

He could not allow himself to have feelings for her.

But he did.

CHAPTER 45

"I'll be back in a little while." Austia held the door of the office open for Annie as she started across the parking lot with a stack of files and a take-out bag from Olive Garden dangling from her arm. "I'm just on my way to visit the Rahmans."

Annie raised her eyebrows and a broad grin spread across her face. "That's answered prayer, isn't it?"

"It sure is." Austia gave her friend a decisive nod, then raised her hand, palm heavenward. "Thank You, Lord. But I'm running late."

As soon as Annie stepped into the back hall, Austia released the door and hurried to her car.

Besides the Lord, Annie was the only one who knew of Mr. Rahman's interest in Jesus and how the elderly man had been intimidated by Imam al-Ansari to the point of distancing himself from Austia. Austia had so hoped that after the terrible scare that sent Mrs. Rahman to the hospital, Mr. Rahman would contact her and renew their friendship. But until now, he hadn't. She pulled out of the parking lot and on to the street.

This morning's phone call from him had been to tell her that Mrs. Rahman was asking for her, and would it be possible for her to stop by. He'd suggested she could come between noon and one thirty.

The time frame was the exact time of noon prayers for all Muslims. She was sure Mr. Rahman had chosen that time for her visit because many Muslims would be in the mosque and it would reduce the chance of someone seeing her at his house. Out of respect for him, and fully understanding his fear after the imam's unexpected appearance the last time she'd visited, she'd already decided to park at the grocery store a few blocks from the Rahmans', buy a small basket of fruit to take with her, and then walk to his house. Seeing the little market on the right side of the street ahead of her, she slowed and pulled up in front of it.

In a few minutes she had the fruit basket in hand and paid for it. The clerk handed her her purchase and she set out for the Rahmans'.

As soon as she stepped on the porch, Mr. Rahman opened the door.

"Welcome, Austia."

"Al salamu alaikum." Smiling, she lifted the small basket toward him, and Mr. Rahman took it from her.

"Wa alikum alsalam. You are so kind." He stepped awkwardly to the side, revealing a crutch under his right arm. "Come in."

"Oh, dear." She eyed his bandaged foot and ankle. "What happened?"

Crossing the threshold, she stepped out of her shoes and quickly reached for the basket. "Let me hold that."

Mr. Rahman closed the door and gestured to the couch. "Please, sit down."

Austia set the basket on the coffee table as Mr. Rahman hobbled to his chair. "May I help you?"

"No, no. I'm fine."

Respecting his wishes, she seated herself.

"What happened?"

"I can hardly say." He absently rubbed his knee. "I was on my way to the pharmacy yesterday afternoon. And there was a snake in my car."

"A snake!" Austia felt her jaw go slack.

The elderly man nodded his head, the hand on his knee knotting into a fist.

"I have no idea how that snake got in there. My windows were up and the car was in the garage."

"Did it bite you?"

"When I saw it, I'd just backed onto the street and was pulling forward. That's when I saw it come across the floor from the passenger's side."

Austia pressed her hand to her chest. "What did you do?"

"I opened the door and jumped. Twisted my ankle."

"I'm so sorry, Mr. Rahman. What happened to the car?"

"It rolled forward, jumped the curb, and stalled." His knotted hand relaxed. "There was one good thing."

"And what was that?"

"Faruq bint Alwalid and his wife, Cala, from the mosque, happened to be driving by. He stopped and helped me. Got the car back in the garage. And his wife stayed with Safia while he took me to the emergency room." He furrowed his brow. "Never did find the snake though."

"Do you know what kind it was?"

"I have no idea, but it was black." He slowly shook his head. "I've never seen any snakes around here."

Neither had Austia, and the whole story seemed extremely odd. Not only the part about the snake but also the news that Faruq, who owned a small bakery in town, had happened to be driving by. His wife was in her ESL class, and as far as Austia knew they lived above the bakery, which was nowhere near the Rahmans, and they didn't own a car. Cala's husband always walked her to and from class. Well, whatever, it seemed Mr. Rahman was going to be fine.

"Please let me know if there is anything I can do for you."

He nodded toward her.

"And what about *Khalama?* Is there anything I can do for her right now?"

Mr. Rahman's eyes shifted to the hallway. "No, but let's go see if she's awake. She was so delighted when I told her you were coming."

Austia followed Mr. Rahman down the hall. How she wished she could put her arm around his waist and let him lean on her. But that would cross boundaries that were to be maintained at all cost and only bring him discomfort of a different kind.

"Safia?" Mr. Rahman whispered his wife's name as he neared her bedside.

Austia caught her breath at the sight of her sweet friend. She had not seen her since the night the ambulance had taken her to the hospital, and it was clear that the episode had taken its toll on her. Safia looked so tiny beneath the covers, white hair framing a drawn face.

Her lids fluttered open, and dark brown eyes first focused on her husband, then moved to Austia. A flicker of recognition became an ember. "Austia." She lifted her thin arm, extending her hand.

Austia gently grasped the gnarled fingers, then bent and kissed her precious *khalama's* cheek. She felt the old woman's weak smile beneath her lips.

Austia straightened and gently stroked the top of Mrs. Rahman's hand.

"You have taken much trouble to come see me." Mrs. Rahman patted the mattress. "I am so happy you're here. Please, sit a while."

Mr. Rahman moved toward the door. "Excuse me. I'll leave you two now."

As he left the room, Austia lowered herself to the edge of the bed. "It was no trouble at all. I've missed our visits and time cooking together."

"Oh, so have I. But I believe you have been keeping me in your prayers."

"Yes, *Khalama*, I have." The reference, acknowledging Austia's prayers to Jesus, the Holy Prophet known to Safia as Isa Al-Masih, touched Austia. "With your permission, I would like to say a prayer for you now."

The ember in *Khalama's* gaze glowed. "Please, I would like that."

Austia lifted her hands, with palms up, to just below her chin. Then, with her eyes open and looking into her palms, she prayed. "O God, full of mercy, full of compassion, help us in our time of need." She felt God's presence surround her. "I pray for dear *Khalama* that You will take her pain away. I pray that in a special way, through Your Holy Servant Isa Al-Masih, You will restore her to full health. May You be glorified and forever praised. *Amin.*" Then, she reached over with her right hand and touched Mrs. Rahman. "In the name of Isa Al-Masih, be healed."

Austia felt her beloved friend relax beneath her touch. *Oh, Lord God, let Your Holy Spirit draw her into the kingdom. I beg You not to let her die lost.*

"Thank you, Austia."

Hearing the tiredness in Mrs. Rahman's voice, Austia stroked the frail woman's forehead, then rose. "I'll let you rest now."

As Mrs. Rahman's eyes drifted closed, she whispered, "Please come and pray for me again soon. I feel so much peace when you pray."

Austia paused a moment, then slipped from the room.

"You must have a cup of tea before you leave." Mr. Rahman's voice greeted her as she entered the living room.

The cup's placement on the coffee table not only directed her where to sit but signaled that Mr. Rahman had something on his mind. "Only for a moment." She sat where directed. "I can't resist a cup of your tea."

"Do you think Prophet Jesus will heal Mrs. Rahman?" His words, carefully measured so as not to betray Islam, failed to mute the hope in his voice.

"Yes, I believe with all my heart that Jesus the Messiah will heal her."

The doorbell rang.

A frightening sense of déjà vu flashed through Austia. She rose.

Mr. Rahman's eyes widened. "Who is it?"

"Imam al-Ansari."

"Just a moment. I'm coming." Mr. Rahman reached for his crutch.

There was no need for discussion. Austia turned and fled to Mrs. Rahman's room. Stepping behind the open door, she listened.

The men exchanged greetings.

Zaki. Why was he here?

At the sound of what must be the men removing their shoes, she backed against the wall. She was helpless to do anything and could only pray her shoes would not be noticed. At least her purse was still on her arm.

The imam's voice was easily discernable. "I heard of your unfortunate accident."

She couldn't make out Mr. Rahman's answer, but she could hear the men moving across the room.

The tea!

"Do you have company?" The imam's words were crisp.

The silence seemed to stretch clear to the bedroom.

Zaki's voice cut in. "Or were you about to have tea with your wife?"

"Yes. Yes, I was. But when I went to get her, I found she was sleeping. Please sit and join me."

Say no. Say no.

"Yes. We will be happy to."

Austia tried to get a hold of herself. The imam would never ask to come into Mrs. Rahman's bedroom, but still she felt weak in the knees. She drew a steadying breath. She just needed to stay quiet and wait until they left. With her car at the market, they would have no reason to suspect she was there.

"Austia?"

Mrs. Rahman's voice seemed to boom across the room.

Austia tiptoed to the bed. "Shh, *Khalama*. Yes, it's me," she whispered.

The imam's voice slithered stealthily down the hall. "What was that?"

CHAPTER 46

"Wait here," Hussein had instructed Fatima when he left her. "I'll be coming to speak to you later."

The sun had not yet risen when he'd given her the order. Now it was high overhead.

She had no idea where he had gone. But for the last few days he often came to bed late or left in the middle of the night. She knew nothing of his business, but she knew everything about the rhythm of his life. He was rigidly methodical.

One of her duties was to keep his clothes in order. Meticulously keeping the closet to please him consumed a part of each day. She'd arranged things first by item: All shirts in one place, to the left starting at the wall. All pants folded on the leg crease, zippers facing out. All jackets, fronts facing right. And then within the group they were ordered by color. His long, one-piece *dishdashas* had a special place on the side wall, ironed to his specifications, hanging with the front to the right and separated by fabric weight, beginning with cotton. Above them perched a shelf for head coverings, *ghutras* on the left and *shumags* on the right.

He'd demanded the same uncompromising structure for his meals, as well as the beginning and ending of his day: to bed at midnight, then rising at five a.m. for the dawn prayer, starting his routine again. But recently something had changed.

She had never been part of his life outside the kitchen and the bedroom and had never concerned herself with his comings and goings. But now, for reasons she could not explain, she had begun to take notice. As though a still, small voice were prodding her.

She set her thoughts aside. How Hussein spent his time was meaningless to her. What mattered to her was Sami. If only there was something she could do to save herself and her son. She had thought of nothing else since Hussein had first told her of his hateful plan. But the only possibility that had occurred to her was too terrifying to contemplate.

The sound of the bedroom door opening scattered her thoughts and drew her full attention to Hussein. As he closed the door behind him she sat on the edge of the bed, lowered her head, and dropped her gaze to the floor.

"I trust you had a good night's rest." Without waiting for her response, he continued. "I bought your plane ticket, and I'll arrange for someone to escort you and your sister to Qatar. I will make your family aware of your homecoming in the next few days."

Fatima's cheeks burned with humiliation. The disgrace she would bring to her family was unforgivable.

Hussein walked toward the crib. "I want Sami moved to my mother's house Sunday. You leave Monday."

A cry escaped Fatima's lips. That was only a few days away.

"Silence."

She felt the force of the word more than she heard it. His voice was muffled by the pounding of her heart in her ears and the rush of blood that pulsated through her body.

Slowly, everything around her faded away. Gone were the drapes, carpet, and furniture. Gone was the evil that her husband wielded with such practiced expertise and boundless pleasure. The walls of terror and intimidation that had held her captive in the hell that was her life suddenly crumbled.

Nothing remained but Hussein, his words, and the fire that burned in her breast to fight for her son.

She lifted her head, the possibility that was too terrifying to contemplate forming on her lips.

"I know you and Faisal killed Sabirah. If you take Sami from me, I'm going to report it to the police."

Hussein's eyes darkened. Rage twisted his face.

Rising, Fatima held his gaze.

The blow of his fist across her face took her to her knees. Her vision blackened briefly as she fought unconsciousness.

Swallowing the metallic taste of blood, she straightened her back and lifted her chin.

As her eyes again met Hussein's, her words seemed to come of their own volition.

"Don't think that killing me will stop them from finding out."

The kick to her stomach sent her to the floor.

Gasping for her breath, she braced herself. But instead of the assault she expected, she heard the sound of Hussein crossing the room, followed by the slam of the bedroom door. She didn't move as she listened to his footfalls fade down the hall.

The enormity of what she'd done overtook her.

How much time passed she didn't know, but as her breathing came easier, she struggled to her feet. She stood silently a moment, trying to get her bearings. Everything looked exactly the same. But everything was inalterably changed. She locked the door, then sat on the edge of the bed.

Slowly, she began to order her thoughts, and as the consequences of what she had done began to occur to her, terror gripped her.

No.

Girding herself to stop the trembling, she swallowed the fishbone of fear in her throat. She would fight for her son with every fiber of her being.

But how?

She searched frantically through limited options.

She dare not draw Najah into it. Her stomach clenched at the thought of bringing her own fate to her sister.

None of the women she'd come to know outside the house would want any part of her plight.

She lowered her chin to her chest.

Jesus was willing.

His words flitted through her mind. How foolish that thought seemed now. The prophet appeared only in dreams and visions. Hussein's plans were laid and he could not be stopped. Jesus couldn't help her now.

"Don't think that killing me will stop them from finding out." Her words replayed in her mind.

That had been an empty threat. Why she had even said such a thing escaped her. Besides herself, there wasn't anyone outside Hussein's inner circle who knew what he and Faisal had done. All Hussein's deeds were cunningly hidden. Beyond the view of any man. She chewed on her lower lip.

Maryam.

She rose.

She would write a note and give it to Maryam at the next ESL class. Hope sparked in her heart. She turned to the table beside her bed and opened the little drawer where she kept the pencils and paper for her schoolwork.

As she picked them up, reality intruded. Hussein would never let her go to class. She was trapped in Hussein's tangled web.

Despair settled over her. Why had she dared to think she could fight him? She limped to the window.

Below she saw her mother-in-law. She was holding Sami and talking to a neighbor.

At just that moment Sami looked up. Seeing his mother, he smiled and reached toward her.

Fatima's heart wrenched in her chest. "I love you," she mouthed through the window.

Tears stung her eyes. She would never give up. She would find a way to save herself and her son.

Suddenly, clear as a voice, a thought came to her. Like a beam of light piercing the darkness, an idea formed. Dropping to her knees, she opened her notebook and laid it on the nightstand.

She eyed the bedroom. Holding her breath, she listened. Hussein could return at any moment.

She pressed her pencil to the paper.

CHAPTER 47

Zaki pulled into the bakery parking lot. There weren't many cars and he found a parking space easily.

It would have been better if the bakery café were bustling. It would have made it just that much easier to go into the men's room unnoticed and drop the cylinder into the toilet's water tank. And then that much easier for his FBI contact to retrieve it so a meeting could be arranged. Though Mr. Rahman's recounting of his encounter with the bakery owner, Faruq, had almost convinced Zaki to hold off on coming today. Especially in light of the fact that his wife had been with him when he'd stopped to help Mr. Rahman. One of them always stayed at the bakery. Just one more reason for Zaki to talk to his contact.

There were a lot of things about the trip to the Rahmans' with Imam al-Ansari that made him uneasy. Not the least of which was seeing Austia's shoes by the front door. He'd seen her wear the distinctive flats with the silver-colored block heels many times. Fortunately, the imam had been so obsessed with the fact that Mr. Rahman was slow to answer the door, he hadn't noticed.

The cup of tea on the table had cinched his suspicion. Without a doubt Austia had been in the house and had hidden when she heard them at the front door. He sighed. She was in way over her head. Fortunately, when Mrs. Rahman cried out, Mr. Rahman's explanation that she sometimes had bad dreams satisfied the imam. The whole thing had only confirmed to him that she had to be removed from the scene. The sooner the better. She was only one casual conversation away from exposing her activities at the Career Center to Dave Miller. Zaki parked, climbed out of the car, and headed to the front of the bakery.

Closed. The bold handwritten letters shouted from the sign posted on the door.

Zaki looked at his watch. There was no reason for the bakery to be closed in the middle of the afternoon. As he neared the sign he could see smaller letters handwritten across the bottom of it: *due to illness.*

Backing away from the door, Zaki looked up at the apartment above the shop. The windows, usually open, were closed. Even if Faruq or his wife were ill, why weren't the employees working?

Jamming his hands in his pockets, he headed back to his car. He'd left work to attend a meeting in Hussein's office. There was no time now to try to find out what had happened. Hopefully the illness was not serious, and the bakery would reopen soon. Losing his connection to the outside world at this particular moment could have far-reaching consequences. Especially for Austia.

Zaki made the short drive to the duplex in record time. As he parked across the street he noticed an unfamiliar car in the driveway. With long strides, he hurried to the front door and then up the stairs to Hussein's office.

He knocked twice. "Zaki."

The door was opened by one of Hussein's nephews, a boy not more than twelve years old. He stepped to the side so Zaki could enter.

Zaki nodded to the men assembled. *"Al salamu alaikum."*

They responded to his greeting. Then, scanning the faces of the men, he took a seat in the last empty chair that surrounded Hussein's desk. The chair was directly to the left of Hussein, putting him just a foot or two from the autocrat. Almost as if the seat had been left for him.

Zaki acknowledged the man sitting at Hussein's right hand. Ma'amoon Abdullah.

Ma'amoon Abdullah nodded toward another man at the table. "This is my son, Taj."

Taj leaned forward. "Good to meet you."

Zaki smiled at the clean-shaven, handsome young man whose English was clearly his first language. Undoubtedly he'd been born and raised in the country he now secretly warred against. A second-generation *jihadist* who was trained to use all the freedoms that made America great—the legal processes that he had surely used to change his name to Dave Miller, the judicial system that protected his privacy, and the passport that let him travel freely in and out of the country—to plot against her. Dave was radical Islam's answer to racial profiling. He turned Zaki's stomach.

Now he knew whom the car belonged to. Zaki had been trying for months to learn exactly what information Ma'amoon Abdullah was responsible for disseminating. Directly in front of Ma'amoon was a small black leather box.

Hussein put his hand on the black box and pulled it in front of him. "As I was saying, America is the land of opportunity. Thanks to their democracy, it is our right to practice our faith and preserve our culture. We can operate here with impunity." He paused, leveling his penetrating gaze at each man. One by one, he moved through the group. Ending with Zaki, he let his gaze linger just a little longer than he had with the others. "And with the help of our theocracy, we will conquer them."

He spent the next thirty minutes spewing vile condemnations about the country that offered him her hospitality and the benefits of her freedom. Zaki swallowed the bile that rose in his throat, acutely aware that the show was designed not only to fire up the faithful who surrounded the desk, but for the young boy standing guard at the door. All part of the relentless indoctrination that was used to ensure another generation of *jihadists*. The boy's fate had been sealed from his first breath. He would learn to pervert the goodness of America into her greatest weakness.

Zaki eyed the boy, who stood straight, feet apart, hands clasped behind his back, his young, serious face reflecting his steadfast commitment to the important task his uncle had given him and the cause it promoted. At twelve, he had already given up the right to himself. Not by choice, but by being born into the death culture of radical Islam.

As a flame of anger flared in Zaki's chest, he turned his attention back to the meeting. It was better not to feel too much or too deeply.

Hussein had each man give a report on his particular assignment. Most involved watching the many moderate Muslims who had found America to be a good and willing partner in their dream of a better life. Missing mosque or making choices that Hussein considered too "Western" would trigger a visit from his father, the imam.

Finally, he brought the meeting to a close. "Ma'amoon and I will be gone tonight and tomorrow, working for the cause of Islam. Good day."

The group, well fed from the trough of Hussein's political rhetoric and filled with spiritual hubris, began to rise.

"Oh, Zaki." Hussein turned to him. "You can take Rasha and Najah to their class while I am gone. Fatima won't be going."

Zaki gave a quick half nod. "As you wish."

"Also"—Hussein's cold eyes rested on Zaki—"tomorrow we will have our first delivery of bottled water. Be sure someone is here to receive it. Have dispensers put in the kitchen, in my office, and in my bedroom bath."

Hussein caressed the small black leather box.

"I've noticed the quality of our tap water is deteriorating."

CHAPTER 48

Austia squared the stack of lessons and rose from her desk. Her students had already started to arrive.

Turning off her office light, she stepped toward the door to grab the doorknob and pull it shut. Just then, three people hurried past her office, making their way to the conference room. She stepped into the hall behind them.

Zaki!

She paused. Apparently he was bringing some ladies to class. Her eyes flew to the two women with him.

Neither one was Fatima. She breathed a silent sigh of relief.

Just then Zaki stopped and turned toward her. The women stopped as well.

Zaki introduced the women as Rasha and Najah. Then he nodded toward the woman named Rasha. "I think you know her father, Imam al-Ansari."

With a calm she didn't feel, she nodded toward the women. "So nice to meet you." Then she stepped around them. "Come with me. It's time to start class."

There was something about the delivery of Zaki's words and the specific words he'd chosen to use. He hadn't said, "I think you know *of* her father." He'd said it as if Austia knew the imam in some capacity. Other than the uncomfortable exchange in the Rahmans' living room when he'd brought the flyers about the call to prayer, she'd never met him face-to-face.

The imam's unexpected visits to the Rahmans'!

Her heart lurched. Zaki had been with the imam when she'd hidden in Mrs. Rahman's room. Had he somehow known she was there? Was he trying to scare her? Had he told the imam's daughter to watch her? The hair on the back of her neck rose as she realized that there seemed to be no area of her life he could not intrude on. Well, that was going to backfire. She would be extremely cautious in her dealings with Rasha ... and Najah for that matter.

Entering the conference room, she put the lessons on the corner of the front table. The two women found seats for themselves.

Austia's gaze lingered on Najah. There was something vaguely familiar about her face, especially around her eyes and mouth. Though Austia searched her memory, she couldn't place her. Just then Najah raised her hand.

Austia went to her side and knelt beside her chair. "Yes?"

The young woman smiled demurely. Then spoke slowly in English. "Hello, Maryam."

The sweet, earnest effort touched Austia's heart. "Good evening."

The woman continued in Arabic. "I have a question."

After a little discussion, Austia realized that the woman had brought in someone's homework. Apparently the person could not attend but wanted to turn in the last assignment.

Najah's eyes sparkled. "Can you help?"

"Of course." Austia accepted the notebook from Najah, then rose and walked to the front of the class. "Welcome." She waited for the room to quiet down. "I'm so glad you have come to learn English. My name is Austia, but please call me Maryam." As she had done hundreds of times over the years, she gave her introduction, then stepped to a nearby table, set down the notebook that Najah had given her, and picked up the evening's lessons.

For the next hour she taught her ladies the common names of pieces of furniture, then they broke for study time. As usual, the study hour flew by.

After dismissing class, Austia picked up the notebook and went to her office. She would give her students time to clear out of the building, then she'd lock up.

After seating herself at her desk, she opened the notebook and looked at the inside flap. Carefully printed was the name Fatima. Austia gasped.

But there was no last name.

Under it was an address. The numbers leapt off the page.

1836 Twenty-Seventh Ave.

Zaki's street. She would never forget that day she'd driven by his house and seen his holstered gun. This address was within a house or two. The thought was more than disquieting.

Najah. What was it about her? She narrowed her eyes, recalling the young woman. Najah.

Austia's eyes flew open. That's why she looked familiar. Fatima.

Yes. A knowing filled her. Najah must be Fatima's sister or some other close relative. There was a definite resemblance.

And Zaki had brought her to class.

Suddenly Austia felt faint. Zaki was directly tied to Fatima, who had asked about the inscription in Sabirah's Bible, and the imam. The same imam who had come to Mr. Rahman's house twice while Austia was there. What did Zaki and the imam know about her relationship with Sabirah? Did they know she was the one who had written in the book? Blood began to pound in her temples. Was this what had brought Zaki to the Career Center in the first place?

Quickly thumbing through the first few pages of the notebook, she found the handout folded in half, tucked in the middle of it. She opened the paper.

The blanks next to the pictures had been filled in. She quickly scanned them, each one correct, nothing unusual. She turned the paper over.

Help me.

She stared at the words, her mind racing.

She needed to get a hold of herself. She closed her eyes and took a steadying breath, focusing on the bottomless well of strength and faith that was God's promised provision.

Peace settled over her. Slowly folding the paper in half, she turned it sideways.

Had the homework been done and then the paper folded and the words written to mean "help me with this"?

The completed work showed no evidence of struggling.

Or …

She read the words again.

Help me.

Austia felt a quickening in her spirit. Or did this woman who had close ties to Zaki, and some tie to Sabirah, mean *she* needed help?

Austia flashed on the brief encounter they'd had when Fatima had asked about the inscription. Had it been some kind of a setup?

Austia couldn't be sure. But she had worked with young Muslim women for years. Fatima was not some sophisticated operative. Everything about her demeanor had been sincere.

And now this message.

She thought about calling Annie. But sharing this information would only further convince Annie to go to the police.

She pressed her fingertips to her forehead. There was no way to be sure if reaching out to Fatima was God's will or Satan's trap. But there was one thing she *was* sure of. God was her protector and her shield. He would deliver her from her enemies. That was not just *a* truth, it was her truth. The gates of Hell would not prevail against her if she was in His will. She would not bow to the sword of fear wielded by the prince of this world if this young Muslim woman needed her.

She reopened the sheet of paper and wrote "Good job" in English and Arabic at the top, then refolded the paper and put it back into the notebook.

She knew what she was going to do, but first she had to get the notebook back to Fatima.

Frowning, she considered her options. She didn't dare go anywhere near the house where she'd seen Zaki, the gun, and the imam. If they saw her there it would raise all kinds of questions in their minds.

She would think of something.

A blood ransom had already been paid for Fatima. Austia would hold the ground Christ had already taken.

CHAPTER 49

The rumor was that Faruq, the baker, had become very ill and had been moved to a hospital in Los Angeles. Information Zaki'd had to glean from casual conversations at the mosque, since asking too many questions would only draw attention to himself and raise suspicions.

He had no alternative access to his sole FBI contact, which left him completely cut off from the outside world. Something he had known from the beginning could happen. Working as an informant in an operation not officially sanctioned by the government of the United States meant he was on his own for now. He took a deep breath as a cold knot formed in his stomach.

There were just too many little things lately that didn't seem quite right: David Miller's sudden arrival on the scene, Mr. Rahman's bizarre accident, and now the baker's sudden illness. Any one of those alone would not have bothered him, but combined with the general sense of uneasiness that he hadn't been able to shake since his visit to the bakery, he'd decided to do a little investigating.

Zaki drove around Austia's block one more time, then turned his car on to the main street and headed for the freeway. He'd already studied the aerial and close-up shots of Austia's house on the Internet. But he'd wanted to come to the house at night to note such details as ingress and egress to the property, how light fell from streetlamps, and which neighboring homes could view the comings and goings at her house.

One surprise had been the alley behind her lot. It ran the length of the block, and he'd walked it. Her uncurtained kitchen window had been lit and he'd been able to get an idea of the layout of the small house. He made mental notes, feeling in his gut that the time was coming when he might need the information.

As he pulled on to the interstate, he rolled down the window of the car and let the cool night air in. It was now almost midnight and he had at least an hour's drive in front of him.

It had been sheer luck that he'd caught sight of Austia out of the corner of his eye as he was walking down the hall with Najah and Rasha, and he hoped tipping her off to the fact that the imam was Rasha's father would serve the purpose he intended of putting her on guard regarding the woman.

While she was in class, he'd used the unexpected access to her office to follow a hunch. And it had paid off. He'd gone through her desk and calendar and found a note with Dave Miller's phone number. The number was different from the one he'd tracked down through the baseball roster. As he suspected, Dave had followed Hussein's protocol and activated a phone to be used exclusively for phone calls with her. The phone would be disconnected at some point. Zaki grinned. The very step that was supposed to give one more level of removal may have given Zaki exactly what he wanted. Dave had registered the phone with a home address. At least that was what it looked like. Zaki would know shortly. He stepped on the accelerator.

Moving this quickly was risky, but he'd had no choice. He had to take advantage of the fact that Hussein was away. As he continued to drive, he found himself in a middle-class residential area. Slowing the car, he saw the address he was looking for. Several cars were parked in the driveway.

After parking a block away, he stole back to the house. He crept around the cars, snapping pictures of the license plates.

As he approached the car closest to the garage door, he caught his breath.

It belonged to Ma'amoon Abdullah. His eyes cut to the house. So this is where Hussein and his courier had gone.

CHAPTER 50

"Mamma." Sami reached toward Fatima as she cleared the plates from the table.

"Yie. Yie. Yie." Hussein's mother lifted the baby in the air. "Your *jeddah* is right here." She jostled him up and down, making him smile, though his eyes were still on his mother.

Fatima blinked rapidly as she fought the urge to grab Sami and run out of the house. But to where? To whom?

She hadn't had a moment alone with Najah to ask her if she gave the notebook to Maryam. She glanced at her sister, who was wiping down the stove. Surely she would have said something if she hadn't.

Fatima began rinsing the plates and stacking them. But even if Maryam did have her notebook, it didn't mean that she would respond. It didn't even mean she'd seen the words on the back of the homework paper.

Rasha's voice broke into her thoughts, "Hurry, Najah. We want to get to the park in time for the ice cream truck."

Fatima turned on the faucet and began filling the sink with hot water. "It won't take me long to get these d—"

"There's really no need for you to go." Her mother-in-law's edict cut her off. "You've neglected many of your chores for quite some time. While we're gone, I want you to shake the floor rugs and wash the cushion covers."

Fatima bit the inside of her cheek. She was powerless to argue. Any objection, no matter how valid, would be met with opposition.

This wasn't about going to the park. For Fatima it was about being with Sami. And her mother-in-law knew it.

Najah stepped next to her sister and dropped her rag in the sink to rinse it. "It's awfully hot today. Maybe Fatima could help carry the folding chairs. And won't you want to take the umbrella in case there is no room under the trees? Remember, that happened last time."

Fatima recognized her sister's suggestion for the clever ruse it was. She felt for Najah's hand under the dishwater and squeezed Najah's fingers.

"That isn't necessary." Hussein's mother rose. "I'll go get them. Then we'll leave." Carrying Sami, she left the kitchen with Rasha at her heels.

As soon as the women were gone, Fatima broke down.

Najah laid the rag down, wiped her hands on a dish towel, and then turned to Fatima and put her arms around her. "I'm so sorry."

Fatima pressed into her sister. "I can't bear this. I can't."

Najah stroked Fatima's hair. "Shh. Shh. I know. I understand."

At the sound of the front closet door opening, Najah stepped back from Fatima and put her hands on Fatima's shoulders. Looking her in the eye, she whispered, "I took your notebook to Maryam. I checked to be sure the homework was in it."

Najah's eyes, filled with compassion and fear, told Fatima more clearly than words that she had seen the plea for help.

"Come now, Najah. We're leaving." The voice came from down the hall.

"I'm coming." Najah kissed her on the forehead, then disappeared out the door.

Tears streaming down her cheeks, Fatima rushed to the front window to catch a glimpse of Sami. Just as she parted the sheer curtains, the stroller passed in front of her. The women didn't notice her. But Sami did.

"Mamma," he cried out.

Rasha shushed him.

"Mamma." His voice grew louder and he began twisting in his stroller seat. "Mamma."

Fatima stepped to the side of the open window where she could not be seen but she could observe the women.

Sami's cry became a wordless scream.

Hussein's mother picked him up from the stroller, trying to quiet him.

He would have none of it, and his flailing arms hit the old woman right in the face.

Grinning, Fatima leaned forward. "Yes, Sami."

As though he heard his mother, Sami began kicking his legs and arching his back, screaming at the top of his lungs. Two women from next door, who were apparently also on their way to the park, stopped in front of the house.

"Mamma. Mamma." Red-faced and sobbing, Sami let the bystanders know his wishes.

Najah stepped next to the stroller and spoke to Hussein's mother. "Why not let Fatima come? It will quiet Sami down and everyone will see what a good *jeddah* you are."

Just then, as he arched his back and twisted his body, the old woman nearly dropped him.

Bending down, Hussein's mother managed to get Sami into the stroller. "Go get her."

CHAPTER 51

Austia picked up her empty lunch bag and put it in the trash can under the sink. "I'm going to run to the post office now."

Annie swallowed the bite of apple she was chewing. "You walking? It's awfully hot."

"I am. I've got my tennis shoes in the car. I've just got to get more exercise."

Annie smiled at her. "Can't you do it when it's not so hot?"

"Oh, if it's not too hot, then it's too cold or too late or too early. You know what I mean?"

Annie huffed a sigh and nodded. "Yep, I know *exactly* what you mean." The two women shared a laugh.

Austia gathered the mail, then stopped at her car to change her shoes. She really didn't mind the summer heat and was looking forward to taking a walk. As she set off for the post office, her thoughts returned to Fatima. When she finished at the post office she was going to Fatima's house.

As she passed the park, she noticed that there were a lot of women with their children out to enjoy the afternoon. Some of the women waved to her. She waved back. A block later she was at the post office. She dropped the mail off and picked up the letters in the Career Center's box, then started back to the office.

The musical bells of the ice cream truck caught her attention. "Just keep walking," she chided herself, then stole a glance to see exactly where the truck had stopped.

It was one block up, across the street, in front of the park.

She would just keep walking. Buying ice cream would defeat the whole purpose of getting more exercise.

She glanced at the line that was forming. She recognized many of the ladies from the ESL classes. It would be lovely to visit with them … just for a moment. She didn't have to buy ice cream.

She jogged across the street, then began greeting the women she knew, using their names when she could, and speaking to them in English. It delighted the women to answer her.

"Good afternoon, Leila. How are you?"

Leila gave a bright smile. "I am fine. And you?"

Austia nodded toward her. "I am fine."

Austia spotted a young woman behind Leila who was new at the last class. "Good afternoon, Atiya. How are you?" The young woman glanced at the elderly woman with her, then answered loudly, "Thank you very much."

"And thank you." Austia nodded toward her. "Very good effort."

She loved these precious women and their immigrant spirit. Most had come to America with their husbands for a better life. They loved their families and wanted more for their children than they had had. And Austia wanted more for them too. In every way. They were God's children and He coveted their hearts.

She wiped her brow as two little girls walked past her eating their ice cream. Cool … sweet … wonderful ice cream.

She walked to the back of the line. She would get vanilla—that wouldn't be too bad. The line continued to lengthen as she walked to the end of it.

As she took her place, she saw Najah, Rasha, and the imam's wife. Her stomach knotted. Another young woman stood directly behind them.

Fatima.

Fatima's eyes met hers.

"Oh, Fatima. I checked your homework. You did a good job."

A look of terror flashed across Fatima's face.

There was no longer any doubt what "Help me" had meant. Austia had seen the look many times on the faces of women who had been belittled and intimidated by their husbands and family. She studied the young woman's face. Barely visible, just where Fatima's *hijab* rested on her cheek, was a yellowish shadow. Austia knew what that meant as well.

If only there were some way to speak to her privately. Then it wouldn't be necessary to go to her house. That would be safer for both of them.

Maybe …

Austia put her hand to her cheek. "My, it's so warm."

She began to fan her face. "I … I … really don't feel well."

Her knees gave way and earth and sky switched places.

"Ya Allah."

"Get water."

"Move back."

Austia heard excited voices around her.

Fatima squatted beside her, fanning her hand next to Austia's face. "Are you okay?"

As Fatima leaned over her, Fatima hooked her hair behind her ear, moving the *hijab*. Austia saw that the yellowish shadow that she had only glimpsed turned deep purple by Fatima's ear. The ear itself was swollen.

Help me. The two words written on the back of the paper called out as clearly as if Fatima had spoken them. Austia caught her eye and whispered, "I won't betray you."

Raising herself on one arm, Austia accepted a cup of water from one of the concerned ladies. "Really, I'm fine. I should have worn a hat. I just got too hot." With some help she rose. "Please don't worry, I'm fine. Thank you."

She took another sip of water, thankful that the opening she'd hoped her performance would give her had materialized. If nothing else, Fatima now knew that Austia had heard her cry for help. What more she could do, she didn't know. But what she did know was that nothing is impossible for God.

As the excitement died down the line for ice cream began to form again. Austia observed Najah, who was standing right behind her, talking to Rasha and the imam's wife. "Let's go get in the shade. Fatima can wait in line for the ice cream."

The women quickly agreed.

"Will you join us, Maryam?" one of the ladies asked.

Nothing is impossible for God.

"I would love to, but I need to get back to work. And I need to get out of sun." She giggled. "But I'm going to get my ice cream first."

The woman nodded and smiled as Najah herded them away, leaving Austia and Fatima in line.

Austia turned her gaze to Fatima. The young woman was staring at her. Fatima's face showed a mixture of fear and hope.

With her eye on the women walking across the grass, Austia whispered, "I want to help you."

Fatima's face contorted as she tried not to cry. It was all Austia could do not to grab her and hold her. "Can you come to the Career Center?" she mouthed.

Fatima gave an almost imperceptible nod of her head.

The line moved forward.

"When?"

Fatima's face filled with uncertainty and she blinked back tears.

The line moved forward again.

For a moment, Austia thought the girl was going to turn and run. But instead she lifted her chin and met Austia's eyes.

"Tonight."

CHAPTER 52

Zaki climbed into his car and headed into the twilight toward Faruq's house. He had to connect to his FBI contact. Faruq was his only link to the outside world.

Eyes riveted on the road, he turned up the radio. But the sound of the announcer's voice didn't silence Fatima's muffled cries that had sounded across the street from the duplex to his house. From what he could make out, Rasha had seen her talking to someone at the park. And Hussein was making sure that never happened again.

His thoughts went to the mean streets of New York where he'd grown up, and the singular ray of light and love that had sustained him through his childhood. His mother. Then to Neryda who had stepped in at his mother's passing, when he had faith in neither man nor God. She lived with the steadfast belief that what was meant for evil God would turn for good. He had almost believed her. But after her murder, his tenuous hold on the idea that good would triumph over evil, that God would prevail in this dark world, was put to death.

And this evening that lesson had been reinforced.

Listening to Fatima's cries had kindled a rage in his belly. Had he not left, he would have intervened. That would have ended her suffering … and his. Forever. But nothing would have been accomplished. It would only have set Hussein free to continue his crusade with impunity. And that was when Zaki had realized in a way he never had before that radical Islam was a movement championed by such evil and darkness that without God's help it would sweep the world.

A violent maelstrom of depravity designed to destroy the God-given liberties of mankind.

He slammed his fist on the steering wheel. "So God, where are You?"

If the West did not win this battle, there was no hope. Not for Christians, Jews, moderate Muslims, or any faith of peace and tolerance. All would be crushed by the iron fist of radical fundamentalism.

He knotted his hands at the sudden realization that everything was at stake. He'd been walking on the razor's edge for years now. He was tired, discouraged, and worn out. His mission was beyond his capabilities. But to quit now would be to betray every principle he'd lived by.

He raised his eyes to the watchful evening sky that arced over the setting sun and came face-to-face with the truth he had tried to ignore since Neryda's death. He needed God's help.

For a moment, he wanted to break down, let go, turn back to God and trust Him. But instead of a prayer, the bitter taste of pain and loss filled his mouth. He turned up the volume on the radio. He would leave prayer to the women. Right now there was nothing more important than reaching his contact.

As Zaki neared the downtown, it occurred to him that it would be wiser to park at the Career Center and walk to Faruq's. Then, if there were lights on in the upstairs apartment, he would decide what to do.

Traffic was light and he quickly made his way to the Center's parking lot.

As he pulled in, he was surprised to see Austia's car parked across the street. He scanned the building, but the only lights were those that were left on every night. He frowned.

After parking his car, he walked the few blocks to the Café Bakery. The building was completely dark. He made his way to the back and silently moved up the wooden steps to the baker's apartment. Crossing lines that shouldn't be crossed, he tried the door. It opened to a service porch.

Inside the porch, he pulled the door shut behind him, then reached in his pocket and pulled out a small flashlight. Flashing the light around him, he saw the second door that opened into the residence. He tried it. It was locked.

Looking through a sidelight, he was able to see mail had been dropped through a slot cut in the door and was scattered on the floor. There was no indication anyone had been there for days.

He turned off his flashlight and returned to the street. The casual inquiries he'd made since he'd first seen the sign *Closed due to illness* had revealed nothing. In fact, he'd slowly realized that no one had actually talked directly to Faruq or his wife. Everyone had heard of Faruq's illness and circumstances from someone else. And from all Zaki could glean, the actual source of all the information was the sign in the Café Bakery's window. Zaki's gut churned. Had the FBI connection been discovered? If it had, had he been identified?

Arriving back at the Career Center, Zaki noted Austia's car was still parked on the street. A glance at the building revealed nothing. He dug his keys out of his pocket as he headed to the back door. Careful not to make any noise, he unlocked it, then slipped into the back hall.

Once inside he realized that the office was dark and quiet. Maybe Austia had met someone earlier and then left with them.

He stiffened as he felt, rather than heard, movement in the front lobby. In one silent motion he ducked into the supply room, stopping just inside its door. Hearing footsteps in the hall, he shallowed his breathing and tilted his head for a broader view. A light came on in Austia's office. He listened closely.

A woman was crying.

He waited a moment, not sure what to do. Finally, he stepped back into the hall, opened the back door, and let it slam shut. Then, as though he'd just arrived, he walked down the hall toward his office.

Austia tore out of her office, a notebook in her hand. "You made it."

Eyes widening, she stopped in her tracks when she saw him.

Apparently she *was* meeting a girlfriend, and from the tears on her cheeks it must be about some woman thing.

"I came in to print out the ads I need for tomorrow morning."

"Oh." Austia stepped back toward her office. "I see."

She turned on her heel and closed the door, but not before he saw the fear in her eyes. His gut wrenched at the sharp reminder of how well he'd done his job.

She was upset and hurting. She needed someone to comfort her. In an unexpected surge of emotion, he knew he wanted to be the one to do it. His gaze shifted to the doorknob.

He resisted the urge to step toward the door. Ambivalence and yearning coursed through him. He clenched his jaw. He was a professional.

Lips forming a silent O, he exhaled, cooling his thoughts.

Since he'd told her he was here to print ads, he moved on to his office and turned on his computer. It had been an easy lie; there weren't any ads for tomorrow morning. After finding the file with last week's ads, he clicked Print. As the printer dutifully fulfilled his request, he stepped back into the hall and walked soundlessly to Austia's office door. She was talking on the phone. He leaned closer.

"She didn't come." Austia's voice caught. "I know she's being abused by her husband and I'm afraid for her life."

Zaki heard what sounded like a drawer opening and closing.

"She wants help. And—I don't know. Right now it seems the only way I can possibly help her is to report it to the police."

There was a pause.

"Yes, Annie, I know that could make it worse for her. Don't think that I haven't thought of that. But I can't stand by and do nothing."

"Well, right now I'm going to go home and think about it. Besides, Zaki's here."

Zaki quickly backtracked to his office and picked up the printout from the computer's tray. When he heard her door open, he stepped into the hall and started toward the copier, wanting to see if she was carrying the notebook.

Her hands were empty. She raised her eyes to his, her gaze raw and vulnerable.

Something deep inside him stirred. He pushed it down. He was deeply mired in the politics of death and destruction, his one link to the outside world had been cut off, someone he deeply cared about was the target of a maniacal despot, and his chance of completing this mission alive was diminishing with each passing day.

"Good night." She pulled the office door shut behind her.

As she turned toward the back door, the overhead light glistened in a tear on her cheek. That tiny drop of deep compassion and selfless love captured him, closing the distance between them, piercing the vault that protected him from feeling, from caring, from needing. Her tears were for the innocents of this world. For the Nerydas, the Fatimas. For injustices never avenged, for the hopelessness and helplessness that daring to love invited. For every sorrow that being human engendered.

And the remnant of that single tear was seeping into the hidden places of his heart. Touching him, moving him, breaking him.

He loved her.

Drawing on more discipline then he'd ever needed to carry out his mission, he stood staring after her as her footsteps faded and the back door slammed.

With his free hand, he raked his fingers through his hair. Forcing his thoughts back to the present, he shook his head to clear it.

There was too much at stake. Her life was in the balance.

He glanced at his watch. He needed to get back to the duplex. But first he wanted to see what had been in the notebook she'd had in her hand when he'd first seen her.

Taking quick steps to a nearby window, he watched her drive away, then returned to her office door and tried the knob. It was locked.

He reached into his pocket and removed a credit card. With one swipe he opened the door.

There was enough light from the hall to see that the notebook wasn't on her desk. He moved behind the desk and began to pull open the top drawers. The second drawer held the notebook. He picked it up and looked at it in the dim light. Opening it, he glanced at the cover.

There in bold print was the name Fatima.

And beneath it, Hussein al-Ansari's address.

Austia had been waiting for Fatima.

He moved into the hall light and started thumbing through the pages. In the middle of the book was a paper folded in half and the words *Help me* written in pencil. Zaki's heart began to pound as the pieces fell into place. Austia had been waiting for Fatima, who hadn't shown up because she had been beaten and was locked in her bedroom.

The revelation stunned him. Austia understood radical Islam in a way few Americans did and clearly she knew what it would mean if she tried to help Fatima. When he'd first come to the Career Center, he'd felt sure that her connection to Senator Amende and the ESL classes being started so soon after her husband's death were somehow linked. It had been impossible for him to believe that someone would desire to help the very people who had killed her loved one. He'd been convinced that it all was a front for the government, giving them a way to gather information on the foreigners living in Agua Viva. He'd been wrong. She saw people as human beings, not as Muslims, or killers, or "other." His admiration for her deepened. She was on her own mission.

His mind flashed on the Bible he'd seen hidden in her desk. She answered to a much higher authority.

He shut the notebook and put it back in the drawer. Still, Austia had no idea the danger she was in. She didn't realize she had raised Hussein's suspicions and that he was having her watched. Not just by Zaki but by David Miller. Or that Hussein knew of her relationship with the Rahmans and had that base covered too. It was just a matter of time before he found out everything. Not only that she was secretly ministering to Muslims, but that she was planning on taking Fatima from him.

And when he did, Austia would be a dead woman.

CHAPTER 53

Austia pulled the sheet up under her chin and turned her head toward the bedroom window. The sun was just coming up, and the day was starting whether she was ready or not. The unsettling events of the night before had left her unsure of Fatima's safety and very sure that Zaki ben Hassan was watching her.

She didn't believe that a two-minute print job was what had brought him to the office. And she'd felt his eyes on her as she'd left. She'd even driven through town before going home to make sure that he wasn't following her. Everything about him felt threatening.

Thank goodness she was meeting Dave tomorrow afternoon for lunch. She threw her feet over the edge of the bed and pushed herself up. Everything about Dave, how she'd met him, his interest in the Muslim people, even his name seemed to be a provision from the Lord. He was so attentive. They talked on the phone every day, and she felt that she was really getting to know him. She started toward the kitchen. She would talk to Dave about Zaki when they met.

After making a cup of hot cinnamon spice tea, she stopped at the front door and picked up the newspaper, then settled onto the couch. A small headline caught her eye. Deep Spring Bombing. The article was about the killing of Pastor Brown and his wife. Apparently the authorities believed that the Christian extremist Jake Richards, who'd been arrested, had not acted alone. They were seeking a person of interest. A woman. Her grip tightened on the paper.

The article reported how a surveillance camera at the nearby bus station had recorded a gray Taurus slowly cruising by the Browns' store just hours before the blast, and then leaving the scene just minutes before the explosion.

Her throat closed. She couldn't breathe. It was her. They were talking about her.

She dropped the paper. How could this be happening? She had nothing to do with Jake Richards. She suddenly realized Jake Richards had seen her there. What if he identified her? What if he tried to implicate her in some sort of defense strategy that he hadn't acted alone? She tried to catch her breath.

Even though she was completely innocent, all of this would draw attention to her and her visit to Deep Spring. It could potentially expose everything she was trying to do—on a national stage.

She had to calm down. If the authorities had been able to determine who owned the gray Taurus, they would have already contacted her. And besides, she had nothing to hide. Maybe she should call them and explain everything.

Explain what? That she'd been there to set up a network of safe houses. If anything, that kind of clandestine activity would only raise their suspicions about her. And if that got in the papers and on the news shows, everyone in Agua Viva would know about it. Better to just let it alone. Right now Fatima needed her help. And the truth was Austia had no idea exactly how she was going to get the young woman to safety. She didn't even know how she was going to meet up with her.

That thought brought another ominous harbinger to mind. Fatima hadn't shown up last night. Suppose she'd arrived while Zaki was there. Austia's heart lurched. That could have raised all kinds of trust issues and most likely frightened Fatima away. Her hand flew to her mouth. What if Fatima had been followed and it had all been discovered by some relative? The possibilities were endless and every one of them incredibly dangerous.

Austia rose and folded her arms across her chest. The fact was that Fatima, or someone close to her, had been in possession of Sabirah's New Testament after Austia had written in it. She shuddered again at the thought that Sabirah's killer must surely have been in the loop at some point. But Fatima asking her to translate the inscription almost surely meant she had no idea Austia had written it. Still, the whole thing made her uncomfortable. A Muslim family so conservative that they felt compelled to avenge their honor by killing their daughter would not just forget about it. They would become even more vigilant over their other family members. And if those family members were attending the ESL classes, then they would be watching everything that went on. Icy fingers of fear made a fist in Austia's stomach as each thought magnified how truly dangerous helping Fatima was. She reached across the coffee table for her Bible and put it in her lap.

"You haven't given me a spirit of fear, Lord." She spoke the words out loud with more confidence than she felt. Look at the fear Fatima lived in every day. That thought filled her with resolve. She had to find a safe house and soon. But how?

As she took a sip of her tea, she noticed her hands were shaking. She set the tea down, firmly clasped her hands in her lap, and bowed her head. "Lord God, help me. Show me what You would have me do. Open a way for me." For the next half hour she prayed for Fatima and all the Muslims of Agua Viva. Asking God to send His warring angels to do battle for the hearts and souls of the lost. She knew it was not enough for her to serve them, she must allow God to serve them through her. That was the difference—the difference that brought souls to Christ. She'd given up the right to herself when she'd taken up a ministry to Muslims, and Fatima's cry to her only deepened that commitment. "Please, Lord, don't let me fear. Give me a spirit of power, love, and a sound mind fully surrendered to You. Amen."

She settled back into the couch and opened her Bible. Thumbing through, she stopped at Joshua. Feeling the presence and peace of the Lord that her prayer time always brought her, she began to hum. Boy, did she relate to the story. If only she had two people to send out into the land to help her find safe houses. She smiled to herself. She had God to help her, and the Spirit of God could go where no man could.

She began to read about Joshua's preparations for the conquest of Canaan. *And they went, and came into an harlot's house, named Rahab, and lodged there.*

Wasn't that like the Lord to use a Canaanite harlot to hide the two spies? Rahab believed that the God of Israel was the true God, and He used her for his purposes. Austia put the Bible down. An unlikely choice, Rahab. Something nudged Austia. She read the verses again.

This time it occurred to her that Rahab had not only played an important role but she had become part of Jesus' lineage. Who would have thought that a prostitute would be in the line of Christ? God's ways were mysterious. Again she felt like there was something important that the Lord was trying to show her. But she didn't know what it was. She read on.

Finally, gaining no new insights, she put the book away and went into her bathroom to get ready for work. It happened that Zaki wouldn't be in the office today. She was glad. She had no idea what she would say to him. He was supposed to visit some accounts in a nearby town and see how the employees that the Career Center had placed there were doing. A brilliant idea Annie had come up with to keep him out of the office.

As she put on her makeup, her thoughts returned to the need for safe houses. She had contacted all her Christian friends, and none had expressed any interest. She had contacted Christian churches far and wide, and except for the Browns, she had come up empty. There had to be someone, somewhere, who had also heard the Lord's call about this.

She needed to get creative. Where would be the last place on earth that someone would look for a Muslim? She giggled. "On Rahab's roof."

She dropped her hands to her sides and straightened.

In the house of a Jew.

"Yes." She pumped her fist. "Thank You, Jesus."

She knew what she was going to do.

CHAPTER 54

The day had been very productive and Zaki had learned that the people the Career Center had placed in the neighboring town had worked out extremely well. So well, in fact, that the employers were expanding their advertising to attract more Muslim customers, which would increase business, and in turn mean they would want to hire more workers from Austia.

Ordinarily that would have been good news. But bringing more Muslims to the Career Center right now only broadened Austia's exposure to Hussein. The more Zaki thought about Austia actively helping Fatima try to escape from Hussein, the more he believed Austia was never going to be safe in Agua Viva. He had to get in touch with his FBI contact. Once Faruq alerted the FBI they would deal directly with her and get her to safety.

Actually, he'd thought about a lot of things today. He shifted in his seat. If he survived this mission, he would find her and they would start over.

As soon as he hit town, he drove to the Café Bakery.

It was open.

Relief flooded through him.

He swung into the parking lot. Finally, he would be able to reconnect to the outside world, tell them about Hussein's recent trip to Los Angeles with his courier and Hussein's increasing interest in Austia. If Hussein uncovered Austia's ministry, it would immediately cast suspicion on Zaki because he was supposed to be monitoring her from the Career Center. It could unravel everything he'd worked for the past two years. Taj had told him he was seeing Austia tomorrow. Just one more unwanted complication. Thank God the Café Bakery was back in business. He strode through the front door.

A steel weight dropped into his stomach.

The man behind the counter wasn't Faruq. It was Zahid Zafar. Zaki had seen him in the bakery from time to time. He lived next door to Austia.

Zaki waited his turn, then ordered a Turkish coffee. "When will Faruq be back?"

The man shrugged. "I'm his cousin. He and his wife are staying with my uncle in LA."

Zaki waited for his drink, paid, and then left. When he got to his car he dumped the coffee, climbed behind the wheel, started the car, and jammed it into gear. Things were unraveling.

Faruq was dead and probably Cala, too.

Faruq didn't have relatives in Los Angeles. That was part of his cover story as Zaki's FBI contact. Faruq, a practicing Muslim, had grown up in Michigan, attended an Ivy League school, and graduated at the top of his class. He joined the FBI after 9/11 and quickly moved up the ranks. One of the best and the brightest. He had passed information under the cover of the bakery for over two years.

Zaki slowly shook his head. How many Americans had come into the Café Bakery for special Middle Eastern pastries and quietly judged him? How many whispered criticisms and stares of distain had he endured in his travels outside of Agua Viva? How many would have been shocked to learn who Faruq really was because it was impossible for them to believe a Muslim could love America?

And he'd done more than that. He'd given his life for his country.

CHAPTER 55

Austia stood at the sink in the darkened kitchen at the back of the Career Center watching students arrive for class. She hoped and prayed Fatima would come tonight. Austia wanted to reassure her that she would help her and then set up a new time to meet.

During her lunch break she'd searched the Internet for messianic Jewish temples and congregations. She'd immediately found a small *shul* located in northern California called Beth Shalom, House of Peace. She'd felt in her spirit that it was no coincidence that it had come up on the first page of 10,773,000 thousand possible sites, and that was further confirmed when she read their Statement of Faith: *The gifts of the Holy Spirit are given with Authority to all those who ask God and obey His commandments.* This was a congregation who knew the Messiah Yeshua well. And a note from the rabbi stated it was his desire to work toward repentance, restoration, and reconciliation in the whole body of Messiah. Clearly a man with a heart for God who would recognize that the "body" had many parts, including Muslim Background Believers. And even though Fatima was not yet a believer, Austia had complete faith God had placed her in Fatima's path and that He would prosper what He ordained. In fact, if Fatima didn't come to class tonight, Austia had a plan. It was incredibly risky, but there were so few options. She'd emailed Rabbi Lohrer and—

She caught her breath as a car pulled up directly in front of the kitchen window. She could see Rasha and Najah in the back seat. The driver got out.

Fatima wasn't with them.

Had Zaki come to the office the other night suspecting Fatima had planned to meet her? Had he intercepted Fatima and pieced things together? "Oh, my God." She clutched the cross beneath her blouse. "Help me."

For a moment, she felt at a complete loss as to what she should do. Then, she grabbed the phone from the kitchen wall and dialed Annie's cell.

Annie answered on the first ring.

"Could you come down to the office and teach the class tonight?"

"Uh. Sure, sweetie. Is something wrong?"

"I'm almost positive that Zaki ben Hassan is working with the people who had Sabirah killed."

Annie gasped. "What?"

"I'm not sure what's going on. But I'm convinced that Fatima is in danger and I need to help her. Go ahead and teach the class and at the end announce that classes are being suspended for now. Tell them it's time for a summer break."

"Are you going to be okay? I should call the police."

"Don't do anything yet. I'll let you know more later. Right now I'm going to go home and try to figure out what to do." An idea suddenly occurred to her. "I'm meeting Dave tomorrow. I'm going to tell him everything and ask him to help me."

CHAPTER 56

"Faisal died last night."

Fatima nodded at Najah from across the freshly stripped bed. "Hussein was at the hospital when it happened. He's over at Faisal's house now. The family is cleaning and wrapping the body."

"I didn't know him well. But I am so sorry for his wife." Fatima unfolded a clean sheet and snapped it toward her sister. "Najah, I need your help."

Najah straightened, concern filling her face. "Help?" She glanced toward the open bedroom door.

Fatima quietly moved toward the door and closed it. "We fly home Monday."

"Yes, I'm packed."

"That's just two days away. Tomorrow Hussein and his mother are moving Sami to her house.

Najah's eyes filled with tears. "I know."

Fatima limped around the bed and took her sister's hand, pulling her with her as she dropped onto the edge of the mattress. Lowering her voice, she leaned into Najah. "Tonight I am going to leave, and I'm taking Sami with me."

Najah's eyes widened. "Leave to where?"

"I'm not sure yet. Maryam said she would help me."

"Maryam! How can she help you?"

Fatima shrugged. "I'm not sure. But I have to leave today or I'll lose Sami forever." She tightened her grip on her sister's hand. "I didn't want to tell you anything because then you would be innocent when they ask what you know. But I have to have your help."

"I'm so scared for you. Let me come with you."

Fatima could feel her sister's hand trembling in hers. "No. It's too dangerous. Anything could happen. You can go home and have a good life."

She could see Najah was not convinced.

"How can I help?"

"I need you to bring me bottles and formula for Sami. Hussein had that good bottled water put in our bathroom. I'm going to mix it in here. That way there will be none missing from the refrigerator. And I need two plastic sacks, like from Walmart."

Najah's eyes widened.

"But I need to get my passport. I have no idea where Hussein keeps it."

Najah's face lit up. "I bet I do." She put her hand on Fatima's arm, clearly desperate to help her sister. "Hussein asked me for my passport yesterday. Said he wanted it to be sure everything was in order for Monday. When I brought it to him he opened his desk drawer and laid it on top of another one."

"Which drawer?"

"The one in front of where he sits in his office."

The thought of going into Hussein's office was terrifying.

"But where will you go? You can't just walk out the door and wander down the street." Najah's eyes drifted to Fatima's leg.

Of course her sister was right. But Fatima had no answer to give her. She'd planned to meet Austia, and when Austia agreed to help her this could have been much easier. But Hussein beating her had shattered that plan. And now there was no more time.

"Najah." Fatima sought her sister's eyes. "I want to share something with you."

Najah placed her free hand on top of Fatima's. "I'm listening."

"The Qur'an says Prophet Jesus performed miracles. He healed the leper and the blind."

Najah nodded.

Fatima hesitated. "I saw Jesus in a dream. He reached out his hand to me and called to me."

"What?" Najah's brow creased and she drew her head back.

His eyes had been filled with love and compassion and he'd spoken to her in her own dialect. "*Ta'ali ya binti*" he'd said when he called to her.

"He spoke as if he knew me. He said, 'Come.'"

"That *was* a strange dream." Najah folded her hands in her lap.

That movement, Najah pulling her hands into her own lap, drew Fatima's attention. Though she couldn't say why, it seemed magnified, abrupt, deliberate. As though Najah were distancing herself from more than Fatima's grasp.

"Yes, it was a strange dream." Suddenly, her tongue felt thick and she couldn't remember what she was going to say. She rose. Just then the door swung open. It was Rasha.

"What are you two doing?"

"I'm just helping Fatima with the bedding."

Rasha glanced at Fatima and frowned. "Well, hurry and finish. We have a lot to do. After the burial everyone is coming here. There is cooking and cleaning to be done."

Najah tilted her head. "Isn't that someone at the door?"

Rasha left the room and hurried down the stairs.

Fatima took up her spot on the other side of the bed and began to tuck the sheet in. Najah was not going to help her discern what Jesus' words had meant or why he had appeared to her. She kept her eyes on the task at hand. Perhaps the Prophet himself would help her understand. With faith small as a mustard seed, she had been asking him to do so. Right now there was no clear means of escape, no place to go, and no plan of survival. It would take a miracle from the Prophet to save her and her son.

"This is for you." Rasha's voice broke into her thoughts. "The person at the door was the lady who taught the ESL class last night."

Fatima's heart leapt. Maryam.

Instead of handing the notebook to Fatima, Rasha began thumbing through it.

Black fright threatened to smother Fatima as Rasha casually perused the opening pages.

Najah turned to Fatima and their eyes locked. "Maryam wasn't there last night. It was a lady I'd never seen before."

Finally, Rasha handed Fatima her notebook, then waved her hand toward Najah. "Let her finish. You come and help me in the kitchen."

As soon as the women's voices faded down the staircase, Fatima closed the door and leaned against it. She opened the notebook and found her homework paper folded in half, tucked into the middle of the book. Her heart jumped. Below the words she had written were new ones written in Arabic: *The park this afternoon at three.*

Fatima drew a deep breath. That was only a few hours from now. Turning, she opened the door a crack and looked down the hall toward Hussein's office.

She had to get her passport.

CHAPTER 57

Austia set the plate of sandwiches and pitcher of tea on the coffee table, then went to the living room window again. She looked at her watch. Dave would be here any minute.

She mentally reviewed her plan to meet Fatima and escape. There hadn't been much time to plan things, but she'd come up with an idea she was sure would work. It would be an incredible relief to get Fatima out of Agua Viva, though as of right now she still didn't have a place to take her. After glancing up and down the street one more time for Dave, she turned on her heel and went to her office.

One look at her inbox told her Rabbi Lohrer had not answered her email. This was potentially a huge complication. The doorbell interrupted her thoughts.

She glanced out the window as she hurried to the front door, then slowed her steps. She didn't recognize the truck in her driveway. She looked through her peephole. It was Dave. She swung the door open. "New truck?"

He nodded. "Got a promotion at work. Now they provide the truck."

"Congratulations." Stepping toward Dave, she gave him a quick hug, then she gestured toward the coffee table. "I made us some sandwiches and there's chips and dip, too. That pitcher has iced tea in it." She closed the door. "I hated to cancel out for the restaurant, but I really needed to talk to you." She paused. "Privately."

His startled expression reminded Austia that what she was about to tell him would probably sound shocking. For a moment she reconsidered what she was about to do. By involving Dave, she could be putting him at risk. The thought gave her pause.

Dave seated himself on the couch and she sat next to him.

She poured some tea and handed him the glass. She would tell him everything, then let him decide.

"Remember how I told you I teach ESL classes to Muslim women?"

He nodded.

"Well, there's more to it than that."

His eyes widened.

"Sometimes the women ask me about Christianity, and sometimes those conversations lead to discussions about Jesus."

"Isn't that great." He took a sip of his tea.

"Yes, you can imagine how that thrills me. Especially when the Holy Spirit leads and opens ways for me to share the gospel with them."

"I'm sure it does." He lifted his glass to her as if offering a toast. "Tell me more."

Somehow his words lacked feeling. As though perhaps he had never experienced a direct leading of the Spirit. Well, in time the Lord would take care of that. "A young woman came to class not long ago. She asked me to translate something, and I was shocked to see that it was the exact inscription I had written in a New Testament that I had given to another student named Sabirah."

For just an instant, Austia saw a flicker of anger in Dave's eyes. Had he read about Sabirah's death in the newspaper? Had it angered him as it had angered her? "She was killed recently. You probably read about it. I'm almost sure it was an honor killing." Tears stung her eyes.

Dave set the glass on the table and leaned forward. "I did read about it."

She waited, but he made no further comment.

Regaining her composure, she continued. "You can imagine how I've agonized over it. That could happen to any of the women I talk to who find the truth about Jesus Christ. It's the reason I continue to try and find safe houses to place them in."

Surprise registered on Dave's face. "Kind of dangerous for you to do, isn't it?"

"It is so worth it, Dave. Do you realize that they're living in bondage, without hope? Even the Jews have the hope of a coming Messiah. These Muslim women have nothing. They believe they are doomed to Hell unless they keep every letter of Sharia law. And they can't. Even though by doing good deeds they can try and cancel out their sins, it's a losing battle, and they know it. When they find out that Jesus died for their sins, that He has paid the price they could never pay because He loves them, they fall on the ground and worship Him. The truth sets them free in a way that we as Americans will never fully understand."

"But Christians believe in three gods. How do you explain that to them?"

Austia stared at him a moment, the phrasing of his question and the edge in his voice confusing her. "You mean, why do the Muslims believe that?"

"Of course." He flushed and picked up his tea.

"They know there's only one God, just as we do. The Qur'an speaks of the God of Abraham. Our Bible speaks of that same God. So I start there when I talk to them. But the reason I wanted to talk to you was because of that young woman who came to class recently. Her name is Fatima."

"Did she ask you about Jesus?" He seemed stunned, though this reaction she understood. It was how she had felt the first time her husband had told her that an Arab friend had asked him about his faith.

"No, she asked me to help her. She's being abused by her husband and she's going to try and escape from him."

"Really?" Dave straightened and moved to the edge of the couch.

"I'm going to try and help her and I'm not sure what's going to happen. I was hoping, if I needed to, that we could come to your house."

"Well. Uh." Dave drummed his fingers on his glass.

"Just for a short time. This all came about so quickly I haven't been able to plan things out as well as I'd like to."

"When exactly is this happening?"

"Later today."

Surprisingly, he seemed to relax. "Yes, I'll help you any way I can. Let me give you my address."

A wave of relief passed over her. "Thank you so much."

She went into the kitchen and returned with a piece of paper and a pen. She handed it to him and he wrote out the directions to his house.

"Oh, there's one more thing."

He waited for her to continue.

"Please don't mention this to Steve. It upsets him terribly that I minister to Muslims."

"Your secret is safe with me. Does anybody else know about this?"

"I hope not. Though there is a man at my office that might have some idea that something is up."

"Who's that?" The two words fired from his lips like bullets.

She put her hand on his arm, touched that he felt so protective of her. "His name is Zaki ben Hassan. He works for me."

"Does he know what you're doing there?"

Austia released a deep sigh. "I'm not sure. I consider him to be a dangerous person. I think he is connected somehow to the people who killed Sabirah."

"Why do you think that?"

"There's been several things. But I'm pretty confident that he knows nothing about Fatima's plan. That's just one more reason I want to get her out of here tonight. Before he learns something."

"This all sounds incredibly dangerous. I should go with you to get her. I could drive and keep the car running."

Austia considered his words for a moment. "No, I have a plan that I think will get us out safely. I'll call you as soon as I have her."

Dave rose. "Guess I should get going."

"Here." Austia took a napkin and put a sandwich in it. "Take this with you."

She walked with him to the door. "It feels so good to share all this with someone." She rose on her toes and kissed his cheek. "Thank you. I'll see you later."

He nodded toward her. "I'll be waiting."

CHAPTER 58

Austia watched Dave get in his car, then shut the door. She poured herself a glass of iced tea and then went to her office. A glance at the computer told her there were no new emails.

She stood staring at the screen. Within hours she would have Fatima in her car, and as of right now she had no place to relocate her. Thank goodness they could at least stop at Dave's temporarily. "Lord, You're the only one who can help me." Catching her bottom lip between her teeth, she bit down. *Or you, Rabbi Lohrer.*

Suddenly dread filled her as an obvious fact occurred to her. Rabbi Lohrer was not going to be answering her email today. It was Saturday. Shabbat. The Sabbath. Friday sundown until Saturday sundown, the period of time Jewish law mandated was to be devoted to the Lord. Her original email had been vague and businesslike. Doing business on Shabbat was forbidden.

She sat down in front of the computer and clicked on the Sent Messages icon. Looking at the email she'd sent him, she realized it would have been delivered early yesterday afternoon, before the beginning of Shabbat. But who knew if he'd checked his email and read it.

She opened her Favorites, went to History, clicked on the Beth Shalom website address, and found the "Contact Us" information. She opened her cell phone and dialed the number. A machine picked up.

"This is Austia Donatelli. You don't know me, but I sent you an email yesterday. I'm in a very urgent situation and need your help. I minister to Muslims and a young Muslim woman needs shelter for at least a few weeks. Is there any possible way you could help? Please call me as soon as you get this message." She left her phone number and hung up. Fear and doubt welled up in her.

This was all happening too fast. She didn't know this rabbi. For all she knew he wouldn't want to get involved, and the drive to his location was hours from Agua Viva. Still, she had to take Fatima somewhere. There was no possible way she could leave her alone with Dave, a single man.

After typing the site address for MapQuest into the browser, she printed out the directions to the shul.

She rose and walked into the living room and sat on the couch. Surely the Lord would not have put Fatima in her path only to abandon them both now. The stakes were so high and both their lives hung in the balance.

Immediately a memory returned to her. The day she had sat in her car in the parking lot of the coffee shop, defeated and discouraged, and recommitted herself to this ministry to Muslims. She had distinctly discerned God's voice that day. "Trust Me," He had said.

She lifted her eyes heavenward. The sweet, gentle reminder lifted her spirits and a sense of peace settled on her, filling her with certainty. This was God's call on her life. And it was worth the cost. She would go to battle with the enemies of His kingdom because He desired that none die lost.

"I am willing, Lord." *On earth as it is in Heaven.*

Rising, she drew a deep breath. It would soon be time to go to the park to meet Fatima. She grabbed a sandwich and turned on the television. As the picture came into focus, her heart lodged in her throat.

Filling the screen was a picture of her in her car. The voiceover hardly registered. "If you know who this woman is, or recognize the 2004 gray Taurus, contact the authorities at the number on your screen. She's wanted for questioning in connection with a bombing in Deep Spring, Nevada. She has been positively identified by a number of witnesses as being in the building only moments before the bomb went off." The picture cut to a FOX News anchor.

The sandwich slipped from Austia's hand. She was the focus of a nationwide manhunt. How long had the alert been broadcasting? This changed everything. She didn't dare drive her car up the state's well-traveled highways now. Yet, she had to get Fatima out of the area. Her mind raced. She had to move quickly. There was no time to wait for Fatima in the park. And somehow she had to get a different car. It was no longer only about hiding Fatima; now Austia's identity put them both in danger.

Annie.

She got her cell phone and called her friend. There was no answer.

Flying into her bedroom, she went to her closet and pulled out the clothing she'd bought to take, as well as a long-sleeved, ankle-length dress of her own that should fit Fatima. Things were happening too fast. She felt like she was forgetting something. She grabbed the small valise she'd put her makeup in that morning. After quickly scanning the room, she ran through the kitchen to the garage. She put everything in the backseat except the outfit she'd bought for herself, which she put in the passenger's seat. She tried Annie again. Still no answer. She opened the garage door and started the car.

The directions!

She ran back to her office, grabbed them off the printer, and returned to the car. She hesitated. She couldn't shake the feeling she was forgetting something. But there was no more time.

Backing slowly out of her garage, she saw the neighbors were sitting on their front porch. She pasted a smile on her lips and waved casually, thankful they could not see she was trembling. Had they just been watching FOX and stationed themselves to watch for her? The thought sent a wave of fear up her spine.

One of the men pulled out a cell phone.

She forced herself to take slow, deep breaths. "Lord, I need to feel Your presence. Please guide and protect me." She had never prayed so earnestly in her life.

Careful to observe the speed limits and do nothing to draw attention to herself, she drove toward the park and parked on a street a block away. She tried Annie again. This time she left a message, briefly telling her what had happened, then turned the phone off and dropped it into her pocket.

After eyeing her surroundings and feeling sure that no one was watching her, Austia took the clothing from the passenger's seat and slipped the burka over her head. Then she opened the car door. Standing, she shook out the long dress and tied on her headpiece, making sure the veil fully covered her face.

She couldn't wait for Fatima to come to her. She would have to take her chances and go to the young woman.

Covered from head to toe, she started toward the park. As she neared the tree-lined grass, she saw the sunny summer afternoon had drawn out many of the neighborhood ladies and their children. The park was bustling with an inordinate amount of activity as people came and went. She soon saw why. It was Saturday and the pony rides were open. By the time she reached the street to Fatima's house she was but another Muslim woman walking on the sidewalk enjoying the beautiful summer day.

Austia lifted her eyes heavenward … and prayed.

CHAPTER 59

Hussein still wasn't answering. Taj closed the phone. Pausing, he considered calling some of the other cell members, but then thought better of it. No one could act without Hussein's instructions, and Hussein would be furious if the unbelievable information Austia had given him was passed to subordinates before he was notified. Taj shoved the phone in his shirt pocket as he headed to Hussein's house.

His mind was racing. Austia was proselytizing. The woman was waging war against Islam. Hussein's suspicions had been right. He'd thought something was going on at the Career Center and that that was where Sabirah had been deceived.

Taj flashed on Austia's face as she was telling him about the Muslim women. She was one of those Christians who believed that Christianity was the only true religion. Her eyes had come alive, but instead of hate he'd seen compassion. He lifted his chin. She was a weak woman who had been duped by a lot of foolish talk about love. With God there was no compromise. There was only Islamic law and complete submission.

A grin pulled at the corner of his mouth. He'd outsmarted Austia by giving her the directions to his house. If for some reason she escaped with Fatima before they were able to stop her, he would know right where she was going. And he and Hussein would meet them there. He nodded absently at the thought of how proud his father would be of him. This would surely raise his standing in the cell. As would the news about Zaki. He tried Hussein's cell phone again. But there was no answer.

Zaki's loyalty was the other thing that Hussein had been intent on learning. Hussein had told Taj to report directly back to him on everything he told Zaki and everything Zaki told him. It had been clear to Taj that Hussein didn't trust Zaki. Then, only a few nights ago, Hussein had been at Taj's house in Los Angeles and had hinted that he wanted to try out the poison in the vials that had been couriered from Yemen. That there was someone in the cell who Hussein believed was a problem and would be a perfect candidate. Though Zaki's name was never spoken, the context of the conversation had made Taj feel certain that Hussein was talking about him. Hussein would be pleased to learn that the integrity of the cell was intact.

Taj pulled up in front of Hussein's duplex, climbed out of the car and rushed to the front door. He rang the bell. Hussein's sister answered.

"Where's Hussein?"

Over Rasha's shoulder he saw three women peering at him from around the corner of the entry. He recognized the shorter one as Hussein's wife, Fatima, and the woman holding a toddler as Hussein's mother.

"Hussein's still at Faisal's funeral."

Of course. He should have thought of that. "When will he be back?"

"He didn't say."

Taj clenched his jaw. As he walked to his car he pulled out his phone and tried Hussein again.

He answered.

"This is Taj. I have just learned that Fatima is planning to escape with the woman at the Career Center this afternoon."

"Where are you?" Hussein's voice was terse.

"I'm sitting in front of your house. The women and your mother are here." Taj glanced in his rearview mirror. "Someone just pulled up behind me." He craned his neck. "It looks like Yunus, Faisal's wife's cousin, and his family."

"I've invited all the family to come this afternoon."

For a moment Hussein said nothing. Taj watched as the men, women and children trooped to the duplex. Finally, Hussein spoke.

"This simply means I must move up my plan. Go to my office. The black box with the vials that your father brought is in my desk in the bottom drawer on the right side. There are gloves there, and a special syringe. Put on the gloves and extract a half milliliter of liquid from the vial. Be sure you don't let it touch you. It can be absorbed through your skin. Reseal the vial and put it back in the box. Go into the bathroom off my bedroom. Inject the water bottle there with the liquid, just above the water line. Then put the gloves and needle back in my drawer. You understand?"

"What about the women?"

"The women will be in the kitchen or waiting on the guests. No one will be upstairs. Tell Rasha I left something for you in my office."

Taj's heart was pounding. "I understand."

Hussein hung up.

Taj wiped the sweat from his brow and got out of the car. He drew a deep breath. He was a warrior. He had trained for this in Yemen.

With long, deliberate strides he returned to the duplex and rang the doorbell again.

When Rasha answered the door, he told her Hussein had left something for him in the office. Then he bounded up the stairs, entered the office and knelt beside Hussein's desk.

He opened the bottom right drawer. Everything was exactly as Hussein had described it. He removed one of the vials from the black box and then picked up the gloves and the syringe and sat in Hussein's chair. He laid everything on the desktop.

Taj raised his head and slowly scanned the room. Straightening his back, he squared his shoulders. This was Hussein's view. He knotted his right hand into a fist, then slammed it down on the desktop as he'd seen Hussein do many times to drive home his point. The metal desk vibrated and the vial rolled into the gloves.

He grabbed for it.

After nearly dropping the vial, he secured it in his hand, then quickly placed it back on the desk. He put on the gloves and picked up the small glass cylinder. He carefully examined the lid to be sure none had leaked out. Then he unscrewed the top, set it on the desk, and withdrew a half milliliter of the liquid.

After quickly screwing the lid back on, he returned the vial to the black box and shut the drawer. Then he took quick steps to the office door, opened it a crack and listened to determine if there was any movement on the stairs or in the hall. Hearing nothing he went door to door, looking in the rooms that lined the hall until he found the master bedroom. He stepped into it and shut the door behind him. Then he went into the bathroom and found the water dispenser.

The bathroom smelled like baby powder. He glanced around the bathroom and through the bathroom door he glimpsed a crib. A teddy bear's innocent shoe-button eyes peeked at him through the white wooden bars.

He was killing someone's mother.

Fighting the urge to vomit, he put the back of his hand to his mouth and swallowed hard. He couldn't let his brothers down. Thoughts of his own mother intruded. Quiet eyes, filled with love. A gentle touch on a fevered brow. He swallowed the hard pit in his throat. He was Allah's servant. With sheer force of will he choked back his emotions. The cause of Allah must prevail … no matter what the cost.

As his emotions warred within him, he plunged the needle into the bottle just above the water line and expelled the poison into the water. Then he pulled the needle out, and without a backward glance, returned to Hussein's office. Kneeling beside the desk, he placed the gloves and syringe back in the drawer exactly as he had found them. He rose and left the office, looking neither right nor left. With his eyes focused on the floor in front of him, he went down the steps, nearly colliding with someone at the foot of the stairs.

It was Fatima.

Her sudden appearance sent an explosion of adrenaline racing through him and he felt weak in his knees. He dropped his gaze and went out the front door to his car.

Just as he reached the driver's door he saw Hussein pull into the driveway, open the garage door, and drive in. Nasser, Hussein's cousin, was with him. Zaki pulled in next to them. Jahi, another member of the cell, was in the passenger's seat and Hussein's father was in the backseat. The men got out of the cars. Taj waited for them to come out of the garage, then started across the street.

Hussein jerked a finger toward him. "Follow me."

Taj glanced at Zaki. Zaki's face was a stony mask.

Suddenly Taj realized that he had said nothing to Hussein about what Austia had told him about Zaki. Hussein knew only that Austia was helping Fatima escape. He had assigned Zaki to watch her. He could think that Zaki knew about the plan.

Jahi was walking so close behind Zaki that there was no daylight between them. As Taj drew closer, he saw why.

Jahi had a gun to Zaki's back.

Hussein radiated hostility. "Nasser, you stand guard here at the front door. Stop anyone you don't recognize and notify me." He opened the front door and stepped through it. "Jahi, stay here in the entry, at the corner of the stairs. Keep your eye on the back hall. Be sure Fatima doesn't leave the house."

CHAPTER 60

Zaki had been stunned when he got out of the car in the garage. Hussein had exploded, telling his father he'd just learned that Fatima planned to escape and that Austia was helping her. The implication was that Zaki was somehow involved. It wasn't until they had all come to the office and Taj had reported every detail of his conversation with Austia and answered repeated probing questions from Hussein that Hussein had calmed down … and the gun had been put away. Still, Zaki wasn't foolish enough to believe he was in the clear. From this day forward he would never be completely above suspicion in the mind of Hussein. The first time something happened that sparked an episode of paranoia, Hussein's focus would return to Zaki. But that didn't matter now. Zaki knew what he was going to do.

His eyes drifted to Taj. Something had changed. He was different in a way Zaki couldn't put his finger on. He'd seemed to go out of his way to exonerate Zaki in regards to Austia. It had been subtle, but Zaki had picked up on certain phrasing that Taj used that emphasized Zaki's innocence. Unnecessary words that bolstered Taj's statements. Things like Austia had revealed *absolutely* nothing to Zaki about the plan she'd made with Fatima. That Austia was *deathly* afraid of Zaki and had *gone out of her way* to conceal her activities from him. It was almost as though Taj didn't want to be a part of the fallout Zaki might suffer as a result of the whole incident. Why a guilty conscience now? Taj had willingly, even joyfully, trained in Yemen and committed himself to helping the cell bring terror to the United States. Something had happened to mute his passion.

Hussein entered the office and seated himself behind his desk. Zaki eyed the small drop of liquid by Hussein's elbow. Zaki had noticed it as he first sat down. For a split second his line of vision had been even with the desk and the small circle of liquid had caught the light. From his current vantage point, he never would have noticed the little circle with a hole in the middle. But now that he had, he couldn't help himself. It bugged him. It didn't belong there.

Hussein reached down and opened the bottom drawer of his desk. He lifted out the black leather box and set it in front of him. "Well, it seems we may soon have the results of our first test. Right, Taj?" Hussein glanced at his father. "Taj just got a promotion at work." He raised his eyebrows. "Perfect timing."

Zaki recognized the box as the one he'd seen at the last meeting that Ma'amoon Abdullah had attended, right before he and Hussein had gone to Los Angeles. Zaki glanced at Taj. The color had drained from his face, sweat beaded on his brow, and in his lap, where Hussein couldn't see them, he twisted his hands. Zaki knew immediately what wasn't being said. Indeed, something *had* changed in the young man who'd been born and raised in America and tasted of her goodness, insulated from the hardening that took place in the disenfranchised youth who were recruited from the *madrasas*. The cell's mission had moved into the next phase. What had been fun and games in Yemen had become real war. And Taj's naive fantasy of fighting jihad was its first casualty.

Hussein opened the box, revealing a row of vials. He removed one, his thumb on the bottom, his forefinger on top of the small black lid.

Zaki's eyes shot to the small circle on the desktop. Hussein's elbow was a fraction of an inch from it.

Hussein held the vial up to the light. "Odorless and tasteless." He looked at the three men, one by one. "Which allows it to be ingested without being noticed. And—" he gave a dramatic pause— "it can be absorbed through the skin. Less than a drop can kill a man." He beamed. "It gives us a variety of ways to use it." Smiling gently, he carefully placed the vial back in its niche. "And it has some very special properties." He leveled his eyes at the men again. "Time release. It takes a full twenty-four hours to kill a human being. Those who try to find out where a person came into contact with it will have to retrace every move of the previous twenty-four hours."

He paused, his tongue darting across his lips, as though savoring his words. "The first sign is slurred speech, then drowsiness. Then as the body starts to shut down, a coma is induced. And then death." He shrugged. "Quite painless, really."

Hussein tilted his head, eying the bottle fondly. "Father, are the speakers installed and working?" His father nodded.

The call to prayer! The speakers were really for a call to jihad. The ability to blast a message of hate and war in Arabic across Agua Viva, or from any mosque with impunity. This was the real reason Hussein had fought passionately to get city council approval for the speakers for months. They were going to be used to carry out the attack Hussein had planned. He could mobilize every radical Muslim within hearing distance at a moment's notice. Instructions and information could be given to any cell member within listening distance, while thousands of non-Arabic speakers innocently went about their business.

The moment was surreal. Two years of work and now Zaki knew the method of the attack planned by the cell, as well as the location of the physical evidence. Without a doubt, a plethora of other details were contained in the computers and files within the office. He had to get the information out to the FBI.

His mind flashed back to the City of Los Angeles file in Austia's office. Many of the cell's members worked for the city, which provided sevices for millions of people.

A self-satisfied smile spread across Hussein's face as he folded his arms on the desk. "Only the best for our American friends." He leaned forward, his right forearm rolling over the tiny liquid circle. "Right?"

Zaki met his gaze and nodded. "Just as it should be."

Hussein settled back in his chair, not a trace of dampness where the circle had been.

CHAPTER 61

Fatima flattened herself against the wall behind the open door of her bedroom, her passport in her hand. Through the crack between the jamb and the door, she saw Hussein, his father, a young man, and Zaki walk down the hall toward Hussein's office. Her eyes widened as she saw the man behind Zaki had a gun pressed into Zaki's back. She heard Hussein's office door open, then slam shut.

She closed her eyes to pull herself together. This was exactly why she had left the bedroom door open. If Hussein returned and came upstairs he would wonder why the door was closed, since she was supposed to be serving guests. Her knees were so weak she couldn't move.

Forcing her thoughts to Sami, she drew strength from her purpose. She would not fail her son. Her eyes cut to the bed.

Najah had hidden the sacks, two cans of powdered formula, and three empty bottles under the bed. Fatima needed only to prepare the bottles and put them in a sack, then fill the other sack with diapers and clothes for Sami, and she'd be ready to leave for the park. Holding her breath, she listened. She could hear muffled voices coming from the direction of Hussein's office.

Fatima limped to the bed and knelt beside it. As she reached for the sacks, she heard a door open and the men's muted voices became loud. Scrambling, she managed to crawl under the bed.

The floor vibrated beneath her from the heavy footfalls of the man coming down the hall. To her horror, he came through the doorway.

The heavy breathing was Hussein's. The ragged breaths a sure sign he was highly agitated.

His leg brushed the bed as he walked past it and into the bathroom. Panic seized her. She had to get out of the room.

The toilet lid clicked against the tank.

Her fingers dug into the rug as she tried desperately to hang on to her sanity. She knew him. He would sense her presence. During her time with him she'd learned he had a mysterious way of knowing things, as though he could read people's thoughts and knew their plans. Warning spasms of fear ricocheted through every fiber of her body.

The toilet flushed.

Had he come to the room already knowing she was hiding? The floor quivered as he stepped out of the bathroom. The thought clarified into certainty. He knew.

She was going to die.

He walked around the bed and sat on the edge of the mattress. She heard him slide out the drawer in his nightstand. Opening her eyes, she saw his feet only inches from her face. He strapped a small holster to his ankle. He was so close she could see the gun's trigger.

His labored breathing was punctuated with the terrifying grunts that housed his explosive temper.

As he rose from the bed, she squeezed her eyes shut and held her breath.

The floor trembled beneath her as he lumbered toward the door and then down the hall. Only after hearing his office door close did she open her eyes and dare to breathe.

Her mind raced. Why had he taken the gun? What was the meeting about and when would it be over? She needed to be gone before then. With no other options, she gathered the things from under the bed, crawled out, and hurried to the bathroom, keeping her attention focused on the voices down the hall.

Shaking badly, she opened the formula and scooped it into the bottles. Then, one by one, she filled the bottles from the water dispenser. Sparkling, pure water. Only the best for Sami. The thought of her son sharpened her resolve and calmed her.

As each bottle was filled, she capped the nipple, and dropped it into the sack. Next she wrapped each bottle in a diaper and then filled the rest of the sack with clothes. Finally she crammed more clothes and diapers for Sami into the second sack.

Listening, to be sure no one was coming, she stepped to the window and opened it. A quick scan of the area below assured her no one was nearby. She dropped the sacks from the window into the flower bed between the house and the driveway. They landed among some blooming bushes.

Knowing time was running out, she raced to the closet, grabbed one of her burkas, folded it in half twice, put her headpiece and veil in the middle of it, and then made it into a roll. She took one of the cords that Hussein used to hold his *keffiyeh* in place and wrapped it around the bundle to secure it. Then she retuned to the window. As she was about to drop it into the flowerbed, a van pulled into the driveway. More guests. She shrank back from the open window.

Curtailing her breathing, she listened to the men's voices still muted behind the closed office door. After a moment she looked to the drive. The family had left the van and was walking to the front of the duplex. She held the burka on the windowsill, waiting for them to disappear around the corner.

The floor vibrated beneath her feet.

The father and mother were still in view. The sound of the office door opening, then closing, plunged a dagger of fear into her chest.

She was going to be caught.

Help me. Someone, help me ... Prophet Jesus ... save me.

She whirled and faced the open bedroom door, keeping her hands behind her back, gripping the burka. As Hussein came even with the open door, his head swiveled toward her.

She let the burka fall from the window ledge.

"What are you doing?" His eyes moved past her to the open window.

CHAPTER 62

"I came up to use the bathroom and I got a drink of water." She could barely hear her own voice. She bit her lower lip to keep it from trembling.

To her amazement a broad smile spread across Hussein's face. "I was going downstairs to tell you to get Sami ready to go to my mother's house. When I'm finished meeting with my father, they're taking him home."

She dropped her gaze and nodded. Hussein walked toward her.

She braced herself, flinching as he pushed her to the side.

Standing at the window, he looked to the right and to the left.

Fatima's heart began to beat erratically as a black wraith of fear threatened to render her unconscious. Hussein looked down.

She forced herself to measure her breaths.

"More guests have arrived. Go take care of Sami and then you can return to serving."

Fatima nodded. She could feel Hussein's eyes upon her, but she kept her gaze riveted to the floor.

He followed her to the stairs, stopping at the top and calling down to Jahi. "Where's my mother?"

"The women and children are in the backyard."

"Fatima is going to get my son ready to go home with my parents."

Hussein turned on his heel and strode from the room, humming.

What the exchange meant, Fatima didn't know. But Jahi moved out of her way as she descended the stairs. Holding raw emotions in check, Fatima took measured breaths and walked past him, then headed down the back hall and out the door to the backyard. She quickly found her mother-in-law amid a group of women, holding Sami, who was drinking from a bottle.

He screamed with delight when he saw her, kicking his legs, chubby hands splayed in excitement as he reached for her. His bottle dropped to the ground. One of the women picked it up.

"Hussein has asked me to get him ready to go home with you. Hussein's almost finished with his meeting."

The woman handed the baby to her. Sami's dark eyes, wide with joy, searched her face, as though assuring himself she had returned for him. Fatima cupped the back of his head in her hand, nestling him to her neck, then walked back into the house.

As she stepped through the door and started toward the utility room, Jahi eyed her from the entry. With sheer force of will, she managed to appear calm while she groped for something to say. "Hussein's mother has asked me to put the car seat in her car."

Jahi nodded.

Fatima stepped into the utility room and out the door that opened to the garage. Trembling so badly she could barely turn the knob, she managed to lock it before pulling it shut. Once in the garage she dashed to the back wall and opened the door that led to the alley where the garbage cans were kept. Once again she locked the door before stepping through it and pulling it shut.

She hesitated a moment. Across the alley, a woman in the yard of a neighboring house was standing by some trash cans watching her. Fatima knelt and picked up a few stray pieces of paper around her own cans. When she rose, the woman was gone. Fatima held her breath and listened. Hearing nothing, she stepped around the corner of the garage and with uneven steps covered the few yards to where she had dropped the sacks and her burka. Juggling Sami in one arm, she managed to gather everything from the flower bed. A quick glance around her assured her that for the moment she was safe.

Suddenly, a piercing scream sounded above her.

Jerking her head back, she saw her mother-in-law leaning out the upstairs window, pointing directly at her. "Stop her. Stop her."

All three men jumped up and tore out of the office. Hussein's mother was in the hall, pointing toward Hussein's bedroom. "She's taken Sami."

Hussein's words came out hard and evenly spaced. "What are you talking about?"

"Fatima. I saw her in the driveway with Sami. She was carrying packages. She ran to the alley."

Hussein tore down the stairs, Zaki, Taj, and the imam behind him. At the bottom of the stairs, Jahi stumbled out of the way. Without breaking his stride, Hussein struck him across the face. "Fool." Zaki heard a crack as the man fell, his head hitting the entry table.

Hussein continued his rampage down the hall and into the utility room. Finding the door to the garage locked, he flew into a rage. Throwing his body against it, the jamb splintered, loosening the knob so the lock no longer held. He jerked the door open and sprinted across the garage. The door to the alley was locked.

With a speed and agility that shocked Zaki, Hussein reached down and in seconds was holding a gun. He shot the doorknob. Then kicked the door open.

Seized by a strength she didn't know she possessed, Fatima, carrying everything—the sacks, the burka, and her precious son—fled back around the corner of the garage. After laying Sami down, she tore the cord from the bundled burka and threaded the sacks on it, then she tied the sacks around her waist. She pulled the two sacks directly over her stomach, then slid the burka over her head. A moment later she had on her headpiece and veil. She scooped Sami into her arms.

She'd taken only a few steps when she heard the locked garage door rattle. As she tried to flee, her bad leg threatened to buckle under the added weight of the sacks and her son. *Help me. Help me, please.*

A wind seemed to spring up around her. Breathing on her. Her legs felt stronger and her steps became even. Her feet began to fly over the ground and down the alley. Strong and sure, her legs carried her to the street that lay at the corner of her block.

"Fatima." A low, urgent call came from behind her.

She ran faster.

"Fatima, it's Maryam."

Turning her head as she ran, she realized a woman was at her heels. Glimpsing the veiled eyes, she slowed her steps. She'd seen them before … loving and compassionate … Maryam sitting beside her at the ESL class. One memory spliced into another. "Come, my daughter," He'd said, speaking to her in the dialect of her homeland, "*Ta'ali ya binti.*" The love and compassion in His eyes unconditional, consuming, life-giving. Now those same eyes were looking at her through the veil.

He had heard her cry. And in a way she could not understand, He was with her now.

She stopped.

"Fatima, give me the baby."

Fatima handed Sami to her. He grinned as Maryam cradled him in her arms.

"Try to calm down. We must walk to the park now. Two friends. A pregnant woman and a lady with a baby."

Fatima nodded as they crossed the street, smoothing her burka over the sacks tied beneath it.

She matched Maryam's stride step for step. The telltale limp that had cursed her all her life was gone. She glanced at the woman beside her.

Maryam's gentle eyes met hers. "Love's touch heals," she whispered.

Just then, Fatima heard a commotion behind them.

Terror filled her at the sound of Hussein's voice shouting orders to his minions.

CHAPTER 63

Hussein pointed to the left. "Taj, go back down the alley. Check out every woman you see. Fatima's limp will be easy to spot."

Zaki and the imam followed Hussein as he turned right and headed up the street. Across the street and to his right were two women. Directly ahead of them was a woman carrying an oversized bundle. In a few strides Hussein had her by the arm.

Following behind him, Zaki scanned each side of the street in both directions. His eye caught a sudden movement. Across the street, one woman grabbed the other woman's hand. Their steps became stiff, deliberate, hurried. He stared at them. Neither one limped. But there was something very familiar about one of them.

Suddenly, Taj appeared from around the corner. He jogged toward them.

Hussein released the woman and followed Zaki's gaze.

"Nothing," Taj called out as he neared them.

"She has to be here somewhere." Hussein's ragged breathing punctuated his words.

Looking past Taj, Zaki saw the two women he'd observed round the corner toward the park. "Maybe Austia already picked her up. Maybe she was waiting here in the alley in her car?"

Hussein turned to him. "What kind of car does she have?"

Taj cut in. "Faisal and I followed her once from her brother's house. It's a 2004 gray Taurus. License plate number is SLD-OUT."

Hussein stared at him for a moment then turned to the imam.

"Go to the mosque. Get on the call-to-prayer speakers and broadcast that my wife has been kidnapped by the woman at the Career Center. Include a description of the car. And give my cell number to be called if she's spotted." He started back down the alley toward the duplex, still barking orders. "Taj, you take him to the mosque. Then go to Abdur Rahman's house; my father will tell you how to get there. Zaki, you go to that woman's house. If she's not there, go inside and see what you can find out about her plans." He stormed into the garage. "I'm going to drive the streets around here. She may still be on foot."

Stepping over the safety beam, Zaki ducked under the garage door as it rose and tore to his car, Taj and the imam right behind him. By the time Zaki reached his car, Taj was pulling away from the curb. As the truck sped past him, Zaki caught his breath.

Displayed prominently on the side of the door was the logo for the Los Angeles Department of Water and Power. The last piece of the puzzle fell into place. Hussein's numerous trips into Los Angeles, the vials of poison from Yemen, Hussein's cryptic remarks to Taj about a "first test."

Zaki reached for his cell phone as he punched the gas. Drawing deep from his memory he keyed in the phone number Faruq had given him to use if Zaki's cover was ever blown. With his contact dead, it was his only option.

Speeding toward the park, with the phone to his ear, Zaki's eyes shot left and right, desperately searching for the woman with the gold-tinged head scarf and her companion.

The voice on the other end of the cell phone captured his attention. "Senator Amende's office."

To Zaki's right were the two women. He took in the full length of the taller woman. His eyes caught a glimpse of the heels of her shoes as she walked. Flats with silver-colored block heels. Austia!

He glanced in his rearview mirror.

Hussein was right behind him.

CHAPTER 64

With Fatima on one arm and Sami in the other, Austia hurried toward the park.

Zaki had looked right at her. Still, there was no possible way he could have known it was her ... she hoped. The sight of her picture being broadcast all over the country by national television had rattled her so much she feared making some fatal mistake. *Protect me from my enemies.*

A car cruised slowly past them. It was Zaki. She turned her head toward the park.

He was on the phone. He was probably talking to the other men who were looking for them. Her eyes darted to the stop sign not far ahead. If he turned right at the end of the block he would find her car. In fact, if he even looked right when he stopped he'd be able to see it from there.

She heard Fatima gasp.

A glance back to the street told her why. There was a second car cruising slowly behind Zaki. In it, with the driver's window down, was the man who'd grabbed the woman by the arm just outside the alley when she and Fatima had fled. She could feel Fatima's hand trembling in hers. Zaki rolled down his window and pointed over the top of the car toward the curb, signaling the man behind him. A bolt of fear shot through Austia as the two cars pulled over only a few yards ahead of them.

Willing herself to remain calm as the distance between the

hunters and the hunted closed, Austia felt a change in Fatima's stride. The bolt of fear hardened into a dagger.

Fatima was limping.

Austia slowed her steps as she watched Zaki jump out of his car and hurry to the other driver's open window. He leaned against the driver's door, his back to them.

Praise You, Lord. The angle of his body was such that neither the driver nor Zaki could see them.

"That's my husband, Hussein al-Ansari." Fatima's voice died away.

Still holding Fatima's hand, Austia turned around and began walking quickly in the opposite direction. At the corner they stood with a number of people waiting to cross the street. Moving to the far side of the group, Austia was able to observe the two men. Hussein had climbed out of his car and was crossing the street to the park. Zaki had returned to his vehicle and was driving forward … toward the stop sign.

As the women crossed the street, Fatima's limp became as pronounced as it had ever been, the cover its absence had provided now gone. Austia set her lips in a firm line. God was with her. Why He had withdrawn this provision she didn't know. What she did know was that He would not fail her. He knew his plan for her life. The beginning … and the end. She ignored the tears that stung her eyes and tightened her grip on Fatima's hand.

She quickly decided that they would continue straight ahead, walking west, away from the park, then, at the next intersection, loop up to the road past the park, where her car was located.

As they neared the street and her car, the number of people on the sidewalks thinned. By the time they reached the corner, they were alone. Austia dropped Fatima's hand, handed her the baby, and signaled her to wait. Then Austia stepped off the sidewalk and into the landscaped strip that lined the roadway, walking only far enough to get a view of her car. Her heart jumped in her chest. Zaki was driving slowly by it. And directly toward her.

She crouched down, calling to Fatima to join her. Fatima had barely knelt before Zaki approached the intersection only a few yards away. He made a U turn.

Austia watched as he cruised by her car a second time. Her blood boiled at the thought of how she had initially trusted him. *Lord, give him what he deserves.*

She captured her thoughts. There was no time to waste on denunciations. So he wanted to find her. Fine. She pulled out her cell phone and went to her contact list where she kept the cell numbers of her employees. She scrolled to his name and pressed Send. She watched as he pulled to the curb behind her car. He answered the phone.

"Zaki, it's Austia. I need your help."

"Where are you?"

She could hear the concern in his voice. What an actor. "I'm at the Career Center. I can't give you details now. I had to leave my car near the park. I took a cab. Could you come and give me a ride home?"

She watched as he pulled into the street and sped off.

"I'll be right there."

She snapped her phone shut and as soon as he was out of sight, she and Fatima walked across the street and toward her car. Seeing no one else around, Austia unlocked the passenger door. In the distance she could hear the call-to-prayer speakers broadcasting. It wasn't time for prayer and the speakers were never used for any other purpose. She looked at Fatima. "Can you make out what they're saying?"

Fatima listened, then shook her head.

As Fatima climbed into the car with Sami, Austia walked around the car and seated herself behind the wheel, the speakers still sounding in the distance.

She retrieved her cell phone from her pocket and turned it on. She had a voice mail—Annie. Maybe Annie had returned her call. She pressed Send and listened.

It was her friend, but the message dashed any hope of help. Annie had driven to San Diego to visit her daughter the night before. After receiving Austia's message, she had left immediately and was now heading back to Agua Viva.

That didn't help. Austia couldn't wait for Annie to arrive. She pressed Send.

Annie answered. "You're on television."

There was no way out. "When did you see it?"

"My son-in-law called my daughter. He was at Best Buy leaving his computer for repair and stopped to check out those flat-screen televisions. He told her he was almost positive it was you. Especially since the car in the picture looked exactly like yours."

Austia's stomach churned. She, her husband, and brother had shared holidays with Annie and her family after Austia's parents died. But still, the thought of someone she saw so seldom recognizing her and her car drove home the reality that she would not be safe anywhere. "I've got to get a car somehow. I'll call you back when I know more."

"I'll be praying." Annie's voice quavered. "Hard."

Austia closed the phone and put it in her pocket. The assurance of Annie's prayers strengthened her.

"Mr. Rahman."

Fatima looked at her.

Austia paused a moment, getting her bearings, thinking through the best way to cross town to the Rahmans while avoiding as much traffic as possible. Settling on a route, she drove as quickly as she dared toward the Rahmans' house.

CHAPTER 65

Taj pulled away from the mosque and headed toward the Rahmans' house. He tightened his grip on the steering wheel, eyeing the gun the imam had retrieved from the mosque and placed on the seat next to him.

Until now, things had always been abstract, somehow distant. He had been an actor in a play in the training camps of Yemen. He had been an ardent observer of the frontline activities of his father. He had embraced the edict of Muslim domination of the world and the idea of jihad to accomplish that most holy mandate. And he'd often spent time dreaming of victories and accolades yet to come. The power and the glory would be his.

Yet, suddenly, it was different. No longer distant.

He had put the poison in the water. *He* had tacitly agreed to be Fatima's killer. But now the euphoria of his visions eluded him. Instead he felt remorse.

He chastised himself. All he was doing, he was doing for true Islam. Fundamentalism. The ways of the moderates were foolish and weak. People who said otherwise didn't know what was in the Qur'an. They were misguided. He lifted his chin and brought his thoughts to the matter at hand. He would perform his mission, make his father proud, and gain the favor of Allah. His reward awaited him in eternity. He reached across the seat and put the gun in his jacket pocket.

As he approached the Rahmans' street, he noticed there was a small market to his right. He pulled into the parking area, as far from the street as possible, and turned off the ignition. After considering a number of plans, he finally decided the way to proceed would be on foot. He had no idea if Austia and Fatima were at the Rahmans' house. It seemed highly unlikely since Austia would have wanted to get Fatima out of the area as quickly as possible. But there was no way to be sure.

Taj climbed out of the truck and went into the market. He selected a box of Arabic sweets and paid for them. Within moments he was on the sidewalk, a friendly visitor bearing a gift.

He crossed the Rahmans' lawn and knocked on the door. An elderly man answered, a crutch under one arm.

"*Al salamu alaikum.* Are you Mr. Rahman?" Taj looked past Mr. Rahman, trying to get a broader view of the room.

The old man smiled. "*Wa alikum aslsalam.*"

"I heard of your unfortunate accident." Taj stepped through the door.

Mr. Rahman took an unsteady step back. His smile vanished.

Leaning against the inside of the door, Taj pushed it shut. Then, reaching into his pocket with his free hand, he pulled out the gun. "Go sit on the couch." Taj's eyes darted around the room. "Is anyone else here?"

He saw Mr. Rahman's eyes cut to a hallway. "Just my wife. She is very ill. *Please,* don't hurt her."

Though he couldn't say why, he sensed the fear in Mr. Rahman's voice was for his wife and not for himself. "I'm not going to hurt anyone. Just sit down and be quiet."

Keeping his eyes on the intruder, Mr. Rahman hobbled to the couch and sat down.

Taj followed him. After dropping the box of sweets on the coffee table, he looked down the hall. "Don't move."

"I will do exactly what you ask." Mr. Rahman raised his hands as if trying to calm Taj. "Just don't hurt my wife."

It took only a few seconds for Taj to dart down the hall and look in a small bathroom and two bedrooms. When he returned to the front room he once again leveled the gun at Mr. Rahman, then backed across the carpet and quickly scanned the kitchen. Satisfied they were alone, he returned to the living room.

The phone rang.

"Answer that." Taj waved the gun toward the phone.

Mr. Rahman hobbled to it and picked up. "Yes." The color drained from his face. "I see."

Taj stepped to the small table that held the base of the phone. He recognized the number on the caller ID. It was Austia.

Taj leaned next to the earpiece.

"So could I use it? Just for the next couple of days?"

Taj elbowed the old man.

"Yes." Mr. Rahman's voice was calm. "Of course."

Austia's voice came over the line. "Thank you so much. I'm desperate. So much has happened. I'll explain when I get there." She hung up.

"What is it she wants?" Taj motioned Mr. Rahman back to the couch.

"She said she needs to use my car."

Taj smirked. A lucky break. He walked to the front window and squatted by the sill to watch for her.

"She's gotten herself in a pile of trouble." Taj glanced at Mr. Rahman. "You seem awfully tight with her. How's that?"

"My wife and I have known her for years." Mr. Rahman moved back into the cushion, sitting erect, his hands in his lap.

"Did you know she was using that Career Center to proselytize?"

Mr. Rahman didn't answer.

"We've been watching her. Finally caught her. There'll be a price to pay now."

Mr. Rahman's voice, strong and even, came across the room. "The Qur'an claims there is no compulsion in religion. Surely Islam is grand enough to stand on its own."

His grandfather's words. Taj's eyes shot to Mr. Rahman. The thin, white-haired man sat quietly, no trace of fear on his face or in his demeanor, only an air of quiet dignity. A man of deep conviction, sure of his faith.

"You're a foolish old man. You know nothing of true Islam."

"I know true Islam is not about guns and bombs. The Qur'an instructs us to invite outsiders into the House of Islam with cordial words. What outsider will want to enter when all he hears from you are words that speak of death and hatred? Islam teaches us to reach out to the widows and orphans. But the brand of religion you advocate only creates widows and orphans."

"Justice demands strong measures and sacrifice."

Mr. Rahman turned toward him, his expression peaceful, his eyes searching Taj's face. "Son, do you not remember the words of our Prophet, peace be upon him, who taught us that the greatest *jihad* is the *jihad* of the soul? The struggle against evil in the heart, against prejudice, hatred, greed, and hypocrisy. What good does it do to wage war on others if you fail to defeat the Enemy of your own soul?"

Taj turned his face away. "Shut up."

Taj rose, moving away from the old man's words. As he began to settle his shoulder against the window's edge, he heard a car. Austia was pulling into the driveway. Fatima was with her. "Let them in." He stepped toward the hall. "Don't do anything that tips her off that I'm here. If you do, I'll kill your wife."

Mr. Rahman pulled himself up. Leaning heavily on the arm of the couch he faced Taj. "The Qur'an begins every chapter invoking the name of God, the Merciful, the Compassionate. If you follow the spirit of Islam, you will not kill anyone."

Foolish, stupid old man. Taj turned on his heel and stepped into the hall, positioning himself so he could hear what was being said in the living room, but could not be seen.

He should call Hussein and tell him he'd found the woman. Reaching into his jacket pocket, he pulled out his cell phone.

He stared at the screen, then slowly closed his eyes. The sound of his grandfather's voice whispered to him, encouraging him as he memorized the last *khutba* of the beloved Muslim saint Chishti. *Love all and hate none. Mere talk of peace will avail you naught. Mere talk of God and religion will not take you far. Bring out all of the latent powers of your being and reveal the full magnificence of your immortal self.*

His grandfather had whispered the words, so that Taj's father, who was waiting for him at the front door, could not hear them.

Taj bit down on his lip, squeezing his eyes shut against the tears that stung them.

What he realized now, that he had not realized then, was what his grandfather had known that day. Taj was being groomed for *jihad*. He would never be permitted to see his grandson again.

CHAPTER 66

Austia pulled into the Rahmans' driveway and pointed toward the garage. "Wait here while I open the garage door."

After putting the car in the garage, the women got out.

"Fatima, let's put everything in Mr. Rahman's car. You can take those sacks out from under your burka now and put them in his back seat." Austia had marveled at Fatima's ingenuity when the young woman told her how she'd come to have a "baby bump."

"No, wait." She put her hand on Fatima's arm. "Why don't you bring the sack with the bottles into the house? We can take a few minutes to heat Sami's bottle and change him if you need to."

Fatima nodded.

The women hurriedly pulled the double garage door shut and moved their things to Mr. Rahman's car. All the while Austia kept her ear tuned to the street traffic. When Zaki found out she wasn't at the Career Center, he'd probably go to her house, but she was sure that eventually he'd end up looking for her here. The clock was ticking, and their lives were in the balance. As soon as they finished, they lifted the garage door high enough to scoot under it, and then hurried to Mr. Rahman's porch.

Mr. Rahman opened the door before Austia could ring the bell.

She smiled in relief at the sight of her dear friend. *"Al salamu alaikum."*

Instead of responding, Mr. Rahman waved the bottom of his crutch at her. He looked ill.

"Is something wrong?" Austia asked.

Mr. Rahman's eyes widened and he shook his head in short jerking motions as he spoke. "No. No, not at all. *Wa alikum alsalam.* Come in."

Austia and Fatima stepped into the room and he closed the door behind them.

"Thank you so much for helping. Something has happened." Austia hesitated, not sure how much to say. "We can't stay long. This is Fatima." She turned toward the young woman and made the introduction. "Some terrible things have happened to her and I'm helping her find a new home."

Mr. Rahman's gaze rested on Sami. "May Allah protect this child."

Austia heard the concern in his voice and was glad she hadn't told him more. "I was hoping she could heat her baby's bottle in the kitchen before we leave."

Mr. Rahman eyed the front doorknob. For a moment she thought he was going to speak, but instead he only nodded.

Austia led Fatima to the kitchen. Fatima laid the sack of bottles on the table, then dug one out. As Fatima changed the baby's diaper, Austia heated a bottle in the microwave. Then she handed the bottle to Fatima, and the women went back into the living room.

Mr. Rahman was sitting ramrod straight on the edge of his chair. Austia noticed he'd laid his car keys next to a box of sweets on the coffee table. She picked them up and put them in her purse.

Fatima shook Sami's bottle.

"You might want to splash some of that formula on your wrist before you feed him to be sure it's not too hot. I wasn't sure how long to heat it."

Austia laid Sami on the couch, then turned to Mr. Rahman. "Thank you so much for all your help. I'll be in touch with you as soon as I can." Austia glanced out the window. "I wish it was dark."

Fatima knelt down, set the bottle on the coffee table, and took off its cap.

"That wouldn't make a bit of difference."

Austia turned toward the voice. Dave was stepping out of the hall, his hands in his jacket pockets.

At the sight of her friend, Austia's heart leapt. "Da—"

Fatima's scream cut her off.

"Fatima, don't be afraid. I know him. He's going to help us." She rushed toward him. "This is too good to be true. How long have you been here?"

He answered her by stepping back and pulling a gun from his pocket.

Fatima rose, grabbed Sami, and stumbled away from him, shielding Sami's face with her hand. "He's here to kill us. Hussein must have sent him." Her eyes were wild with fear. "He's going to kill us. He's going to kill us all."

Austia gasped as reality splintered into chaos—Dave holding a gun on them—Fatima screaming he was going to kill them—Mrs. Rahman's frantic voice coming from down the hall, calling her husband—Mr. Rahman struggling to his feet.

Finally, a single stark truth emerged. Dave had deceived her. As had Zaki. Nothing that she had believed about them was true. No one was going to help her. Right now, Fatima's and Sami's lives depended on her … and the sovereignty of God.

Adrenaline surged through her as she fought to get her bearings. "What do you want from us?"

Dave's face was grim. "I'm taking you to Hussein al-Ansari."

Austia heard Fatima whimper. Stepping back, she positioned herself between Fatima, Sami, and Dave.

"Hussein is Sabirah's uncle." Dave's face hardened. "You might remember her?"

A myriad of emotions flooded through Austia. Loss, anger, fear, and panic all battled to seize the moment.

Facing a gun, with the lives of those in the room inextricably intertwined with her actions, she must choose to surrender to the paralyzing emotions that held her in a death grip or choose to believe that God had called her to this place, exactly at this moment in time … And He would never leave her or forsake her.

From the midst of the melee rose a singular truth. This battle against the rulers of darkness, wickedness in high places, and supernatural agents of depravity belonged to the Lord.

As she searched Dave's face, a blade of ruby-red light cut through her line of vision, separating the physical world from the spiritual world. Love, strengthened by the spittle, steeled by the nails, girded by the thrusted spear, brought Heaven to earth. And for one fleeting moment she saw Dave through the eyes of Christ. His expression was one of fear, his eyes haunted and empty. Heavy chains were wrapped about him, scales covered his eyes, and tongues shaped like tines whispered in his ears.

Compassion so powerful that it seemed a living thing filled her heart as God's truth revealed the deception of radicalized Islam incarnate in the man before her. Without love, zeal degenerates into fanaticism—justice degenerates into unbridled revenge—righteous anger into hatred—just punishments into cruel atrocities—religious piety into religious hypocrisy. Without love, divine rule is despotism.

Tears running down her cheeks, she pled for his life. "You don't have to do this. There is another way. God is more than a God of power, judgment, and vengeance. He is a God of Love."

Dave waved the gun toward the couch. "Sit."

Oh, Lord God, don't let him die lost. "Please don't do this. I beg you."

He pulled out his cell phone with his free hand.

Austia stared at him. He could not hear her. He couldn't see the truth. "If you're going to kill me, you'd better do it now, because I'm taking Fatima and leaving."

She moved toward Fatima and grasped her hand. "Let's go."

The click of Dave cocking his gun was the last thing she heard as she stepped toward the door.

CHAPTER 67

"Yes, that's everything I can tell you right now, Senator." Zaki tightened his grip on the steering wheel.

The senator let out a low whistle. "I've kept tabs on Austia's situation since the death of her husband. Take this number. If there are any more developments, call it. The man who will answer is part of the interagency communication team. He is very familiar with Austia's situation."

Zaki made a mental note of the number, then disconnected. Should the worst happen, all the most important information he had garnered about Hussein's al-Ansari's cell would not die with him. And just as importantly, Faruq's and Cala's deaths would not have been in vain. He keyed the contact number that the senator had given him to use in the future into his phone and saved it.

Now, his primary concern was to save Austia, Fatima, and the baby. Austia hadn't been at the Career Center. He tried her cell again. No answer. He gripped the steering wheel and leaned forward as he pressed on toward her house.

When he'd left Hussein, they'd agreed that Hussein would search the park and Zaki would drive the surrounding streets looking for the women or Austia's car. He could only hope Hussein hadn't stumbled upon Austia's vehicle, which was within sight of the park. Zaki glanced at his watch. He'd better check in.

Hussein answered before the phone rang, his voice agitated and demanding. "Where are they?"

"They're not on the streets. I found no sign of them." Zaki bit the inside of his cheek. If Hussein had seen her car, it would complicate things.

"Meet me at her house."

For a moment, fearing the women might be there, Zaki considered telling Hussein he'd already checked with no result. But the truth that Hussein was as sly as Satan himself suddenly pushed forward and Zaki thought better of it.

"I'm on my way."

The phone went dead.

Zaki jammed his foot down on the accelerator. What if Austia had left the Career Center and gone home? His stomach wrenched at the thought of Hussein finding the two women. As he careened around the corner of her street, her house came into view and a wave of nausea washed through him. Hussein's car was in the driveway. So, the viper *had* been at her house when Zaki had called.

Zaki parked at the curb and climbed out of his car. As he approached the door, he could hear the muffled sound of a woman's voice. Anger rose in his chest and his blood pulsed through his veins as he felt for the gun jammed in the back of his waistband. He knocked.

Hussein unlocked the door and opened it. To Zaki's surprise the TV was on and he immediately realized that the woman's voice he'd heard was coming from the television. He quickly scanned the room. There was a partially eaten sandwich on the coffee table.

Hussein turned toward him, jerking his thumb toward the screen. "It was good of her to have left the television on for me. Look at this." Hussein's use of the past tense signaled Zaki that Hussein had already searched the house for the women. He sent up a silent word of thanks.

For now, the women were safe.

It took a moment for Zaki to realize that the person the reporter was talking about was Austia. And when Austia's picture flashed on the screen, there was no doubt about the identity of the person of interest.

Hussein's icy eyes observed Zaki. "Sadly, Fatima and my son are with the woman they're after. It's imperative we find them first." A confident, smug smile lifted one corner of his mouth. "Fortunately I have some information no one else has."

The hair on Zaki's arms rose.

"I know where they've gone." Hussein looked at Zaki as though he thought Zaki might also know things about Austia that no one else knew; the insinuating look making him wonder if any secret was safe from Hussein. Terror, slick as blood, sweated in Zaki's palms. The evil despot seemed privy even to a person's most private thoughts.

"That is fortunate."

Hussein turned and left the room. Zaki followed him to Austia's computer. On the screen was a MapQuest page. At the top were the words: Start—Agua Viva, CA. End—Las Castas, CA.

Hussein tilted his head, his eyes excitedly scanning the screen that exposed Austia's escape route. "So good of her to leave us an address."

Blood raged through Zaki's veins at the thought of Austia's plight. Everything she was doing was in an effort to save Fatima and her son from this monster. And Zaki was powerless to protect her.

Hussein clicked on the printer icon at the top of the screen. The moment the printer ejected the paper, he grabbed it. "Her destination is just south of San Francisco, near the coast."

Hussein opened his cell phone and pressed a button. "Get me two tickets to San Francisco. Book it round trip on the first available flight. I don't care which airline. Bring two carry-on bags packed with men's clothes, my alternate papers, and identification for Zaki ben Hassan. He'll be traveling as Michael Doran. When you have the tickets, call me. We'll meet you at the curb in front of the airline." He snapped the phone shut.

Hussein's cell ran like a well-oiled machine. Fear and intimidation were powerful motivators when perfection was not expected but demanded. The margin of error allowed was just wide enough to hold a dead body.

Fake IDs would be produced within the hour with names lifted from stolen credit cards. The credit cards would become the second piece of matching ID. It was certain that whoever had been on the other end of the line knew the drill.

A little box popped from the bottom right of the screen. Hussein grabbed the mouse and clicked on it. Dread blanketed Zaki as he read the note that appeared before them.

> *Austia—I just heard your phone message. I tried to call you but it went straight to voice mail. Your request is an answer to prayer. I will tell you more upon your arrival. Bring your Muslim friend. We welcome her and will help her in any way we can.*

Hussein scrolled down to read the attached thread.

Rabbi Lohrer,

My name is Austia Donatelli. The Lord has given me a special ministry and I find myself in need of help. I am looking for churches that would be willing to adopt immigrants who have recently become Christians. They will need to be housed and will need assistance in finding a job.

Hussein clenched his fist and rose. "See how the Jews and the Americans conspire to destroy Islam?" His face hardened and his tongue darted across his lips. "Sit! You write like an American, don't you?"

Trapped in the birthing of Hussein's demonic plan, Zaki nodded.

"Good, because she's going to send him another letter."

As Zaki took Hussein's place behind the computer, Hussein's phone rang and he answered it. "What time does the Alaska flight arrive in San Francisco?" He listened. "Book the Southwest flight at 6:25." Hussein disconnected, then looked at the printout of the directions again. "According to this, those women have about a seven-hour drive."

He turned to Zaki. "Write."

Zaki clicked on the rabbi's email address and the template popped up. His mind raced for some way he might code in something to signal the rabbi that he was in danger.

Hussein paused. "Tell him she'll arrive tomorrow. That her friend Michael Doran is meeting her there and will arrive before she does." As Zaki typed, Hussein continued to dictate. "Tell him she wants him to call Michael and give him the directions to the house.

Then give him your phone number."

Zaki began to type. With Hussein reading over his shoulder he dared not attempt anything that might draw Hussein's attention.

Stroke by stroke, Zaki crafted the message that would set up the woman he loved to die.

CHAPTER 68

Austia sped away from the Rahmans' house and headed toward the interstate. She wasn't sure if Dave had watched her drive away in Mr. Rahman's car. If he had it would only be a matter of minutes before every Muslim in Agua Viva would be looking for it. The sooner she left town the better.

As she merged onto the interstate she dared to think that they might actually make it out of the area.

Then a sudden thought made her gasp.

Fatima jostled Sami, who was beginning to whimper. "What's wrong?"

Austia heard the quaver in the young woman's voice. "What if Dave makes Mr. Rahman report his car as stolen?"

Fatima began to cry. "I'm so scared. There is no hope. No one can stop my husband. He will find us. He has ways that you don't understand."

Austia reached across the seat and put her hand on Fatima's shoulder, then glanced at her. "Fatima, God is with us."

Shaking her head, Fatima lowered her eyes. "I have not obeyed my husband. The angel has recorded that in the book and Allah will punish me for it."

Austia's heart went out to Fatima. The simple words spoke volumes. Not the least of which was the power Hussein held over Fatima. It had taken an incredible amount of courage for her to take her son and leave Hussein. She had done so understanding fully the

348

penalties in this life … and the next one.

"God is merciful and compassionate." Austia paused, letting the familiar words register with Fatima. "He loves us and He has provided us with a Savior."

Again she paused, asking the Holy Spirit, the only purveyor of truth, to empower the words and speak to Fatima's heart. "Even if you have disobeyed Him, you can call on the name of Jesus. God has not only given Prophet Jesus the authority to heal the body, He has also given Him the authority to heal the heart."

From the corner of her eye Austia saw Fatima slowly smooth her skirt over her shorter leg. Tears sprang to Austia's eyes at the silent reference to the miraculous intervention of the Lord that had hidden them from Hussein during their escape. "And so He will forgive the sin of your heart. And He will protect you and help you. But you must call on Him."

Fatima raised her eyes. "You speak as though Prophet Jesus is like God, but there is only one God—he is Allah."

The stumbling block. The Trinity. The concept that was almost impossible for a Muslim to understand. How many had been denied union with God because of it? Austia took Fatima's hand in hers. "Jesus is God's love become man. Yes, there is only one God, but He shows us His mercy and compassion in many ways."

A flicker of hope sparked in Fatima's eyes, but then she straightened and faced the windshield. "What if Mr. Rahman did tell the police we stole his car?"

Knowing that only Jesus Christ can change the heart, Austia let the subject drop. "Then they will be looking for us."

"Can we fly to where we are going?"

Austia's eyes cut to her companion. Why not? "Why, yes. Yes, we can. That's a great idea." A thought occurred to her. "You have to have ID."

A smile spread across Fatima's face. "I have my passport." She patted her chest.

Austia slowly shook her head, again impressed by the young woman's resourcefulness and forethought.

Sami began to cry in earnest. Fatima lifted him to her shoulder and began patting his back. "He's getting hungry and we left in such a hurry I forgot all the bottles at Mr. Rahman's."

Austia quirked her mouth. They needed to stop, get Sami some food, and decide on a plan. Taking the next exit, Austia drove until she saw a grocery store. Keeping an eye out for the police, she pulled into the parking lot of Safeway and stopped. She opened her purse and took out some money.

"Fatima, go in and get Sami some food. It's better for me to stay out of sight. I'll call the airlines and see about getting us tickets to San Francisco."

Fatima took the money from Austia's hand.

As Fatima climbed out of the car, Austia opened her cell phone. She had traveled to San Francisco and Seattle several times. Southwest Airlines had daily flights up the coast. She called information and got the number. The reservation line put her on hold. Austia was still holding when Fatima returned with a small sack of groceries.

Fatima laid Sami on the front seat, then took the sack from the back seat. After taking the lid from the can of powdered formula, she scooped some into a baby bottle. Then she opened the water she'd purchased and poured it into the bottle. Sami began to squeal and kick his chubby legs. She shook the mixture, put both bags on the floor, scooped Sami up into her arms, and climbed back into the car.

Fatima nodded toward the grocery bag at her feet. "There's some juice and candy bars in there for us." Sami pulled the bottle from her hands and began to suck on it.

A beep from the phone drew Austia's attention. She pulled the phone from her ear and looked at the screen. "Oh no. My battery's low." She didn't charge the phone every night and she hadn't thought about charging it the night before.

Last night seemed a lifetime ago. Then she hadn't known that she'd be using her phone to run for her life, or that she was being hunted for the bombing in Deep Spring, or that she would be driving a car that would be considered stolen. Rushing out of the house hadn't been part of her plan. She'd thought they would drive up the coast, free to stop along the way, making the drive in two jumps. Her heart skipped a beat. The phone charger. She had forgotten the phone charger.

She put the phone back to her ear and started the car. "Hurry, please hurry and answer." The phone beeped again.

As she pulled out of the parking lot, a woman came on the line. "How can I help you?"

"Could you tell me what flights you have to San Francisco this afternoon? I need a reservation for two adults and an infant."

As she listened, Austia glanced at the clock on the dash. "6:25 will be perfect." Just as she finished giving the woman her credit card number her phone went dead.

"Hello. Hello." She glanced at Fatima. "My phone is dead." She dropped it into her purse. "Oh, Lord God, get us on that flight."

A twinge of doubt pricked her. Unexpected complications, from her face being shown all over the country to leaving the bottles at Mr. Rahman's to her phone going dead, seemed to be lapses in God's faithfulness. Things were going wrong and every one of them increased the danger they were in.

The twinge of doubt rooted. Maybe she had completely misread God. Everything going wrong sure made it seem so. She released a deep sigh. It was too late now. She had to see this through. Once they were on the plane, they would be safe.

"Austia?" Fatima's voice broke into her thoughts.

"You said in class that you and your husband spoke Arabic at home."

Austia nodded.

"Why?"

David.

Suddenly feelings of longing rose in Austia's chest. If only he were here with her now.

"We spoke Arabic at home because that was his native language." She glanced at Fatima.

Fatima knitted her brows and her eyes sharpened. "Where was he from?"

Austia felt a swelling in her spirit and goose bumps rose on her arms. She knew exactly what it meant. The Holy Spirit was prompting her, telling her He had prepared Fatima's heart and was drawing her. Austia had no idea how that preparation had been done, or why it would begin by Fatima asking about David. But she knew that it was, for this moment, an open door that she was to walk through and tell Fatima about Christ.

CHAPTER 69

Dave crumpled on the couch, the gun in his hand. He hadn't believed her. No one would walk away with a loaded gun in her face.

This wasn't how it was supposed to end. His cause was noble and right. Islamic rule of law, God's law, would be established throughout the world. Allah was greater. He let the gun slip from his hand to the floor.

At the sound of the garage door closing, Dave opened his cell phone and pressed Send.

Hussein answered.

"They aren't at the Rahmans'. They didn't come here."

He closed his phone, then turned to Mr. Rahman. Their eyes met, but the old man said nothing.

Dave opened his cell again. Closing his eyes, he searched his memory. In a deep and distant place he found what he was looking for.

He entered the numbers into his keypad.

His heart stirred at the sound of the voice on the other end of the line.

His grip tightened on the phone. "Grandfather? It's Taj."

CHAPTER 70

Austia glanced at Fatima across the front seat. "My husband was from Kuwait. His name was Dawud al-Baraka. He was raised a Muslim, but he became a follower of Prophet Jesus because someone who cared talked to him about God when he was a young man coming to the United States to attend medical school. The seeds that laborer planted, God bless him wherever he is, bore fruit later on. David became totally devoted to Prophet Jesus. He became a true Christian. But he loved his people. In the end, he gave his life trying to save them."

Her mind drifted back to the moment over two years ago when the phone next to her bed had rung in the middle of the night, and a heavily accented voice told her that her husband had earned his fate by returning to his family's home and speaking blasphemy. A capital offense. And there had been a veiled reference to the vigilant network of radical Muslims that stretched worldwide, right to the town she lived in. The next day she'd changed her phone number, the locks on her house, and returned to her maiden name. She blinked rapidly.

Fatima reached across the seat and rested her arm on Austia's. "I'm sorry. And I'm sorry"—her voice broke—"for the trouble I bring you now."

The helplessness in the crippled, abused young woman's voice touched Austia in a way she couldn't explain. Fatima had been born into the hopelessness of radical Islam and, but for the grace of God, Austia could have been born into that faith too. The truth about

David's life suddenly struck her in a way it never had before. That is what drove him. He understood the dark finality of one born into radical Islam. If no one outside the closed, segregated culture reached them, they would never hear the gospel. But for a missionary crossing his path when he was a young man, he, too, would have been lost for eternity. This was the provision God had made for the Muslims. Sanctified believers, vessels of His Holy Spirit, to do Christ's work here on earth so that none would die lost.

"Fatima, you haven't brought me any trouble. Prophet Jesus is with us."

As they drove to the airport, Austia turned her thoughts to the rabbi. With the phone dead there was no way of reaching him now. She glanced at the clock—time was running short. If she couldn't call him before they boarded the plane, then she would call him from San Francisco when they arrived. Austia turned her attention back to the road as they entered the maze that was the Los Angeles airport.

After parking the car, she turned to Fatima. "I brought you a dress to wear so you will blend in." Austia turned and pulled her knees under her and leaned into the backseat. She grabbed the dress and handed it to Fatima. "This isn't going to be easy, but slip off whatever you have under your burka and put this dress on. Then take your burka off and we'll leave it in the car."

Austia held Sami as Fatima managed to change her clothes in the confined space. When she finished her face was flush with color. Austia wasn't sure if it was from Fatima exerting herself or from finding herself in a Western-style dress. Austia handed Sami back to Fatima. "Why don't you change him and I'll get our stuff together."

Austia stepped out of the car. After a quick look around to be sure no one was looking in their direction, she pulled her burka over her head and threw it in the back seat. She grabbed the broad-brimmed hat she'd brought and pushed it down over her hair. Then she took out her carry-on and lifted her purse from the front seat.

Fatima put Sami on her hip and gave Austia a tentative smile. "I'm ready."

Austia smiled back at her, realizing Fatima was using what looked like a rectangle of thin cloth that might have been brought to wrap Sami as a *hijab*. For a moment Austia considered asking her to take it off, but then thought better of it. In her simple dress and headscarf, she looked no different from many other women who would be passing through the LA airport. "Come on. We've got to hurry."

Fatima stared out the window of the shuttle taking them to the Southwest terminal. She could see Austia's reflection in it. Austia had suffered much in her life, yet she was still willing to help. Such selfless courage was impossible to understand. Why would a person be willing to risk her life for another? Especially since Austia hardly knew her and Fatima wasn't even a Christian.

Austia's revelation that her husband had been a Muslim who had become a Christian was startling. Dawud had grown up Muslim, but when he came to America and was free to choose, he'd chosen Christianity. Why? Probably, like her, he found that the Christians were nothing like the monsters that he'd heard about all his life. Austia was compassionate, kind, and loving.

Fatima felt something stir in her heart. A seed, taken root, bloomed. Austia had said that Jesus was God's love become man. Fatima studied Austia's reflection. *God's love become woman?* she wondered.

Austia's words returned to her: *God has not only given Prophet Jesus the authority to heal the body, He has also given Him the authority to heal the heart.*

Fatima had no idea what the future held. She had done many wrong, unforgivable things to escape her husband. She looked at Sami. There wasn't a doubt in her mind about Jesus' power to heal the body. He had healed Sami in her womb and even strengthened her leg when she'd run for her life. She wanted to live to raise her son and did not want the wrath of Allah to fall on her.

Austia had said Jesus would forgive the sin of her heart and would protect her, but she must call on Him. A fiery dart of fear shot through Fatima. That was blasphemy.

Fatima closed her eyes. All her life she'd felt Allah had never cared for her. But then Jesus had come to her in her dreams and called to her. Her heart began to pound as her thoughts coalesced. She tightened her hold on Sami and pressed her cheek against his. *Oh, Prophet Jesus, forgive the sin of my heart and take care of Sami and me.*

The bus groaned as the driver pulled it to a stop at the curb. Fatima rose and followed Austia from the bus. They were the last ones off. The door closed behind them.

As the bus was about to pull out, a cab cut directly in front of it. The bus driver laid on the horn. Austia grabbed Fatima's shoulder and pulled her back from the curb, sending them both into a group of people walking behind them.

The cab screeched to a halt at the curb and a man jumped out from the passenger's side. He stepped to the back passenger door and opened it. Holding the door open, he faced them.

As Hussein al-Ansari climbed out of the cab, Zaki looked directly into Fatima's eyes.

CHAPTER 71

Austia's God must have been watching over her. Austia and Fatima ending up not twenty feet from Hussein at the airport could have had deadly consequences for them all. Zaki fought an involuntary shudder. He couldn't deny that in a very diabolical way things always seemed to work in Hussein's favor. As though a war strategized in Hell was being played out on earth.

Still, he had been the one to step out of the cab and see the two women. Giving them precious seconds to fade into the group of people passing behind them and then disappear into the terminal.

Even now, as he and Hussein sat waiting to board their flight, he kept his eye out for them. Apparently Austia had changed her mind and was now flying to San Francisco. He'd managed to get by himself in a stall in the men's room earlier, and had tried to call her, but voice mail picked up on the first ring. Either her phone was off or it was dead. He'd then started to call the number Senator Amende had given him, but Hussein had moved directly in front of the stall door. There was no way he could have talked. The sound of his cell phone interrupted his thoughts.

Hussein grunted and turned toward him.

He flipped the phone open and a glance at the screen told him it was the call he'd hoped wouldn't come. "Hello."

"Michael Doran, please."

"This is Michael."

Hussein scooted close in so he could hear what the caller said.

Hatred for the man rose like bile in Zaki's throat.

As Zaki listened, the rabbi recounted receiving "Austia's" email informing him of Michael Doran's arrival.

Zaki responded, "Yes, I'm at the airport now and will arrive in San Francisco later tonight."

"Let me pick you up."

Hussein poked him and nodded.

"Thank you. I arrive at 9:55."

"I'll wait at baggage claim. I should be easy to spot. Probably the only one there with a *kippah* and a beard." He chuckled. "I look forward to meeting you. God be with you."

Zaki lowered his gaze. "May God be with you, too, brother." He hung up. When he turned to Hussein he found the despot's beady eyes observing him.

"You sounded very convincing." Hussein's unblinking stare bore through him.

"It's my job."

The first call to board the aircraft sounded overhead.

His eyes still on Zaki's face, Hussein reached in his pocket and retrieved his cell phone. Without looking at the keypad, he pressed a number.

A moment later he spoke. "We're leafing. Do you haf our 'supplies'?" Confusion crossed Hussein's face and he cleared his throat. "Perfect. Phase one was just completed. Cut his lines."

Zaki heard the slur in Hussein's words.

The poison. The drop on the desk. *Yes.* Hope pulsed in his chest.

Hussein rose. "Our brothers from the Sacramento cell will be meeting us."

Zaki nodded and followed Hussein to the boarding gate.

As the plane landed in San Francisco, Hussein turned to Zaki with final instructions. "Go meet the rabbi at baggage claim. I'll catch up with you later."

"As you say."

When they deplaned, Hussein hurried to the men's room, leaving Zaki to continue on to meet the rabbi.

Just as Hussein was about to disappear through the bathroom doorway, he looked back at Zaki. When their eyes met, an impression so strong it became a certainty razored through Zaki's gut.

Hussein knew Zaki's true identity!

Zaki glanced around. The order to cut the rabbi's phone lines meant that Hussein already had people in place at the rabbi's house. And it had not escaped him that Hussein's instructions left Zaki unarmed. In fact, it was highly likely that members of the Sacramento cell were observing him at this very moment.

He took out his cell phone. He dialed the number Senator Amende had given him. A man answered on the first ring.

"Zahid Zafar."

Zahid Zafar. The familiar name stunned him for a moment. Austia's neighbor. The man in the bakery who'd told him when Zaki had asked about Faruq's absence, *"I'm his cousin. He and his wife are staying with my uncle in LA."*

The words that had tipped Zaki off go the fact that Faruq was dead. Pieces fell into place. At the time Zaki had thought it was a poorly thought out response to satisfy his curiosity about what had happened to Faruq. Now he realized the words had been carefully chosen to let him know Faruq was dead without revealing that the speaker had been working with Faruq through the FBI.

"This is Zaki ben Hassan."

Zahid responded, "I've been briefed."

"I'm just leaving the San Francisco airport. I'm in route to a Rabbi Lohrer's house in Las Castas. Notify—" A firm grip on his right elbow ended his conversation. A second man in a security guard's uniform took his phone.

The man on his right, wearing street clothes, whispered to him in perfect English. "It would be extremely unwise to resist."

They escorted him out of the building to a waiting car. The car door was opened and he was pushed into the backseat. The man in street clothes got in with him and closed the door.

Seeing the bearded man at the wheel wearing a *kippah*, Zaki put it all together. The Sacramento cell had identified Rabbi Lohrer and taken him hostage either at his home or at the airport. They were now in control of the rabbi, his house, and his phones. The blond man sitting in the front passenger's seat undoubtedly held a gun.

The door next to Zaki opened. Hussein pushed his way in. "Where are the supplies?"

The blond man answered. "In the trunk."

Hussein slammed the car door. "Go."

Flanked by the enemy, Zaki's mind raced. Why was Hussein taking him to the rabbi's house to meet the women? He was of no further use to Hussein. Icy points of fear prickled along the back of his neck. Who knew what the maniacal despot had in mind for him.

The rabbi made his way out of the airport and headed west. Before long they turned off the highway and Zaki saw that they were entering a hilly treed area. Finally the rabbi turned down a gravel drive and pulled up in front of a modest home. The light fixture outside the front door dimly lit the area and Zaki could make out a fairly large structure to the side of the house.

Hussein opened his door and ordered everyone out, his slurred speech obvious now. Zaki saw Hussein's cohorts exchange glances as the blond man took the rabbi's car keys from the ignition and threw them to the second man. The second man walked around the car and opened the trunk.

The blond man, gun now fully exposed, ordered Zaki and the rabbi to back up and stand with their hands clasped in front of them.

As Zaki stepped back, he heard movement in the trees behind him. His body tensed. He shot a look at Hussein. The big man slowly turned his large head in the direction of the sound, then turned back to the man standing by the open trunk and nodded.

Without speaking, the man reached into the trunk. He pulled out a handgun and extended it toward Hussein. Hussein misjudged the distance between them and his first swipe missed the weapon, throwing him off balance. After a stumbling step forward, he managed to grasp the gun.

The sounds of movement behind Zaki increased, and within moments ten or so men appeared. No one spoke, and the only sound in the eerie silence was the labored breathing of the rabbi who sucked air in jagged, terrified breaths.

In the darkness, Zaki couldn't identify any of the men who had joined them. All wore black clothes and black hooded masks that shaded their eyes. He could see those nearest him held AK-47s. Grim reapers holding iron scythes. No light was needed for him to know they had other weapons hidden beneath their clothes. Perhaps even vests packed with explosives to be detonated if they were captured.

Why so many men? Why so much fire power? Did Hussein with his freakish powers of perception know something? Feel something? Zaki lifted his chin. Whatever was going on, his own fate was a certainty.

God, save my soul.

He squared his shoulders, lifted his chin, and leveled his eyes on his captors.

Hussein looked in the direction of the hooded men. "Go back to your posts. When the women arrive, take p-positions to fire." He wiped his hand over his mouth, then spit. "Once they leave the car, if they go anywhere but to the front door, intercept them, take the baby from them, and kill them."

Ten men to fire on two unarmed women. Whoever found the bodies would get a clear message. For a moment Zaki considered trying to wrest Hussein's gun from him and shoot him with it. Zaki was more than willing to lay down his life to rid the earth of this satanic monster. As well to die now as to die later. But as the thought surged through him and the muscles in his legs began to coil, a field of force seemed to drop in front of him. And though he couldn't say how, he knew he was not to act of his own volition. He slowly settled back onto his heels.

As the men faded into the night, Hussein turned to the blond man. "Go back to the street and radio us when the women arrive.

They should be in a gray Taurus." The man set off at a jog down the driveway.

Hussein stepped toward the trunk, his eyes and the gun on Zaki and the rabbi. "Shair, take the rest of the supplies into the house."

The man by the trunk nodded.

While Shair gathered what looked like guns and ammunition, Hussein herded Zaki and the rabbi into the house. When Shair joined them, Hussein dropped heavily onto a couch. He directed Zaki and the rabbi to sit on the floor with their backs against the wall across from him. Then he directed his attention to Zaki.

"When the women arrive, I'm going to lend you a gun." He grinned and raised his eyebrows. "Shair and I will be right behind you to be sure you use it. You will answer the door. You will tell my wife to come in. Then you will kill that woman you work for."

Zaki held the devil's gaze. "As you say."

Austia was on her way to her own execution.

And he was to be her executioner.

CHAPTER 72

Austia turned off the overhead light, stuck the directions to Rabbi Lohrer's house in the visor of the rented car, and pulled out of the rest stop. The highway was empty, as it had been when they'd pulled off.

She dismissed the wave of uneasiness that winged across her shoulders. She was used to the traffic in Los Angeles, but this was probably perfectly ordinary for this area. Still. She pressed the door lock button. Glancing at Fatima, she saw that Sami was sleeping serenely in his mother's arms.

It was only by the grace of God that she and Fatima had escaped. When they'd turned into the crowd of people behind them, Austia had discovered that they were only steps from the door leading into the terminal. And once inside, they'd found a women's restroom only a few feet away. They'd hidden there until they felt it was safe to venture out. Then they'd gone to the ticket counter, and thankfully the TSA inspectors had been preoccupied with an Arab-looking businessman and had given her and Fatima little more than a glance before waving them through.

She felt her shoulders relax a bit, and as she settled back into the seat her thoughts returned to the question that had plagued her ever since she'd arrived at the Southwest Airlines terminal. Why had Zaki and Hussein been at the airport? Why had they come looking for her there? Had the men checked outgoing flights and found her name? Or even Fatima's for that matter. There wasn't a doubt in her mind, from all Fatima had told her about Hussein, that he would have connections able to do that.

But that idea had been proven wrong because when she'd tried to change her ticket to the later flight she'd discovered that Southwest hadn't recorded her original reservation. The one she'd tried to make from the car. That's when she realized that when her phone went dead, it must have cut her off before the reservation process had been completed. They'd ended up getting a stand-by seat on the next flight out. Praise God, there had been no sign of the men anywhere. She grimaced, remembering how she'd doubted God's faithfulness when the phone died.

Still, seeing them had completely shaken her. There was no way they could have known she would be there with Fatima. She herself had only decided to take the flight in the hour before.

She glanced at Fatima. "What a day. But we're on the last leg of our journey now."

Gratitude filled the young woman's sweet, earnest face. "How can I ever thank you for all you've done?"

Austia reached across the seat and patted Fatima's leg. "The glory belongs to Prophet Jesus. He has watched over us every step of the way."

"It's true." Fatima nodded slowly. "I was thinking about Him the whole time we were in the airplane. I feel—" Overwhelmed, tears sprang to her eyes. And as words failed her, she lifted her fingers to her lips. Then she softly kissed them and pressed them over her heart.

Through Fatima's window, in the night sky, a bright light caught Austia's eye. "Look, Fatima, a falling star." She tilted her head. "Or maybe something else. It has a deep red glow around it."

Fatima turned her face toward the window. "Whatever it is, it's beautiful." There was a note of wonder in Fatima's soft voice.

As it faded, Austia turned her attention back to the road. "Why don't you close your eyes and rest a while. According to the directions it's only about another thirty miles."

Fatima gently repositioned Sami in her arms and then laid her head against the seat back. Within moments her breathing slowed.

Austia lifted her eyes to the starry sky. *Tonight the heavens rejoice.*

As the miles passed, the stars faded and the moonlight dimmed. The sense of isolation that had nudged Austia earlier returned. Shifting in her seat, she glanced absently in her rearview mirror.

She started at the sight of distant headlights suddenly behind her, unblinking beady eyes observing her. Then, as she rounded a curve in the road, the lights disappeared.

When the road ahead straightened, she kept her eye on the rearview mirror. But there was nothing behind her except the murky darkness. She rubbed the back of her neck. She was being silly. The car had probably turned off.

But where? She hadn't passed any intersecting streets or even a turnout. She pressed the door lock button again.

As she rounded another curve, thick tendrils of fog floated across her headlights. Leaning forward, she turned on the wipers and slowed her speed as the fog misted her windshield. Her eyes shot to the gauges on the dash. This would not be a good time for the car to break down. Like soldiers at attention, the bright red needles were all holding their positions.

Releasing an audible sigh, she glanced at the young mother and her son resting beside her. She and Fatima and Sami were safe. She began to hum.

Welcome to Las Castas.

The big sign had a spotlight on it. She reached over and nudged Fatima. "Wake up, sweetie. We're almost there."

Fatima opened her eyes and nodded sleepily.

Austia saw an intersection ahead, and as she approached she saw that it was Indian Trail Road. The street the rabbi lived on. The directions stated it was only another two miles to the rabbi's house.

A thought occurred to her. Maybe the men had gone to her house. She dismissed the idea. They wouldn't have found anything to help them. She began watching the mailbox numbers. She spotted the name Lohrer, spelled out with reflective decals. She turned into the gravel driveway.

Suddenly, she flashed on the moment in Agua Viva when she'd run back in her house for the directions—*she'd never turned off the computer. She'd left the directions on the screen.* The men must have gone to her house and seen them! Her heart started to pound and she took her foot off the accelerator. They hadn't been at the airport to find her. They'd been there to fly to San Francisco and meet her. She gasped.

Fatima straightened. "What's wrong?"

Austia tried to keep her voice calm. "I'm not sure."

But the men hadn't found her. Had they? She'd seen nothing unusual at the San Francisco airport and she and Fatima had been on guard from the moment they'd left the restroom until they'd driven off in the rented car.

Headlights appeared behind her.

She felt herself starting to sweat. Unless … unless … they had followed her. "Get down, Fatima."

"Why? What's happening?" Sami started to cry.

"Please, just do as I say."

Austia heard Fatima trying to comfort her son as she slid to the floorboard.

Frantic, Austia realized it was too late to back out of the drive. She had to drive forward. In the rearview mirror, she kept her eyes on the car behind her. Maybe it was nothing. Maybe she would be laughing about it in a few minutes when she parked and found out it was someone who had taken a wrong turn and needed directions.

The car behind her stopped.

That had to be it. Someone was lost. She stepped on the gas and immediately saw the rabbi's house in front of her.

"Austia, what's happening?"

"I'm still not sure. Stay down."

The car in the driveway behind her was still stopped. Austia parked next to the rabbi's car and climbed out.

Leaving her door open, she looked back down the drive, but now she couldn't see anything through the thick fog. Either the car was gone, or the lights were off. She considered walking partway down the drive to see if she could determine if the car was still there.

An owl hooted somewhere behind her.

She shuddered at the eerily human voice and thought better of it.

As much as she hated waking the rabbi in the middle of the night, under the circumstances she didn't want to wait in the car until morning. "Fatima, stay here. I'll be right back."

Austia shut the car door and started toward the house.

CHAPTER 73

As headlights fanned across the living room wall, Shair leapt out of his chair. Hussein staggered up from the couch, breathing heavily and swaying from side to side, trying to get his balance and his bearings. Like his captors, Zaki was keenly aware that there had been no call from the man Hussein had sent to watch for the women.

Zahid had alerted the FBI.

"Whozze it?" Hussein took unsteady steps to where Shair stood looking through the slice of space where the curtains ended at the window's edge.

"A woman."

Hussein pushed him aside. "Itz her." Hussein pulled his gun from his belt. "That's not the car. Where's my son?"

Shair kicked Zaki with his foot. "Get up."

Zaki rose.

Prodding Zaki in the back with his AK-47, Shair followed Zaki to the door. Shair started to hand Zaki a revolver.

"Wait. Somzhingz wrong. No gun for him. You." He pointed at Zaki. "Open the door and pull her in."

A surge of adrenaline pulsed through Zaki. Suddenly, the aura of past battlefields, trenches, and missions charged the air. The present fused with the past. His mission became clear as his training took over and he prepared to die for his country, his faith, and the woman he loved. In what seemed like one motion, Zaki opened the door, grabbed the gun from Shair, and pulled Austia to the ground.

"FBI. FBI," sounded from across the drive.

Austia fought Zaki as he tried to shield her with his body. Clawing and biting him, she managed to break from his hold and run toward the car.

From behind him, Zaki heard Hussein shout to Shair, "Kill her."

A gunfight as violent as any battle Zaki had ever been in erupted.

Stepping through the door, Shair lifted his AK-47 and fired at Austia.

Rolling onto his back, Zaki shot Shair in the chest. As his body fell, it revealed Hussein in shadowy silhouette, standing behind him. Black eyes glowing red. His gun pointed at Zaki.

In the seconds it took Hussein to steady himself, Zaki fired.

Hussein's legs crumpled beneath him, sending his bulk sprawling across the threshold toward Zaki. Hussein's jowly face landed just inches from him.

As Zaki scrambled to his feet, the fire in Hussein's eyes became dark gray wisps. A helix of black smoke issued from his mouth and spiraled upward.

Gunfire spewed from every direction. A group of terrorists ran toward the parked cars, firing at Austia, and additional heavy fire came from somewhere up the driveway.

With bullets flying, Zaki backed up to the side of the house while shooting at the terrorists nearing Austia.

One of the men returned fire and the other sprayed Austia and the cars with bullets.

Austia fell to the ground.

Zaki saw the spastic jerk of her body as she went down.

Zigzagging through the melee, he went to her. With no bullets left in his gun, he dropped it and wrapped his arms around her, dragging her between the two parked cars.

He cradled her and pushed her hair from her face. Tears stung his eyes. "Fight, Austia. Fight. Don't die. You can't die." Blood was everywhere.

An innocent caught in the crossfire.

He kissed her face with the desperate urgency of a man who knows the finality of death. Pressing her head to his chest, he lifted his face heavenward. Words tore from his lips, cursing God, filled with the emotion of someone who had lost everyone he had ever loved.

He buried his face in her matted hair. "Don't let her die." His voice husky and pleading, he wept. "I love you. Live. You're a fighter. Please, live."

But there was no response.

CHAPTER 74

Zaki knelt beside the simple gravesite and laid the flowers down. When would the killing stop? How many more like her would have to die?

He blinked rapidly. Fatima was in a better place now. Even with Hussein dead, she would never have been safe. Had she lived, she would have been hunted like an animal. And ultimately, if Hussein's henchman had not taken her life, they would have taken her son. To Fatima there would have been no difference.

He rose. But for Austia's fighting spirit and will to live he would have been mourning her death on this beautiful summer morning. Instead he would be sitting with her at her bedside within the hour. His heart heavy, he turned his gaze back to the grave. Sami would grow up without a mother. The mind of God was unfathomable … and cruel. He turned on his heel and headed toward his car.

Stopping at the car door, he looked back through the cemetery gates and searched the distance. His eyes sought the sliver of ground that marked Fatima's plot. He spotted the big maple tree, then moved his eyes to the right. Even from where he stood, he could see the dark mark of the freshly turned dirt.

He hated them. Hussein and every Muslim who supported him. It didn't matter if they were active in the cell or not. There were hundreds of thousands who supported Hussein and his kind by sitting silently by and saying nothing, the carnage and death at Rabbi Lohrer's house a tribute to their silence. Zaki climbed into his car, started it, and headed to the highway.

It had taken time to sort things out that night, but it had finally become clear that the FBI, sent as a result of his call to Zahid Zafar, had arrived at almost exactly the same time as Austia and Fatima, actually following them onto the property. But for a matter of minutes, the women would have been spared hell on earth. The FBI had killed the lookout, but had been forced to engage the Sacramento cell hiding in the woods once the cell started their assault on the women. Exiting the freeway, Zaki drove toward town. The simultaneous raid carried out at the duplex had been far less violent and no one had been killed.

Sami had survived. That was truly a miracle. The car was riddled with bullets and Fatima most certainly had died from those gunshots. She was found with Sami protectively cloistered in her arms. Not a single bullet had touched him. Yet an unsettling fact remained. The evidence showed that Fatima's wounds had not bled, indicating that her body had been lifeless prior to being hit. Zaki slowly shook his head. The coroner had been able to offer no explanation.

A thought fleeted across his mind and he glanced heavenward. "Impossible."

Zaki pulled into the hospital parking lot, parked, and bounded to the entrance.

Not wanting to wait for the elevator, he took the stairs two at a time to the third floor, then pushed the door and walked directly to room A7. He stopped at the threshold and peered in.

Austia was sleeping.

He tiptoed to her bedside and took a seat in the chair where he'd sat vigil day and night only the week before, wondering then after each breath she took if it would be her last. Her eyes fluttered open.

"Hey." She slid her hand from under the sheet and turned it over, palm up.

He accepted the invitation and took her hand in his. Then he scooted the chair forward and kissed her lightly on the lips. "I love you." He paused, his eyes caressing her. "I just took your flowers to Fatima."

"Thank you." Austia's eyes filled with tears, and as they had so many times since that terrible night, he leaned over her, took her in his arms, and let her cry. As she quieted, he gently released her and seated himself.

"I'm s-s-sorry."

"Shh." He handed her a tissue from the dispenser beside her bed. "It's okay. I understand."

She dabbed at her eyes. "Any news?"

Zaki knew she was asking about the additional blood tests that had been ordered to try and determine Fatima's cause of death. The tests had explained nothing. He shook his head.

She squeezed his hand. "Do you believe me now?"

Zaki studied the face of this remarkable woman, her faith not shattered but strengthened by her horrific experience and the death of the woman she had risked everything for.

Austia's eyes met his. "The Lord took her out of a situation that no one else could have. And I believe He did it just before they sprayed that car. I know she would have called out to Him. And I know He answered her."

Zaki tried to keep his own thoughts about such an idea from showing on his face. "I hope it's true. But I hate the men that did this. The more I think about the whole thing, the more I pray to God that every last terrorist is ferreted out, tried as an enemy combatant, and locked up until it's time for him to burn in Hell."

Austia's eyes filled with compassion. "Please, don't hate."

He lowered his gaze. He loved her. He wanted to put away his anger, his hatred. But the truth was he was calling the FBI lab every day to find out which gun had fired the bullet that had almost killed her. The one that had pierced an artery in her neck and missed her spinal cord by a fraction of an inch, leaving her to bleed to death.

He wanted to know whose gun had delivered that shot. If the shooter had survived, then Zaki would personally follow his trial until he was sure that Hell's adherent was sentenced to meet his master. He clenched his jaw. And if somehow he escaped justice, Zaki would personally deliver it.

"Excuse me." A voice at the door interrupted Zaki's thoughts. "It's time to take her for her scan."

He rose and kissed Austia's forehead, then stepped out of the way. "I'll be here when you get back."

As he watched Austia being wheeled from the room he made a silent vow as hatred took root. Whoever shot her deserved death.

And he would make it his business to be sure that that sentence was carried out.

CHAPTER 75

Austia sat in her wheelchair by her living room window watching for Zaki. During the week she'd been home from the hospital he'd waited on her hand and foot. He'd even served coffee and cookies, at her request, to the investigators from Deep Spring when they came to her house to wrap up the part of the Brown bombing investigation that involved her. He'd been the one who had called Deep Spring for her while she was still in the hospital to let them know she was the person of interest they were looking for. Even though by the time they'd arrived it had become clear to them she had no involvement and that Jake Richards had acted alone, it had still been intimidating. Having Zaki by her side had been a blessing.

He adored her and didn't mind showing it. There was something deeply moving about a man who so carefully guarded his emotions publicly holding her tenderly and revealing his most intimate feelings. She felt herself flush. He'd drawn her to places he'd allowed no other human being, and she'd come to understand the complex tapestry that was his life. The deep wounding he'd experienced that made him afraid to love. The deep love he had for her that made him willing to risk it all again.

Still, she knew he couldn't get past the feeling that he should have stopped Hussein. That he should have done more. That if he had, Fatima would not have died and Austia would not have been injured.

She settled back in her chair. Knowing what she did about how it had all gone down, it was clear that there was nothing he could have done differently that would have changed the outcome. Besides, it was all going to work out. Yes, it would be months of physical therapy, and she would probably always have a limp from the bullets that had shattered her right leg and arm. But overall, she was going to be fine.

If only the same could be said of Zaki.

In the weeks since that night, she had watched him develop a seething hatred toward Muslims. From the ayatollahs who had forced his parents to flee Iran, to the deaths on the battlefields of Yemen, to the shot that had almost killed her—all had linked into a single steel chain that encircled his heart.

She knotted her hands as conflicting emotions rose in her chest.

Sometime during those long nights at the hospital with him beside her comforting her and encouraging her, she'd realized that she was falling in love with him. Then he'd kissed her.

The touch of his lips had sent a flood of emotions surging through her. But the one that had stood out was that of breathtaking wonder as she was filled with a knowing. This was the man she had been waiting for ... and who had been waiting for her. The attraction both spiritual and physical merging into a beautiful whole. A foreshadowing of a oneness and purity meant for the temple of God.

But she fought it. They could never have a future together. God's call on her life to allow Him to love Muslims through her had not changed. Sharing that call with a man who had hardened his heart toward the Muslim people would be impossible.

Tears stung her eyes. Why had God allowed this to happen? It was as though Satan himself had orchestrated the chain of events that had culminated in Zaki's hatred toward Muslims, making a mockery of the prayers she'd prayed asking for a husband. Not even God could turn back the clock to that terrible night and change to good what Satan meant for evil. Now that hate would only breed more hate.

And more sorrow.

She had to tell Zaki that any chance for a future with him had been put to death that night in the gunfire. She couldn't let him continue to be deeply involved in her life, thinking they were building something together. Only yesterday he'd asked her if she'd considered moving closer to Steve. She recognized it as him really asking what she had already discerned from other comments he'd made. Was she going to cut her ties with Agua Viva and her ministry?

The sound of a car door shutting drew her attention. It was Zaki. He was carrying flowers. Wheeling to the door, she tried to gather her thoughts. He knocked.

"Come in."

He stepped into the living room and closed the door. The minute his eyes settled on her, his smile vanished. "What's wrong?"

She rolled her chair toward the couch. "We need to talk."

He laid the flowers on the coffee table and sat on the edge of the couch cushion and leaned forward, facing her. "I'm listening."

She searched for a way to start the conversation. Coming up empty, she asked, "Did you pick up Najah's brother from the airport last night?"

Zaki knitted his brows. "Yes."

"I want to be sure and meet him and see Najah and Sami before they leave. I'm going to miss that precious little boy so much."

Austia saw a shadow pass across Zaki's eyes, the charred remains of deep sadness. She should have been more sensitive. Zaki had told her he couldn't have children and how it was something he'd desperately yearned for. She understood that desperate yearning well. But if she had learned anything in the last few weeks, it was that God hears and answers prayers in His own way and in His own time. There was a child waiting somewhere with a prayer of its own. She felt it in her heart.

Zaki nodded. "Of course. Let's take them to dinner tonight. They leave tomorrow." He paused. "In fact, I was hoping you'd feel like coming with us to the airport tomorrow. It isn't that far from Steve's. Why don't we stop by and see him?"

Their last visit with her brother had been filled with veiled questions and pointed suggestions about her future plans. It had been clear to her that Zaki and her brother had had some previous conversation and formed an alliance for the purpose of setting her life in a new direction. This was her opening.

"Since you bring up visiting with Steve ... The last time we did, it made me very uncomfortable. He's never liked the fact that I minister to Muslims. He started pressuring me to close the Career Center the day I opened it. When we were with him last time, I felt like that was *still* his agenda." She tilted her head and looked directly into Zaki's eyes. "And frankly, I got the feeling you were one hundred percent behind him."

Zaki's eyes held hers, though his expression was gentle. "America's war against fanatical Islam is only going to intensify in the coming years. More and more moderate Muslims are going to become radicalized. This is going to become a full-fledged clash of civilizations." He reached across the space between them and took her hand. "I love you, Austia. There's nothing more important to me than your safety." His handsome face held the raw emotion of someone who loved her deeply and unashamedly. "Your life is worth more than a thousand of those hate-filled, death-loving radicals."

Her heart wrenched. "Not to God."

He withdrew his hand from hers and rose. "Austia, this has to stop. You're being naive and foolish. Those who are born into Islam make their choices and they deserve to live with the consequences. It's only a matter of time until the moderates are radicalized. They'll be no different than the godforsaken soul who shot you. What they deserve for their actions is death. You're wasting your time trying to minister to them."

His words cut her deeply. "I can do nothing less."

He was tearing her apart. She couldn't deny it. She loved him as she had not loved since David's death. But to deny her ministry would be to deny God. "Leave. Please. Leave now."

She spun her chair around and wheeled to her bedroom. Alone, the desperate hopelessness of the situation crashed over her. How much more would following God cost her?

Zaki could hear Austia's sobs coming from her bedroom. He raked his fingers through his hair. Why couldn't she see the truth? She was on the losing side of a spiritual battle.

The sound of his phone interrupted his thoughts. He flipped it open and glanced at the screen. It was the lab.

"This is Zaki."

"Harry here. The bullet that severed Austia's artery was from a revolver."

Zaki felt like he was breathing through mud. He knew from the investigation that he was the only one who had a revolver that night. "What are you saying?"

"She was hit by a bullet from a revolver."

He drew a sharp breath.

His mind filtered back to that moment—shooting at the thugs who were shooting at her. It had all happened so fast. There had been so much confusion. The image of her body jerking as she fell expanded in his mind's eye until it shut out everything else.

He was the one who had shot her.

He cursed his name. He had done that to her. He clenched the phone in his hand, then threw it against the wall. "No!" The keening wail pierced the air.

She had almost died.

He felt like he'd been hit in the stomach with a two-by-four.

"What's going on?" Austia's voice came from down the hall.

As he turned toward it, she rounded the corner. "What happened?"

Seeing her sitting in the wheelchair, face tearstained, frightened, and fragile, his mind reeled.

He was responsible.

His own words, spoken only moments before, returned to him and condemned him. *Those who are born into Islam make their choices and they deserve to live with the consequences. What they deserve for their actions is death.*

That night he'd chosen his course of action. And now he would have to live with the consequences of his choices forever.

Like a light through a prism, truth illuminated his heart. But for the grace of the God he had cursed, he would have killed her. The unfathomable mind of God had given *him* mercy. What he would not give others, God had given him.

He crossed the room to Austia and sank to his knees beside her. "The bullet that nearly killed you came from a revolver. My revolver. It was me. I'm the one who shot you." Barely able to speak, his voice came out an urgent whisper. "Forgive me. Please, forgive me. I'm so sorry. Please, say you forgive me."

As he searched her face, her eyes met his. Loving and compassionate, they held no judgment. "I can do nothing less."

CHAPTER 76

The months of recovery had been long. First a wheelchair, then crutches, and through it all, endless hours of physical therapy. Zaki had been her rock through the emotional ups and downs that the doctors had told her would come as part of healing from the massive trauma her body had suffered. And though she still couldn't walk unaided, today marked the official end of her therapy sessions.

Zaki pulled into the driveway. "Home, safe and sound." He turned off the engine and faced her. Instead of speaking he gave her a mischievous smile. "Let's go in, shall we?"

Something was up. Austia glanced around her yard, then turned to observe the street.

Nothing.

Zaki climbed out of the car, hurried to her side and opened the car door. Then he lifted her out.

"Put me down, please. I want to practice on my own. I expect to be driving myself to work next week."

"As you wish." He grinned and handed her her crutches.

Austia leaned against the car door and pulled her crutches under her arms. After managing a few steps back, she balanced on one foot and poked the car door shut with the tip of the other crutch. "Sheesh. I hate these things."

Zaki rounded the front of the car ahead of her, smiling with encouragement. "You're doing great. It won't be long before you don't need them."

She noticed how he hung back, giving her plenty of room to maneuver. God bless him, he never lost his patience with her. She turned toward her front door.

The next step sent her sprawling on the front lawn.

Zaki was by her side in an instant, scooping her up in his arms. "Let me get you into the house, then I'll come back and get the crutches."

She felt like a feather in his strong arms. A princess rescued by her knight. "Thank you." *Thank You, Lord, for this wonderful man.*

She felt tears sting her eyes. "I love you so much."

He stopped where he was and kissed her on the lips.

Suddenly, she felt heat start in her neck and move up as the reality of where they were rudely nudged her and sent her careening into the present. "Zaki! Stop it. What if the neighbors see us?"

"Why shouldn't I kiss the woman of my dreams?" His dark eyes danced with amusement. "Besides, thanks to that big oak tree, they can't see us anyway."

She looked at him with as much disapproval as she could muster, then turned her head into his shoulder, not wanting him to see that she found his independent, maverick attitude totally appealing. In a few strides he was at her front door.

Before Zaki could reach for the knob, the door opened.

"Steve." Austia caught her breath. "It's so good to see you. What a wonderful surprise."

The terrible ordeal she had been through had devastated Steve. That his efforts to protect her had been the door through which evil had come had nearly destroyed him. In the early weeks, he had spent hours by her bedside, begging God to spare her life, and through the months of recovery had constantly asked for her forgiveness, but despite her assurances, somehow he never seemed able to accept it.

But something had changed since the experience. Though he was still adamant that she stop her ministry at the Career Center, he had begun to speak about the need to reach out to Muslim children and model the love of Christ to them. He had even cultivated a relationship with a young Muslim boy, Kalid, in his condo complex and spoke of him often. Steve had become friendly with the father and helped the boy with his homework. He said their friendship was changing the boy's attitude toward Christians. She smiled to herself. The boy wasn't the only one being changed.

She pulled away from Zaki to look at him. "You knew about this, didn't you?"

His dark eyes were filled with amusement. "Here, Steve, would you put this special delivery package on the couch while I go get her crutches?"

Steve took his sister from Zaki's arms and stepped to the side. As Zaki ran to get the crutches, the front door seemed to close of its own accord. *"Al salamu alaikum."*

"Mr. Rahman!"

The elderly man stepped into her view. *"Masha'allah."*

Austia had not seen Mr. Rahman since she'd left the hospital. They'd spoken on the phone during the days she'd been confined to the house. Though they'd spoken little about what had happened in Las Castas, other than how Zaki had managed to alert the FBI and destroy the cell. There was no need to bring up to the gentle old man the dark side of Islam. It would only upset him.

As they walked toward the living room, she heard the door open behind her. Zaki stepped in front of them, crutches in hand. His eyes sparkled. "Let's sit down."

Steve strode into the living room and turned toward the couch. Austia stared at the visitor sitting there as a warm glow flowed through her. *"Khalama!"*

Mrs. Rahman was propped up on the cushions. She reached her thin arms toward Austia as Steve set her gently beside Mrs. Rahman. The two women embraced.

After sliding Austia's crutches under the coffee table, Zaki gestured to Steve and Mr. Rahman to sit on the loveseat. Then he took a seat on the recliner at the end of the couch.

Austia took her dear friend's frail hand in hers. "This *is* a surprise. It's so wonderful to see you up."

"Oh, I wouldn't have missed this for anything."

Austia furrowed her brow. "What do—"

"Tea, anyone?" Annie entered the room from the kitchen carrying a tray, cups steaming.

"Annie." Austia's hand flew to her mouth. "What are you doing here?"

"Heard there was a gathering of your closest friends." She winked. "And I wouldn't have missed it for anything." She set the tea on the coffee table.

Austia turned to Zaki and raised her eyebrows, silently asking him what was going on. He rose.

"Austia." He moved toward the couch and stopped just to the left of her legs. He sought her eyes and with raw emotion on his face, he dropped to his knee. "I love you."

A trill spiraled through Austia's stomach. This intensely private man, who had only whispered those three words once during their relationship, desired to declare his love for her in front of the people she loved most. Tears stung her eyes.

He lowered his gaze. "For years I didn't know if life was worth living." He raised his face to hers. "Now I know life isn't worth living without you." He drew a steadying breath. "I want to be part of your life and part of your dreams and serve our God with you for the rest of my life."

He pulled a ring from his shirt pocket. The glittering shards of light that reflected off the solitary diamond seemed to punctuate the clear purity of his words.

"Will you marry me?"

Austia smiled through her tears. The room faded from her vision and she was alone with him. Aware her answer spoke not only to Zaki but to the God of Abraham whose call on her life continued.

"I will."

after words

... a little more ...

When a delightful concert comes to an end,

the orchestra might offer an encore.

When a fine meal comes to an end,

it's always nice to savor a bit of dessert.

When a great story comes to an end,

we think you may want to linger.

And so, we offer ...

AfterWords—just a little something more after you

have finished a David C Cook novel.

We invite you to stay awhile in the story.

Thanks for reading!

Turn the page for ...

- **A Conversation with Nikki Arana**

A CONVERSATION WITH NIKKI ARANA

Q: Was this novel based on a true story?

A. *The Next Target* was inspired by work I have done in the Christian underground in Egypt and now in the United States. God led me to start a ministry, A Voice for the Persecuted. Besides helping persecuted Christians, we make presentations to educate American Christians about Islam, and we have resources for individuals and organizations that need cross-cultural training.

Q: How did you first get involved in your ministry?

A: My third novel, *The Fragrance of Roses,* was about a child with leukemia. I needed help with the medical aspects of the story. I connected with a Dr. Dorak, who was exceptionally knowledgeable about childhood leukemia. He agreed to be a resource for the book. He was a Muslim. He knew I was writing a "Christian" novel, but he agreed to help me. He was completely dedicated to helping children with leukemia. He didn't care if they were Christians, Muslims, or Jews. He worked with me for ten months on the book. By the time we finished, I considered him a good friend and I truly respected and loved him. The reality that he was lost really weighed on my heart. I began to pray about that, and during that prayer time God caused me to see that what was true for him was true for all Muslims. He gave me a love for the Muslim people. That was when I began to ask God to show me how He wanted to use me.

Q: How did He do that?

A: I was aware of the practice of "honor killings." That is, the practice of family members killing others in their family who convert to Christianity. I felt that God was calling me to reach out to the Muslims who live and work among us and to be a vessel to give them what Islam can never give. But I wondered what good it was to evangelize Muslims and then leave them to be murdered. I knew I had to set up a network of safe houses for them. I got involved helping support former Muslim women in Egypt who had converted to Christianity and now helped hide other women who had converted. Sadly, within two years they were all dead. With no other contacts there, I turned my focus to America. God opened many doors and used me and others to help persecuted Christians here. Many Americans don't realize that there are Christians in our country under the threat of death. I hope my book raises public awareness about this issue.

Q: What are some first steps readers can take to reach out to Muslims?

A: Education is critical. The media has been the primary source of information for most of the American public. Sadly, it often gives the impression that Muslims are terrorists. That isn't true. Many are seeking, especially those who live here, and we have what they are looking for.

Form friendships. Evangelizing Muslims is a friendship ministry. Look at them through the eyes of Christ. Be a reflection of His love for them. Reach out to them. Extend a helping hand where needed.

Be available. What I mean by that is, seek them out by going to places they might be, like Middle Eastern restaurants, sports events, or Muslim celebrations. When you show up, the Holy Spirit shows up with you. He will orchestrate everything. Watch what He is doing and respond to that.

Q: Could you recommend a few nonfiction books for those interested in learning more about Muslim-Christian relationships?

A: I sure can. I coauthored one with Harry Morin titled *Through the Eyes of Christ: How to Lead Muslims into the Kingdom of God.* It is written for the layperson and answers many common questions. It is available on my website: www.nikkiarana.com. I also recommend *Daughters of Islam: Building Bridges with Muslim Women* by Miriam Adeney.

ACKNOWLEDGMENTS

Bringing this book to publication was a long journey. I started the first draft in 2007 and wrote the book as women's fiction. Then I rewrote the book as a novel of suspense. During that same period of time, my agent was presenting it to publishers. The subject, evangelizing Muslims, frightened some of them, and there was a period of time when we thought we might not find a home for this book. It required the commitment and help of many people to bring this novel to print. God's ways are mysterious, but His love never fails.

First, I want to thank my agent, Natasha Kern, who always encouraged me, believed in the book, looked toward the day it would be on bookshelves, and worked tirelessly for two years to find a publisher. Love always protects, always trusts, always hopes, always perseveres.

Second, Harry Morin who provided cultural context and read every scene of the book for accuracy regarding references to Muslims and Islam. He helped watch for bias to ensure that the distinction was made between Muslims, the people, and Islam, the religion. Christ covets the hearts of the Muslim people. Harry has dedicated his life to reaching those hearts. Love does not rejoice at injustice and unrighteousness but rejoices when right and truth prevail.

Also, my family, especially my husband, Antonio. My steadfast partner for thirty-six years. He makes all the rough places smooth. Love is patient, love is kind.

And of course, Don Pape and the fantastic team at David C Cook. Their excitement about the story lifted me up. Their hearts for the Muslim people and their desire to serve Christ and proclaim His message through the written word brings glory to God's name. Love rejoices with the truth.

I am passionate about encouraging Christians to reach out in friendship to the Muslims who live among us, model the love of Christ to them, and then with the leading of the Holy Spirit give them the Gift that Islam can never give. Thank you all who made this book possible. With a special thanks to Joe and Austia Hickey. You all have been the *via* of Christ's love for me. As you hold this book in your hands, a book that encountered obstacle after obstacle, you are the living words of the spiritual truth … Love never fails.